STOLEN HOPE

D.R. CAMPBELL

STOLEN HOPE

Published in the United States of America
ISBN: 978-0692887547
1. Fiction / Thrillers / Crime
2. Fiction / Mystery & Detective / General

I dedicate this to my girls, Sydney and Natalie. Thank you for showing me what love, fear, grace, strength, faith and courage look like every day.

I love you with my every breath,

Mom

Table of Contents

PROLOGUE

"There!" Adena pushed the last bobby pin in her sister's hair. She stepped back and looked in the mirror. "What'd ya think?"

"They're not too big?" Deandra asked, moving her head from side to side. Large, chocolate brown eyes fringed with long, curled eyelashes gave the new hairdo the once-over in the mirror. Deandra was sixteen years old, and had only been in Texas for four years, moving with their mother from Saint Elizabeth parish in Jamaica shortly after their father died. Having begged her mother for an entire year, Deandra was ecstatic when she was given permission to live with her sister last summer.

Adena ran her fingers over the braids she coiled over her sister's head. Tilting her head to the side, she said, "No, you look great!"

"Yeah, I know!" Deandra's chubby cheeks gave way to deep dimples.

Adena laughed as she walked to her bed and busied herself moving things from one purse to another. She reached across the bed, grabbed her cell phone, checking the charge.

"I have to leave for work." Absently, she glanced back at Deandra. "Don't forget to put your contacts in."

Deandra rolled her eyes. "I hate wearing those things," she murmured.

"You look cute in your glasses, but the contacts up the cuteness." Adena slipped her foot into one of the black wedge shoes she wore to work. They weren't attractive, but they were very comfortable.

"Do you think Raymond will be there?" Deandra fingered the diamond pendant on her necklace, still looking in the mirror. It hadn't been difficult for her to make friends, and she was excited she was invited to the coach's victory party celebrating the basketball team's winning season.

"He's the team star!" Adena's voice was muffled from inside the closet. "He'll be there!" Adena reappeared, smoothing down her hair as she grabbed her purse. "Do you want help with your makeup?"

"No, I got it. Go to work. I'll call you later."

"Okay." She ran by, planted a quick kiss on her cheek. "Call me when you get home." "Have fun," she yelled from down the hall, and slammed the front door.

Deandra walked into the bathroom, placed her glasses on the counter. "Up the cuteness," she told herself in the mirror. She sighed as she picked up the contact case and began to get ready for the party.

●●●

Later that evening, Deandra was laying upside-down on her bed, feet resting on the headboard, cell phone to her ear.

"Did you wear the contacts?" Adena asked on the other end.

She pushed her glasses up onto the bridge of her nose. "Yeah, yeah, I wore the contacts." Scratching between the braids, she added, "Oh. Tiffany liked my hair. She wanted me to ask you if you could do hers?"

"Sure. Remind me who she is again?"

"She's the one that has the dog I want."

"Oh, yeah, right," Adena responded. "Was Raymond there?"

"Yeah, he was there," Deandra giggled. "And guess what? He asked me. . ." Deandra heard a loud thud outside her room. She turned her head towards the direction of the noise, wondering if she imagined it.

"He asked you what," her sister asked. "What's wrong?"

"I'm not sure. I thought I heard something."

Deandra slid off the bed and walked slowly to the door. Her sister continued asking questions, talking about the party, but Deandra wasn't paying attention. Her fingers grabbed the doorknob a little harder than necessary, and she turned the knob. The door gave a little "creek," when it opened. She strained to hear something, but was met by silence. Shrugging her shoulders, Deandra gave the obligatory "uh-huh" to her sister as she turned to go back to her room.

She put one knee on the bed but stopped when she heard another thud on the other side of the closed door. Cautiously, she approached the door a second time, and turned the knob, willing her heart to slow down. She opened the door and began down the hall towards where she thought the sound came from, the back door. She stopped and listened, but heard nothing.

"Deandra, are you listening to me?!" her sister demanded.

"Shhh," Deandra whispered into the phone.

"Huh?!"

Suddenly, she heard another sound, only this time, it came from the patio door. Her brown eyes were huge as she turned towards the noise. Two figures clothed in black were pushing a huge object into the patio door.

Deandra's heart stopped. She could not believe her eyes! "Someone's trying to break into the house!" She whispered frantically into the phone at her sister.

"What?" Adena yelled. "Where are they?"

"They're outside! I am looking at them! I'm looking at them right now!" She watched as the robbers heaved the object into the door again, jumping as it made contact.

"Grab the house phone and go hide!" Adena instructed.

Without another word, she grabbed the cordless phone from the nearby table, and ran back into her room. She slammed the door closed, fumbling with the lock. She then ran into the closet, slamming its door behind her. She buried herself in the back, hiding among the various sleeves and dresses hanging from the racks. She closed her eyes, heart racing.

"Where are you," Adena asked. She ran her fingers through her hair, and began to pace the cubicle as far as the office phone cord would let her.

"I'm in the closet! Adena, help me! What am I going to do? Please come home! Why are they here?!"

Adena dug her fist into her eyes, uselessness growing inside of her as she listened to her sister plead for her help. "Okay, listen to me. Call 911 from the house phone. Keep me on the line, but call 911. Do it now!" Adena flopped back in her chair, helpless.

Deandra dropped the cell phone and dialed the number as instructed.

"911, what's your emergency," the operator answered.

"Someone's trying to break into my house!" Deandra yelled into the phone. Her eyes widened and fresh panic washed over her when she heard glass shatter from the other room.

"Calm down, ma'am. Did you say someone broke into your home?"

"They're in here right now!" Deandra screamed. "Please help me!"

"Where are you, ma'am," the telephone operator asked.

"In my closet! Please send someone! They are trying to get in!"

The bedroom door crashed open. Deandra screamed into the phone, "They're inside! Oh, my god, they're inside! They're inside!"

"Okay, ma'am, I'm sending police over right now. Ma'am, don't hang up!"

"Please hurry! They are right outside the door!"

In one abrupt moment, the closet door flew into the wall. Deandra screamed as two dark-clothed people rushed inside. Deandra screamed again. "Help me, somebody!"

"Get that bitch!" One of the robbers yelled, as the other lunged at her. Deandra dug her feet into the floor, pushing herself into the wall, pulling clothes down all around her. "Somebody help me! Adena! Help me!" she screamed.

"Deandra!" Adena yelled, knocking over her chair as she stood up. Her co-workers swung around in her direction, startled by the sudden outburst. She clutched her throat defenseless as she listened to the struggles and screams coming through the receiver.

"Ma'am, ma'am, are you there," the 911 operator called out.

One of the robbers put his hand over Deandra's mouth. She bit down on his palm, and he yelled, yanking his hand away. She screamed again as all three scuffled against one another and she clawed the air, striking one of robbers on the jaw.

"Bitch!" The bitten attacker back-handed her across the face. For an instant, she was stunned and stopped struggling. Using this to their advantage, both attackers took her arms and dragged her out of the bedroom. They headed down the hall towards the broken patio door as Deandra came out of her daze.

She was acutely aware of what was at stake if they took her through that door. Shaking her head with new determination, she dug her feet into the floor. She wiggled and twisted in the hands of her attackers. She screamed with everything in her, jerking and flapping her arms in protest. They tried to pick her up, but with the bucking and squirming, they were only able to pick up one leg. One hand back over her mouth, the attackers struggled to not lose their holds. She screamed at the top of her lungs against the hand, her throat burning. Stinging tears filled her eyes as she flung her head aimlessly from side to side.

A third assailant walked in through the broken door. He approached the three of them, towering over Deandra. The crunching glass under his shoes echoed throughout the room. Also dressed in black, he wore a black ski mask over his face, so all she saw were his eyes. They were black ice, cold and frigid. She implored him with her own eyes, but there was nothing there in his. Tears streamed down her face, Deandra whimpered against the hand covering her mouth.

Without a word, the third attacker looked away. He then reached back and backhanded her across the face. A white light flashed behind her eyes, the images of the attackers outlined in little stars, faint and distant. He stretched his arm back, then stepped forward, and slapped her again on the opposite cheek. Her whole body vibrated and stung. Her head lobbed to one side and the images of the invaders swam before her.

The lead assailant looked at the other two and said, "Now, get her and let's go."

Deandra sucked in one last breath and mercifully blacked out.

STOLEN HOPE

CHAPTER ONE

The shrill ring of the telephone cut through the silence of the early morning hour. Marissa jerked, bolting upright in the dark. The phone rang a second time. Collapsing back onto the bed, she flung her hand to the source of the noise. She cleared her throat once and clicked the 'talk' button mid-third ring.

"Hello?" she mumbled.

"Maury, I think I have something you need to see," the male voice on the other end responded.

"You think or you know, which is it?" Marissa opened one eye and looked at the florescent blue display on the night stand. 4:45 a.m.

"Positive," he replied.

"Gavin, this better be good. Are you wearing your watch?" Frustrated, Marissa glanced at the time again before she flopped her head back on her pillow.

"We're ten minutes from your place."

"Excuse me?" Marissa shot up again, this time all remnants of sleep gone.

"We will be there in ten minutes. Get dressed." The line went dead.

Dammit, she muttered. Marissa flopped back once again onto the pillow, growling as she punched her fists in the air in a mini temper tantrum.

From the time she was a little girl, Marissa Elliot always knew she wanted to be a lawyer. She spent hours watching detective or legal eagle shows on television, and then went to her room to reenact the show. Marissa always played the lead role. She didn't have any brothers or sisters to play with, so she used her dolls for the other characters. Marissa's mother watched and worried. As a single parent, money was always tight. She worked two jobs, and she knew it would take years of schooling and a lot money to make her daughter's dream become a reality. She tried to talk to Marissa about other careers, but Marissa would not be swayed. She felt a certain passion and thrill whenever she saw the attorney give their final, convincing argument. She was most positive it was her calling in life.

It was this determination that made Marissa work hard in school. She excelled in English and history, was a member of the National Honors Society, and awarded a full scholarship to Ohio State University. She received a double bachelor's degree in political science and English literature where she graduated a semester early at the top five percent of her class. After graduating law school, summa cum laude, she served as a judicial law clerk for two years before accepting a position at the District Attorney's Office in Dallas, Texas.

There, Marissa breathed, ate and slept the law. For five years, she specialized in crimes against children and domestic violence, producing a stellar conviction record which earned respect not only among her co-workers but also with the defense attorneys that went up against her. She gave lectures during career week at the various community colleges in the metroplex, and every odd month gave pro-bono advice at The Family Place, a local women's shelter. A friend of a friend introduced her to the United States Attorney, who had already heard of her impressive career. He offered her a position as an Assistant United States Attorney which she has held for the past seven years. Her mother was constantly telling their friends that Marissa's success was due to the fact that she never listened to her and always did things her way.

Her male colleagues not only respected her for her legal expertise, but admired her smooth, café au lait complexion and eyes of brown velvet. She had been the homecoming queen during her senior year in high school, and was named Ms. African-American History Month during her junior year in college. She had the looks and grace of a runway model, slender, and naturally curly hair, the only thing she liked about her absent Caucasian father. Everyone around Marissa thought she was beautiful, kind, and sincere. But she never flaunted her looks, adding to her appeal. Her friends worried that she wouldn't slow down long enough to fall in love and get married. Marissa insisted that she just never had any time to devote to a serious relationship, which left just casual dating. She didn't feel she was missing anything. She enjoyed her work, enjoyed her friends, enjoyed her life, and enjoyed things just the way they were.

Marissa swung her legs over the edge of the bed. In an effort to wake up, she stood, yawned and stretched, and made her way to the bathroom, where she splashed water on her face and brushed her teeth. She brushed her brunette, shoulder-length curls into a ponytail, and headed into her closet where she jumped into a pair of jeans, a faded Ohio State t-shirt, and her favorite slip-on tennis shoes.

Her pulse quickened at the sound of pounding on the front door. She made her way out of the bedroom and down the hall as the pounding continued. "I'm coming! I'm coming!" Jogging across the living room, Marissa yanked open the door.

Gavin smiled at her on the other side, and stuck out a cup of Starbucks coffee. Gavin Wright was 6'2", African-American, and a former offensive end for the former Houston Oilers. Trading the football for a shield, Gavin served on Dallas Police Department's SWAT for four years before joining the FBI eight years ago. His size was still impressive, still very fit even after having been out of the game for over thirteen years, and he sported a shaved head and an easy smile. But at five o'clock in the morning, his easy smile only further annoyed Marissa. Without a word, she took the cup, grabbed her keys from the bowl on the table, and walked outside. Gavin held the storm door in equal silence as she locked the main one. He followed behind her as they made their way to the dark, obvious-looking government car in her driveway. She stood there, smelling the coffee.

"This better be good." She looked at him over the brim.

"It is," he responded a little too cheerful. He opened the back passenger door for her, then rounded the back of the car, sliding into the backseat beside her.

Marissa continued to sip her coffee in silence as the car streamed towards their destination. They didn't travel far when the lamp posts that lined the streets gave way to alternating white and red blinking lights. She looked out the window to what looked to be just a field in the dark, yet saw more lights. They had arrived at the municipal airport not far from where she lived. The car continued to drive across the parking lot of the airstrip, and stopped very close to a small Gulfstream 550. Gavin glanced at her while he ate his croissant.

"Where are we going?" Marissa arched an eyebrow.

Gavin put his coffee cup to his mouth, and said, "Oklahoma" into the cup, then jumped out of the car. Marissa followed suit.

"What's in Oklahoma?" Marissa slammed the door, then opened it again, retrieving her coffee. "Gavin, what's in Oklahoma," she repeated.

Gavin continued to walk towards the aircraft. Its engines were alive, its door already open. "I'll tell you on the way," he yelled behind him. He took the stairs two at a time and disappeared into the aircraft.

Marissa stopped walking. She brushed a few loose curls from her eyes, and looked up at the airplane, not sure if she was fully awake.

"Ms. Elliot? The captain's ready to take off whenever you are, ma'am!" The cabin attendant stood at the door.

She flashed him a thumb's up and walked up the stairs. Oh, yeah, this *better* be good!

●●●

Adena's fingers shook as she scrolled her phone's directory looking for her mother's number. She forced herself to listen for an answer on the other side as she observed the chaos around her. There were uniformed officers coming in and going out the front door, the ones going out carried brown paper bags and wore blue latex gloves. The ones coming in were talking on cell phones and wore blue disposable shoe covers. There were several plain-clothed officers also inside, two stood in a near-by corner comparing notes. The phone rang two more times. When the front door opened again, she saw an officer huddled with Vivien. She was pointing in the direction of her place, the officer writing in his notepad.

"Hello?" The voice was soft from sleep.

Her stomach dropped as she brought her attention back to the telephone. For a moment, she couldn't breathe.

"Hello?" This time, the voice was tinged with impatience.

"Mama." Adena closed her eyes.

"Adena, are you okay? What's wrong?" The impatience was replaced with alarm.

"Mama, there's been a break-in at my place." She heard the quiet gasp on the other end.

"Are you okay? Were you hurt?"

Tears ran down Adena's face as she spoke. "I'm fine, mama, I'm fine. I was at work." Taking a jagged breath, she forced the words out of her mouth. "It's not me, it's Deandra."

"Is she all right?"

She closed her eyes and forced the words from her lips. "She was kidnapped."

"Wait, what? I, I don't understand. What did you just say?"

Adena's voice was raw and hoarse as she repeated, "Deandra was kidnapped, mama. Someone broke into my apartment and they took Deandra."

"Oh, my god! Where are you? What happened?" Greeted with silence, her mother repeated louder, "Adena, what happened!?"

Adena took deliberate, slow breaths and told her the events of the evening as she knew them. She stifled her own cries as she listened to her mother's.

"Do they have any idea where she is? Where they might have gone?"

"Not right now." Adena's eyes darted around her, watching the officers buzz about. "The police are here now."

"How are you holding up?"

"I'm scared, mama." She pressed a hand to her closed eyes. "I can still hear her screaming. I couldn't get here. I couldn't get to her." She dropped her head with guilt. Tears squeezed themselves out of her closed eyes.

"I can be there in fifteen minutes."

"No," Adena her head snapped up. Her eyes cut around the room at the officers and the portable lights placed in the bedroom and hallway. There were lights and police everywhere. She watched an officer delicately remove loose black powder off the bedroom doorframe with a brush. "It's nothing but craziness here, and you don't need to see this."

"Nonsense, . . ." her mother started.

"Mama, no!" She replied a little too sharp.

"Come over here, then," her mother said.

Adena pressed the back of her hand over her mouth against the sob that threatened to escape. She closed her eyes, nodding as she said, "Okay."

•••

"Three days ago, a young girl was kidnapped from her sister's apartment." Marissa was seated across from Gavin as they flew in the night. He leaned forward, placed a small tape recorder on the table between them. Without introduction, he pressed "play." For a few seconds, there was silence.

"911, what's your emergency?" A voice crackled from the recorder.

"Someone's trying to break into my house!" A young girl yelled into the telephone hysterical.

"Calm down, ma'am. Did you say someone broke into your home?"

"They're in here right now," the girl cried. "Please help me!"

"Where are you, ma'am?"

"I'm in my closet! Please send someone! They are trying to get in!"

"Okay, ma'am, I'm sending police over right now. Ma'am, don't hang up!"

There was a terrific bang. The girl screamed for help, and a male voice yelled, "Get that bitch!" Marissa made out the name "Adena" among the screams and rustling in the background.

"Ma'am, ma'am, are you there?"

The girl screamed again, and there was more scuffling in the background. A male voice yelled out, and then the line beeped and went dead. The operator continued, "Hello? Hello, ma'am?"

Gavin stopped the recorder and looked at Marissa, her eyes glued on the tape recorder. After a few seconds, she cleared her throat, interrupting the ire quiet that followed.

"What was that?"

"That was the 911 call she — . . .,"

"Who is 'she'?" Marissa interrupted.

"Oh, right. Deandra Knight. Sixteen, living with her sister. She was at home alone at the time of the break in. She was on the phone with her sister when she heard pounding at the door. Her sister told her to call 911. When her sister got to the house, the police were already there, but the patio door around back was broken, and the place was in disarray. No sign of Deandra."

"How long ago was this?"

"She's been missing for three days."

"And Oklahoma?" Marissa grabbed the tape recorder and rewound the tape. The girl's voice sounded so young to be sixteen, she thought, listening a second time.

Gavin swallowed, his eyes bore into hers. "I've been back and forth over the past forty-eight hours already, working with the police and a couple of the suspects in Ponca City,

Oklahoma. Late last night, and then earlier this morning, we were led to a grave in the brush at a local lake." His gaze never left hers. "We have recovered a body that we think is Deandra."

"You think or you know?"

"We strongly believe it's her."

"Wait. Back up," she said, holding up her hand. "Are you telling me you've been up there already and you flew back just to get me?"

"Yep," he nodded. "There were warrants involved, judges, and a lot of frequent flier miles that don't count." He threw her a wicked smile. "Besides, Maury, I knew you'd want to get involved as soon as possible."

The cup stopped mid-way to her lips. "I had asked you not to call me that."

Gavin burst into a hearty laugh. Several years ago, they had worked on a federal drug case that revolved around a state domestic violence case. With all the fighting and arguing and cousins and brothers-in-law that were involved, in a fit of frustration, Marissa mentioned it all reminded her of an episode of Maury Povich. Gavin took an instant liking to the reference, and thus, her nickname was born. The thing is, though, she hated nicknames, she found them childish. But he reveled in the fact that he was the only one who paid no attention to her protests. The name stuck.

Resigned, she sat back in her seat. She looked out the window, concentrating on the blinking lights of the aircraft as they made their way through the darkness. Only now, she knew where they are headed. And why.

She turned her attention back to Gavin. "What's the back story?"

He paused, sat back in his chair and clasped his hands behind his head. "Basically, there was a drug deal gone bad. A couple of punks were given a sum of cash in exchange for marijuana. Only, they never showed up with the drugs. Instead, claimed they were robbed of the drugs, the front money, and their car. But the geniuses were seen by an accomplice of the head dope dealer driving around in the 'stolen' car." He made air quotation marks to punctuate the word "stolen."

"Nice." Marissa shook her head.

"Oh, wait, there's more," Gavin continued, sitting upright again. "The head dope dealer rounds up his posse to go to their apartment. I guess to try and make the crooks confess, right? They go over to where they live, break in, except no crooks. Just their little sister. They take the sister, thinking she's covering up for where the brothers are, right? Only she doesn't know anything. They don't believe her, and now..."

"And now we are going to look at the body of a dead girl," she finished.

●●●

Trance-like, she hung up the phone, yet couldn't move from the side of the bed. Her mind flooded with all kinds of images and pictures of Deandra being dragged to God knows where with God knows who. Fear and panic blended together until they created a physical pain in her chest. Lydia placed her hand over her heart, subconsciously pushing it back in place, it was beating so fast surely it moved from its chamber! Over and over, she kept thinking how? What could have happened? Who could have wanted to harm Deandra, and more important, why?

She and Norrece had decided to retire here in Texas to be closer to their older children. Her husband of thirty-seven years, once a vibrant teacher in the primary school system in the parish of Saint Elizabeth, was dead after eight weeks of being diagnosed with stage II gastric cancer a year after leaving Jamaica. In those last weeks, with love, she bathed him, changed him, massaged his arms and legs when they ached. When he couldn't eat, she ground up his food so he could take it in a straw. She walked to the window, reminisced how he liked to be rubbed with baby powder because he liked the smell, it calmed him and reminded him of when the children were little. It wouldn't surprise her if he kept his being sick a secret to spare her the pain.

Lydia never thought she would again experience a pain like losing her beloved Norrece. Tears streamed down her face and her chest ached, her heart literally hurt over the thought of harm coming to Deandra. She covered her mouth and tried to keep the awful thoughts at bay. She trembled in her paper-thin nightgown, yet it had nothing to do with the air. Her throat stung, and her pounding head felt heavy. She just could not believe what Adena told her. Deandra, missing!

Lydia turned from the window, using the back of her hand to dry her eyes. She took her favorite terry-cloth robe off the nearby bench and walked out the room. She put on the robe, rubbing her arms as she walked down the hall to the kitchen.

She reached behind the refrigerator and flipped on the light switch. The pretty kitchen was painted a cheery yellow with white cabinets and trim and appliances. There were pops of green where plants were growing in corners and on the windowsill in pretty porcelain planters of rich blues and reds. She crossed the kitchen to the gas stove and retrieved a tea pot. The busyness of making tea kept her mind in the present, her thoughts on the task of measuring the tea and pouring the water. While it perked, she got down two cups, not sure if Adena was up for tea, yet needed something to do to not think.

•••

An hour later, the plane landed in Oklahoma. As she got up to depart, Marissa scooped up the recorder that was still on the table and put it in her pocket to listen again later. She followed Gavin to the door of the plane, who gestured for her to go first. She smiled at the attendant and stepped outside. A police officer leaning against a squad car scrambled to the stairs. He was tall and thin, almost lanky.

"Agent Wright?" The officer shouted over the plane's engine.

"Yeah," Gavin poked his head from behind Marissa.

The officer gave a gangly wave as they walked down the short stairs. "I'm Officer Hamilton. I didn't meet you when you were here earlier." The officer shook hands with Gavin. "I'm here to take you to the site." He tilted his hat to Marissa. "Ma'am," he said.

"This is Marissa Elliot, the AUSA assigned to this case," Gavin introduced.

"Ma'am," he repeated, tilting his hat to Marissa. "Welcome to Ponca City." Officer Hamilton opened the passenger door for her. Up close, she pegged him for being fresh out of the academy, probably no older than twenty-four years old.

"Thank you," Marissa smiled and slipped into the squad car.

Once inside, Officer Hamilton maneuvered the squad car off the tarmac, onto the highway. The sun struggled to be seen between the thick trees as it rose, signaling a new day. Gavin leaned forward, positioning himself between the officer and Marissa.

"Do we have a cause of death yet," he asked.

Officer Hamilton glanced sideways at Gavin, looked back at the highway, and said, "The initial cause of death reported was blunt-force trauma to the back of her head."

Marissa remained silent, watching the world outside continue on as if nothing was wrong.

Before long, the squad car pulled into a motel. There were several other squad cars in the lot. In the distance behind the motel, trees were lined with yellow tape. There were police officers in the woods, some were pointing to an area in front of them, some had shovels, and a medical examiner's van was parked off to the side.

Marissa got out of the car, looking up at the sky. It was clear, not a cloud to be found. Beautiful day, she thought, I should be bike-riding, swimming, anything but doing this. But she silently followed in step behind Officer Hamilton and Gavin towards the yellow-taped woods.

Sitting a part from the field of officers was a kid. Couldn't have been any older than seventeen, eighteen years of age, she guessed. An officer was flanked on either side of him. His hands were cuffed behind his back, his legs stretched out in front of him, crossed at the ankles. He had a black bandana over his head, and braids were peeking out from underneath.

"Who's that?" Marissa ran a little to catch up with Gavin.

Glancing over, he responded, "That's Calvin Stewart. He's the one that told us where the body was."

Marissa looked back over at him. Simultaneously, he turned in her direction. She wasn't close enough to read his eye, but Marissa could feel their darkness. Cold. Caught off guard and slightly flustered, she dropped her eyes, shifting them ahead. She refused to look back, but she felt him still looking.

They arrived to an area marked with small red flags. It was a small grave, slightly shallow with a pile of dirt and leaves off to the side.

"This is where we found her," Gavin said. "We have pictures of the undisturbed area prior to our recovering the body." Turning to Officer Hamilton, he asked, "Where are they?"

"Back at the motel. We commandeered a lower-level room as an on-site command post."

"And the body?"

Officer Hamilton pointed. Gavin and Marissa followed his finger to the van pulling out onto the street. "She's headed to the state crime lab."

"There's nothing else to see here.," Marissa said, peering down in the hole. "I'm going up to the motel."

"I'll go with you," Gavin responded. After a brief discussion with Officer Hamilton, he patted him on the back and followed.

"Why is he still staring at me?" She looked back at Calvin Stewart, still sitting off with the officers on each side, his stare still fixed on her.

"I dunno, Maury," Gavin shrugged, looking back over his shoulder. "Maybe he thinks you're pretty."

She glared at him, and was even more annoyed when he laughed.

They headed towards the room where they spotted officers coming and going. Inside were four or five more officers, some in uniforms, a couple wearing t-shirts that read "Ponca City Police" on the back. They all looked up when Gavin and Marissa walked in.

Gavin held up his identification and said, "Gavin Wright, Federal Bureau of Investigations. This here is Marissa Elliot, Assistant United States Attorney in Dallas. Who's in charge?"

"I am." An older gentleman got up from the desk holding a cup of coffee. He smiled, offered his other hand to Gavin. "Didn't think you'd be back so soon." Turning to Marissa, he said, "I'm Sergeant Dave MacGregor. Welcome to Ponca City." Sergeant MacGregor extended his hand to Marissa.

"Wish we were meeting under different circumstances," Marissa said, shaking his hand.

"Would you folks like a cup of coffee?" Sergeant MacGregor gestured toward the back of the room where a make-shift coffee bar was assembled, along with pastries and muffins.

"Thank you." Gavin walked over to the counter and helped himself to a Danish. Marissa poured herself a cup of coffee. Tasting it, she grimaced, pouring more sugar into the Styrofoam cup.

"Where are the photos of the victim," Gavin inquired. Licking one set of fingers, his other hand reached for another Danish.

Sergeant MacGregor walked over to the desk he vacated earlier, and picked up a digital camera. "Damn shame," he said, handing it over to Gavin.

"Allow me." Marissa took the camera instead. The girl was naked, her body half-curled in the fetal position in the grave. The skin of her arms, torso, and one breast were burned, visibly peeled away from the muscle and bone. Splotches of peeled skin sprinkled her face. She was wearing a gag sealed to her face with duct tape. Maggots were present in her ears and coming out of her nose cavity. She clicked through picture after picture. There were pictures of the body inside the grave, the grave once the body was removed, and pictures of the covered body beside the grave. Such a shame, Marissa thought. More than a shame, it was a waste.

"I need to talk to the boy again." Gavin called out over his shoulder. She handed the camera over to him which he snapped through quickly. "Damn, he murmured.

"We'll set him up back at the station for you whenever you're ready," Sergeant MacGregor responded. "Same place as before. He's already on the way."

"Thanks." Gavin handed the camera back to him. Turning to Officer Hamilton, he said, "We need to get to the station."

"Yes, sir." Officer Hamilton held the door open for Gavin.

"Uh, you coming?" Gavin looked at Marissa, who had taken the camera again.

"No, I'm going to stick around here, get some more information." He watched as she went through the photos carefully, pausing to view each one up close.

Gavin walked over to Marissa, and lowered his voice. "Maury, you okay? Some of these are pretty morbid." He nodded at the pictures.

She smiled at his concern. He was close enough that his cologne tickled her nose. Nodding, she touched his arm. "Of course. I'll be fine."

Gavin looked at her, weighing her answer. "Okay. Well, then, I'll meet you at the lab. Let's go!" He slapped Officer Hamilton on the shoulders as they walked out the door.

CHAPTER TWO

Gavin rubbed his forehead in frustration. He looked in the mirror on the wall and shook his head. The earpiece in his ear crackled and a voice said, "What do you wanna do?"

He looked across the table and said, "Okay, one more time."

"Look, big man, I told you everything." He glared at Gavin. He looked all of fifteen, maybe sixteen years old, wearing the standard orange jumper selected for inmates. He wore the same black bandana he had on earlier, and his hands rested on the table uncuffed.

"What, Calvin, you got somewhere to go?" Gavin jerked a nearby chair and straddled it backwards. "Let's take it from the top." He rested his chin on his hand. With the other, pressed the "record" button on the tape recorder on the table. He gestured to Calvin to begin.

"Me and Blade was to meet these two dudes behind this carwash, and, you know, we was supposed to buy some weed."

"And then what?"

"We, you know, waited for 'bout twenty, thirty minutes, and, you know, Blade kept saying 'where they at, man?' I kept tellin' him to, you know, 'be cool, dawg, they coming.'"

"So, you guys waited," Gavin propelled his free hand in the air, prompting him to continue.

"Yeah, we waited another ten, fifteen minutes." Calvin licked his lips and fidgeted in his chair. "Blade got, you know, real mad, right? And dude just got out the car. He just started walking 'round, you know, cussin' and saying 'I can't go back yet,' know what I mean? He was just, you know, cussin' and going off and stuff."

"Okay, what happened after you went back to your apartment?"

"Later on after that, we was at Vanessa's house sitting out back, drinking beer, right? And Blade was, umm, mumblin', saying some shit like he was gonna kill 'em."

"And that would be?" asked Gavin.

"Rider and Mac."

Gavin looked back at him with a blank stare.

"You know, Rider, as in Knight Rider?" Calvin clicked his teeth. "The TV show?"

"Okay, we'll come back to that in a minute." Gavin rolled his eyes. "Go on," he prompted.

"Later on, we texted Mac, you know, to find out where they were, right?" Calvin licked his lips again. "He called, and him and Mac was talking at first, but then Blade said Rider took the phone, told Blade they had, you know, got jacked or some ol' bullshit like that. That the dudes stole the money and the car."

"How do you know they weren't telling the truth?" Gavin suggested. "Maybe they really did get jacked."

"Man, we scoped out they crib for like, a couple days, know what I'm sayin? These dudes, "Calvin scoffed, "man, they drove up one night real late, right? But check it, they were in the car they said was stolen, man!" He chuckled at the memory.

"Now, after you and Connors found out they lied about getting jacked, who's idea was it to kidnap the girl?"

"Man, we didn't set out to, you know, grab her, like we planned it and shit." Calvin's finger jabbed the table. "We was tryin' to get the dudes that jacked us. When we went in, we was aiming at getting them dudes to tell us where the money was. But they weren't there. So," Calvin shrugged his shoulders and leaned back in his chair, "we took they sister."

Gavin continued to record Calvin's confession for the next hour. Every once in a while, he looked at Ted, the officer sitting in the corner of the room. Afterwards, Calvin looked Gavin up and down and said, "Now, what's in this for me, playa? Am I gonna get my deal now?"

"We'll do what we can," Gavin responded.

"Hey, man, you said you'd get me a deal!" Calvin slammed his fist on the table, knocking his chair onto the floor as he stood up, leaning across the table towards Gavin.

Ted grabbed Calvin's arms behind his back and slammed him face-first into the table.

"You got it, Caesar." Gavin put his hand on Calvin's shoulder.

Calvin looked up when he heard his nickname. Ted eased his hold and Calvin stood up, massaging his wrist. He looked at Gavin long and hard.

"You got it," he repeated, patting his shoulder again. "You earned some help. I'll see that the right people hook you up."

Scooping up the tape recorder, Gavin left the room.

• • •

Marissa walked into the crime lab and looked around. The room was white, almost too white. She saw two large, walk-in refrigerator doors to the far right of the room. The walls were lined with cabinets, some held various containers and some housed books. There were several rolling tables, and she was relieved no one was on them. Until she spotted the table off to the left. A body was lying on it, still in the black bag it was delivered in. Marissa started towards it.

"Excuse me, may I help you?"

A tall man walked towards Marissa, wiping his hands with a towel. He was wearing green hospital scrubs, and his hair was short, blond and spiked. He looked to be in his late forties, early fifties, she guessed. He tossed the towel onto a nearby empty table and planted himself between her and the dead person's table, folding his arms across his chest.

Glancing back at the body, she said, "My name is Marissa Elliot. I'm an Assistant United States Attorney from Dallas, Texas. This body," she pointed, "may be the victim of a missing person's case that I'm investigating."

The man pondered her answer a moment before he stuck out his hand and said, "Welcome to my lab, Ms. Elliot. I'm Cliff Miller, chief medical examiner for the state of Oklahoma"

"Thank you, Doctor." Marissa gave a small smile and shook his hand. "I take it you haven't started the autopsy yet?" She tilted her head in the direction of the table behind him.

"No, I was just about to."

"To be sure, is this person male or female?"

He took a clipboard from a shelf under the table. "Umm, female, African-American, approximately fourteen to sixteen years old."

"Looks like I'm in the right spot."

"Are you . . .," he hesitated.

"I'm fine with observing your examination, doctor," she said, straightening her shoulders.

A slender man with dark hair and a solid build walked up to Marissa. "Hi. Kenneth Adams," he introduced himself, stretching out his hand to her.

"Marissa Elliot, Assistant U.S. Attorney in Dallas," she replied, extending her own.

Kenneth was in his early thirties, and had kind eyes. He appeared relaxed in a pair of jeans and a white button-down shirt with the sleeves rolled up to his elbows. She noticed he was holding a camera. She looked from it to him, raising her left eyebrow in question.

"No, nothing obscene," he chuckled. "I'm a crime scene investigator for DeSoto PD. I'm here to photo document the autopsy."

"Ah." Marissa nodded.

Doctor Miller motioned to an attendant dressed just like him who came forward as two others stood at a large sink just behind him. The attendant and Dr. Miller pushed the table with the body to the sink. Unzipping the bag, the attendant cautiously first unwrapped a white sheet-like cloth and then green plastic underneath before he and Dr. Miller gently lifted the body as the second attendant slid the bag from under her, stowing it on the shelf underneath. Kenneth took snap shots of all the actions while the third attendant spoke into a mini tape-recorder. Doctor Miller started the cleansing process, gently sprayed her with water. The first attendant removed twigs and brushed dirt from the body, putting samples of each in little bags which the second tagged and marked them to be reviewed later.

"Can I see you for a moment outside, please?"

Marissa jumped and twirled around to face Gavin. He immediately held up his hands to ward off an attack. "Whoa! Maury, I'm sorry! I'm sorry! I didn't mean to startle you! But," he lowered his voice, "can I speak to you outside, please?"

"We'll continue to clean her off, Ms. Elliot," Dr. Miller called out. "I'll bring you back in when we are ready to begin."

Without waiting for a response, Gavin took Marissa's arm and steered her towards the door.

Once out in the hall, she jerked from his grasp and growled, "What? What!?" from between her teeth, still shaken from him scaring her.

"Her sister is on her way." He shoved his hands in his pockets.

"Who's," she asked.

"Her's," Gavin nodded towards the examination room.

"What!?" Marissa sputtered. "But...but what if it's not her?"

"Seriously?" Gavin dropped his head as he looked at Marissa.

"Seriously. What if it isn't?"

Raking his hand across his head a couple times, Gavin huffed. Marissa crossed her arms over her chest.

"Okay, look," he said. "In all likelihood, we are in the presence of our victim, Deandra Knight. Now from my understanding, her sister has been calling the bureau in twenty-minute intervals since her sister disappeared. Whether we do it here, or we do it in Dallas, we are going to have to deliver the news whether or not this is indeed her sister."

The door of the examination room opened. "Ms. Elliot, we're ready to begin." Doctor Miller stood waiting. Glancing at Gavin, Marissa walked toward Dr. Miller in silence. Shaking his head, Gavin followed.

"I did not remove the gag from her mouth. I thought you would want to be present for all points after cleansing."

"Thanks, Doc," Gavin responded. Doctor Miller frowned at Gavin.

"Oh, I'm sorry. Gavin Wright, FBI," Gavin flashed his badge and smiled. "I'm lead officer of the investigation of the, uh, victim here."

"Of course. Follow me, please." The doctor handed them both surgical masks, turned and walked back into the room. Marissa pulled on her surgical mask as she fell in step behind Dr. Miller, stopping at the table.

Marissa saw the girl's face for the first time. Hair still beaded with water, her face was ashen, her lips purple around the gag. Marissa felt an odd brush of sorrow as she looked down.

"We are ready to begin the external examination," said Dr. Miller. He nodded, and an assistant appeared at the foot of the body. She first looked at the victim, then looked at Marissa. Marissa nodded her head. The assistant made various notes while Dr. Miller talked, looking up periodically at the clock. Another assistant gathered more items from the body such as hair samples, pieces of skin, and scrapings from under her fingernails, putting them in small plastic bags and recorded the contents. Kenneth, also wearing a surgical mask, moved around quick and quiet, only the click of his camera interrupting the silence.

"Hey, doc, do you smell that?" Gavin asked, eyebrows drawn together. "What is that?"

"That smell, Agent Wright, is gasoline. I believe that is what led to this." He pointed to her right shoulder, torso and various parts of her face and neck where the skin had fallen away.

Gavin made notes in his notebook. He leaned closer to the victim's face.

"Doc," he asked, "what made these groves on her cheek here?"

Doctor Miller leaned down alongside Gavin, looking from the top of his glasses. Stepping back a bit, Dr. Miller stood upright, glancing at Marissa. "Those 'groves,' Agent Wright, were made by her tears."

"Oh." Gavin stood up.

The doctor retrieved a pair of tweezers from the near-by tray, and gently peeled away the tape, then the gag from her mouth. Pieces of string from the cloth dangled from her bottom lip. The attendant continued to record all steps performed by Dr. Miller, while the other bagged the tape, gag and marked them. Kenneth continued taking pictures. Doctor Miller retrieved more string from around the victim's mouth.

A scream from the door startled everyone. Gavin whirled towards the door, hand on his holstered gun. A petite black woman, one hand holding onto the door, stood there screaming at the top of her lungs. She was doubled over, her other hand pressed into her stomach. The screams were deafening.

Recovering from the initial shock, Marissa and Gavin ran to the woman. Marissa put her arms around her shoulders, Gavin pried her hand from the door, both of them walking her backwards out of the examination room. They sat her down on a nearby bench. The woman continued to scream, rocking back and forth, her arms wrapped around her midsection.

After a few seconds, Marissa said, "Ma'am, . . .ma'am!" She half-screamed herself to be heard. "I'm going to have to ask you to calm down."

The woman continued to rock back and forth sobbed, but the screaming ceased.

Moments passed before the woman's cries slowed down. Marissa and Gavin shared a glance over the woman's head.

"That's better," Marissa said. "What's your name?"

The woman wiped her eyes and straightened, easing back into the bench. Without looking at either of them, she said, "Adena. Adena Knight." A tear fell down her cheek.

"Okay. Well, I'm Marissa Elliot, and this is Special Agent Gavin Wright."

Gavin cleared his throat. "Umm, Ms. Knight, you really shouldn't be here." Shifting his feet, he said, "We have not identified the body yet. We are still very early in this investigation."

"It's her," Adena whispered.

"Ma'am," he started, "I know you are upset, and ...,"

"That is my sister in there!" Adena shouted, big tears leaked from behind her eyes and rolled down her cheeks.

"Okay, okay, just calm down." Marissa said. Turning to Adena, she said, "Pardon me for saying so, but you weren't at the door for very long, yet you're sure that is your sister?"

Reluctant, Adena nodded. "I did her hair," she turned sad eyes to Marissa.

Marissa shot her eyes up at Gavin. He nodded, and walked off, going back into the examination room. She put her hand on Adena's back. She was petite with a pretty Pixie haircut. She looked just a little older than her sister, no more than twenty-five, twenty-six years old. She looked . . . like a nice person, Marissa concluded.

"I am so sorry for your loss," Marissa began. "I will not even say that I understand what you must be going through."

"Have you found who did this to her?" Eyes looking forward, Adena's voice was barely audible.

"As Agent Wright said earlier, we are so very early into this investigation. I am going to have to ask you a few questions, though."

"I need to call my mama." Adena dropped her head. "I have to tell my mama Deandra is dead." Her shoulders shook once more, and she pressed a hand to her eyes.

"Wait, before we go any further, we do have to make a positive identification on the victim. I know this is difficult for you, Ms. Knight, but . . . can you do that? Can you identify your sister for us?"

There was a long pause, long enough that she didn't think she heard her. As she was about to ask again, Adena raised her head and looked at Marissa. Her eyes were sad, the burden of the question visible within their depths. Nodding, Adena swallowed, tears streaming down her face. Both women stood up, and walked back towards the examination room.

Gavin met them at the door. "Ms. Knight is ready to give us a positive ID of the body," Marissa whispered.

He looked back at the doctor and nodded his head. Without a word, Dr. Miller pulled a sheet over the body, stopping at the top of her shoulders. He stepped back, and Adena moved into his place. Her eyes were closed at first. Taking a deep breath, she opened them and looked down at the body. She reached to touch the body, but abruptly withdrew her hand as if burned. Reaching out again, she placed her hand on the victim's chest. She made her way upward, touching her chin, then her cheek, careful to avoid the deteriorated skin spots from the gasoline. Adena caressed the side of her head, fingered a braid, shaking her head as her face crumbled.

Gavin stepped forward. "Ms. Knight, is this your sister, Deandra Knight?"

"This is my sister," Adena responded without looking at him. "This is Deandra." Her sobs grew louder as she continued to stoke her sister's face. "This is my baby sister. This is my baby sister!" she repeated over and over again. Adena put her forehead on Deandra's chest, sobbing.

Gavin and Marissa both removed her from Deandra's body, and Dr. Miller covered the rest of her remains. Marissa cradled Adena into the fold of her arm, and walked her back through the door.

"Thanks, Doc. I think we're done here. We'll be in touch," Gavin shook his hand and followed the two women.

They went back to the bench and sat down. Adena held her head in her hands.

Marissa decided to plunge in. "When was the last time you spoke to your sister?"

"I was on the telephone with her when she started screaming that someone was trying to break in," Adena replied without raising her head.

"Did you hear anything," Gavin asked.

"I heard a big bang or boom in the background."

"Any voices? Someone besides your sister's?"

Adena paused for a moment, then answered, "No. Just the bang. I told Deandra to hide and call 911. I heard some rustling, and then the phone went dead." Adena rocked back and forth.

"Wait, I don't understand. You were on the phone with your sister during the break-in?" Marissa asked.

"Deandra called me from her cell phone. She used the house phone to call 911. I wanted to stay on the line, on the other phone, so I told her to get the house phone."

"Hang on a second, we're missing something." Gavin raised his hands. "How did you find us? Here, now? How did you know Deandra was here, and how did you get here so fast?"

After a short but significant pause, Adena looked up at him. "I'm sure you know I've made a pest of myself with the DeSoto police. I may have overheard conversations about the investigation heading in this direction." She hesitated, avoiding his eyes. "I just asked the officer that took my last call whether it was true or not, did the police think she was taken up here."

"Do I even wanna know how you were led here?" He stepped in front of her so they were facing each other.

"Well, the first place I checked was the hospital. After that, . . ."

"No, no, no." Gavin shook his head. "I mean how did you get in *here*, past the front guard?"

"I guess there was an emergency or something on another floor," Adena shrugged her shoulders.

"Okay, okay. I get it." He waved his hand in the air.

"Is there anything else you remember about that night?" Marissa asked.

"No," she shook her head, "that's all I remember. The boom. I just dropped everything at work and ran to my car. I tried to get to her," she cried.

"I know, ma'am. I really appreciate you talking to us during this difficult time," Gavin said.

"Who could do this? Why would anyone want to hurt her? She was just sixteen years old! Who would want to hurt her?!"

"Ma'am, we're going to find out," Gavin replied.

●●●

Later that afternoon, Marissa stood in the motel room surveying the mess. The bed was unmade. There were soda cans and take-out bags on the night stand. The lamp was still on, as well as the inner bathroom light. One curtain was drawn, the other partially meeting its mate. She looked on the floor, observed a towel lying next to her feet. Using her foot, Marissa rolled the towel around and saw splotches of dried blood. On the television stand were empty chip bags, another soda can. Walking into the open bathroom, she came across another towel with more dried blood on it. Sitting in the trash were opened condom packages, in the sink was a presumably used condom. The shower curtain was pulled back, the bathtub dirty. Looking up and around at the ceiling, Marissa turned and walked backed out.

Gavin stood by the front door. Hands on his waist, he, too, looked around, shaking his head. "Man," he said.

Marissa spotted a chair on the opposite wall of the bathroom counter. There were pieces of duct tape hanging from one side. A shoe was underneath. She looked out into the main room. This is where Deandra spent her last moments, she thought. Marissa could only wonder what took place in this room, who's blood was on the towels. She knew some of the things that happened as she looked again in the sink. How scared she must have been, not knowing if she was going to see her sister, her family again.

Marissa looked at Gavin, nodding her head once. Gavin waved his hand forward and said, "Come on." Uniformed officers came into the room and began collecting evidence. One officer collected the soda cans and the towels off the floor. These items were placed in bags, and passed to another officer that wrote its contents on the tape before sealing it. She watched another officer retrieve the condom from the sink and one of the packages from the trash.

"Are you serious!?" Gavin exclaimed. He walked to the officer, taking the bagged condom from her. Holding it up to the light, he examined it closer. Shaking his head, he handed the bag back to the officer and looked at Marissa. "These dudes weren't too bright. Did they really leave behind a fucking used condom?"

"That, and blood, not to mention finger prints I'm sure are all over the soda cans and in this room."

"Wow," was all he could say.

Looking around, she could not imagine what must have happened there for the last three days and three nights of Deandra Knight's life. She ran her fingers along the opened curtain.

Exhaling a heavy breath, Marissa walked past the officers and outside. Wow was right.

STOLEN HOPE

CHAPTER THREE

Adena sat in the car, head on the steering wheel. Images of Deandra lying on the table danced behind her eyes. She remembered the coldness beneath her fingers as they skimmed her face, the hardness of her body when she laid her hand on her heart. It didn't beat. It was still. Adena opened her hand and, through unshed tears, looked down at the necklace. Deandra's necklace. The lady from the morgue, the attorney, gave it to her with the promise she would give it back. She smiled looking at it. Deandra had been proud of it because it was her first purchase with her own money. She babysat often for Adena's friend, Vivien, who lived in another building at the apartment complex. She loved those two little boys. Often times, Deandra had not referred to it as work, and almost felt guilty when she got paid. Smiling wider, Adena looked at the little diamond at the end, and she could almost hear Deandra laugh as she said, "I said I *almost* feel guilty!"

Moments later, Adena opened the door at last and got out. She paused, closing her eyes and offered up a quick prayer for strength. She walked up the sidewalk and the quick stairs to the front door. With a deep breath, she rang the doorbell. She didn't realize she was holding it until the door opened. Her voice quivered as she said, "Hey, mama."

The woman on the other side search Adena's face. Her hands flew to her mouth as she screamed, "No!" over and over. She must have been washing dishes or something because the dishtowel and mug in her hand both fell to the floor, yet neither woman heard the mug break.

Adena walked across the threshold, forcing her mother to step back into the room. Closing the door with one hand, she embraced her mother with the other. She cradled her, held onto her as Lydia continued to scream that one word over and over. Her mother's body shook with grief, and the screaming crossed over to wails.

Fearing her mother would faint or fall, Adena led her to the worn yet still comfortable sofa and they both sat down. Still hugging her mother, she rocked her back and forth.

After a few moments, Lydia gently pulled away from the embrace. She looked at her daughter and said, "How?"

"I don't know," Adena looked into her eyes, grief masking her vision. She touched her butter-soft chocolate face and shook her head. "They don't know."

"Where is she?"

"Right now she's in Oklahoma City."

"What? How did she get there? What happened!?" Lydia started to get up. "Are you sure it was Deandra? Maybe, . . . "

"Mama, I saw her." Adena pulled her back down. "It was her." She looked into her mother's eyes.

Lydia searched her daughter's face, yearning for any sign that she was wrong.

Adena took her mother's hand. Heart heavy, she laid Deandra's necklace in her palm and closed her fingers around it. Lydia looked down and opened her hand. Through her tears, the diamond sparkled. Clutching her hand and the necklace to her heart, she dropped her head.

A few seconds later, she straightened and put her free hand on her daughter's cheek. "How are you?"

"Oh, mama," Adena nuzzled her cheek deep into her mother's hand. "She looked so peaceful lying there. Her body was so hard, like the table she was on. I keep hearing her voice yelling in the phone, yelling for help. I couldn't get to her." She dropped her head and sobbed, shoulders shaking. "I couldn't get to her."

Lydia circled her other arm around her daughter's shoulders. She rubbed her back, and Adena gave into the tears and guilt and pain. Moments later, she pulled from her mother's embrace and wiped her eyes.

"I'm sorry you had to see her like that." Lydia took her daughter's hand, squeezed it. "That should not be how you see your sister for the last time."

Adena stood up and walked over to the fireplace. "I talked to the attorney that is going to be handling this."

"Does he know anything?"

"She, mama," Adena smiled.

"Well, does she?"

"It's too early in the investigation to know anything, mama," she replied, mimicking the FBI agent's response he gave her. She rubbed her hands on the front of her jeans. "Umm, I also spoke with the doctor that, . . . " she took a gulp of air, "that had Deandra. He said they should be able to send her home in a few days. They are still doing some tests."

Lydia nodded. She watched her daughter pick up a picture frame from the mantel. It was Deandra, sitting in that very room, taken a couple years ago. She hated taking pictures, yet Adena had just gotten a camera and was practicing shooting. Deandra smiled and held up two fingers in the 'peace' sign. She smiled, remembering all the coaxing it took to get her to take the picture. She did it, though, and didn't protest as she sat for several more until her sister was satisfied with the results.

"I want her buried alongside your father."

"I kinda knew you would," Adena nodded, putting the picture back among the others on the mantel. She turned and faced her mother. "I think Daddy would like that." She took her mother's hand and squeezed it. "I cannot think of another place where she should be."

• • •

"Grace, could you pull the Benson file? I have court in ten minutes!" Marissa grabbed her jacket off the hook behind her office door. Her assistant appeared with the requested file. Grace Bennett was a pretty brunette, her hair in a high ponytail. She was shorter than Marissa, and dressed very stylish in a plum suit with a side slit in the skirt that carried into the side button jacket and black patent-leather high-heel pumps. She handed Marissa the file just as her phone rang. She glanced back as Grace picked up the ringing telephone.

"Ms. Elliot's office," she answered.

Marissa mouthed "I'm not here," and put on her jacket, grabbing the other files she needed from the top of the nearby file cabinet.

"Sir, one moment, let me see if she's left for court yet." Placing the call on hold, Grace said, "It's Mr. Waterman."

Marissa paused. Jack Waterman was not just her boss, he was *the* United States Attorney. It was Jack that hired her from the District Attorney's office, and took her under his wing while she was still learning and growing as an attorney. He didn't micro-manage his team, he gave all of his attorneys the rope they needed to work their cases, yet he was approachable for problem-solving and assistance. She considered him not only a great mentor, but a great friend.

"Tell him I just left and I'll call him when I get back," Marissa ask, glancing at her watch.

"No need. We can talk now." Jack walked up behind Marissa.

Marissa whirled around, almost bumping into him. She looked from him to Grace, still holding the receiver, and back at Jack again. "How did you...," she sputtered. Grace raised her shoulders as she replaced the receiver.

"We need to talk." Jack walked into the office and sat down in a chair in front of her desk as Grace exited, closing the door behind her.

"Can we talk a little later," she asked. "I have several arraignments in five minutes."

Jack unceremoniously picked up the telephone. "Ben, can you come in here for a second?" He paused, then said, "Thanks, buddy," and hung up.

Within seconds, a quick knock was followed by another lawyer entering her office.

"Ben, could you take care of these arraignments for Marissa," Jack asked. He walked over and removed the files from her hands, handing them over to Ben. Marissa was too dumbstruck to say anything.

"Of course, sir." Ben took the files and opened one as he retreated out the door.

"Now, let's talk." After closing the door behind him, he helped Marissa off with her jacket as she still stood there. He gave her a little push on the small of her back, and she walked in silence around her desk and sat down in her chair. He sat down in front of her. "How was the trip?" he asked.

"Umm, . . . it was fine."

"'Fine?'"

"Well, besides the fact we viewed a dead body, had to calm down a hysterical sister, and interrogated a suspect? Yeah, it was fine."

Marissa gave him a brief synopsis of the previous day's events. After she finished, Jack sat silent for a moment, just long enough for her to get edgy.

"Jack, did you really come down here to clear my morning just to hear about my trip?"

"No, not really," he smiled.

"So, what's this all about?"

"You weren't the only one that was awakened at an unlawful hour yesterday." He chuckled and leaned back in his chair. "I was briefed by the FBI's supervising agent about your requested presence, not to mention I received a call from a judge about warrants and, in turn, have been in contact with DOJ."

"Justice? Why?"

"With the extenuating circumstances surrounding this kidnapping and murder, they, quite frankly, want to take the prosecution a step further." At her quizzical stare, he continued. "This case is now being reviewed by the Capital Case Unit at the Attorney General's office to prosecute under the death penalty act."

"I don't understand."

"As you know, there is a new law on the books, The Federal Death Penalty Act of 1994 that basically gives us permission to seek the death penalty on a multitude of federal crimes that result in death. There is particular interest with it amongst the law-makers because it revises the previous Act, placing heavy emphasis on crimes that are drug-related."

"Really?"

"Really. We can now ask the judge for a sentence of death."

"We can do that?" She was stunned.

"DOJ has considerable interest in this particular case because, from our side of the table, this was a vicious crime, an intentional kidnapping resulting in murder. Not only that, it stemmed from a drug crime." Jack rocked back in his chair. "According to the suits, we are sitting on all of the ingredients for a well-baked death penalty case under this new Act."

"How do we go about this?" Marissa picked up a pencil, tapping it on her desk.

"For one, this law requires notification to the family of the victim once the decision to seek the death penalty is made. How much or how little contact you keep, I'll leave that strictly up to you. You'll need to appear before the Unit in Washington to give them an overview of the case, answer any questions they may have about the investigation or status." He paused, clearing his throat. "Under this statute, it also means there will be an automatic severance if there are multiple defendants."

"You mean if there are three or ten defendants, there will be three or ten separate trials!?" Her eyes widened. "Aww, man," she groaned.

"I know, I know." Jack held up his hand, warding off the oncoming questions. "This will involve a lot of red tape.

There will be a lot of eyes watching this, both here and from the East Coast. But from my point of view, she deserves this. That girl was sixteen years old, just talking on the phone. Just because she was home, she died. She deserves this," he repeated before standing up. "I'll get Grace the details for you."

Jack walked to the door, but then stopped and turned around again. "I should also tell you that under this new Act, there are only two cases in the United States that have met the Unit's criteria to prosecute."

"Really?" She tilted her head to the side. "Which ones?"

"Ironically, there's a case also here in Texas where a civilian was found dead on a military base."

Mouthing the word 'wow,' Marissa paused. "And the other one?"

"The other one is yours." Without another word, he walked out, closing the door behind him.

Marissa laid her forehead on her desk, a little overwhelmed. She thought about their conversation. This undercurrent of excitement grew inside of her.

This was why she went to law school, this is why she chose this side of the law to represent. On the prosecution side of the game, she created an avenue of justice, representing people who were unable to speak for themselves. At the District Attorney's Office, she helped countless women who were victims of domestic violence put their accusers behind bars. She heard the pain in their voice when describing their living environment and the beatings that took place almost daily. She remembered the hope in their eyes when a prison sentence was handed to the abuser, hope that they could then put their situation behind them and begin a better life. Yes, every person under the blanket of the United States Constitution deserved to be viewed as innocent until proven guilty. But viewed as innocent and actually being innocent are two very different things. Marissa understood that murderers, rapists, drug dealers, and carjackers deserved their day in court to have it proven whether or not they were guilty of these crimes. But she liked being an advocate for the people without voices, people who were not really listened to. Now here, at the U.S. Attorney's Office, she was given the opportunity to be that advocate for people again. People who deserved to be heard, no matter how little their voice or how loud their accuser yelled. People like Deandra.

Marissa heard tapping on the door.

"Are you taking a power nap?" Gavin asked.

"I'm finding my Chi," she responded without raising her head from her desk.

"How's that working for ya?"

"I'm still here instead of Cabo, so it's not," she sighed. Hearing him take a seat in front of her desk, Marissa raised her head. Stretching her neck, she looked at him. "What's up?"

"Got an ID on all the finger prints lifted from the hotel room in Oklahoma. Calvin Stewart was there." The perp from Oklahoma, she remembered. Gavin flipped through some papers. "We got prints on Roland Connors, also known as 'Blade.' The others are listed here." He handed her the report.

"Well, this looks like enough to get us the rest of our warrants." Marissa scanned it. "I already have an appointment for us to visit Magistrate Duncan. Grace just has to plug in these names, and they're done."

Gavin nodded. He looked around the office, gazing out the window before saying, "The lab is not quite finished with its analysis, but we believe the blood is Deandra's. That's all we have so far."

Marissa called for Grace. Once she arrived, she handed her the report. "This includes the names for the arrest warrants. We see Magistrate Duncan in fifteen minutes."

"I'll get them to you right away." Grace took the report and walked out.

"I want to go talk to the sister again. Make a visit to the mother, too."

"Why?"

"Well, I've just been informed that we are going to pursue this case under the Federal Death Penalty Act. And one of the provisions of doing that is to talk to the family of the victim, and make them aware of this office's decision and procedures involved moving forward."

"We can do that?" Gavin arched an eyebrow.

"Yes, we can do that," Marissa smiled. "And we're one of the firsts to put our feet in the water."

"So, what does that mean?"

"It means we try this case like we normally would, only a lot more red tape. Should be an interesting ride."

"Yippeekayay!"

Marissa couldn't suppress a laugh. A light tap at her door interrupted them. "Come in!"

"Here's the manual from Mr. Waterman. And the arrest warrants." Grace put the documents on the desk.

"Thanks. It looks like this will be a big one." Grace nodded her head and left the office. Marissa thumbed through the manual. It was thick. Thick enough to know she couldn't finish reading all of it at work, and thick enough to know the suits were going to get very involved. Marissa sighed, putting it in her briefcase. A little light reading before bed, she mused to herself.

Checking her watch, she stood up and said, "Well, let's go talk to a judge about some bad guys."

● ● ●

Frank paused outside the apartment door. He looked to his right, saw the agents run to the back of the building and the point officer standing ready to "open" the door. He glanced to his left at the crouching agents beside him.

He took several deep breaths and banged on the door. "This is the FBI! Open up!" Their guns were drawn, and hearing no moment inside, he beat on the door again. "FBI! Open up!" he repeated.

Inside the apartment, an older woman came from a bedroom. She was wearing a robe and a shower cap, still wet from her recent bath. The banging on the door made her jump. She ran to the boy lying on the couch. *How he could sleep through all of that,* she thought. *Didn't he hear them banging?!*

She started for the door. It burst open and three agents swarmed into the apartment. "Freeze!" the point agent yelled.

The lady screamed, threw her hands to her face. "Step aside, ma'am," another agent ran past her, checking down the hall.

"Wake up, sleeping beauty!" Frank and two agents tilted the couch until the boy rolled onto the floor. The boy cried out as he landed face first on the ground.

"Hey, who the hell are you, man?" He looked up from Frank to the other two agents, each pointing guns at him.

"We're your wake-up call," Frank replied, relieved that this did not involve any gunfire. He looked up as the other officers came from down the hall.

"We're clear. There's no one else here," they reported.

"Are you Nikko Hollis?"

"Who's asking?" The boy held his hands out in front of him, still lying on the floor.

"Nikko! What have you done?" The older lady stood beside the agents looking at him and began swatting his legs.

"I didn't do nuthin', ma'!" Nikko used his hands to shield his mother's arms while still eyeing the guys with the guns. "Stop hitting me, ma! I didn't do nuthin'!"

"That's what they all say," Frank retorted. "Pick 'em up." Turning to his mother, he said, "Ma'am, we have a warrant to arrest your son here." He handed her the documents.

"Nikko Hollis, you are under arrest for the kidnapping and murder of Deandra Knight. You have the right to remain silent," Frank recited the Miranda rights while putting Nikko's wrists in the handcuffs.

"Wait! Wait, what's going on," Nikko's mother lunged at Frank, wrestling with his hands, trying to stop him from handcuffing her son. An agent grabbed her arms and pulled them behind her and away from Frank. She looked from Frank to her son. "Wait, murder? What is this all about? Stop!"

"Do you understand the rights I have just read to you?" Frank finished.

"Yeah, now where's my lawyer?" Nikko glared at Frank. His nostrils flared and he was breathing hard.

"Oh, you'll get your lawyer, all right," Frank replied, stepping aside. "Take him down to the car, will ya?" An agent took Nikko by the arm and out the door.

"You can let her go," he told the agent still subduing Nikko's mother.

"Please," she said, jerking her arm from the agent's hold, "tell me what's going on!"

"Ma'am, please read the arrest warrant. Here's my card," he said, handing it to her. "I'll be able to answer any questions you may have after we take your son down to the precinct and talk to him. We should have him booked in a few hours."

He nodded his head at a nearby officer, and they righted the over-turned sofa.

She looked down at the card. Frank raised his arm and made a circle in the air with his finger. He and the remaining agents walked past Nikko's mother.

"Have a good day, ma'am," Frank said to her and walked out the door.

●●●

He walked out of the convenience store and pulled his baseball cap low. He made a quick look to the left then right before jogging across the street to the motel. Walking up the stairs, he took a swig of the orange soda and unlocked the door. He stepped inside, closed and locked it behind him. He peeked out the window. Satisfied he wasn't followed, he tossed the hotel key and his hat onto the dresser across the room. *This time tomorrow*, he smiled to himself, *I'll be chilling with a new job in Jersey, cash in my pocket, and leaving all of this behind me*. He flopped across the bed and turned on the television with the remote control. He opened the bag of potato chips and flipped channels. *A football game, perfect*, he thought as he threw the remote near his feet. Reaching for the orange soda on the night stand, he took another swig.

All of a sudden, the door burst open, crashing into the wall behind it.

"Freeze! FBI!" Three agents swarmed in, at once filling the room. He spit out the orange soda and scrambled to the other side of the bed. He tripped on the bedspread, and an agent tackled him to the floor.

"I ain't done nuthin'!" He yelled, squirming under the agent. But he could barely move, the agent had his elbow in his back, pinning him to the ground.

Two other agents ran into the room, guns drawn. One jumped over his flailing legs and ran into the bathroom. Seconds later, he came out. "Clear," he announced. "There's no one else here."

Gavin stood in the door. Crossing the threshold, he put his gun in his holster. He removed his sunglasses and said, "Malcolm Connors, you are charged with the kidnapping and murder of Deandra Knight."

"Man, that's not me! My name Jamal!" He continued to squirm under the agent.

"Jamal, huh," retorted Gavin. He walked over to him, raised him up from the floor by the back pocket of his jeans, and removed his wallet. Gavin let go of the back pocket, and the boy fell back to the floor with a thud.

He fished inside the wallet and pulled out his driver's license. He picked the boy up again by his back pocket and put the driver's license in front of his face. "Is this you?"

The boy refused to look at the picture.

"Well, it kinda looks like you." He looked at the picture again. "What do you think?" He held out the license for a nearby agent to review.

"Yeah," the agent nodded, "it looks like him to me."

"I think so, too," Gavin said. Once again, he let go of the back pocket, and once again, the boy fell to the ground with a thud.

"Okay, let's try this again. Malcolm Connors," Gavin put the license back into the wallet, "you are under arrest for the kidnapping and murder of Deandra Knight." As he read Malcolm his rights, an agent picked him up off the floor. Malcolm glared at Gavin. "Do you understand these rights as I have read them to you?"

"Man, fuck you!" he spat.

"I'll take that as a yes. Get him outta here!" The agent holding Malcolm took him out of the motel room and down the stairs.

Gavin's cell phone rang. He fished it from his pocket and checked the caller ID. It was Marissa.

"Maury," he answered, smiling. "What's going on?"

"You are," Marissa said on the other end. "Hey, I have the final warrant signed. You'll need to swing by here to pick it up. The plane lands at 10:45 in the morning."

"Cool." He looked at his watch. "5:30 alright?"

"See you then," Marissa said and hung up.

●●●

Gavin leaned against the squad car and watched the plane taxi down the tarmac. He looked up and around at the sky. It was a gorgeous sunny day, just the right amount of wind and a clear blue sky. The plane continued to taxi towards him. He looked at his watch. 10:50 a.m. *A little late, but,* he shrugged his shoulders, *what are you gonna do?* He removed his sunglasses, cleaned them with his shirt. He put them back on and watched the plane get closer and closer still to his car. He crossed his arms and waited.

The plane was a beautiful Cessna Citation VII, very sleek and fast, this Gavin knew. The nose of the airplane stopped just a few feet from where he stood. The pilot took off his sunglasses and looked at him, bewildered. Gavin didn't move. He saw a flight attendant enter the cockpit and talk to the pilot. They both looked back at him. Gavin grinned and threw up a wave. The flight attendant looked at the pilot again and withdrew from the cockpit.

Moments later, the door of the aircraft opened, and the stairs folded out onto the tarmac. The flight attendant Gavin saw in the cockpit appeared at the door. She was tall, a pretty redhead with a pretty smile and a pretty short mini-skirted uniform. She raised her hand to guard her eyes against the sun.

"Hi," she called out. Gavin waved again. "Can I help you?" she asked.

"Thank you," he shouted back. "I'm looking for Roland Connors. I believe he is a passenger on this flight."

The pretty attendant didn't say anything, yet lost her smile. Visibly clearing her throat, her smile returned, and she said, "One moment, please," and retreated into the plane.

Gavin looked down at his boots. *Man, I need to replace these things,* he thought as he looked at the scuffed-up toes. Sighing, he looked back up to the empty door of the plane.

The flight attendant returned. "Mr. Connors will be deplaning in a few moments," she reported.

Nodding, he checked his watch again.

Seconds later, a young man walked out to the door. The distinguished black man looked to be in his mid-twenties and about six feet tall, give or take a couple inches. He had on a tailored navy blue suit and a crisp white button-down shirt opened at the neck. Gavin couldn't see his eyes past the chic, dark sunglasses he wore, but he felt them staring back at him.

"Hey, are you Roland Connors?" He asked, waving.

"Who wants to know?" he yelled back.

Gavin looked around, puzzled. "Uh, I do," he replied, looking back at him.

"Look, I don't know what this is about," the man said, looking around, "but I don't want no trouble."

"Hey, I'm not here to give you any trouble." Gavin held up his hands.

"Oh, yeah? Then what's all this," the man gestured behind Gavin.

There were four squad cars and a half-dozen police officers and FBI agents behind his vehicle. Some were posed behind the cars, guns drawn, all pointing at the plane.

"Oh, that," he jerked his thumb behind him. "Well, they're here in case you gave any trouble. But, seeing that you don't want any trouble," he walked over to the bottom stairs of the plane, "why don't you come on down and let's talk."

Roland sighed and looked around at the officers again. He reached for the bag the flight attendant handed to him, but Gavin said, "Uh, no. You won't be needing a bag. We provide everything for you."

Smiling, Roland retracting his hand and reached into his pocket. The officers behind Gavin cocked their guns, getting into position. Gavin rested his hand on his own gun at his side. Roland heard all of the guns click and looked out at the officers. He held up his free hand and removed a wad of cash from his pockets with the other, waving it to the officers. He peeled off two one hundred-dollar bills and handed them to the flight attendant.

"Thank you, sir," she replied.

He kissed her on the cheek and descended down the stairs.

STOLEN HOPE

CHAPTER FOUR

She knocked on the door a little more persistent this time. Marissa took a quick look at Gavin alongside her, who smiled and then rolled his eyes. It got a chuckle out of her, but she coughed it down as the lock clicked and the door opened.

"Hello, Mrs. Knight. I'm Marissa Elliot," she introduced herself. "We spoke on the phone earlier."

Lydia was a little shorter than Marissa, but her head wrap gave her two more inches. Her skin was smooth chocolate with sharp cheekbones and chin. Her head wrap matched the royal-blue figure-less smock she wore. She looked from Marissa, then to Gavin in silence.

"Ma'am, my name is Gavin Wright," he said, handing her a business card. "I'm with the FBI, and I'm working with Ms. Elliot here on the murder of your daughter."

She did not give a word of greeting, yet took the card and stepped aside, granting them permission to enter.

The living room was bright yellow, decorated with worn earth-toned furniture. There were bold, big-leafed plants sprinkled throughout the room. Family pictures were placed on end tables and the mantle across from where they stood. There was a worn rug on the floor, the edges held evidence of how vibrant the oranges and rust and reds were long ago.

Lydia led them into the room, gesturing for each to sit down, and then walked out. She still had not spoken a word. Marissa looked around at the knick-knack shelf which held figurines of a couple holding hands, a child tossing a ball, and Jesus petting a sheep.

Gavin poked her in the side. She looked at him, and he nodded his head towards the far wall. On a table in the corner was a picture of Deandra surrounded by candles. There was a small cup with three burning incense sticks, the smoke billowing around the picture and into the air.

Marissa walked over to it. She fingered the rosary laying beside the picture. She looked into the smiling eyes of Deandra. Such laughter in those brown eyes, such hope, she thought. Her smile was infectious, and Marissa found herself smiling back.

"Thank you, ma'am," Gavin said.

Marissa turned around as he stood up and took the tray Lydia carried. She looked at Lydia, but she was looking past Marissa at Deandra's picture.

"She took that picture two years ago," she said, the sorrow in her voice strengthening an accent, one that Marissa couldn't place. "It was her favorite. She hated taking pictures, yet she liked that one."

"I am so sorry for your loss." Marissa walked back to the sofa.

Lydia smile. She handed her a glass of iced tea, offered one to Gavin, then took one for herself. "Thank you. I and my family appreciate your words of condolence."

"Ma'am, thank you for agreeing to meet with us today," Marissa started. "I know this is a difficult time for you, so I will make this brief. By law, I am required to tell you that the United States Attorney's Office has made the decision to prosecute this as a crime against the United States."

Lydia paused. "I don't understand," she stuttered. Confusion arose in her eyes. "How is this, how is her death a crime against the United States?"

"They took Deandra against her will across state lines, ma'am," explained Gavin. "Texas was robbed of Deandra against its will. That places the state of Texas as the body that was harmed. Because the federal government is the prosecutor of the state, it is the federal government's responsibility and duty to respond to this robbery."

"I still don't understand. So what does all of this mean, exactly?"

"Mrs. Knight," Marissa explained, "because this robbery resulted in murder, Deandra's murder, the United States is requesting permission to seek the death penalty against all persons directly involved."

Lydia set her glass down on the table. She looked first at Marissa and then Gavin. The questions that appeared in her eyes changed her posture. Looking back at Marissa, she said, "Do you know why this happened to her?"

"We are familiar with what could have prompted this, yes," she replied.

"But you won't tell me." Lydia looked at Gavin.

"Ma'am, we are still in the early stages of this investigation. We cannot go into specific details, yet, as family to the victim, we can tell you arrests have been made."

"And that's another reason why we are here," Marissa added. "We, of course, want to keep you informed of the progress as much as possible. My office will be in constant contact with you every step of the way, and answer any questions you may have."

"Who did this," she whispered, eyes closed.

"It really is too early to determine that." Marissa put her hand on top of Lydia's curled fingers on her lap. "We have made arrests," she said, "yet we are still sorting out the details and assigning responsibility." Shaking her clasped hands, Marissa repeated, "We've made arrests."

"You said you were asking permission to use the death penalty." Lydia opened her eyes, tears threatening to spill over their brim. Marissa nodded. "Permission from whom?"

"Headquarters. Washington, D.C."

"Do I need to do anything?"

"Well, I need you to look over these documents." Marissa retrieved them from her portfolio and handed them to her. "It explains what charges we will be seeking, the government's responsibility, as well as the rights of the victim's family. After you have had some time to review them, perhaps discuss them with your family, please sign and mail them back to my office."

Lydia read over the documents, pausing every now and then to read a section more closely. Without a word, she stood up. Gavin and Marissa took that as their cue to leave, so they got up, too, and started toward the door.

"Wait." Lydia held out her hand. She walked over to the nearby desk and signed the last page before handing the documents back to Marissa.

"Ma'am, are you sure you don't want to discuss this with Adena, or anyone else in your family? Have some time to think about this?"

"No." Lydia stood ram-rod straight, looking from Gavin to Marissa with unwavering eyes. "Okay," Marissa said, replacing the documents in her portfolio. "Okay. Before we go," Marissa stopped walking and looked at Lydia. She felt bad for this woman and, in a gesture of heartfelt compassion, she gave her arm a gentle squeeze. "I understand the medical examiner released the body – I'm sorry. Released Deandra to the family and that she'll be flown here soon. I won't pretend to know what you are going through or the amount of pain that you are in. My sincerest condolences to you and to your family."

"I appreciate your words. Thank you very much."

"Again, Mrs. Knight," Gavin said, "sorry for your loss."

"Thank you," Lydia repeated, opening the front door.

"We'll be in touch," Marissa said, as she headed down the stairs. The door closed followed by the click of the lock.

"Well, that went well," Gavin said, opening the car door for Marissa.

"Yes, it did," she responded as Gavin slid into the driver's seat and started the engine. She looked back at the house, just as the curtain to the front window fell back into place.

•••

Four days later, the defendants were all in court together for the first time for their arraignments. The courtroom was crowded: there were lawyers for each of the five accused who, in turn, appeared to each have either an assistant or associate to add to the air of their importance. The accused men were sitting in the jury box, all wearing orange jumpsuits, the uniform of the incarcerated. The stenographer sitting in front of the bench was busy readying her equipment. Her hair was in a messy bun, the glasses on the tip of her nose threatened to fall at any moment, and she couldn't get the last leg of her stenography machine to stay in place. The bailiff bent down to assist her. Just as the machine clicked into place, the small red light in the far corner of the courtroom flashed. The bailiff, who looked to have seen action on a football field, straightened to his full six feet, four inches, and gave the universal command for attention: "All rise!"

Shuffling feet and screeching chairs echoed throughout the courtroom as everyone stood. The door behind the bench opened, and out walked the judge. Magistrate Judge Rosalyn P. Thresher was a petite woman, newly-appointed to the bench fifteen months ago, and the only Hispanic judge to serve on the federal bench. Marissa worked with her at the District Attorney's Office at one point and found her personable, holding great knowledge of the law. Magistrate Thresher also had a wonderful sense of humor, but none of that showed today as she sat down and put on her glasses.

Marissa glanced behind her as she took her own seat. Gavin sat directly behind her just outside the well. From what she could see, he was court-ready, wearing a crisp light-blue button-down shirt and a navy blazer. He winked at her before she turned around in her chair.

"This is the case of the United States of America verses Roland Connors," Magistrate Thresher began. "Paul, please bring the defendant to their table."

Roland stood up and walked down from the jury box. Surveying the courtroom, his eyes stopped on Marissa. He gave her the once-over, slowing taking her from her Gucci-leather black pumps all the way up until he reached her face. As he got closer, he nodded. Marissa's eyes never left his as he made his way to the table on her left. He stood at the chair right next to her.

"Are you defendant Roland Loenthal Connors," the judge asked.

"Yes, ma'am," his voice raspy and soft.

"You have been charged in an indictment with kidnapping, conspiracy to commit kidnapping, interstate travel in aid of a racketeering enterprise, and carrying a firearm during and in relation to a crime of violence. Do you have a copy of the indictment?"

"We do, your honor," a voice responded from the back of the courtroom. Marissa swiveled her chair towards the voice. A portly gentleman bounced into the courtroom, waving the indictment in the air.

"Did we interrupt your previous engagement, counselor?" Judge Thresher asked. She looked over the rim of her glasses at the newcomer.

"No, your honor. I went to the wrong courtroom. May the court please accept my most humble apologies," the gentleman gave a slight bow to the bench. "Cecil P. Montgomery for the defendant, ma'am."

Oh, great, Marissa thought to herself. Cecil P. Montgomery is recognized as a legal genius throughout Texas and Oklahoma, board certified in criminal law. He was a walking powerhouse, notable for defending high-profile clients in cases throughout the Dallas/Fort Worth area for over thirty years. Not only has Montgomery established his place in legal history, he came from a distinguished line of attorneys. His father, Daniel P. Montgomery, was a very well-known state court judge who recently passed away, but not before Southern Methodist University renamed a wing of its law school after him. His mother, Justice Patricia K. Montgomery, retired from the Texas Supreme Court several years ago, following the footsteps of her twin brother, Justice Patrick K. Montgomery. Montgomery was also known to be a slick talker and a self-imposed ladies' man, with a particular fondness for women of questionable youth.

"Very well, Mr. Montgomery. Let's start over," Magistrate Thresher shifted her glance back to Roland. "Are you defendant Roland Loenthal Connors?"

"Yes, ma'am."

"Within the last twenty-four hours, have you used or taken any alcohol, drugs, or medication?"

"No, ma'am," Roland responded.

"Now, I will tell you about your certain constitutional rights."

Marissa listened as the judge read aloud. She looked out to the jury box at the other defendants. Calvin Stewart was the only one that was looking at her, the same look he gave her when she first saw him in Oklahoma.

"Mr. Montgomery, are you prepared to proceed with the arraignment?"

"Yes, your honor." Montgomery's thick Southern drawl made Marissa's flesh crawl, and she tried not to shutter.

"Very well. Please allow your client to look over the indictment," Magistrate Thresher instructed.

Montgomery's cufflinks clanked against the table as he laid the indictment in front of Roland. They huddled together, whispering among themselves, and it took every effort for Marissa not to roll her eyes at the show.

"Are you correctly named in the indictment," the judge asked a few moments later, "with the correct spelling of your name?"

"Yes, ma'am," responded Roland.

"Would you like me to read the indictment aloud into the record?"

"No, ma'am."

"So you waive formal reading of the indictment?" the judge asked, looking at Montgomery.

"Yes, ma'am, I believe we will waive that reading."

Now looking at Marissa, Magistrate Thresher said, "Ms. Elliot, would you please advise the defendant of the statutory penalties that would apply if he were to be convicted on these charges?"

"Yes, your honor." Marissa stood up. Roland didn't take his eyes off Marissa throughout the entire reading.

"Mr. Connors, do you understand what you've been charged with?"

"Yes, ma'am."

"Very well. How do you plead to count one of the indictment?"

"Not guilty, your honor," Montgomery responded.

"How do you plead to count two of the indictment?"

"Not guilty," he repeated. Magistrate Thresher continued through all counts, and Montgomery echoed his "not guilty" response.

"Your pleas of not guilty are accepted. This case is scheduled for trial before the. . ."

"Your honor, if I may," Marissa interrupted, standing up.

"Yes, Ms. Elliot?" Magistrate Thresher removed her glasses and looked at Marissa.

"Your honor, the government has made the formal request to the Department of Justice to seek the death penalty against all named-defendants in this action."

"Okay, Ms. Elliot. The court will appoint co-counsel for defendant Roland Loenthal Connors according to the capital punishment procedures of the Criminal Justice Act."

"Your honor," Montgomery interrupted, "I am on the panel of attorneys for court appointments, so there will be no need to go through with that assignment."

Magistrate Thresher put her glasses back on and looked at Montgomery. "Mr. Montgomery, you aware of the facts of this case, correct?"

"Why, yes, I am, your honor," he twanged.

"I have no doubt that in the very near future, the government will want to declare this a complex case, am I correct?"

"That is correct, your honor," replied Marissa.

"Mr. Montgomery, although your reputation in this legal community is very well known and deserved, I am still of the opinion that co-counsel should be appointed to assist in this case." Magistrate Thresher reached over and took the papers handed to her by her courtroom deputy. "I hereby appoint Ms. Gretchen Williams of Widder, Williams and Smith as co-counsel according to the CJA requirements. Ms. Williams will be notified and the appointment packet will go out today. Mr. Montgomery will retain lead counsel status."

"Thank you, your honor." Montgomery returned to his seat.

Turning back to Marissa, Magistrate Thresher asked, "Has the issue of detention been decided during an earlier proceeding?"

"No, your honor," Marissa responded.

"Is there a detainer against the defendant?"

"Yes, ma'am. May I approach?"

"Yes."

Marissa walked to the front of the bench and handed her motion to the courtroom deputy. The deputy file-stamped the document and handed it to Magistrate Thresher. On her way back, Marissa stopped at the defendant's table and laid a copy in front of Montgomery. He smiled at her, and as she took her seat, she couldn't help thinking that he looked like a snake.

"All right," the judge said, "I hereby order the defendant detained without a hearing. although I'll hold a detention hearing if the defendant's lawyer requests one." She gestured to the defendant's table. "Mr. Montgomery, does your client want a detention hearing scheduled at this time?"

"We do, your honor," he replied.

"Okay. A detention hearing is set for Monday morning, September 6, at 10:00 a.m. The defendant is to remain in the custody of the United States Marshal's Service until a determination of detention is made." Magistrate Thresher made a formal thud with her gavel.

"Next on the docket, . . ."

Marissa gathered her notes and motions for the next defendant and thought to herself, one down, four to go.

CHAPTER FIVE

Marissa rolled her head from side to side, stretching the kinks out of her neck. With one eye open, she glanced at her watch. 8:19 p.m. It was several days after the initial appearances of Deandra's killers, and Marissa was scheduled to take the case back to the grand jury in two days, adding more charges.

Her cell phone vibrated and danced on her desk. Stifling a yawn, Marissa pushed the 'talk' button. "Elliot," she answered.

"Maury, I think you want to come meet me at the police station," Gavin said on the other end.

"You think, or you know?" Marissa fished around under her desk with her foot for her red peep-toe pumps. "And stop calling me that."

Gavin gave her his location, then said, "See you in ten minutes," before the line went dead.

Well, at least it's not five o'clock in the morning, she grumbled, locating a shoe. She saved her work and shut down her computer. Making a mental note to start checking its caller I.D., she threw her phone in her purse, turned off her desk lamp, and stood up, fumbling on her other shoe. She flicked her suit jacket off the chair in front of her desk and walked out the door.

Moments later, Marissa walked through the doors of Precinct 11. There were people everywhere, even at this late hour. A couple was sitting on one of the benches, the woman's head on the man's shoulders. She looked as if either she had been or was on the verge of crying. Another man absently looked out the frosted windows, obviously thinking on other things, as the window held no view. There were people sitting in chairs, and on the benches along the walls. In an opposite corner, a lady, probably no older than seventeen years old, breast-feeding her baby.

Spotting the information desk, she walked across the room. "Hi," she smiled. "I'm Marissa Elliot, I believe . . ."

"Maury." Gavin walked through the sliding doors behind the officer's desk. He handed her a visitor's badge. "Thanks, Jimbo." He patted his shoulder. The officer nodded and buzzed the sliding doors open.

"So, what's going on?" Marissa inquired.

Gavin led her down the hall in silence. He stopped at the elevator bank, pushed the 'up' button.

"Another piece of the puzzle," he finally responded as the elevator doors opened. She stepped inside. They rode in silence.

The car stopped on the third floor. Marissa stepped out first and almost ran smack into Robert Madison. He carefully grabbed her arms before she hit his chest. His eyes wrinkled in the corners when he smiled and said, "Is this what it took to get you in my arms?" Robert was a fellow colleague at the U.S. Attorney's Office, a senior attorney. He was tall and very distinguished looking. He had a head full of hair that was, at one time, coal black but now held more salt than pepper. Robert was well-liked around the office because of his Paul Newman blue eyes and wicked sense of humor.

"Robert, what are you doing here," she laughed. She liked Robert, always respected his advice.

"Well, we made an arrest on some guys that may be related to your Oklahoma case."

"The Deandra Knight case?" All smiles vanished, his *and* hers.

"Yeah. Walk with me." He guided her down another hall to a room marked 'Interview 2' and opened the door. It was empty save a long table and a few chairs. Robert pointed to one and Marissa sat down. He sat across from her, and Gavin leaned against the wall behind him.

"So, what's going on," Marissa cut her eyes first at Gavin, then Robert.

"About three hours ago, I was given enough evidence to bring to Magistrate Tyler a criminal complaint and get arrest warrants issued for some local drug dealers." Robert sat forward and folded his hands.

Marissa blinked several times, saying nothing.

"They were arrested with 578 pounds of marijuana in the trunk, along with 36 grams of cocaine in their possession."

"I still don't understand what this has to do with my case." She was tired and could feel her patience evaporating, still uncertain why she was brought down to the station.

"The DEA just arrested David Anchorman, Ryan Knight and Kyle MacKenzie," Robert finished. He sat back in his chair.

"Who," she sighed, now annoyed.

"Mac and Rider," Gavin answered.

"You mean . . .," she stopped. Her eyes widened as she looked back at Robert.

"Yes," Robert supplied. "The brothers and a cousin of Deandra Knight are now in custody."

"Do they know about her?" It was Marissa's turn to sit back in her chair.

"I'm not certain. This is why I wanted you down here. It's clear they were the catalyst to your case, but I don't think we have enough to supersede what you have to add them to yours."

"I'm going in to begin interviews, if you wanna watch," Gavin chimed in.

"Absolutely."

"Let's go." Robert pushed back from the table and stood up.

The three of them walked down the hall to another set of rooms. Robert and Marissa went into a room marked 'Interrogation C,' Gavin entered the room next door.

She stood at the window looking into the room Gavin was in. He sat on the opposite side of the window at another long table, waiting. He seemed to know right where she was because he looked at her and waved. She instinctively waved back, then felt silly because she knew he couldn't see her. How does he do that, she wondered. As if answering, he chuckled.

The door to Gavin's room opened. A plain-clothed officer walked in first, and then Marissa watched a young man behind him come into view. His hair was braided up and back into a ponytail, and he was wearing a white tank top and sagging black jeans. His hands were cuffed behind his back. His right bicep had the initials K R under a large M. His left forearm had a picture of an ace of spades with "Mac" written underneath. The front officer pointed to a chair across from Gavin and the young man sat down. He looked at Gavin for a second, then rolled his eyes to the floor.

Gavin read him his rights and asked if he wanted an attorney present. He said nothing. "Are you Kyle MacKenzie," Gavin asked.

Still nothing.

"Do you know why you were arrested?"

Kyle crossed his ankles, stretched his legs out in front of him, still silent.

"Is Ryan Knight your cousin?" Again, silence.

"What were you doing with all of that dope in the car?"

More silence, but he shifted in his seat a little.

"Is there something that I can ask that you will answer?"

"Yea, when you gon' get the fuck outta my face," he scoffed.

"You just want to skip all of the pleasantries, huh," Gavin laughed back.

He returned a silent stare.

Gavin sat back in his chair, stretching his long legs under the table. "Who's idea was it to steal the money," he asked. He bore his unwavering glaze at Kyle, who still said nothing.

"Where'd the dope come from," Gavin pressed.

Still nothing.

Marissa could have sworn she saw Gavin's nostrils flare, just a little.

"You know they saw you flossin' around town, right," Gavin needled.

"Yeah, whatever, man," Kyle said, shifting in his seat.

"And, didn't you tell 'em the car you were riding in was stolen," Gavin pushed.

"You got the wrong dude, bruh." Kyle looked at him and smirked.

In a flash, Gavin stood up, knocking his chair back. He grabbed Kyle by the shirt and pulled him half-way across the table to within inches of his own face. "A girl is dead because you and your bitch-ass buddies decided to stiff a dope dealer."

"Gavin, take it easy, man," a voice in his earpiece said. "Stand down."

He pulled Kyle closer, his eyes black steel.

"Wright, stand down!" The earpiece cracked again.

"And not just any girl, punk-ass," Gavin lowered his voice. "The girl you helped kill," he jerked Kyle still closer, and in his ear, whispered, "was Deandra," then pushed him back, staring into his eyes.

There. Gavin saw a flicker of confusion, recognition, and then regret washed through Kyle's eyes and across his face. His mouth tightened a little. He shoved him back in his chair, and Kyle almost fell over backwards from the force. Gavin walked to the door.

"Hey, yo, hold out," he called out. Gavin stopped without turning around. "Are you for real? Deandra's dead?"

Gavin turned around and said, "You should have showed up at the car wash, bruh."

"Hey, man, that's not on me." Kyle sat up and leaned forward. "What they do to Dee, man?"

"Nuh-uh." Gavin shook his head. "This is how it's going down." He walked back to his chair, turning it around to straddle it backwards. "You first tell me what happened that night."

"Man, it wasn't my idea to leave them dudes hanging at the car wash back there."

"Why don't you just start from the beginning." Gavin pushed 'play' on the recorder.

●●●

Marissa listened as Kyle gave his account of what happened prior to the kidnapping. Gavin had long before removed his handcuffs, so she also watched his body language and hand gestures throughout the interview.

"So, what are you thinking?" Robert asked Marissa.

"I think he's telling the truth," she sighed, rubbing the back of her neck. "I believe he didn't know Ryan was not going to show up to make the deal. And I don't think he knew that Deandra was kidnapped."

"What are you talking about?"

Marissa turned around and saw Lydia standing behind her, Adena close behind. Her mother was dressed in traditional African clothing, a royal blue tunic with mustard slacks and blue and mustard headdress. Adena, on the other hand, had on jeans and a pink casual sweater.

"What are you doing here?" Lydia stood before Marissa and waited.

"Mrs. Knight, Adena, you really shouldn't be here."

"Nonsense," she replied. Her accent was thicker than Marissa remembered. "My sons have been arrested, and I demand to know why."

"They were arrested for drug possession."

"But you were discussing Deandra," she probed.

"Do you think they had something to do with my sister's murder?" Adena stepped forward a little.

"I really can't answer that at this time," Marissa responded, her gut tightened.

"Why? Why can't you tell us what's going on?"

Before she could respond, Gavin walked into the room. "We're going to take them . . ." He stopped when he saw the Knights. "Oh, hey, . . . Hello, Mrs. Knight. Adena." He shook first Lydia's hand, then her daughter's. He pulled Marissa close to him. "What's going on," he whispered in her ear.

"The Knights are here to get information on the new arrests," she looked at him.

Robert stepped up from behind them. "Mrs. Knight, ma'am," he said, looking at Adena, "my name is Robert Madison, the prosecutor over your sons' arrests. They have been processed and we are transporting them to federal court down the street for their hearing."

"Wait. What!?" Adena stepped forward again. "What are you talking about? What kind of hearing? What is going on?" She glared at Robert.

"I don't understand," Lydia pressed. "Please tell me what is going on, and what does this have to do with my daughter?"

"Okay, let's everybody calm down." Gavin steered Adena away from Robert. He handed her a card and said, 'Ma'am, you and your mother can meet us here, and I'm sure some answers will be provided for you."

Reading it, she shot her eyes back at Robert. "Fine," she dumped the card in her purse. "We'll be there in ten minutes!"

●●●

It looked like a typical day in court, except that it was almost midnight. In this case, instead of the judge wearing a black robe, he wore a black tuxedo, the tie undone, hanging around his neck. Magistrate Judge Douglas Gregory was at least thirty-four years old, had fire-red hair, his face sprinkled with freckles, and his green eyes fixated on Robert.

"I suppose I should say thank you for rescuing me from this benefit I was attending," Magistrate Gregory began, "but I don't think my wife is thrilled about it. So, this better be good."

"Your honor," Robert stood up, "the government is thankful that you made yourself available at this late hour to conduct this hearing."

"You're welcome, counselor. Although, I'm going to hold applause for my escape until later." Magistrate Gregory folded his hands and leaned forward, looking from Robert to Kyle MacKenzie at the opposite table. He was flanked by two deputy United States Marshals. "The complaint and affidavit sitting before me lends itself to being your garden-variety drug case. Even though I must say these are rather large amounts, did it really warrant an emergency hearing?"

"Your honor, the government believes the facts of this case, yes, on the surface may read routine, but evidence shows that this is truly not the case."

"Okay, and what might that evidence be," the judge asked.

"The government has reasons to believe that the actions and activities of these defendants were the catalyst that created another heinous crime against the government."

The judge stared blankly at Robert, who cleared his throat. He looked at Marissa sitting behind him, and she gave a slight nod. He then proceeded to explain the interlocking incidents between his case and her's. During Robert's presentation, Kyle did not look at his mother. Neither did Ryan or David, who were sitting in the jury box. They stared straight ahead, almost without blinking.

After Robert finished, Magistrate Gregory sat back in his chair. He looked first at the jury box, then at Kyle sitting at the defense table.

"Deputies, bring the other two defendants down to the defense table. There's no need to go through this three separate times."

After they were seated, the deputies returned to their positions. The courtroom door opened. Marissa turned around to see a third deputy take up post at the back entrance.

"I take it since lawyers are not present for the defendants that they need one appointed?" Magistrate Gregory asked. Without waiting for an answer, he turned to the defense table and asked, "Are either of you able to hire your own lawyer?"

One by one, each responded "no."

"Would you like me to appoint one to represent you?"

"Yes, sir," they answered in unison.

"Very well. I order that a lawyer be appointed to represent each defendant here today from the list of lawyers qualified to handle this type of case. These appointments are subject to my review of a completed financial affidavit, which is to be submitted to me within the next forty-eight hours. Each of you should understand that the information you provide on the affidavit is subject to the penalties of perjury." He looked at each defendant. "Meaning," he explained, "that you could be prosecuted for lying to me if you give false information on the affidavit. Is there a detainer against the defendants?"

"Yes, your honor," Robert replied.

"Okay. I hereby order the defendants detained without a hearing, although I'll hold detention hearings if the defendants' lawyers request one."

"Thank you, your honor," Robert said.

"All rise," the bailiff called out as Magistrate Gregory stood up.

"This hearing is concluded," he said and rapped his gavel. "Have a good night," and he exited through the back door.

●●●

Lydia didn't move when the hearing concluded. She looked to the opposite side of the courtroom as the deputies gathered the defendants. Her stomach fluttered as the clanking of the handcuffs seems to bounce off the expansive walls around them. To say that it was difficult to bring herself to look at them was an understatement. She felt a surge of emotions run through her: anger, disappointment, shock, sorrow. In her disappointment, she didn't want to look at them. Yet, her maternal insides won over her hurt, and she sighed as she turned her gaze onto her sons in sorrow.

It was at that moment that Ryan and David looked out into the galley at them. Adena sadly looked from one to the other. Shaking her head, she turned and bolted out of the courtroom. David lowered his head and walked ahead of Ryan, following one of the deputies out of view. Ryan looked at his mother and offered no words, no smile, no excuses. Lydia offered no words as well, just gave a nod of her head. The second deputy nudged Ryan, and they followed David. Lydia stared after them as they were led through a door and beyond.

●●●

Marissa gathered her coat and briefcase. It had been a long day made even longer by tonight's unexpected events. She turned to Robert as he walked by and said, "We'll talk soon."

He nodded and pushed open the courtroom doors. Marissa started toward the door, yet was stopped at the hand on her shoulder. It was Lydia.

"Yes, Mrs. Knight?"

"The other day when you came to my house, did you know then? Did you know then that my sons had something to do with this?"

"No, ma'am," Marissa answered. "I had no idea of any of this prior to tonight. I am so sorry for your troubles."

"The documents that I signed," Lydia continued, "is that giving you permission to kill my boys?"

Marissa looked at her. Her eyes were red and a little swollen. But, most of all, they were sad. Marissa could only imagine the pain of trying to fit these pieces together and make sense out of it all.

"Mrs. Knight, although interlinked, this case cannot be joined with mine," she assured her. "The facts of this action are their own, separate entity and does not carry the same sentencing conditions."

A small spark of relief appeared in Lydia's eyes. She said nothing else as she turned. Marissa looked after her as she walked out of the courtroom. Sighing, she followed.

CHAPTER SIX

Marissa looked out the window into the sky. The clouds were thick and plentiful, so thick she believed they would hold her if she walked on them. The sky was flawless, blue and open. The sun was shining on the other side of the plane, but its rays sparkled off the wing Marissa sat next to.

It had been six weeks since she first received Gavin's phone call so early in the morning. Six weeks since she first learned of Deandra Knight and was assigned to bring her killers to justice. Six weeks since she met Deandra's sister, talked with Lydia, and learned of Robert's connected case with her brothers.

Marissa presented another indictment against the accused killers to the grand jury three days ago. In a rare occurrence, all twenty-three members of the grand jury concurred to bring additional charges against all of the defendants. On the same day, Marissa received word that the Capital Case Unit had reached its decision on her death penalty request, but wanted to discuss some matters with her in person. Jack reassured her that sometimes these requests to come to Washington were not unusual.

Two fingers clicked in front of her face. She blinked and looked at Gavin.

"Hel-lo," he said. "Where did you go?"

"Oh, just thinking. A lot has happened in these past few weeks. Just taking it all in."

"You nervous?"

She shrugged her shoulders. A little. There's a lot riding on this." She then turned her full body to face Gavin. "Tell me. Why are you here, again?"

"Moral support." Gavin sat back in the seat next to her. He flipped the pages of his magazine, more out of something to do rather than actually reading it.

"Moral support?" She arched an eyebrow.

"Yeah, you know. In case you need someone to hold your hand during the hard questions," he said without looking up.

She continued looking at him, mute.

"All right," he said, lowering the magazine. "I was 'invited' to this shindig to answer any questions the committee has about the investigation." He air-pumped quotation marks when he said 'invited.'

Marissa nodded her head and turned back to the window.

"Hey, are you sure you're alright?" Gavin leaned closer.

"Yeah, yeah, I'm fine." She nodded again, touched by his concern. "I know we aren't supposed to take cases personally, but," she hesitated, shrugging her shoulders, "this one is different. Forget the fact that she was just sixteen years old. I'm also looking at the scope of setting precedent here. I mean, hel-lo, Washington, D.C." She jerked a thumb towards the window.

"I get what you mean." Gavin settled back into his seat. "That feeling is what had me flying back and forth for interviews and being in on the search and recovery. But," he shifted closer, and Marissa found herself leaning closer to him, biting her lip. "I figure if you have feelings like that, then you still care and the job hasn't taken away that human side of you."

Up to that point, they hadn't broken eye contact. But now, she looked down, then looked back at him and smiled.

Gavin gave her a gentle head butt and went back to looking through his magazine.

Feeling somewhat at ease, Marissa turned back to look at the clouds beyond the window.

●●●

Heart heavy, she watched the plane back up the tarmac. This was the moment she had been dreading all week. The heavens echoed her pain as peels of thunder rung the sky. She had refused an umbrella and let the rain kiss her skin. She shivered inside her raincoat, but she didn't know if it was because of the cold rain or the dreaded anticipation inching towards her.

The plane continued to crawl backwards, coming to a complete stop just yards away from where Lydia stood. She took a heavy, unsteady breath and walked towards it. The stomach flips coincided with her steps, creating a hypnotic rhythm as she continued to walk. When she reached the plane, she stopped and looked up. The rain grew harder, and she blinked away the drops. Her spleen leapt into her throat as she stood there. She closed her eyes and waited.

Moments later, the mouth of the plane's belly opened, and she jumped when the lip hit the concrete with a thud. A man on the inside walked over to one side of the opening and pushed a button. The chains of the conveyor belt attached to the lip began to churn. The clanking sound pierced Lydia's very soul.

Before long, the dreaded moment arrived. She felt it before she saw it. The coffin rolled to the front of the plane's opening and stopped. Her heart caught in her throat, and for a moment, the heavens and the earth swirled together. She tried to catch her breath, but the vice clutching her lungs made it too painful to breathe. Her stomach churned, and suddenly she felt hot, a wave of nausea crashed inside of her. Her eyes stung from the acid and bile that raced up her throat. Flushed, she doubled over just in time to retch the awful concoction onto the concrete, barely missing her shoes. Her insides continued to spill out until it was empty, yet her body still went through the motions. Finally spent, she straightened herself, wiping her mouth with the backside of her hand.

As if on cue when she stood up, the coffin gave the tiniest dip and proceeded to roll down the conveyor belt towards her. Her head pounded, the violence of the sudden headache almost blinded her. She watched the coffin proceed towards her, and for a split moment, she wanted to run. Run from the truth, run from the nightmares, run from the ever-looming sadness that filled her recent days. Just...run.

The coffin stopped at her side, and with trembling fingers, she touched the spot where she believed her daughter's heart lay inside. The slickness of the wood to her fingers made everything real. Her heart raced, and her whole body shook, and she knew. This was really happening. This box held the body of her baby. It was final, there was no more hoping or pretending. The realization of that moment caught Lydia off guard. Although her head knew it and she had lived it over the past few weeks, it still thoroughly unearthed her. She could not find the air to catch her breath.

She put both of her palms on the casket, and her eyes welled until everything shimmered behind her tears. She laid her head on the coffin and let the pain overcome her. The deep force of loss inside her very being produced an involuntary shaking of her body, and she cried out in agony. She wailed over the loss of life, a life that will never experience true love's first kiss, children of her own, or see the fulfillment of her dreams. Her soul ached over the stolen hopes the moment her daughter died. She allowed herself for the first time to be what she was, a grieving mother.

●●●

The cab ride down into the Federal Triangle was uneventful. Traffic cooperated as they headed north on Pennsylvania Avenue. The cab stopped in front of the building named after the late Attorney General Robert F. Kennedy. The block-long building did nothing to calm Marissa's nerves. Gavin nudged her back, and she gave a lop-sided smile as she was guided through the high aluminum doors. She went through the security checkpoints, removing the necessary items as instructed.

She put her watch back on and gathered her purse and briefcase from the conveyor belt of the X-ray machine, watching as the officer gave Gavin back his credentials and locked away his gun. She jumped when a gentleman all of a sudden appeared to her left and said, "Ms. Elliot?"

"Yes," she hesitated. "Marissa Elliot."

"Good morning. I apologize for startling you," the gentleman smiled. "My name is Erik Stone. I'm the personal assistant to Mrs. Hamilton." Erik Stone was tall with the upper body of a swimmer, broad shoulders and chest, slender torso. The navy pinstriped suit was tailor-made and expertly matched with a paisley yellow tie. His blond hair was cut close just above his ears yet hung long from the top and swooped to one side. The silver Calvin Klein glasses completed his preppy look.

He shook her hand first and then Gavin's. "Allow me to show you the way," he said, sweeping his hand forward. Without another word, he turned and walked away from the magnetometers, and they followed. They crossed the Great Hall and headed to the elevator bank. He then turned to Marissa and said, "The committee will be convening in twenty minutes, but Mrs. Hamilton would like to talk to you first."

"Really?" Marissa arched her right eyebrow. "This is a surprise, I thought I would just be talking to the committee." Amanda Scott-Hamilton was the Attorney General. Her boss's boss.

"This is the first case of its kind. I mean," Erik stammered, "the first of two cases being considered under this renewed piece of legislation."

Once they arrived on the appropriate floor, Erik led them down the extensive hallway, lined with grand murals and granite pillars. He stopped in front of a wood door. He looked back over his shoulder and smiled. "Don't be nervous," he said and opened the door.

The interior offices were just as grand with plush carpet, rich woods, and giant pieces of art. There were people buzzing about, telephones ringing, conversations here and there, all contributing to the organized chaos. Erik pushed open another door, and behind it was a conference room. The table was long and made of thick onyx glass. There were at least a dozen chairs framed in black wood with deep navy seat cushions and back rests. The walls were adorned with giant paintings of different buildings in D.C., all night visions of the buildings in the snow.

"Please, have a seat." Erik gestured to the chairs. "Mrs. Hamilton will be in shortly." He left the room, closing the door behind him.

Marissa put her briefcase and purse on a chair and pulled another out from the table and sat down. Gavin wondered over to one of the paintings.

Moments later, a side door opened. The gentleman that entered were clearly Secret Service, complete with the dark suit, short haircut and scoping eyes that surveyed the room in a matter of seconds. He stepped aside, making way for the woman that followed behind him. Amanda Scott-Hamilton was the most powerful woman in the current administration, and wore it well yet unassumingly so. She was all of five feet tall, petite with stylish blond hair and sea-blue eyes. She wore a brilliant red suit, and carried the power of the color well. She was polished, crisp, yet warm. She smiled and said "thank you" to the agent, who then retreated and closed the door.

"Good morning. I'm Amanda Scott-Hamilton." She walked up to Marissa and stretched out her hand.

"Good morning, your honor." Marissa took the lithe hand in hers. "Marissa Elliot."

"It's a pleasure to meet you, Ms. Elliot." Her blue eyes twinkled. She turned to Gavin and repeated the introduction.

Mrs. Hamilton walked to the opposite side of the table and gestured toward the chairs. "Please, sit," promptly doing so herself.

"I wasn't expecting to meet you, ma'am, so this is a very pleasant surprise," said Marissa.

"How is Jack doing," asked Mrs. Hamilton.

"He's great, your Honor, running the office well."

"Jack's a good man. I miss our days at the firm." Mrs. Hamilton folded her hands in front of her. She looked from Gavin to Marissa and said, "On behalf of the entire Department of Justice, I want to thank you for prosecuting this to the fullest extent of the law. I've read all of the literature generated between our offices. The circumstances of this particular action are especially grave and heinous, and, forgive me for saying so, are exactly why the Federal Death Penalty Act was revised and re-established."

"She was an innocent girl, just talking to her sister on the phone. If anyone deserves to be avenged to the fullest extent of the law, it's Deandra Knight," said Marissa.

"I understand you have suspects in custody?"

Marissa filled her in on the current status of the case, with Gavin giving the overview of the investigative side.

There was a short knock at the door and the same agent entered. "Excuse me, your honor. The committee is ready."

"Will you be attending the meeting with us, ma'am?"

"No," Mrs. Hamilton stood up. "I have a previous commitment, but I have my strongest confidence that you will do fine." She shook Marissa's hand once more. "It was a true pleasure chatting with you."

"Thank you, your honor, but the pleasure was mine," Marissa replied.

Mrs. Hamilton gave one last smile, and then left the conference room.

Almost instantly, Mr. Stone appeared at the opposite door.

"The committee is ready for you now. Shall we?" And he turned and walked out of the room.

Marissa looked at Gavin. He gave her a quick wink and said, "Let's go do what we came to do!"

●●●

The fingers that wrapped around Lydia's arm startled her, yet she allowed them to hold her as she raised her head from the coffin. Her own hands rubbed it lovingly one last time, and with pain in her eyes, she nodded at the plane's crew members who then continued to take the coffin to the hearse waiting nearby.

"Mrs. Knight, are you all right now?" Lydia looked up into the eyes of the man who still held her arm and gave him a shaky smile. Pastor Derrick Nash was the senior pastor of her church. The bald African-American pastor towered over her at six-feet, four inches tall. He had perfect straight white teeth surrounded by an artfully crafted goatee. He often describes himself to his congregation as the ruggedly handsome yet approachable pastor, but they all know he only has eyes for his lovely wife, Evelyn. He and Sister Nash had been a tremendous support to her and the family, nothing but strength and encouragement during this difficult time.

His other hand held an umbrella over them, and his eyes watched her with genuine concern. "I'm sorry. Maybe that was the wrong thing to say," he stammered.

Lydia patted the hand on her arm, as she watched the man close the door to the back of the hearse. Her heart sank as her eyes followed the car driving away from them, headed to the funeral home.

"Thank you for coming out today," she said, as Pastor Nash steered her towards the waiting car. She was grateful for his support, for she still felt weak and a little dizzy. Her brain was fuzzy and her feet felt heavy and almost twice their size. She saw Adena standing by the car, ready to bolt to her side.

When they reached the car, Adena simply put her arms around her mother, placing her cheek to Lydia's. As hard as it was for her to watch, she respected her mother's wishes to greet the plane alone.

Pulling herself back, she kissed her forehead. Pastor Nash opened the car door, and Lydia thankfully sank down into the seat. When he closed the door, her mind snapped to the one hundred and one decisions that needed to be made. Her thoughts swirled a thousand miles a minute, all of the decisions vying for her undivided attention.

Turning to Adena in the back, she said, "I want Deandra to wear the purple dress."

"What? What dress?" Adena looked at her confused.

"The purple one from last Christmas. And when the family walks in, I want the casket to be closed," she directed to Pastor Nash. He nodded as he steered towards the airport exit. "None of that open-and-close mess I've seen at some funerals," she continued. "And I think we should have the reception away from the house. I don't want to kick anyone out that doesn't know when to leave. When I get home, I'm going to want peace and quiet."

Pastor Nash chuckled.

"Wait. You want to start dealing with these decisions now?" Adena was a little shocked. "Maybe you should rest awhile and meet with the funeral home director in the morning."

But Lydia was thinking just the opposite. She was more than ready to start taking control of the situation. She felt energized somehow.

"Now is perfect." She turned back to Pastor Nash. "Will you go with us? To the funeral home? I feel the need for another person to be there to make sure my wishes are carried out."

"Absolutely," he smiled. Spotting the hearse a few cars ahead, he turned into the same lane.

Adena let out a long sigh. She sat back in her seat, but not before she patted her mother's shoulder.

"Well, you remember Joscelyne Parker? She's the party coordinator at Sullivan's."

Lydia displayed the first light-hearted smile Adena had seen in weeks. "Little Josie!? Oh, I haven't seen her in ages!"

"I'll give her a call." Adena giggled herself, her mother's spirit infectious.

●●●

Several days later, Marissa was sitting in the courtroom, waiting for the day's proceedings to begin. She scratched some notes on the pad in front of her, but then she simply put her pen down, realizing she was scribbling because she was nervous. She watched as Austin reached over and wrote a grid on her pad and put an 'O' in the upper left corner of the grid. She smiled and marked an 'X' in the lower right corner.

Austin Gregory had been assigned as second chair in Marissa's case. More than ten years her senior, Austin had been at the U.S. Attorney's Office for over twelve years. He owned an impressive record of prosecuting – and winning – death penalty cases on the state level back when he was an assistant District Attorney, which is what prompted Jack to assign him as co-counsel on this case. Austin appeared calm and unnerved as he marked an 'O' in the lower left corner of the grid.

Marissa moved to mark her 'X' when the court security officer entered the courtroom and ordered, "All rise!" In sync, she and Austin rose as the high door in front of them opened.

"Hear ye, hear ye, hear ye! The court of the Honorable Thomas H. Stagner, III is now in session."

The courtroom fell silent as Judge Stagner walked through the door and made his way to his chair and remained standing. The judge was African-American and stood over six feet tall. He had a reputation for being quiet and reserved, yet behind his glasses were the eyes of a man that saw everything. Judge Stagner was known for running his courtroom in equal fairness to all that came before him, and his interpretation of the law was highly praised by the higher courts. The legal community as a whole give him high marks for his competence in being a steadfast executor of fair justice.

Judge Stagner bowed his head, and everyone followed suit. "God bless this proceeding and everyone here present today. You may be seated," the bailiff concluded.

"Good afternoon, ladies and gentlemen," Judge Stagner began, his voice deep and solemn. "This is a status conference in the matter of the United States verses Roland Connors, et al. Three weeks ago, the government filed its Notice of Intent to Seek the Death Penalty." He looked over at Marissa. "Is this still the government's intention, Ms. Elliot?"

"Yes, your honor," she replied, standing up.

"To which defendants is the government wanting to impose the sentence of death, should that defendant be found guilty?"

"The government is seeking the death penalty on defendants Roland Loenthal Connors and Nikko Benjamin Hollis, your honor."

"And the other defendants," the judge inquired.

"Your honor, it is the government's position that the three remaining defendants, Jeremy Dwaine Spencer, Malcolm Robert Connors, and Calvin Michael Stewart, were involved to help facilitate the plans of the other two. Quite frankly, your honor," said Marissa, "the government believes this plan to kidnap and murder Deandra Knight would have been carried out with or without the assistance of Malcolm Connors, Jeremy Spencer, and Calvin Stewart." She then turned to the defense table. "They were only along for the ride."

"Mr. Montgomery," the judge said, "do you have any response to the government's intention?"

Standing, he flexed his arm just enough to flash an expensive cufflink to his audience. "Your honor," he drawled, "the defense is very much aware that the government desires to seek the death penalty as to my client. I guess it now becomes my responsibility to make sure that he is found not guilty." He then looked at Marissa and gave a slight nod.

Pompous ass, she thought to herself.

"Do any of you have anything else to add," Judge Stagner asked, looking at the other lawyers at the table. Each stood and replied, "No, your honor."

"Okay," the judge said. The courtroom deputy handed him some papers. "Since the death penalty is now going to be the sentence should the named defendants be found guilty, the court determines that second attorneys for the penalty phase should be appointed. It looks like Magistrate Thresher has already appointed second attorneys for these defendants, so I am not going to disturb her orders. Accordingly, this court upholds the appointments of Gretchen Williams as co-counsel for Roland Loenthal Connors, and Brandon C. Whitfield as co-counsel to Mr. Parkenson to represent Nikko Benjamin Hollis." He wrote on the papers and handed them back to his courtroom deputy.

"Also pending before the court are also several motions for continuance. The government has timely filed its response to these motions, and it looks like we are in agreement here." Again, Judge Stagner looked at Marissa.

"Yes, your honor. Now that the Notice of Intent to Seek the Death Penalty is proper before the court, it adds additional, complex issues that need to be resolved before a trial can begin in this case."

The judge now turned his attention to the various lawyers sitting at the defense table. "Does the defense have anything to add?"

Montgomery stood up. "On behalf of the defense lawyers present, no, your honor, we do not." He returned to his seat.

"Okay, first up. We have an agreed motion for continuance of the current trial date." Judge Stagner looked out to the attorneys. "Is everyone still in agreement?"

"Yes, your honor," Marissa and Montgomery responded in unison.

"Okay, it looks like the other motions are pretty much the same, filed on behalf of each defendant. I'm not going to read each of them just to put them into the record of this hearing. That's not necessary."

Judge Stagner again looked to the attorneys. "After careful consideration of the motions, the responses and replies, the indictment, and the record, as well as the potential punishment of death now sought by the government, the court finds that this case is sufficiently complex due to the number of defendants, the nature of the prosecution, and the existence of novel questions of the law. It is unreasonable to expect adequate preparation for pretrial proceedings and the trial itself within the limits established by the Speedy Trial Act. The opinion of the court is that the ends of justice served by granting the continuance outweighs the best interest of the public and the defendants in a speedy trial.

"Therefore, the court finds that this action should be and is hereby continued from its current trial date of January 6, 2003. I remember ordering the attorneys to synchronize your calendars and give me several dates. No one had a problem with May, correct?"

"Correct, your honor," Marissa replied.

"Good. The trial in this case is hereby reset for Monday, May 5, 2003." Again, the courtroom deputy handed the judge some papers. He wrote on each one, and handed them back to her as the attorneys busied themselves recording the new trial date into their various electronic devices.

"Next up, we have several motions for severance of the defendants. And, it looks like these also are agreed to."

"That is correct, your honor," Montgomery said.

"All right, then. Trying these defendants together could create potential prejudices against them, not to mention the defendants have a right to a fair trial. Therefore, invoking Rule 14 is proper, and the court hereby grants the defendants' agreed motions to sever as a whole."

Looking out into the well, Judge Stagner asked, "Does anyone have a problem with that?"

"No, your honor," Ms. Williams replied.

"Great. Now, in light of the trial being moved, these pending motions for extension of time to file pretrial motions are also granted." The courtroom deputy handed the judge some papers, and he read the new deadlines into the record. "Is there anything in further need of discussion?"

"Nothing from the government, your honor," answered Marissa.

"Same for the defense, your honor," Montgomery replied.

"Then court is now in recess." The judge stood up and the entire courtroom stood up in response.

After the judge left the courtroom, Marissa gathered her notepad and briefcase. She looked at Austin, who smiled and said, "Time to get to work!"

CHAPTER SEVEN

The sky was a brilliant pale blue. Not a cloud in it. The wind was gusty, but not overly so that it was inconvenient. The grass was rich, a deep green, and the oak trees that dotted the landscape were tall and sturdy, their dark trunks just as rich as the grass.

A couple feet from where she stood, several squirrels played chase. Marissa watched them dart over the flat grave markers of the people that have passed on. Leaning against a large cross headstone, she observed the grave side service from the distance.

There was a fair amount of people that came to say goodbye to Deandra. Marissa was particularly drawn to the number of children that were there, a couple dozen in total. Some were crying, most had their heads down, the boys looked a little uncomfortable. She caught sight of the school bus among the cars, and was moved that the school made arrangements for the children to come pay their last respects to their fellow classmate, their friend.

Adena was sitting in the middle on the front row, and there was a man standing behind her, his hand on her shoulder. She wore a simple black dress, no frills, and a smart pair of dark sunglasses, and her hands were clasped tight in her lap. Even from where she stood, Marissa could see the tears falling down her face.

Lydia sat off a little from the others. he chose a deep purple suit, almost eggplant, which piqued Marissa's curiosity as to why. She did not take her eyes off the elegant wood coffin, and she sat straight as an arrow on the edge of her seat as if ready to bolt once the service was complete. Marissa observed her dab her eyes once and again with a white handkerchief, and her heart again went out to her.

The pastor signed the cross over his body, signaling the end of the service. Marissa repeated the sign. She watched the children, one by one, walk over to the coffin and lay a pink or white flower on top. They then walked over to Lydia, some offering a handshake or a pat on the shoulder, others leaning down for a heart-heavy hug. Some stopped to offer Deandra's sister the same measure of condolence, and the man standing behind her accepted the boys' handshakes.

After speaking with a couple of mourners, the pastor walked over to Lydia, helping her to her feet. She watched them hug, Lydia nodding over something he shared. Marissa straightened up, preparing to leave herself. Lydia broke her embrace with the pastor and spoke a few words, and suddenly turned and looked right at Marissa! Their eyes locked for what seemed like an eternity. Marissa stopped breathing, embarrassed for being caught observing a painful, private moment. The pastor then turned and looked at her also. After they exchanged a few words, he walked away as Lydia began to walk towards her.

●●●

She saw her standing there, alone out in the distance, leaning on a monument. She wasn't sure how long she'd been standing there, but it would not have surprised her at all if she had been there the whole time. Lydia was taken aback, yet touched when she saw Marissa make the sign of the cross along with them.

She looked over into the crowd of people, and her heart swelled as she watched Deandra's various teachers, Mr. Howard, her violin instructor, and Ms. Janice, the bus driver. Her breath caught in her throat as her classmates laid their flowers on her casket. Her insides ached when each came over to offer their condolences, some offering hugs which Lydia returned in hopes to sooth their sorrows as much as it was their intention on soothing hers. Others offered a gentle touch of her shoulder or arm.

Adena walked over and wrapped her arms around her mother from behind. Lydia closed her eyes, and, for a moment, lost herself in the embrace.

"Are you okay, mama?" Adena whispered.

She nodded and patted her daughter's arm.

"We'll stay as long as you want to." Adena kissed her mother's cheek.

"Why don't you wait for me in the car." Lydia turned around, smiling at her. "I want to speak to Pastor Nash and some of the guests."

Adena nodded and let go as her mother stood up. Lydia gave her future son-in-law, William, a warm hug and watched him put his arm around Adena, steering her to the car.

She dabbed her face with a handkerchief and released a heart-felt smile as Pastor Nash stood in front of her with open arms. Walking into them, she sighed and said, "Thank you, Pastor. The service was lovely."

"A lovely service for a lovely soul. May the fullest measure of God's peace be with you and your family." Pastor Nash squeezed her in a good ol' fashioned bear hug. "Are you ready to head to Sullivan's?"

Lydia stepped out of his embrace and looked across the way at Marissa. Looking back at Pastor Nash, she smiled and said, "There's someone here I should speak to," nodding her head over his shoulder in Marissa's direction.

Pastor Nash turned around and spotted the woman in the red raincoat out in the distance. Nodding, he faced Lydia and said, "Why don't I tell Adena and William that I'll take you to the reception, and let them leave. Take as much time as you need."

Grasping his arm one last time, Lydia responded, "I won't be long," before she turned and walked toward Marissa.

●●●

Her heart sped up as she watched Lydia make her way to her. She had hoped to have figured out something to say by the time she reached her, but when Lydia stopped inches away, her tongue was thick and her mouth felt like cotton was stuffed in her cheeks.

Swallowing hard, Marissa stuck out her hand and said, "Hello, Mrs. Knight. Please, I'm so sorry for the intrusion."

The expression on Lydia's face was friendly kindness as she clasped Marissa's hand with both of her own.

"Thank you for coming. You didn't have to stand up here alone," she said, half-turning to look around her. "You could have joined us."

"Oh no, . . . no. It wouldn't have been proper," Marissa stammered, embarrassed.

Lydia chuckled, which sounded almost girlish, and Marissa smiled in return.

"Agent Wright didn't come with you," she stated rather than asked, looking past Marissa.

"No, he's downtown working."

Sensing the unspoken, Lydia nodded her head, deciding it be best not to go down that road. She had since let go of her hands, which Marissa shoved into the pockets of her raincoat.

"Mrs. Knight, I had hoped to know what to say to you when you reached me. Other than apologizing again for my intrusion on your farewell to Deandra."

"Will you pardon an old woman's curiosity if I ask why you came?"

Although thrown off by the question, Marissa didn't sense any anger or resentment in her voice. She looked past Lydia to the casket. The wind moved some of the top flowers around, their petals tickled by the breeze.

"Because her death was unnecessary. Because she mattered. She's not just a file number on my desk, some case I have to close." She shrugged her shoulders. "And I can't explain it any better than that. Can't explain it in any other way than . . . she matters."

Lydia turned and looked at the casket sitting alone amongst the trees. The grounds crew was collecting the chairs, the yellow school bus windings itself down the hill. She saw Pastor Nash close the door to the family limousine, having convinced Adena and William to allow him to drive her to the reception. Her heart sunk a little looking back on the casket. A wave of pain blew through her in the breeze, then dulled but did not vanish.

Without turning around, she said, "You know, when your spouse dies, you're called a widow or a widower. When a parent dies first, you're called an orphan." Turning to face Marissa, her shoulders fell as she continued, "It is such an unnatural thing, when a child dies before their parents. So, what do they call you when your child dies first?" The unshed tears stung her eyes.

"They will call you a mother, because no matter what event life throws at you, that will never change." Resigned, she looked into Lydia's weathered face, her kind eyes, and sighed. "You will forever be a mother."

Through her tears, Lydia reached out to touch Marissa's arm. "I'm glad you were picked to handle her case. I know you'll give it your best because you care. Thank you." She gently squeezed her arm before letting go.

"I better go," Marissa whispered.

"I'm glad you came." Again, Lydia nodded.

"The honor was mine."

Lydia turned and started walking towards the waiting car.

"Mrs. Knight," Marissa blurted. She had no idea why she called out, only that she was grateful that she had paused in her pain to come speak to her.

Lydia stopped and turned around. It took all Marissa had not to run to her and hug her. Instead, she shoved her hands deeper inside her pockets. "I'll keep you posted," she said.

"Thank you." With a slight nod, Lydia turned and continued to the car.

Marissa watched as the pastor held the door for her. She watched as, moments later, they headed down the hill, her eyes followed them until they reached the street beyond. Gazing at the casket, her own eyes filling with tears as she watched it being lowered into the ground.

●●●

A few nights later, Marissa was sitting in her favorite burger joint drafting her witness list for trial. She had, for the most part, a final tally of her expert witnesses, and was now running down her factual ones. Index cards with various names and titles were spread out over the table, numbered in pencil in order of importance.

She took a sip of beer, and almost spit it out again when Gavin slid onto the bench opposite her in the booth. Dressed casual in jeans and a brown leather jacket, he smiled as he took one of her French fries she earlier pushed aside.

"Do you have some sort of radar that tells you when it is the most inopportune time to find me?" Marissa looked at the ceiling over him and shook her head.

"No, I just consider it one of the perks." He threw her a wink as he popped another fry into his mouth.

She shook her head and chuckled. Her waitress stopped at the table and Gavin ordered her another beer and one for himself. After she left, Marissa sat back into the booth.

"So, how did the interview go?" She looked at him across the table.

"Well, we talked to him. He had his lawyer there, of course." Gavin paused to eat more fries. "He gave us the rundown of what happened, well, of what was supposed to happen that night."

Marissa retrieved a notepad from her briefcase and proceeded to take notes. She sprinkled the conversation with questions here and there, and made mental notes to go talk to the detainees and order the transcript of Gavin's interview.

He stopped talking and gave her a curious look. "You still don't read the paper, do you," he asked before partaking of yet another French fry.

"Well, that was random," Marissa frowned. "Why?"

He plopped a folded newspaper on top of her index cards, some scattering across the table with the breeze. He sat back as the waitress returned and placed the beers in front of them. Glancing at Gavin, Marissa unfolded the paper and read the headlines. *A Mother's Knightmare: The Deandra Knight murder*.

She took a long pull from her fresh beer and read the story. Gavin watched her tuck a loose curl behind her ear as her eyes darted over the paper. He waited in silence, drinking his own beer and finishing her fries, watching her.

"Aww, man, I was afraid of this." Finishing the article, she slid the paper back across the table.

"What?"

"This." She pointed at the paper. "The media."

"What part of this did you think would **not** make the news? I mean, think about it! You have a girl kidnapped from her home, found dead hundreds of miles away, and all because her brothers thought they were smarter than a drug dealer. Wow!" He shook his head.

"I'm not a complete idiot." Marissa jutted out her chin in self-defense. "I knew there would be coverage." She took another pull from her glass, glancing down at the newspaper. "It tends to hurt the jury pool if there's a lot of coverage, that's all. So, maybe this is it."

Gavin's glass suspended in mid-air. "Uh, Maury, how long have you been sitting here?"

"More randomness. I dunno." Confused, Marissa looked at her watch. "I think I got here around 4:30, 4:45."

"Then you haven't seen today's newscast."

"Why?" She set her mug down on the table a little harder than necessary.

He nodded behind her. Turning around, Marissa caught a glimpse of Deandra Knight's picture on the restaurant's television before it switched to a map of DeSoto with a highlighted star where what she assumed was where she was taken. She couldn't hear the newscast and the reporter's summation of her case, but she assumed it was just as she read in the paper.

"Great." She turned around to face Gavin, slumped in her seat.

"Well, look at the bright side," Gavin offered. Marissa glared at him, to which he returned a smile. "At least they didn't get a picture of you."

"How is that . . ." She stopped and rolled her eyes. "Never mind. It'll only make sense in your head."

He laughed as the waitress put the bill on the table. She reached for it, but Gavin was quicker.

"You don't have to do that," she said.

Glancing at the bill, Gavin put some cash on the table before returning his wallet to his back pocket. Sliding out of the booth, he stood up and said, "My pleasure, counselor. Besides," he stopped when Marissa followed his lead and slid out of the booth.

"Besides, what?" She stood in front of him and looked up.

"Next time, dinner's on you." He winked at her before he extended his hand, gesturing for her to go first.

She stuck her tongue and led the way out. Laughing again behind her, Gavin followed her outside.

They stopped at her car. Gavin waited while she unlocked the driver's door and threw her belongings on the other seat. Turning, she looked up at him again. "I went to the funeral Saturday," she confessed.

"Aww, man." He looked around, rubbing his hand over his head a few times.

"Don't ask me why, I just needed to be there."

"Okay," he probed. "And?"

"And, what?" She mumbled, fiddling with her keys.

"And, what happened?" Impatient, his eyes waited for the answer.

"Well, Mrs. Knight saw me." Marissa let out a loud sigh and gave him the run-down of their conversation. Her cheeks grew warm remembering her embarrassment. The slight flush did not go unnoticed by Gavin.

He let out a low whistle when she finished. "That is one strong woman."

Marissa nodded in silence.

"Hey," he playfully poked her side with his elbow. "Remember, we got 'em. We got the guys who did this. This trial," he looked off, shaking his head, "this trial is just a formality, Maury. I think this is gonna be a slam-dunk," he grinned.

"You think or you know?"

"I know it." Undaunted, Gavin chuckled. "They'll get everything that's coming to them."

Nodding again, Marissa got in her car. She started the engine and let down the driver's window. Gavin closed the door, leaning in. "You just do what you do, and we'll get 'em."

"Yeah, I know," she replied thoughtfully. Putting the car in 'drive,' she turned and flashed Gavin a warm smile. "Thanks for dinner."

He nodded and backed away.

"G'night!" Marissa tapped her horn a couple times and drove off.

● ● ●

Lydia sat on the floor in the middle of the room. The bed wasn't made, the covers pushed back as if Deandra had just sprinted out of it this morning. She fingered the pretty lilac comforter, remembering the excitement splashed over her daughter's face at seeing her "grown-up" room.

She looked at the various posters and pictures that adorned the walls. The desk chair held a couple of shirts and a pair of jeans. Just like her father, she chuckled, remembering how Norrece threw his clothes on the back of the chair in their room. The desk itself had a couple of school books, some notebook paper and her purse.

Lydia sighed and opened the bottom drawer of the dresser. She removed the clothes, carefully packing them in the nearby box. She fought back the tidal wave of emotions that threatened to overtake her as she packed away Deandra's favorite jeans, and the pajamas she liked to wear when she was sick. Her hands shook as she picked up the goofy lime green socks Deandra thought were so fun. She put the socks under her nose and inhaled deep, blinking away tears before placing them in the box, too.

Her eyes locked onto the closet door. The room suddenly seemed small, the oxygen suddenly sparse as she eyed that door. She sank to the bed, digging into the comforter. The door was closed, but her mind conjured up images of Deandra hiding in there, calling for help, being dragged from inside.

Adena watched her mother clutch the comforter, watched as the anguish enveloped her face, her emotions as she stared at the closet door.

"Mama?"

She wiped the tears from her face as Adena appeared at the bedroom door. Lydia smiled as best she could.

Adena cocked her head to the side and gave her a half-smile. "Aww, mama. I told you I'd do this." She sidestepped the boxes and sat on the bed next to her. Taking her hand, she looked around and sighed. "How are you?"

"You shouldn't have to do this alone." Lydia patted her daughter's hand. Looking around the room, her eyes fell again to the closet door.

"Neither should you," Adena scolded. "Mama, why don't you take a break? Or go home? I can get started on the closet, and William can help me with the rest," she insisted.

"I know." She shook her head. "But I want to." Chuckling a little, she added, "It may not look like it, but it is helping me."

Adena leaned over and kissed her mother's soft cheek. Taking her own survey of the room, Adena said, "Well, it looks like you made a dent out here. Let's finish this, and then tackle the closet. By that time, William will be here."

In silent agreement, Lydia stretched out a piece of tape, securing it over the top of a nearby box. When that box was finished, she moved to the next box and repeated the process.

Adena stood up and walked over to a covered wall. Blinking back her own tears, she reached to remove a poster. A corner ripped, and the tearing sound triggered an odd sense of comfort in Adena. Looking at the poster in her hand, she tore it in half, the sound again bringing about an odd sense of relief.

She reached for another poster, but this time she grabbed it in the middle and yanked it down. The ripping and tearing brought her an even stronger sense of pleasure. She tore down another and another, the sound of the shredded paper personified the anguish and anger in her soul. It externalized the guilt that racked her, the guilt she carried deep inside for not being able to help her baby sister. Possessed, she ripped and shredded the posters with her hands, her fingers flying through the papers. Her throat burned and tears blurred her vision as she listened and was soothed by the sounds of the ripped paper.

Spent, she sunk down onto her knees among the confetti, leaning her forehead against the wall. Her shoulders shook as she sobbed for her sister and for herself.

Lydia stood behind her, heart heavy. She put her hand on Adena's head as she listened to her daughter grieve. She slowly stroked her head, cooing softly as Adena's sobs gave way to soft murmurs.

Adena leaned into her mother's legs, cradling her head in her hands. Lydia continued stroking her head while she cried until there was nothing left.

•••

The next afternoon, Marissa sat barefoot and Indian-style, on the floor in her office. She was surrounded by notepads, note cards and books, going over her notes, putting together a draft of how she wanted her side of trial to run. She took a sip from her coffee cup as she reached for a note card, jotting down a thought when there was a short rap on her door.

Before she had a chance to answer, Grace walked into Marissa's office. "You have a visitor."

Puzzled, Marissa looked at her watch. "Did I forget to update my calendar?"

Grace shook her head. "It's Mrs. Knight."

Marissa stood up, her eyes darted around her office looking for anything that was in plain view from the case that could potentially upset her.

Reading her mind, Grace said, "The photographs are in Conference Room Ten."

"Thanks." Marissa breathed a sigh of relief as she walked over to retrieve her suit jacket from her chair. Sliding into the navy pumps under her desk, she said, "Okay, bring her in."

Seconds after she left, Grace returned followed by Lydia. She looked smaller than Marissa remembered, although she couldn't determine if it was her natural stature or the weight of the events life handed her.

"Hello, Mrs. Knight. Please," Marissa gestured to a chair in front of her desk, "sit down."

She sat where suggested. "Thank you for seeing me unannounced."

Marissa observed her nervousness, Lydia clutched her purse in her lap. Deciding against formality, she sat down in the chair next to her. "What brings you downtown?"

"I had hopes of visiting my sons," she replied, looking down at her lap. Marissa opted not to respond.

After a slight pause, Lydia whispered, "But I couldn't do it. I couldn't go see them. Not yet." She then looked into Marissa's eyes. Sheer anguish reflected back. The tears that welled there threatened to spill over but didn't. There was nothing but pure hurt all over her face. "They are responsible for my baby's death," she continued. "As a mother, how can I rationalize this . . . this act of . . . I don't even know what to call it." Some of the anguish was replaced by anger. Again, she wrung and then rewrung her hands on her purse.

"Do you have children, Ms. Elliott?"

Taken aback by the question, Marissa stammered, "Uh, no. No, I do not."

Lydia stood up and walked to the window. "I have experienced a parent's worst nightmare, the death of a child. The circle of life dictates that parents are to pass before their children, and it is the children that are to continue to make life move. When that circle is interrupted, when a child dies before its time," she paused, still looking out the window, "a parent's natural reaction is to question who shall make life move now?"

Lowering her head, Marissa again opted to remain silent.

"It is particularly difficult when that life has been interrupted in such a way that Deandra's has, because of an act of greed or violent cowardness."

"Mrs. Knight, I'm sure neither one of those boys knew that this was going to happen."

Lydia let out a light chuckle. Turning to face her, she smiled. "Please, Ms. Elliott, your colleague is prosecuting those boys. Don't turn to the defense side now." She lowered her eyes, but not before Marissa witnessed the pain inside. "No, regardless of what they were doing, the greed in them took over."

"Perhaps the consequences of their actions were much higher than they anticipated."

Her smile fell. "Indeed, they were." She walked towards the door. "Thank you again for seeing me."

"I appreciate your stopping by." Marissa stood up.

Lydia hesitated, then said, "I'm still not ready to see my sons."

"You deserve the right not to be," Marissa replied nodding.

Without another word, Lydia left her office.

CHAPTER EIGHT

Over the next several months, Marissa worked night and day preparing for Deandra's trial. She conducted interviews of various witnesses, and narrowed down which ones would best benefit her goal. Over greasy Chinese food with Gavin, she viewed countless hours of taped interviews of the suspects when they were in Oklahoma, and read and re-read transcripts of those interviews late into the night before bed. She then interviewed each suspect herself, deciding on who she wanted to testify and who the jury would not hear from. She talked to Deandra's brothers, Ryan and Kyle, and oversaw the disposition of their related cases. She flew to Washington, D.C., twice, both times at the request of the Attorney General to discuss the status of the case in its pretrial stages.

In the months before trial, Lydia arranged for the Salvation Army to remove the furniture and boxes of Deandra's things from Adena's apartment. Adena surprised her one evening, giving her Deandra's lime-green socks, which she stored in her top dresser drawer along with Norrece's wedding band. She delivered some of the plants given in condolence to the local nursing home where she volunteered, and the flowers to various hospitals. She turned down interviews from news reporters and the newspapers. She turned down an interview with Matt Lauer of the 'Today Show,' even when he called to personally invite her to speak on the show.

Over time, she did visit her sons in jail. It was difficult to look at them, to know what they had done. Upon their inquiry, she shared the details of Deandra's funeral, and expressed her sorrow that they could not attend. She wept as they apologized over and over again, taking responsibility for their part in their sister's death. She appeared at their court appearances: she was relieved when Kyle received probation for his part in the crime, and deeply saddened upon learning Ryan would have to serve seven years. Kyle did not ask to live with either she or his sister, to which Lydia was silently grateful. She was sure no one would blame her for saying no if asked, but she was glad it was not a choice she had to make.

●●●

And now, it was the morning of trial. It found Marissa sitting in her chair out on the patio in the quiet predawn hours. Hours before, she'd tossed and turned for a bit, trying to go back to sleep, but the struggle only agitated her. So, she got up. Clad in her favorite boxer shorts and a tank top, she found her way to the kitchen and made a cup of coffee. Tucked in a blanket for extra warmth, she sat on her patio, listening to the birds calling each other. She witnessed a rabbit hopping about in the shadows.

She'd spent the previous week in court haggling over pretrial motions and giving estimates as to how long each side believed their case would last. Three days were spent meticulously picking a jury and arguing with Montgomery and the other defense lawyers whether the jury should be sequestered. Now, the day had come to put on her case.

She had tried difficult cases before. Complex drug smuggling cases, carjacking crimes, sometimes with children involved. She successfully won rape cases and was responsible for securing life sentences for culprits who committed crimes while using cyberspace. Marissa was a seasoned attorney, and was careful not to cross the line of personal attachments to her cases. Yes, the children made it especially difficult to remember this rule, what human being wouldn't be touched to see a nine-year-old smile when she was told she no longer had to be afraid. Those were the most satisfying. Winning justice for someone that was helpless in securing it on their own.

Marissa pulled out the picture of Deandra she had "borrowed" from evidence. She looked at her eyes, how they reflected her smile. It was out here, alone in the quiet predawn of day that she allowed herself to feel the sadness, feel the loss of this beautiful soul. She looked up at the sky, saw it change from violet to soft pink to blue and smiled.

"This is your day," she said, looking back at the picture. Walking back into the house, she put her cup and the picture on the counter, and went to get ready for court.

●●●

The dawn of the day of trial found Lydia at the cemetery. Fragments of the sun peeked through the sturdy oak trees, the dew on the grass twinkled and sparkled. She sat between the two headstones, using her hand to brush away the leaves that had gathered on their tops. Clearing out the flower vase, she placed daffodils in the vase for her Norrece, running her hands with love over the stone. Misty-eyed, she repeated the gesture for Deandra, this time with Gerber daisies.

Turning her head up to the sky, she offered up a silent prayer. Lydia spoke of love for her husband and child, quietly asking for the strength to make it through this final chapter of this painful battle. She asked for justice so that Deandra – and she – could rest in peace. As if in answer, the sun came from behind the trees, warming Lydia's face and drying her tears. She closed her eyes and smiled.

•••

Marissa pushed open the doors of the courtroom and walked in. She walked past the spectators, various family members and friends of the accused. Some reporters the judge allowed inside were sitting in the back of the courtroom minus their cameras, and she was grateful cameras were not permitted on court floors. She walked past a sketch artist, setting up her "work area" a few benches behind the prosecution table, various pencils and a giant sketch pad lay next to her leg. She saw Lydia sitting three or four rows behind the artist. Marissa remembered several months ago when Lydia sat on the opposite side of the room, when her sons pled guilty to the crime that started this whole nightmare.

When she approached the two attorney tables, Montgomery stood up.

"Why, good morning, Ms. Elliot." He wore a coal-black suit and canary-yellow shirt which set off another set of gaudy cufflinks. Ms. Williams sat next to him, and gave a smile, but it was more out of professional courtesy than genuineness.

Marissa directed her smile between them and said, "Good morning," before taking her place at the opposite table. She put her briefcase on the floor next to her chair. Seconds later, the courtroom doors opened, and Austin and Gavin walked in. They walked up to the well, Austin stepping through and Gavin taking a seat on the bench behind them.

"Good morning, Maury," said Gavin. "You're looking lawyerly today." Marissa wore a berry-colored suit, black patent-leather peep-toe pumps and her hair was in a curly up do. She opted to wear her fashionable Donna Karen glasses instead of contacts.

"I want to look like I know what I'm doing," she winked.

"Mission accomplished," he responded. "Very classy."

The side door to the left of the room opened, and two deputy U.S. Marshals walked through, escorting the defendant. Roland was dressed in plain clothes instead of the prison jumpsuit. He did not look at Marissa, but instead kept his eyes forward. He looked out over the crowd, and smiled at the elderly woman waving at him. He stopped at a chair in between his attorneys, and one of the deputies uncuffed him. He shook hands with the attorneys before taking his seat.

The door to the right opened, and the courtroom deputy, courtroom stenographer, and bailiff walked in. As they took their respective places, Austin leaned over and said, "We can make a quick run to Starbucks for a triple espresso, if you're nervous."

A small red light came on, and she smiled and said, "Make him run for donuts instead," nodding her head at Gavin.

"All rise," the bailiff instructed.

"I heard that," Gavin whispered as he stood to his feet.

Judge Stagner walked into the courtroom and stood beside his chair. The bailiff recited the court's prayer and, as Marissa took her seat, the butterflies in her stomach began their dance. Austin adjusted his necktie, more out of nervous habit than necessity, as he looked flawless in his charcoal gray suit with a hint of pinstripes, crisp white shirt and navy tie.

The judge adjusted some papers on his desk, and, after pausing to read from one of them, he looked out into the courtroom.

"Ladies and gentlemen, good morning," he began. "Let me state for the record that this is criminal cause number 5:03-CR-084-S. We are in the last-minute preparations before the commencement of trial. It has been communicated to the court that there was some concern about discussing potential 404(b) material or materials that could be considered evidence of other crimes to show or prove that it is within his character to carry out the alleged crime. If any of those materials are coming out in the opening statements, I think we need to resolve that. Ms. Elliot?"

Marissa stood. "Good morning, your honor. We would attempt to introduce a lot of evidence where I don't consider it 404(b). If I may, let me first state what the evidence would be."

"Keep in mind I've read your brief."

"Yes, sir. To be brief, we're talking about the prior sexual assaults of Deandra, specifically by Roland."

"I don't think there's any doubt that that will be coming in, and you can discuss it in opening statement," said Judge Stagner.

"The second would be the prior dealings with the Knight brothers," continued Marissa, "because that would relate to motive, obviously, for the background conspiracy, and motive for committing the offense."

Judge Stagner held up his hand. "I will allow you to discuss it in opening statements, but I want you to know in advance that my tolerance for that evidence is limited, because I believe it can be wasteful of time, Ms. Elliot, if you spend a lot of time on it."

"I don't anticipate spending a lot of time on it, your honor, but I do think I have to bring it out in trial, and that would relate also to during the time period Roland Connors and Jeremy Spencer had a marijuana business going up in Ponca City. Part of their source was the Knight brothers, and this is all intertwined together in one business enterprise. Those are the only ones we would attempt to bring out in opening statements," she concluded.

"All right. I'm not going to . . .," started Judge Stagner.

"Your honor," Montgomery called out, also standing, "I don't mean to interrupt the court, but before we go any further, we would, for the record, object to the government going into those matters in its opening statement."

Judge Stagner looked over at Montgomery. "Thank you. Overruled."

Dividing his attention now between Marissa and Montgomery, the judge said, "I understand that one of the jurors, Mr. Harold Barry, has an emergency that we need to address before we bring the jury down, so I would like to retrieve him. Any objections?" He paused for a moment. Hearing none, he continued. "Henry, bring in Mr. Barry. Escort him over here so that we can have it somewhat private."

The bailiff left the courtroom, returning with the juror. He was thin, shorter than Marissa, and timid. He walked up to the bench, wringing his hat.

The judge removed his glasses and looked at him. "Mr. Barry, I already know your situation very well, and I appreciate your bringing it to my attention as quick as you did. Could you, please sir, discuss your personal emergency with me and counsel?"

The shy man cleared his throat, straightened his glasses and said, "Well, to be brief, two nights ago, my mother was taken to the emergency room because she fell down at home. She is ninety-six years old, and the doctors do not believe she will survive a surgery. And once the doctors made that decision, the hospital cannot keep her until arrangements are made. So, until I can research and find a suitable nursing facility, she will be released to me." Marissa detected a slight lisp.

"And when will she be released from the hospital," the judge inquired.

"Tomorrow afternoon." He pushed his glasses back into place.

Judge Stagner cleared his throat. "Now, you have been chosen to serve on this jury, and it's an important task. So, it is my job to balance the fact that after everything was said and done, you were one of the persons chosen to be on the jury, for good reason."

The juror raised his eyebrows and started to speak.

The judge raised his hand, stopping him. "Now, Mr. Barry, no one is saying that you could have foreseen this emergency. Certainly, no one here is accusing you of that. But, if I may be frank, Mr. Barry, under these new circumstances, if I may speak for everyone here, we are concerned about your ability to concentrate and follow the evidence. Mr. Barry," the judge put back on his glasses, "can you help me out with that? Will you be able to serve, but more importantly, are you willing to serve on this jury?"

Mr. Barry looked nervous, and his eyes darted to each attorney and back to the judge. He cleared his throat again, then said, "I think my state of mind right now precludes me from being able to concentrate fully on this." His voice softened. "I'm all Mother has, and yet I have to find a home for her that won't make her think I don't want her around. I just don't know."

The judge looked at the attorneys. "Do any of you have any questions," he asked. Each responded "No." Turning back at the juror, he said, "If you don't mind stepping into the jury box, and let us discuss this." As the bailiff escorted Mr. Barry away, the judge turned his microphone to the side.

"Okay, let me say my comment first. This is difficult, his situation is difficult, and I think anybody would have difficulty with that task." The judge looked out at the other attorneys. He spread his hands out palms up, and said, "We do have four alternates duly chosen."

Marissa stepped forward. "Your honor, if I may. Mr. Barry was clearly upset talking about this. I'm concerned with not just his ability to listen and comprehend, but also to focus and pay attention."

"Not to mention the time and effort it will take to make phone calls and visit different facilities and then make the arrangements, on top of her daily care," the judge thought aloud.

Austin stepped forward. "I think he would be unable to concentrate during what would be two of the most important days of our case when we put on some of the testifying co-defendants, so I can see how it could prejudice our case."

Judge Stagner sat back in his chair. He fiddled with his glasses for a moment. Then he looked out to the attorneys and said, "I'm going to excuse him. I just can't see him being able to give the full concentration this trial needs. We have four alternates, so we will move the first alternate to his chair and proceed with trial."

Montgomery, flustered, said "We object, your honor."

"I understand," the judge said. "Overruled. And the first alternate is whom?"

The judge directed the bailiff to bring back the juror, and after a brief discussion, dismissed him from the panel. His relief was evident as he thanked everyone and left the courtroom. Sending the attorneys back to their respective tables, the judge instructed the bailiff to bring in the jury.

After they were seated, the judge looked out and said, "To make sure that we have the right jurors in the jury box, I'll call out the names, and each juror should say 'here' as his or her name is called."

As the judge read the roll of names and they were sworn in, Austin leaned over and whispered, "Are you sure you don't want that coffee?"

"Ask me again in ten minutes," Marissa replied.

Judge Stagner proceeded to give the jury preliminary instructions about the trial. Marissa jotted down some last minute notes, as Austin watched the body language of the jury panel. Both looked up as the judge concluded and asked, "Is the government prepared to arraign the defendant?"

Marissa stood, and said, "The government is ready, your honor."

"Is the defendant ready?"

"Yes, your honor," replied Montgomery.

"The defendant will please rise," the judge instructed. Montgomery made a display of assisting Roland with his chair as he stood before the court. Roland was unmoved, staring straight ahead as Marissa read the indictment into the record.

"How does the defendant plead to the charges of the grand jury set out in the superseding indictment as read today, guilty or not guilty, Mr. Montgomery?"

"The defendant pleads not guilty, your honor," Montgomery stated, a little louder than necessary. Marissa heard snickering behind her in the courtroom.

"Thank you." Judge Stagner glanced at Montgomery. "You may be seated. Is the government prepared for opening statement?"

"The government is ready, your honor," answered Marissa.

"You may proceed."

●●●

Gavin stood and walked to the back of the courtroom. Spotting Adena and her mother, he slid next to Adena and whispered, "Come outside with me."

She squeezed her mother's hand and stood up. Lydia looked at both, confused, but nodded as they walked out.

Surveying the hallway, Gavin spotted an empty bench and led Adena down the hall.

"What's wrong? Why are we out here? I need to be inside with Mama."

"Ma'am, you can't be in there now."

"What!? Wait, why not?"

"The Rule has been invoked."

She blinked. "Excuse me?"

"Rule 615. Witnesses cannot sit in the courtroom and hear the testimony of other witnesses," Gavin explained. "It's so you won't tailor your testimony to another witness's testimony."

She stood up, turning away. Then she whirled back to face him. "So, Mama has to sit in there, and listen to this all alone?"

"Is there someone that you can call, someone that can be in there with her?" Gavin rubbed his neck.

"Well, I can call William." Then Adena shook her head. "No. I just won't testify. I just won't!"

"Now, wait, you can't do that." Gavin also stood up. "You can't just not do your part in putting these guys away."

"Mama cannot sit in there alone, hearing what happened to Deandra, what they did to her," she argued back, on the verge of tears.

"Look, I know this is difficult for you. But from what I've seen, your mother is a tough lady. The best thing you can do for her is to give your testimony when you are called." Gavin sat back down on the bench. "The best thing you can do right now is to call William and wait out here."

Adena sank down beside him. She laid her head back to rest on the wall, and closed her eyes.

Gavin laid his head back on the wall also, and waited.

• • •

Back inside the courtroom, Marissa stood before the jury. Smiling, she quickly looked at each individual juror, then began.

"Ladies and gentlemen, good morning. My name is Marissa Elliot. As I stated during the jury selection, I am an assistant United States Attorney, and I have the privilege of giving the opening statement for the United States in this case. And the United States will prove in this case just what the grand jury charged, that the defendant, Roland Loenthal Connors, was involved in a business enterprise involving the distribution and trafficking of marijuana, and that he traveled in interstate commerce from Oklahoma to Texas to further that enterprise. Also, we will prove beyond a reasonable doubt that the defendant, Roland Connors, participated in the kidnapping of a sixteen-year-old girl named Deandra Knight, who was abducted on April 6th, in the nighttime of that Saturday night while she was home, talking on the phone as most teenage girls do, and taken to Ponca City where two days later she was hit over the head with a shovel and buried in a shallow grave in a park just outside of Ponca City.

"Now, I've told you what we will prove to you. I want to now go into and go through what the evidence will show."

Marissa walked back and forth in front of the jury as she explained the workings of the drug business enterprise. She was calm and poised, and spoke in a clear, soothing tone. The jury watched her, and appeared attentive to the tale she wove.

"The testimony will show, ladies and gentlemen, that in March 2002, Roland Connors came down to Texas to purchase marijuana from the victim's brothers, Ryan Knight and Kyle MacKenzie. The purchase price of the marijuana was going to be $7,000. Roland Connors and Calvin Stewart met with Kyle MacKenzie and Ryan Knight, both older brothers of Deandra Knight, behind a Wal-Mart where they'd met before, and Roland Connors gave MacKenzie and Knight $7,000, which was given to them before the actual delivery of the marijuana took place. These arrangements were not new, business had been conducted in this manner several times before.

"But this time, unbeknownst to Roland Connors and Calvin Stewart, Kyle MacKenzie and Ryan Knight had lost their connection for marijuana months ago. So, the $7,000 that was taken by MacKenzie and

Knight was never delivered. They never purchased any marijuana, and they kept the money.

"After the rip-off by Kyle MacKenzie and Ryan Knight, at that time Roland Connors was embarrassed and he was upset, angry over losing $7,000. So, he contacted an employee he knew, a lady, a part-time girlfriend, if you will, named Diane Murphy. Diane Murphy worked for TXU, and at Roland's request, she obtained the address of Adena Knight, where Kyle MacKenzie and Ryan Knight were living with Deandra Knight.

"Over the next several days, Roland Connors, Nikko Hollis, Malcolm Connors, and Calvin Stewart conducted surveillance in camouflage outfits there at the apartment, waiting and plotting and planning their move to get the money back. They decided to go into the apartment that Saturday night and steal it back. So, Roland Connors carried a .380 semi-automatic pistol. Malcolm Connors carried a two-by-four plank of wood. Nikko Hollis carried a .380 semi-automatic pistol. And Calvin Stewart carried the can of gasoline. And these gentlemen went up to the apartment with these weapons with the intention to get the money back, by any means necessary.

"They went up to the apartment, and at first knocked. Now, whether they heard someone inside or just wanted to break in to literally see if someone was inside is unclear. What is clear, ladies and gentlemen, is they were hell-bent on retrieving their money. You will hear what happened on the 911 tape we will play for you. That in that time Malcolm Connors broke the glass out to the side sliding glass door with the two-by-four. He and Nikko Hollis went in and by force abducted Deandra Knight, took her out of the apartment into their waiting car, where they drove over to another location and dropped off Malcolm Connors, and then switched cars with Deandra Knight screaming in the car the entire time.

"Ladies and gentlemen, you will hear testimony of their interrogation of Deandra Knight, asking where her brothers were, their questions of where was the money. The testimony will show that she was not involved at all in any drug dealings, any stealing of their money, and was a typical teenage girl. The testimony will show how they repeatedly sexually assaulted Deandra Knight both by raping her and making her perform oral sex on them."

Lydia closed her eyes.

"You will hear how Calvin Stewart, Roland Connors, and Nikko Hollis took Deandra, after two days of torture, sexual assault, and beatings, to a grave that had been dug earlier by Roland Connors and Nikko Hollis, yet they couldn't find the grave in the dark."

Marissa paused in front of the jury and spread her arms on the rail, leaning into the box. "Let me say this part again. They took Deandra Knight out of the motel, drove to a park with intentions to kill her, but could not find the grave. So, they took her back to the motel. The testimony will show that the next morning, they went out again to the woods to a grave that they dug with the intention of killing her and dumping her in it. They took her out, and the testimony will show that she was beaten repeatedly over the head with a shovel, and she was buried in the grave."

Still watching the jury, she continued pacing before the box. "Now, I just want to say, in addition to what we will prove and will show you, I want to, for just a moment, and tell you how we will show it. Of course, we will have the police officers and witnesses that were there that saw what happened at the apartment, at the place where Roland hid, and in Ponca City, Oklahoma. We will call accomplices, co-defendants who have entered into plea agreements, and they will testify. Calvin Stewart, who agreed to plead guilty to life without the possibility of release for the kidnapping, will testify. He led the police to Deandra Knight's body. Malcolm Connors, Roland Connors' own brother, will testify. Now, he will not receive the death penalty, but he entered into a plea agreement for the conspiracy. Their plea agreements require them to testify truthfully. You will hear from them. These gentlemen were there. They were involved. And you will hear them admit their participation with Roland Connors, which was pretty severe.

"The testimony, ladies and gentlemen, will go one step further. You'll hear the testimony of Gavin Anthony Wright, who is a special agent with the Federal Bureau of Investigation. Special Agent Wright will testify to his interviews with Roland Connors upon his arrival in the Dallas/Fort Worth area, and the written statement he took from Roland Connors. You will hear from Agent Wright's testimony where Roland Connors admitted to him in his participating in the kidnapping of Deandra Knight and admitted participating in her murder.

"I ask you, ladies and gentlemen, to pay careful attention and listen to the evidence presented not only by the government in this case but by the defense, and I submit to you after you've heard that evidence, you'll have no reasonable doubt as to the guilt of the defendant Roland Loenthal Connors of the kidnapping and murder of Deandra Knight."

Marissa walked back to her seat and sat down. Austin pushed a legal pad in front of her where he wrote 'nice job, counselor.' Without looking, she wrote back 'thanks.' Judge Stagner looked over to Montgomery. "Does the defendant wish to make an opening statement at this time?"

Montgomery stood up and flexed his arms, displaying the gaudy cufflinks. He smiled and replied, "Yes, your honor."

"You may proceed."

Montgomery gave a slight nod towards the bench, and said, "May it please the court." When he walked past the prosecutor's table, he gave another nod. He stopped in front of the jury box, spread out his arms, and gave a theatrical half-bow to his audience. Marissa sat back in her chair and swiveled to face the jury, eager to hear Montgomery weave his client's side of the story.

"Ladies and gentlemen," he began, "as the court has instructed you good folks, the purpose of an opening statement is to outline the evidence as we anticipate it will unfold here in the courtroom. As you've likewise been informed, as we talked about in voir dire," pronouncing it 'voy deer,' "this is a trial with potentially two stages to it. The evidence that you hear during the first stage will be the evidence that you can likewise consider during the second stage of this trial, if it should reach that far." At that, Montgomery waved an arm towards Marissa.

"At this stage of the trial, the burden of proof is on the government of every element they've made, every accusation they've made, the burden of proof is on them beyond a reasonable doubt. Of course, it is Ms. Williams' job and my job, as Mr. Connors' attorneys, to make sure that the government is held to their burden of proof at this stage of the trial. If, at the end of this stage, you twelve folks unanimously decide that they have met this burden of proof beyond a reasonable doubt, that's when the second stage of this trial will start, and there will be new evidence for you to consider and new deliberations.

"Now, I anticipate that some of the evidence in this case will be horrible, shocking. But I also anticipate that the evidence is going to show that there were many individuals that played essential roles in this horrible abduction and murder. There are four named co-defendants, as you heard from the reading of the indictment: Jeremy "D. Low" Spencer, Nikko "Nickels" Hollis, Malcolm Connors, and Calvin "Caesar" Stewart, all of whom played essential roles in this abduction and murder.

"The evidence will show that Deandra Knight's own two brothers, Kyle MacKenzie and Ryan Knight, were not only drug dealers, but through their double-crosses and their rip-offs, they are the ones that created this very dangerous situation for their sister. And that perhaps, even more important, once the abduction occurred, they purposely obstructed the investigation of law enforcement in their efforts to find their younger sister, and this obstruction of law enforcement was motivated by nothing other than their own cowardice, selfishness and greed."

He stopped and leaned on the rail of the jury box, looking at each juror one by one. "Now, the evidence will probably begin with the 911 tape, Deandra Knight calling to the police for help. I anticipate that there will be testimony as to Jeremy Spencer sending Nikko Hollis down here, and Roland Connors and Calvin Stewart to go to this apartment to collect the money from Deandra's older brothers, Kyle MacKenzie and Ryan Knight. There was never any discussion, as the evidence will show, and never any plan, the evidence will show, to abduct Deandra. The plan was to collect the money that these brothers had ripped off from Jeremy Spencer, Roland Connors and Calvin Stewart."

Montgomery began his pacing again. "Ladies and gentlemen, I anticipate that the evidence will show that the other co-defendants, for good reason, were all afraid of Nikko "Nickels" Hollis. The evidence will show that Nikko Hollis had sexually assaulted Deandra Knight before they had even departed the Dallas area, and this was at a time when Roland Connors was at his sister's house. This was at a time when there were three individuals in a car with Deandra Knight, none of those individuals being my client, Roland Connors." Montgomery turned and pointed at the defense table.

"The evidence will further show that it was those three in the car. It was Malcolm Connors who took his turn with Deandra Knight at a time when his brother Roland Connors was nowhere around." Montgomery emphasized each word by hitting the jury rail.

"The evidence will show that Calvin Stewart took his turn with Deandra Knight once they had gotten her to Oklahoma and in a motel. Now, you may or may not hear from Jeremy Spencer, "D-Low" Spencer, but the evidence will show that Jeremy "D-Low" Spencer took his turn with Deandra Knight once they got to Oklahoma, as well. And with the exception of Nikko Hollis, these are all individuals that the government has struck deals with. They will not have to have a trial like Roland Connors. They will not have to face the penalty like the one my client is facing."

Montgomery paused in front of the jury and smiled. "I think the evidence will show that, after taken into custody, Roland Connors gave a full and truthful confession about his involvement in this offense. That he made this confession without a deal, without any promises. And on that same evening, he encouraged his little brother, Malcolm, to do the same, to tell the truth, and that Malcolm gave a confession that same evening. And you'll hear more details about the deals that Malcolm and Jeremy "D-Low" Spencer and Calvin Stewart had made so that they don't have to stand trial in this case, the deals the government made with those individuals.

"We have entered, ladies and gentlemen, into a plea of not guilty. We're going to hold the government to its burden of proof, but in listening to the evidence at this stage of the trial, keep in mind that there could be an additional stage with additional evidence in which you good twelve folks will be deciding whether life without the possibility of release is the appropriate punishment under all the circumstances in this case. And that's what this case is all about."

Montgomery took a moment's pause before retreating to the defense table. Marissa swiveled her chair back towards the bench.

Judge Stagner cleared his throat. "We'll take a ten-minute recess. Try to return here at 10:30 for the first government witness."

CHAPTER NINE

Marissa stepped outside, spotted Gavin and Adena down the hall, and headed in their direction. Gavin stood up when he saw her coming.

"Hey, we're just about to get started. Ready?" She looked from Gavin to Adena, sensing the tension.

Adena stood up. "Wait. He gets to go in? He's a witness, too! Why can't I go in since he gets to?!"

Glancing at Gavin, Marissa put her hands out in front of her. "I know it's difficult for you to wait out here. I genuinely appreciate your patience."

"Why can I not go in there? My mother is in there by herself, and . . ."

Gavin opened his mouth to answer, but Marissa laid her hand on his shoulder. "Gavin is the lead agent in this case, so the Rule doesn't apply to him."

Before Adena could protest further, Marissa took both of her hands in hers. She gave them a couple of gentle but firm shakes and looked into Adena's eyes. "Hey, now is not the time to freak out. I need you to stay focused and strong. I need you to let us do our jobs."

"Okay. Okay." Adena shook her head.

A security guard came up to them. "Ms. Elliott, the judge is ready to go in."

Just then, the elevator doors opened. "Babe, is everything okay?" William rushed to the group.

Marissa let go of Adena, who smiled at him. "Yes, baby. I just have to wait out here instead of being with Mama inside," she explained.

"Thanks," Gavin whispered in Marissa's ear. "She was just about to call off her testimony." He ran his hand over his head.

"Looks like I got here just in time." Marissa looked back at the couple huddled on the bench.

"Ms. Elliott," the security officer called, a little more forceful.

"Thank you. Yes, I'm sorry." Marissa and Gavin hurried into the direction of the courtroom.

Hand on the small of her back, he followed her into the courtroom and up to the well. She pointed to the chair on the other side of Austin, which he pulled out and started to sit.

The door behind the judge's chair opened, and Gavin righted himself as the bailiff announced, "All rise!"

Judge Stagner looked over at Marissa. "Is everything okay, counselor? Are we ready to proceed?"

She gave him a brilliant smile and said, "Yes, your honor."

"Very well. The government may call its first witness." The judge sat back in his chair, fingers laced together on the desk.

Marissa remained standing. "Your honor, the United States calls Amanda Reed. She'll be testifying to the first three counts of the indictment."

"All right," the judge replied. He then turned to the witness. "Ms. Reed, if you'll please raise your right hand and be sworn." After being sworn, he gestured to the witness chair where she sat down.

Marissa walked to the lectern. After arranging her papers, she looked over at the witness and pushed her glasses up onto her nose.

"Ms. Reed, will you state your full name for the record, please?"

"My name is Amanda Reed," she said, her voice only just above a whisper.

"Ma'am, if you could pull the microphone down a little bit, so the jury can hear you," Marissa instructed. Once adjusted, she continued. "Thank you. How are you employed?"

"I am a telecommunicator for the City of DeSoto," she said.

"Ma'am, you're going to have to speak up a little bit. Could you repeat your answer, please?"

A little louder, the witness repeated, "I am a telecommunicator for the City of DeSoto."

"Thank you. How long have you been employed in that position?"

"For approximately a year and a half."

"And what are your duties and responsibilities of that position?"

"I am a police dispatcher."

"What were your duties and responsibilities as a police dispatcher with the City of DeSoto?"

"I was functioning as a 911 call taker, answering emergency and non-emergency calls from the City of DeSoto."

Austin appeared at her side, laying a note on the lectern. After reading it, she looked back at the witness. "Ms. Reed, you'll need to speak up a little louder. It's still a little difficult to hear you."

She nodded.

"A 911 call taker, is that the same thing as a 911 operator?"

"Yes, it is."

"On the night of April 6, 2003, do you remember receiving a 911 call from 3401 Partridge Parkway, The Villa Winds Apartments?"

"Yes, I do."

Marissa turned and took the tape Austin handed to her. "Your honor, at this time I would offer into evidence Government's Exhibit 1-A."

Judge Stagner took a moment's pause, then said, "Hearing no objection, 1-A is admitted."

Turning back to the witness, Marissa continued. "Also in front of you, Ms. Reed, should be an exhibit marked Government's Exhibit 1-B. Do you have that?"

"Yes, ma'am."

"And is Government's Exhibit 1-B a transcript of the conversation contained in Government's Exhibit 1-A?"

"Yes, ma'am," she repeated.

"Now, have you read through Government's Exhibit 1-B and compared it with the conversation on Government's Exhibit 1-A?"

"Yes, ma'am."

"And is it a fair and accurate transcript of the conversation on Government's Exhibit 1-A."

"Yes, it is."

"Your honor, at this time I would offer into evidence Government's Exhibit 1-B."

Without looking up, the judge replied, "Admitted."

"Your honor, at this time I request permission to play Government's Exhibit 1-A for the jury and also to publish Government's Exhibit 1-B to the jury."

"Both requests are granted."

"May I approach the witness, your honor?"

"You may."

Marissa walked up to the witness stand. There was a tape recorder on the desk next to the microphone. Addressing the jury, she said, "I will now play for you the 911 tape." She pushed play and stepped aside to watch the jury as they listened.

●●●

Lydia closed her eyes as the tape began. It gave a glimpse of the beginning of the last moments of Deandra's life, the glass breaking, the scuffling of the intruders. She listened to her daughter's frantic pleas for help. Lydia fought against the tide of helplessness that rose in her as she listened to her daughter's screams. Her heart beat along with the rhythm of the beeping when the line went dead. She couldn't decide if it was mercy or regret she felt when the prosecutor stopped the tape. Then she opened her eyes.

●●●

"Ms. Reed," Marissa continued after the tape ended, "the noise at the end of the tape, could you explain what that noise is, the beeping noise?"

She took a sip of water and then replied, "The beeping noise is the other end of the phone being disconnected. I was still on line. When it beeps like that, the other end has been disconnected."

"When you say, 'disconnected,' you mean the receiver was hung up on the phone?"

"Correct," she responded.

"Did you attempt to call back?"

"Yes, I did."

"And were you able to get anyone at the apartment?"

"I received an answering machine, and after the message had discontinued, I identified myself as the police and asked someone to pick up, but there was no answer."

Marissa looked at the judge. "Pass the witness, your honor."

Judge Stagner, in turn, looked at Montgomery. "Cross-examination?"

"Thank you, your honor." Montgomery walked to the lectern and peered at the witness over his glasses.

"Ms. Reed, did you make any effort to enhance the quality of the audio on the tape?"

Taken aback by his question, the witness blinked several times. "Did I make any effort to enhance it," she repeated.

Montgomery smiled. "Yes, ma'am."

"No, I have not made any effort to enhance it." The witness sat a little straighter, obvious to the jury and to Marissa that she did not like Montgomery's accusation.

"Do you know whether anybody with either the DeSoto Police Department or the federal government has made any effort to enhance the audio to where you could hear some of the inaudible parts of the tape?"

"I do believe the federal government did have the tape in hand, but the police department of DeSoto did not."

"All right." Montgomery paused a moment, looking over his notes. Looking back at the witness, he asked, "Does it sound different here in the court today than it did the first time you listened to it?"

"No, sir, it does not."

"So, the first time you listened to the actual tape recording was after it had been enhanced by the federal government, is that right?"

Irritated, the witness replied, "No, that is not correct."

"Okay, then, when was the first time you listened to the tape, Ms. Reed?"

"The first time I listened to the tape was right after it happened. Approximately two days after."

"All right. Did the enhancement by the federal government improve the quality of the audio?"

"No, not in my opinion."

"It didn't get any better," Montgomery prompted.

"No."

He smiled again at the witness. "Thank you, ma'am," he said and walked back to his seat.

"Redirect, counselor," the judge asked Marissa.

"No more questions, your honor."

Turning to the witness, Judge Stagner said, "You may step down. The government may call its next witness."

"The government calls Vivien Howard, your honor," Austin responded.

The bailiff escorted the witness to the witness stand. Judge Stagner swore her to the oath and she sat down.

Austin smiled at the witness and said, "Good morning, ma'am."

"Good morning," she replied.

"Would you tell us your name, please, and spell your first name for the reporter."

She did so, and then Austin asked, "Miss Howard, what sort of work do you do?"

"I'm a human resources manager for several medical office clusters."

"Now, I want to direct your attention, if I may, back to Saturday, April 6, 2002. Do you recall that particular day, Miss Howard?"

"Yes, I do."

"Where were you living at that particular time?"

"I was living at 3401 Partridge Parkway, Villa Winds Apartments."

"All right. And how long had you lived there as of that time?"

"Almost two years."

"Okay. Now, directing your attention back to that particular day, Miss Howard, let me ask you, also, if you knew an individual by the name of David Mitchell."

"Yes."

"And who is David Mitchell?"

"He was my boyfriend at that time."

"Was he staying at the apartment at that time, as well," Austin inquired.

"Yes, he was."

"Now, do you recall anything particular occurring or happening or that you observed beginning in the morning of April 6 that attracted your attention, ma'am?"

"Yes."

"Okay. Tell us what that was, if you would, please."

Miss Howard cleared her throat and looked first at the jury, then back at Austin. "I noticed a car that I was not familiar with in the apartment complex throughout the day on Saturday."

"When you first noticed this vehicle, where was it, to the best of your knowledge?"

"The vehicle was parked across from our apartment complex, kind of adjacent to our apartment complex but within visual sight from our dining room window."

"And what in particular was it that attracted your attention to this particular car that day, Miss Howard?"

"The car would park, well, it was backed into a parking space and would be there for an hour or an hour and a half at a time. But no one ever got in or out, at all."

"Can you describe the car for us?"

"The car was a tan or brownish color, and it appeared to be an older model car. A Chevy, I think."

"All right. Were you able to notice how many people may have been in the vehicle?"

"From a distance, I could not tell how many people were in the car because the windows were tinted."

"Okay."

Miss Howard continued, "It wasn't until I . . ."

Montgomery stood up. "I'm going to object, your honor, to unresponsive at this point."

Judge Stagner replied, "Sustained." Looking at Austin, he said, "Go ahead, sir."

Austin flipped a page in his notebook. "Did you have an opportunity later on that particular day to get closer to the vehicle?"

"Yes, I did."

"Okay. What was that occasion?"

"I had went to throw trash into the dumpster. On my way to throw the trash out, I didn't pay much attention to or even look towards the car. It wasn't until I had emptied the trash and turned around that I noticed that there were individuals in the car."

"What can you tell us about the way they appeared at the time you saw them there?"

"I really only got a look at one of the individuals, and it was just kind of, just a short glimpse. I think I was startled more than anything."

"Why was that, Miss Howard?"

"From noticing the car from the apartment, it didn't look like people were in it. And once I had approached the car and noticed that there were individuals in the car, I was startled that there were people inside because the car had been parked for like an hour, hour and a half."

"Now, what, if anything, can you tell us about the appearance of the one individual that you were able to see?"

"I noticed that there was an African-American male wearing a baseball hat, and from the distance I could not determine, you know, the height or the body weight of the individual."

"How about age," Austin probed. "Can you give us some idea?"

"The age of the individual was maybe in his early twenties."

"All right. Did you notice what other type of clothing this individual may have been wearing?"

"At that time, I could not determine the clothing that the individual was wearing."

"Were you at a later time able to determine what type of clothing this individual was wearing?"

"No, I was not."

"Miss Howard, can you tell us about any of the other occupants, if there were any other occupants?"

"I noticed that there was an individual on the passenger side and what appeared to be an individual in the back seat, kind of slumped over."

"How would you describe them?"

"Can I have some water, please," Miss Howard asked.

"Please," replied Austin, gesturing towards the decanter sitting on the witness stand.

Miss Howard, after drinking her water, smiled at Austin and said, "Thank you. Can you repeat the question, please?"

"Of course, Miss Howard. How would you describe the individual or individuals you saw in the car?"

"I'm not able to describe those individuals."

"Were you able to see whether they were African American, white, Hispanic, or . . . ?"

"Yes. The individual on the passenger side was an African American, and I believe that the individual in the back seat was an African American, as well."

"Age?"

"Early twenties."

"All right. Clothing?"

"No, I am not able to identify the clothing."

"Did you ever speak to them, or did they ever speak to you?"

"No."

"Did you ever see them get out of the car?"

"No, I did not."

"Now, I can't recall if I asked you, Miss Howard, but do you recall about what time of the day on Saturday it was when you first noticed this vehicle?"

"I think that the time was around 12:00, 1:00."

"And over how long a period that particular day did you continue to see the vehicle where it was?"

"The vehicle was in and out of the complex several times on Saturday, just off and on. I saw the car at three different times on that Saturday."

"All right. Let me ask you, did you say anything to either Mr. Mitchell or anybody else in the complex about this particular car when you saw the occupants?"

"Yes, I did."

"What did you say to whom, please?"

"I called David to the apartment to let him know that I was suspicious of the individuals that were in the car, and told him to take precaution."

"What was he doing at or about the time you told him about this car?"

"David and another gentleman that lived in the apartment complex at the time were working on their cars, doing maintenance work on their cars at the time."

"And this other individual, what was his name?"

"Tony, but I'm not sure of his last name."

"All right. Did you go out to where they were working?"

"Yes, I did."

"From where they were working on this car, that is Tony Douglas and David Mitchell, were you and they able to see this Chevy from time to time?"

"Yes, they were."

Austin shifted gears. "Now, you said it was there off and on during the course of the afternoon. Were you there when it left, or do you recall it leaving?"

"I really can't recall it leaving, but I was there all day."

"All right. At some point in time, I gather the vehicle did leave?"

"Yes, it did."

"And did you ever write down a license number or write down a description of the vehicle?"

"No, I didn't."

"Ever call the police?"

"No."

"I gather, then, you weren't alarmed to that extent?"

"That's correct."

"Okay. Did Mr. Mitchell and Mr. Douglas remain there that evening, or did they leave for a while?"

"Could you repeat the question, please?"

"Mr. Mitchell, David Mitchell, and Mr. Tony Douglas, did they stay there, or did they leave sometime early in the evening?"

Miss Howard took another drink of water. "David Mitchell and Tony Douglas left around 6:30."

"Do you know where they went?"

"They went to the car wash."

"And about what time did they return, as best as you can recall?"

Biting her lip, she replied, "They returned at approximately 8:15."

"And did anything occur at or about the time or shortly thereafter, shortly after they returned from the car wash?"

"Yes. I think after returning they realized that something had happened..."

Montgomery stood up again. "Objection on what they realized, your honor."

Judge Stagner looked puzzled. "Could you restate the objection?"

"Objection on what they realized," he repeated.

Judge Stagner looked back at Austin. "Sustain the objection."

Austin cleared his throat and said, "Let's go back for a second. Do you know an individual by the name of Adena Knight?"

"Yes, I do."

"And how do you know Adena Knight?"

"Adena and I became acquainted through the lady who does our hair. She, Shammah, realized that we live in the same apartment complex and thought we would get along."

"And where did Adena Knight live, if you know, at the time back on April 6, 2002?"

"She lived at the Villa Winds Apartments."

"And you said you lived at apartment number 306?"

"Yes, that's correct."

"Can you give the members of the jury some idea of the approximate distance that separated the apartment you were living in at the time and apartment 212 where Adena Knight was living at the time?"

"I could look out my front door and see Adena Knight's apartment."

"The distance that you're referring to, is that something you could point here in this courtroom and give the jury some idea what we're talking about? Was it as close to the back of this wall here or farther?

"I would say that."

Austin blinked a couple of time. "Say what," he questioned.

"I would say the distance is from where I'm sitting now to the back door."

"Okay. Now, you said you were friends with Adena Knight. Did you come to know an individual by the name of Deandra Knight?"

"Yes, I did."

"And how did you come to meet or know her?"

"I met her through Adena. Then after meeting her and getting to know her, I hired her as a temporary baby-sitter."

"Okay. For whom?"

"For my nephews."

"Okay. So would your nephews come to visit you from time to time, ma'am?"

"Yes."

"Would you need babysitting services?"

"Yes."

"Were you looking for somebody that was trustworthy?"

Montgomery stood up. "Your honor, this is not relevant at this point in time."

"I'm going to allow it for a few more questions." Judge Stagner rubbed his chin. "Go ahead."

Austin looked back at Miss Howard. "Were you looking for somebody trustworthy to leave your nephew when it was necessary?"

"Yes, I was, and I found that individual to be Deandra Knight."

"Your honor," Montgomery said, "we object to what she found. It's nonresponsive."

"Nonresponsive," repeated the judge. "Sustained."

"Did you come from time to time to hire Deandra Knight to babysit your nephews?"

"Yes. She became a permanent babysitter for me during the duration of my nephews' stay."

"Okay. When would that have taken place, approximately?"

"It was around New Year's Day, that weekend."

"Okay. Now, you said you knew Adena Knight, and you got to know Deandra Knight. Did you know either of her brothers, either Kyle MacKenzie or Ryan Knight?"

"I knew of those individuals. I did not know them as well as I knew Adena or Deandra."

"All right. Now, the location where you said you saw the Chevy back in and park and remain, would those have been locations where the occupants could have seen apartment 212, the Knight apartment?"

"Yes."

"And now, let's go back, if we can. I believe you said that David Mitchell and Tony Douglas had gone to the car wash and had returned. Did you have occasion to see Adena Knight later that evening?"

"Yes, I did."

"Where did you see her, around what time was it?"

"I saw her around 8:45." Nodding, she said, "Yeah, between 8:45 and 9:00, she came to my apartment."

"Did you have a conversation with her?"

"Yes, I did."

"Without going into what she may have said to you, was she calm or was she excited?"

"She was crying, and she was excited."

"Now, what did you do as a result of your conversation with Adena Knight that evening when she came to your apartment?"

Montgomery stood up. "Your honor, we're going to object to that as hearsay."

"Sustained," replied the judge.

Marissa noticed Austin clinched his jaw. "Miss Howard, did you go somewhere?"

She gave him a blank stare. "Pardon me," she asked.

"Did you go somewhere after you talked to Adena Knight?"

"Same objection, your honor," Montgomery announced.

Judge Stagner waved his pen in the air. "Overruled."

Miss Howard replied, "After talking to Adena Knight, I did leave my apartment to go out to see what was going on."

"Tell us what you saw, if you would, please."

"When I arrived at her apartment, I saw detectives, I saw police cars, and at that time the crime scene had been marked off."

"All right. Did you have occasion yourself to go introduce yourself to DeSoto police officers?"

"I believe that they came to me."

"Did you tell them pretty much what you've told the members of the jury here today about the vehicle that you'd seen and the individuals?"

"What I stated to the police. . ."

Austin interrupted. "Listen to the question. Did you talk to the officers about what you had seen with regard to the vehicle and the individuals you had seen?"

Nodding her head, Miss Howard replied, "Yes, I did."

Austin looked at the judge. "May I approach the witness, your honor?"

"You may."

Marissa handed him some photos, and Austin shuffled through them, walking to the witness stand.

"Let me begin, ma'am, by showing you what's been marked as Government's Exhibit 21-A. Let me ask you to take a look at that photograph, and I'll ask you if you recognize what's portrayed or depicted in this photograph?"

Studying it for several seconds, Miss Howard replied, "It appears to be the car that I saw on April 6th in the Villa Winds apartment complex."

Addressing the judge, Austin said, "We'll offer Government's Exhibit 21-A at this time, your honor."

"21-A is admitted," Judge Stagner replied, making notes.

"May I publish it to the jury?"

"You may." Austin walked over to the jury box and handed the photograph to the first juror on the end.

"Now, Miss Howard, let me know you also what's been marked as Government's Exhibit 4-B. Let me ask you to take a look at that particular exhibit, if you would, ma'am. Do you recognize the person that is portrayed in that particular photograph?"

"Yes, I do."

"Who is that?"

"Deandra Knight."

"Does that fairly and accurately depict the way she was back when you knew her a year ago?"

"Yes, it does."

"We offer Government's Exhibit 4-B at this time, your honor."

"We object to relevance," Montgomery said.

"Overruled, Mr. Montgomery. The exhibit is admitted."

"May I publish this to the jury at this time?"

"You may." Again, Austin walked over to the jury box and handed the photo to the first juror. The bailiff, in turn, handed him the previous photograph. Walking back to the prosecution's table, Austin took the large poster board Marissa handed him. He set it on the easel already positioned between the witness stand and the jury box.

Directing his attention to the witness, Austin continued. "This diagram is already in evidence, Miss Howard, Government's Exhibit 2-A. Let me ask you if you recognize this as an accurate depiction of the Villa Winds Apartments where you lived back at that time?"

Looking at the diagram, the witness replied, "Yes."

"Okay. Can you point to and show the jury where your apartment was located?"

"I think so."

"Okay. Show us where your apartment was at the time."

Using the laser pointer Austin handed to her, Miss Howard pointed to the diagram.

Austin placed a felt red dot on the spot where the laser touched the diagram. "Now, show us where 212, the building where Deandra's apartment was."

"It's going to be over here," she said, again pointing the laser at the diagram. Again, Austin placed a felt red dot on the spot where the laser touched the diagram.

"Okay. Now, can you give the members of the jury some ballpark idea of where it was that you saw this Chevy that you identified for us on Saturday when you saw it?"

She pointed the laser to the diagram once more.

"Okay. Did you see it only in one place, or did you see it in other places?"

"It was always parked in the same spot."

"I believe that's all the questions I have, your honor." Austin said, walking back to the podium, gathering his notebook. "I'll pass the witness." Turning to Miss Howard, he said, "Thank you, ma'am."

Judge Stagner looked at Montgomery. "Cross- examination, sir. You may proceed."

Montgomery made a show of gathering his notes and other belongings before almost gliding to the lectern. He first looked at the jury and smiled, then focused on the witness.

"Now, Miss Howard," he began, "you had indicated that you knew of Ryan Knight and Kyle MacKenzie, is that correct?"

"Yes, that's correct," she responded.

"Deandra's two older brothers?"

"That's correct."

"And what is it that you knew about them?"

"I knew very little about them. My association with them was on a very limited basis."

"Did you know that they were living there at the apartment at the time?"

"No, I did not."

"Were you familiar with the cars that Ryan Knight and Kyle MacKenzie drove?"

"Yes, I was."

"And what kind of cars did they drive?"

"Well, one of the cars was a dark blue Nissan, and the other vehicle was some type of white car."

"A white car and a dark blue Nissan?"

"Yes."

"And you saw the cars parked there at the apartment complex on several occasions, did you not?"

"I wouldn't say several. I did see the cars parked there."

"Okay, on this particular day, you saw those cars parked there, did you not?"

"Objection, your honor," Austin stood up. "What's the relevance to all of this?"

"Mr. Montgomery?" responded Judge Stagner.

"Your honor, I ask for leniency. The witness said that she knew the brothers, and I am simply inquiring as to how well she is familiar with or how well she knows the brothers of the victim."

Judge Stagner paused for a moment. "I'll allow it." He looked at him. "Very little leniency, Mr. Montgomery. But I'll allow it." Turning his attention to the witness, Judge Stagner said, "Please answer the question, ma'am."

"Could you repeat the question," she asked.

"Of course, ma'am," Montgomery responded. "On the particular day of April 6, 2002, you saw those cars parked there, did you not, Miss Howard?"

"I cannot recall."

"Now, how would they typically park the cars?"

"I would see the cars parked on the back street, backed in."

"Can you point out for the jury on that diagram where that would be?"

She pointed the laser towards the diagram, almost touching a red felt dot.

Montgomery smiled and asked, "May I approach, your honor?"

"Yes, you may."

He walked up to the easel and placed a blue felt dot on the diagram. Walking back to the lectern, he continued. "Okay, now, as I understand it, on this particular day, the cars could have or could not have been parked there?"

"I object." Austin stood up. "That's a misstatement of the testimony. She said she did not see the cars that day."

Looking at Montgomery, the judge said, "Do you want to restate the question?"

"Do you remember, ma'am, whether or not you saw the cars that day," he asked.

"I do not remember," she replied.

"You said you saw this Chevy," Montgomery held up the photograph of the car, "or this navy car several times that day, is that correct?"

"That's correct."

"And that would have been on Saturday, April 6th?"

"That's correct."

"And what time did you first see it?"

"I think it was between 12:00 noon or 12:30, is when I first noticed the car."

"Early to mid-afternoon?"

"Yes."

"Do you recall, Miss Howard, how long it was there?"

"I would say an hour to an hour and a half."

"Did it leave at some point?"

"Yes, it did."

"And when was the time you next saw it?"

"I'm not sure on the time I saw the car again."

"Do you recall, Miss Howard, approximately how much later and how long later? An hour later? Two hours later," he pressed.

"I would say two hours, two hours later."

"Approximately?"

"That's correct."

"And do you recall how long it stayed that time?"

"Again, about an hour."

"And then it left?"

"Yes."

"And the way I understand it, you were shown photographs as part of the investigation of this case by a police officer?"

Miss Howard looked puzzled. "Photographs of what, I'm sorry?"

"Photographs of individuals, Miss Howard," Montgomery smiled.

"Yes, I was."

"All right. And as I understand it, you were unable to identify any of the individuals who you viewed as any of the occupants of that car, is that correct?"

"That's correct."

"Thank you, ma'am." Turning to the judge, Montgomery said, "I'll pass the witness, your honor." He gathered up his belongings and returned to his seat.

"Is there redirect," the judge inquired.

Standing, Austin said, "There is none, your honor."

"You may step down," Judge Stagner instructed the witness. She stepped down from the stand and walked past the two attorneys' tables, out of the well.

"May this witness be excused, your honor?"

"This witness is excused."

Looking at Austin, the judge asked, "Before we call the next witness, do you imagine testimony will run beyond the noon hour?"

"Possibly not, your honor."

Judge Stagner peered at him from the top of his glasses. "'Possibly not, Mr. Gregory?"

"No disrespect intended, your honor," Austin responded. The look Judge Stagner gave him would have made any other attorney stammer and lose their focus. Austin, on the other hand, was calm and unrattled. "The government's line of questioning for this next witness is not very long."

Sitting back in his chair, the judge said, "Well, let's hear the next witness, then. You may go on. Thank you." He nodded at Austin.

"The government calls Mr. Tony Douglas."

After being sworn in, the witness sat down in the witness chair.

"Tell us your name, please sir," Austin began.

"Tony Douglas."

"Let me ask you, sir, back in April of 2002, where were you residing?"

"Excuse me?" The witness inclined his ear towards Austin.

"Where did you live?"

"Villa Winds Apartments."

"What apartment?"

"Apartment 306."

"Let me direct your attention, if I might, Mr. Douglas, to the afternoon of April 6, 2002, and I'll ask you if you had occasion to be out in the parking lot of your complex working on your car?"

"That's correct."

"Do you do that frequently, sir?"

"Yeah, pretty much."

"Anything unusual occur at or about that time that you can recall?"

The witness shifted in his chair. "Yeah. I noticed a car was parted right across from where I was working. One person was in it when I first noticed it, and then a few more minutes, a few more heads started to pop up."

"You noticed one person at first?"

"Yeah."

"And then how many more?"

"Two more, making a total of three." The witness held up three fingers.

"Okay," said Austin, "tell us about the car."

"Camaro, between '81 and '84."

"Are you sure?"

The witness grinned. "Oh, yeah, I'm sure. That car is a classic."

Austin grinned back. "You know a little bit about cars, don't you, Mr. Douglas?"

"Yeah, I like to tinker with them."

"And you said there was one individual, and then you later saw two others pop up, is that right?"

"Right."

"Can you give us an idea of about what time it was you first saw the car?"

"I'm not sure of the time."

"Had you ever seen it over there before, to your recollection?"

"No, I haven't."

"Did you have occasion to get close enough to see any of the occupants?"

"Yeah."

"Okay, tell us about that. How did that happen?"

"Well, I was just working on my car, so they were about 20 yards from me."

"Describe these individuals, if you would."

"They had on camouflage fatigues, military."

Austin feigned surprise. "Sir?"

"Camouflage fatigues, military," the witness repeated.

"First off, how many were there?"

"Three."

"Were they out of the car when you saw them?"

"No. They were all in the car."

"All right. And what was the occasion you got close enough to see they were in fatigues?"

"Well, I could see that from where I was."

"Okay. Camouflage?"

"Uh-huh."

"All right. About how old did they look?"

"They looked to be young, maybe between 18 and 21, somewhere around there."

"Well, did you have occasion to talk to them?"

"No, I did not."

"Did you see them talk to anyone else out there?"

"No."

"Did they remain where they were parked, or did they move around, or what do you recall about the car?"

"They backed in and sat there."

"Did you ever see them drive off at some point?"

"No. They were still there when I left."

"Where did you go, Mr. Douglas?"

"I went to wash my car."

"And when you got back, did something happen?"

"Yeah. When I got back, I was met by a DeSoto police officer who started asking me a few questions."

"Did you give them information about what you just told the members of the jury?"

"The same thing I just told you."

"I beg your pardon, sir?"

"The same thing I just told you," repeated the witness, almost swallowing the microphone. Several jurors snickered.

"Did you ever write down a license number or anything like that?"

"No."

"So when you got back, you told the police what you've told the members of the jury here today, is that correct?"

"That's correct."

"Let me ask you, Mr. Douglas, did you have occasion at some time to view a series of photographic lineups?"

"Yes, I did."

"All right. Do you think you got a good enough chance or a good enough look to be able to recognize and identify anyone or any of the individuals you saw in that Camaro that day?"

The witness rubbed his chin. "Well, just not a very good, but pretty good, you know?"

"Let me put it this way: were you ever able to make a positive identification of anybody?"

"No, just some of them looked like the guys that were in the car."

"May I approach the witness, your honor?"

"You may," he replied.

"Let me show you Government's Exhibit 21-A, and I'll ask you if you recognize that particular automobile?"

The witness looked at the picture, pointed and said, "Yeah, that was the car."

"And what is this in this particular photograph, sir?"

"A Camaro."

"Does it appear to be the same Camaro that you were referring to?"

"Yeah. I mean, yes, sir."

Austin handed the witness the laser pointer, then walked over to the easel. "Mr. Douglas, can you show us approximately where the Camaro was backed in when you saw it?"

The witness pointed the laser to the diagram. "Right here on this corner." The laser dot sat on top of a red felt dot.

"All right. I believe that's all I have. Thank you very much, Mr. Douglas." Walking back to the lectern, Austin said, "And I'll pass this witness."

Judge Stagner sat forward and said, "Is there cross examination, Mr. Montgomery?"

"Just a few questions, your honor," he replied, taking his position at the lectern. Smiling at the witness, Montgomery asked, "Mr. Douglas, could you tell the court how far the vehicle was again from where you were working on your car?"

"About twenty yards?"

"And you testified that you were able to see some individuals sitting in the car?"

"Yeah."

"What were they wearing again, Mr. Douglas?"

"Military fatigues, camouflage."

"And you could see this clearly, sir?"

"Yes, sir."

"Did the car have tinted windows?'

"Yeah."

"Did you ever go up to the car?"

"Your honor," Austin stood up, "objection to relevance."

"Mr. Montgomery?"

"Your honor, I am merely trying to understand how Mr. Douglas, who was twenty yards away from the car, says that not only could he see the individuals, but he could clearly see the type of clothing they had on. And yet Miss Howard testified that she could not make out what they had on, whether a shirt was yellow or black," Montgomery answered, dripping with smugness.

"Objection overruled," Judge Stagner said, sitting back in his chair.

Looking back at Mr. Douglas, Montgomery said, "Now, sir, did you ever go up to the car?"

"No, sir."

"Did the individuals ever get out of the car?"

"No, sir."

"What time of day was it, Mr. Douglas, when you realized there were people in the car?"

"I'm not sure of the time of day." The witness shifted again, this time to the other side of his chair.

Montgomery did not mask his annoyance. "Was the sun up or down, Mr. Douglas?"

"The sun was up."

"Okay, was it more towards the beginning of the day, or more towards the end of the day?"

"Uh, I would say more towards the end of the day."

"So, you were able to see the type of clothes the individuals were wearing in the latter part of the afternoon through tinted windows?"

"Yeah."

"And yet you could not make a positive identification of any of the individuals, is that correct?"

"Yeah."

Montgomery closed his notebook. He looked at the witness and said, "Thank you, sir."

"Re-cross, Mr. Gregory," asked the judge.

"No, sir."

Judge Stagner nodded at the witness. "Very well. You may step down, Mr. Douglas. Mr. Douglas, you are also free to go."

"Thanks, judge," said Mr. Douglas as he stepped from the witness stand, and proceeded to walk out of the courtroom.

"It's about five minutes until noon. We'll take our lunch break until 1:30 p.m." Judge Stagner rose, followed by everyone in the courtroom. Marissa gathered her briefcase, and purse, prepared to leave. She jumped when Austin touched her elbow.

"Your office in ten minutes," he said.

She nodded, and crossed the courtroom to exit. When she opened the doors, she was immediately engulfed by the media. Reporters all began talking at once, each one hollering her name, vying for her attention.

"Ms. Elliot, how do you think it's going in there?"

"Marissa! How long do you think this trial will last?"

"Do you like the jury you've selected, Ms. Elliot?"

Each reporter was shouting her name, and mini tape recorders and microphones were thrust into her face from all sides. The sea of people, both reporters and spectators made it hard for Marissa to take two steps.

"Ladies and gentlemen, please!" She raised her hand and waved, hoping to be heard over the commotion. "On behalf of the United States, I have no comment at this time." That announcement only caused the reporters to shout louder.

Someone tugged on her elbow. Frowning, she yanked her arm back only to discover it was Gavin's hand that held her.

"Come on," he said, pulling her close so she could hear him above the crowd.

Pushing his way through the crowd, he barked at the reporters, "Ms. Elliot has no comment at this time. Thank you." Still holding her arm, he led her the short distance to the elevators, where Austin was waiting with an open car. Gavin half pushed her inside.

"Thank you," she said, a little rattled with the unexpected media blitz.

"I'm here to protect and to serve." He winked at her just as the doors closed.

CHAPTER TEN

On the other side of the crowd, Adena waited for her mother to come out of the courtroom. Spotting her in the crowd, she shouted, "Mama!" as she and William made their way to Lydia's side.

Chuckling, she said, "I'm not as fragile as both of you are thinking I am." She swatted their hands away from her elbows. "I'm fine, you two!" Turning to William, she smiled. "And what are you doing here?"

Giving a sheepish smile, he replied, "Both Adena and I don't think you should be in there alone, Ms. Lydia."

"Well, I will say listening to the 911 tape was hard." Sorrow overcast her vision. "Hearing Deandra scream like that, . . ." she trailed off.

"Excuse me, are you Mrs. Knight?" A tall gentleman with red hair in a dark gray suit approached them from behind. He spoke into a small recording device. "We are in the early stages of the Deandra Knight murder trial, and I'm here with Mrs. Knight, Deandra's mother. Ma'am, if I could just ask you a few questions. How are you holding up in there?"

Lydia gave a blank stare to the young man. She spotted several other people looking in their direction. Before she could answer him, they all started running up to her, each thrusting something in her face to speak into.

"Mrs. Knight, is it true your sons are to blame for their sister's death?"

"Mrs. Knight, how are you holding up?"

"Are you hoping for the death penalty, Mrs. Knight?"

"Hey!" William tried to intercept, but he was engulfed in the throng of reporters contending for Lydia's comments.

She was completely overwhelmed. The questions kept coming, and no matter where Adena tried to lead her to get out of the mess, she was met again with questions. And now, they had caught the attention of random people in the hallway and coming off the elevator.

"Okay, people, knock it off. Let the lady alone." Gavin stepped in between Lydia and a woman reporter who wouldn't let go of her arm. He looked down at the hold, then at the lady holding her, and said, "Ma'am. Please." She let go of Lydia's arm, and he turned to address the crowd.

"This is a difficult time for the Knight family. I'm sure they would appreciate your respect of their privacy."

The reporters were momentary silenced. Gavin put his hand on William's shoulder. "Follow me, man." He steered him back towards the courtroom, then led them to a room just beyond.

Inside, they were greeted by Judge Stagner, only instead of a robe, he was wearing his suit coat. He gestured to the conference room-size table and surrounding chairs. "Please, come in. Sit down," he said. He pulled out a chair, and Lydia sat down, not sure what to make of what was going on. Adena and William sat on either side of her, also confused.

Judge Stagner gave Gavin a slight nod, who reciprocated and stepped outside, closing the door behind him.

William looked from Lydia to Adena and back again. He then looked at the judge, and said, "Why are we in here?"

The judge shoved his hands in his pockets. "This is my attorney-client conference room. I was made aware of those reporters out there looking for an interview. I'm offering this room to you for the duration of the trial. It will be a no-reporter zone."

"Thank you." Adena sat back in her chair, the relief visible on her face.

"It was getting ugly out there," William blew out a huge breath.

"A deputy U.S. Marshal will be here in a moment to see to getting y'all some lunch or refreshments from the cafeteria on eight."

Lydia smiled. "That's very kind of you, sir. We appreciate this."

He put a hand on his chest. "I offer you my deepest condolences for the loss of your daughter. And your sister," he gestured his hand at Adena. "I'm very sorry for your loss."

"Thank you, your honor," said Lydia. The judge did not miss the slight straightening of her spine. Adena also murmured a "thank you."

There was a knock on the door. The judge opened it, and a young woman popped her head inside. Looking over the group, she said, "Hello, everyone. I'm Deputy Centers. Can I get you anything from the cafeteria?"

"Well, I'll leave you to your lunch," Judge Stagner said, and walked out.

●●●

At precisely 1:30, everyone was back in the courtroom. Judge Stagner pounded his gavel, and the courtroom became silent.

"Before we get started, I want to address the media." He took off his glasses and looked out into the audience. "I was informed of the gang-rush on both Ms. Elliott and Mrs. Knight for their attention during the lunch recess. You are this close," holding up his fore finger and thumb less than an inch apart, "to my issuing a gag order in this case. Mrs.

Knight is off limits. Her family is off limits. If and when the family is ready to address the media, I am quite certain she or a member of her family will let you know. Until that happens, I'm not to hear of another incident like the one this morning, or all of you will be banned from this courtroom. Do I make myself clear?"

There were rounds of "yes, sir," and "yes, your honor" heard from the back of the courtroom.

"Very well. Now, let's move on. The government may call its next witness," said the judge.

Marissa stood up. "Thank you, your honor. Your honor, at this time the United States calls Kenneth Adams."

The witness walked into the well and stood before Judge Stagner. He wore a nice tailored gray suit and navy blue tie.

"Mr. Adams, if you'll please raise your right hand and be sworn." Kenneth adjusted his glasses as he was sworn in and then took his seat on the witness stand.

"Would you state your name for the record, please," Marissa began.

"My name is Kenneth Adams."

"How are you employed?"

"I'm a crime scene investigator with the Desoto Police Department."

"What are your duties and responsibilities as a crime scene investigator, Mr. Adams?"

"My duties include the evaluation of a crime scene, search of evidence, crime scene photography, diagram of a crime scene, and latent fingerprint processing."

"And how long have you been a crime scene investigator for DeSoto PD?"

"Approximately seventeen years."

Marissa walked from behind the podium, standing in front of the prosecution table.

"On April 6, 2002, were you assigned to the investigation of the Deandra Knight kidnapping?"

"Yes, I was."

"And when did you get assigned to the investigation on that case?"

"I was called at approximately 9:45 p.m. on Saturday, April 6."

"And what location did you go to as a result of being assigned and called on that case?"

"I went to 3401 Partridge Parkway, apartment 212."

"Mr. Adams, would you generally describe for the jury what you did when you arrived at 3401 Partridge Parkway?"

The witness shifted in his seat. "Upon my arrival, I met with Detective Frank Fargo. He gave me a briefing as to what had happened. After getting my briefing, I made a walk-through of the apartment, then I took photographs of the apartment."

Marissa took the photographs Austin held out. Your honor, may I approach the witness?"

"You may," the judge replied.

Walking up to the witness stand, she said, "Let me show you what's been marked as Government's Exhibit 2-L, and ask you if you can identify that?"

"Yes. That's the front door of apartment 212."

"Did you take the photograph?"

"Yes, I did."

"Your honor," she turned to the bench, "I would offer into evidence Government's Exhibit 2-L."

"2-L is admitted."

Turning back to the witness, Marissa asked, "Would you please describe what you observed at the scene when you arrived at 3401 Partridge?"

"Upon my arrival, I noticed that the west sliding glass door of the apartment was smashed, glass was on the patio, and glass scattered across the room of the living room. Also saw one of the vertical blind slats laying out on the patio."

"Did you process the apartment for fingerprints?"

"Yes, I did. I also made a search of the apartment. We found a .25 caliber Raven auto pistol on the bed. It did not have any ammo or an ammo magazine in it, so I made a search of the apartment to see if I could locate the magazine and the ammo, which I did not. I did find the gun case laying on the floor in front of the dresser. After I collected those items, then I processed both sliding glass doors of the living room for latent or, concealed fingerprints, that may have been missed earlier. And around the bedroom door that was broken, all for fingerprints on the frame and the glass."

"Where is the next location that you went to in relation to the investigation in this case?"

"The next location was 501 Pomegranate Way in Duncanville, Texas."

"And did you collect evidence at that location?"

"Yes, I did."

Marissa held up her hand. "Wait, let me back up. On what date did you go to that location?"

"That would have been on Tuesday, April 9."

"What evidence did you collect there?"

"That was where the location of the '83 Camero was. Upon my arrival, met with Detective Fargo, and he requested that I process the exterior of the vehicle for latent fingerprints and have the vehicle towed and stored for further interior processing. But at the Pomegranate Way location, we processed the exterior for fingerprints."

"When did you process the interior of the Camero?"

"That was the morning of April 9."

"Mr. Adams, I ask you to look at Government's Exhibit 63-A and 64-A, and ask if you can identify those exhibit?"

"Yes, ma'am."

"And what are they?"

"63-A is the left rear floor mat that I took out of the Camero."

"And 64-A?"

"64-A is the front full size floor mat from the Camero."

"Your honor, at this time I would offer into evidence Government's Exhibit 63-A and 64-A."

"63-A is admitted," replied Judge Stagner. "And 64-A is admitted."

"Okay, Mr. Adams. The next location that you went to in relation to this investigation, where would that be?"

"That would be in Ponca City, Oklahoma. I went to two locations there, 745 West Elm Avenue and 730 West Elm Avenue.

"And what date was that on?"

"That was on Thursday, April 11."

"And what did you collect at the 745 West Elm Avenue location?"

"I collected some insurance receipt with the name Roland Connors, a phone bill, and also collected a sports bag with some medication bottles in it."

"Where's the next location that you went to in relation to your investigation?"

"I went across the street to 740 West Elm Avenue. There, I collected a pair of tennis shoes."

"All right. What was the next location that you went to?"

"We next went to the Ponca City Inn."

"And about what time did you get to the Ponca City Inn?"

"It was Friday morning at 2:12 a.m."

"What took place once you arrived, Mr. Adams?"

"On our arrival, myself, Special Agent Wright and other FBI agents went to the motel office and made contact with Ms. Merrell, the property manager. There we found out that Jeremy Spencer had rented an apartment, a room there, room 108. We got consent from Ms. Merrell to make a search of that room. We went to room 108 and at approximately 2:35 a.m., we entered the room."

"Let me ask you to look at Government's Exhibit 53, and ask you if you can identify that?"

The witness took the exhibit. "Yes, I can," he replied. "This is a copy of the registration card signed by Nikko Hollis."

"Your honor, at this time I would offer into evidence Government's Exhibit 53."

The judge replied, "Government's Exhibit 53 is admitted."

Looking back at the witness, Marissa continued. "Now, what did you do when you went into room 108 and processed that room or investigated and searched that room?"

"Well, the first thing I did was photograph the room just as we found it, then I made a search of the room and collected physical evidence out of the room."

"And what evidence did you collect at that time?"

"I collected a cigarette butt, some hairs from the bathroom floor. Umm, a sample of white stain that was on a chair next to the main door, another cigarette butt, a Band-Aid, and I collected the bedspread from the room."

"Now, were you interrupted during the course of your search at all?"

"Yes. While unloading evidence and putting it in my truck, the suspect vehicle that was described to us by the security guard of the motel drove past us, in front of 108. The FBI initiated a stop. The vehicle and the suspect was brought back to the parking area in front of 108."

"Is that when Jeremy Spencer was arrested by the officers that were there and the agents that were working in 108?"

"That's correct."

"Were you present when anything was taken from his pockets?"

"Yes, I was. They reached into his pocket, and they removed a key. The key had a sticker on it with the numbers 108 on it."

"Once Jeremy Spencer was arrested, did you have occasion to either search or assist in the search of his vehicle?"

"Yes, I did. We opened the trunk of his car. There we found a .38 caliber Smith and Wesson pistol that had ammo in it. We also found a .380 automatic that was also loaded, and some license plates, Oklahoma license plates."

"Did you go to another location in relation to this investigation, Mr. Adams?"

"Yes, I did. We went to Watson Wrecking Service to process the vehicle that Jeremy Spencer was driving and where we seized the guns from. There, we collected the floor mats from the car, a candy wrapper and also trace vacuumed the seats, back seat and front seat, the floors. We collected the back and front carpet from the vehicle. I also collected an earring, and a small ring that was underneath the rear seat, as well as an Oklahoma state license plate."

"Did you later that day proceed to an area called Faurot Lake?"

"That's correct."

"And what happened when you got to Faurot Lake?"

"We made a grid search of the park trying to find the location of the grave site, Deandra Knight grave site."

"How long did you and the other officers and agents stay out at the park area that day?"

"From approximately 9:30 a.m. until around 5:00 p.m."

Marissa stepped behind the podium and flipped some notes. "Wait. Let's come back to that in a minute. Mr. Adams, did you go to another location in relation to this investigation?"

"Yes, ma'am. We went to the Gable Gateway motel, room number 219. Then we began to make a search of that room and collect physical evidence."

"Now, would you describe for the jury what items of evidence you collected from the Gable Gateway motel?"

"Okay. From the Gable Gateway motel, I collected the bedspread that was on the bed. We collected carpet samples next to the bed, carpet samples from the dressing area, and a control sample of the carpet from one corner of the room. I found a gold loop-type earring behind the dresser. Also we collected a blanket out of the dresser, a telephone book and a Bible, also collected some mini-pretzels that were behind the dresser. After that, we processed the room for latent fingerprints."

"Let's put a pause here for a moment. Did you have cause to return to the Ponca City Inn that Saturday evening?"

"Yes, I did."

"And for what?"

"Additional processing, and also to use the alternate light source in search of body fluids."

"Anything else, Mr. Adams?"

"We lifted additional fingerprints off the bathroom wall."

"Okay, let's go back to Gable Gateway. Was there anything else collected there that evening?"

"No, ma'am."

"Now, where was the next location that you went to in relation to this investigation?"

"We went back to Faurot Lake."

"When?"

"About 11:00 that evening, we went back out to Faurot Lake to make another search. They had brought one of the subjects out to Faurot Lake to see if he could spot the grave site.

"And were you successful in finding the grave site that evening?"

"No, we were not."

"So, what happened next?"

"On Sunday morning we went to Faurot Lake. Upon our arrival, we learned that the location was found where the victim's clothing was taken and burned. So, I went to that location."

"And where was that location?"

"It's a vacant field."

"Okay. And did you collect any items? Did you find any evidence items in the vacant field?"

"Yes, I did. I found a five-gallon paint bucket. In the bucket was burned debris. A short distance from it, we found a yellow high-lo anti-freeze plastic jug."

"Let me show you what's been marked as Government's Exhibit 24, and ask if you can identify that, please?"

"Yes. This is the jug I collected."

"Your honor, at this time, I would offer into evidence Government's Exhibit Number 24."

Judge Stagner juggled some papers on the bench. "I'm sorry, counselor. Number 24?"

"Yes, your honor," Marissa responded.

"It's already been admitted." Judge Stagner waved his hand, and Marissa continued.

"Now, what happened after you gathered evidence at that location?"

"I returned to Faurot Lake to make the search for the grave site."

"And what did you do when you arrived there?"

"Upon my arrival, I learned that the grave site had been located, and we were waiting for the second subject to be brought out to verify that location."

"Were you present, Mr. Adams, when the grave site was excavated and the excavation began?" She caught the slight shift Kenneth made in his chair.

"Yes, I was."

"And what role did you take once the grave site was found and the excavation began?"

"My task at the grave site was evidence collection and taking photographs."

"And who, in fact, conducted the excavation?"

"Joe Thomas from the FBI and Randy Sternes from DeSoto."

"Do you know approximately what time the body was found?"

"Yes. At 4:37 p.m., the victim's left knee was uncovered. She was fully uncovered at 7:45 p.m."

"And what happened after she was uncovered?"

"After she was uncovered, I took photographs as we had found her. Then she was lifted from the grave and placed on a sheet provided by the Oklahoma state lab."

"And then what happened?"

"The victim was later transported to the Oklahoma state lab by Oklahoma state people."

"Did you go to the Oklahoma state lab?"

"Yes, I did."

"And were you present during the autopsy?"

"Yes, I was."

"Did you take photographs during the autopsy?"

"Yes, I did."

Marissa turned to the bench. "Your honor, at this time, I would like to offer into evidence Government's Exhibits 37-A through -FF, excluding Government's Exhibit number 37-Z and 37-CC."

"Very well. Give me a moment to mark my book."

"Yes sir," she replied.

"Any objections, Mr. Montgomery?" Judge Stagner turned to the defense table.

"Your honor," Montgomery drawled, "we're going to object for all the reasons that we articulated before. And I think the record should reflect that the photographs that the government intends to offer are large, much larger than other photographs they have that are of a much smaller size. And in addition to all the reasons we expressed previously, we would object to them."

Concentrating very hard not to roll her eyes, Marissa responded. "Your honor, I'm not asking to display them at this moment, just to offer them into evidence."

"All right," Judge Stagner said, "37-A through -FF are admitted save and except 37-Z and 37-CC. The objection is overruled."

Montgomery sat down as Marissa said, "Your honor, at this time, I pass the witness."

"Is there cross?" Judge Stagner peered over his glasses at Montgomery.

"No, sir."

"You may step down, sir." The judge nodded at the witness.

"Ladies and gentlemen, I think this is a good place to stop for today." Judge Stagner announced. He turned to the jury then. "Please remember all of the instructions that I have given you about avoiding the media coverage. I expect there will be more so be very vigilant about not discussing the case with anyone at home or among yourselves. Any questions?" No one responded. "All right, thank you. I'll see you all at nine tomorrow morning."

CHAPTER ELEVEN

Marissa clipped on the pearl earring that matched her necklace. She fastened her watch and closed the jewelry drawer of her armoire. She stood in her closet, trying to select shoes to off-set her olive suit when she thought she heard the doorbell. She looked at her watch, 7:35 a.m. She poked her head out of the closet, straining her ears.

I must be hearing things, she thought to herself. Then the doorbell rang again.

Okay, see, I'm not crazy! She made her way across the living room and opened the door to find Gavin on the other side with a cup of Starbucks coffee thrust out in front of him.

Surprised, Marissa leaned against the doorframe and smiled. "Is this going to become a habit?"

"Good morning. It doesn't look like I woke you this time," Gavin smiled back. Marissa noted the charcoal-gray suit and sky-blue shirt, pleasantly surprised that he chose not to wear a tie. She had always thought Gavin was handsome, but this morning, . . . wow.

Flustered, she cleared her throat. "Is that for me," she asked, referring to the coffee.

"Well, I figured this would be the ice breaker if I did wake you."

Marissa stepped aside as he walked across the threshold, taking the coffee as he passed. Her eyes followed him in, gazing on his broad back. Averting her eyes, she busied herself with closing the door behind him, smelling the cup.

Gavin turned to face her. "Since I didn't wake you, what were you doing?"

"Trying to pick out a shoe." She pointed to her bare feet.

"Well, lemme give it try."

The coffee cup froze mid-way to her lips. "Excuse me?" She lowered the cup. "You wanna help me pick out a shoe?"

"Sure, why not?" He shrugged his shoulders.

"Alright, this ought to be good!" Marissa was intrigued. Suppressing a smile, she turned and led him down the hall to her bedroom.

She watched him observe the mint-green walls with white trim and the large dark wood furniture. The sparkling white bedding was splashed with pastel throw pillows, and the colors echoed on the seat cushions of the huge bay window that took almost the entire adjoining wall.

Marissa led the way across the room into a mammoth of a bathroom. He let out a low whistle at the shower wall with showerheads on each end. The focal point of the room, however, was the huge marble bathtub that sat in the middle of the room. The wall opposite the shower displayed two vanity sinks, where he assumed she put on her makeup because of the stool under the kick-out in the middle.

"Fancy," he remarked, looking around.

She threw a smile behind her. "Yeah, it was the master suite that sold me on the house." Standing in front of a closed door, her hand on the knob, and her smile deepened. "This clinched it."

She opened the door and stepped into one of the biggest closets he had ever seen. Rows and rows of tops, skirts, and suits in a rainbow of colors, and jeans and slacks and long dresses had their own section in the back. There was an island in the center with drawers, and an entire wall of shoes, which she stood in front of, arms folded across her chest.

"No wonder you can't make up your mind. There's an entire shoe store in here!" There were rows and rows of shoes in every color there ever was: red, navy, pink, purple, and cream. He saw pumps and boots of various heights, and even spotted several pairs of tennis shoes. They were arranged by graduating color hues and all in clear, plastic shoe boxes.

"Don't mock the shoes." Gesturing towards the wall, she turned to him. "Well? Which one?"

Raising an eyebrow, Gavin walked closer and scanned the clear boxes. Looking over at her olive skirt and cream collarless blouse, he pulled down a pair of Christian Louboutin brown leopard high sling-backs.

"Wow. I'm impressed." Using his arm to steady herself, she put on the suggested shoes. She walked over to the full-length mirror in the corner, donning the matching olive jacket. She caught his eye in the mirror watching her and smiled. "Nice choice. Thanks."

"I aim to please." He grinned as she grabbed the coffee cup before they left the closet. As they walked back down the hall, she glanced over her shoulder. "So, to what do I owe the pleasure of this morning visit?"

"Well, I just wanna make sure there wasn't anything else we need to go over before I testify today." He leaned against the counter and watched as she took her phone off the charger, putting it in her purse on the love seat.

She paused. "Are you nervous?"

"Not really. Well, a little. Not about my part or what I'm up there for. But this is some heavy stuff I'm going to be talking about. With Mrs. Knight in the room," Gavin shrugged, "can't help but think this is going to be hard on her."

"I know." Marissa rubbed his arm, touched. "But she's strong. This will be painful, true, but it will aid in her closure and healing." She leaned into him and added, "I think."

Nodding, he blew out a huge sigh.

"Are you gonna be okay?" She picked up the nearby briefcase and faced him. "I can switch the order around and put you on tomorrow, if you need some more time."

"No, don't do that, Maury. I'll be fine." Gavin shook his head. "Just ready to get this over with."

Smiling, she said, "You know I'll be doing the examination, so I'll go easy on you. And guess what?"

Gavin looked at her, eyebrow raised.

"You get to drive us to court." Grabbing her purse and briefcase, she flashed another huge smile.

"Like I didn't see that one coming!" He chuckled as he walked past her, opening the door.

●●●

Later that morning, Judge Stagner brought the courtroom to order. "The government may call its next witness," he said.

Marissa stood up. "The United States would call Gavin Anthony Wright."

"Please raise your right hand and be sworn."

After taking his oath, Gavin sat down at the witness stand. Marissa walked up to the podium and said, "May it please the court." Addressing Gavin, she said, "Would you state your name for the court and jury, please."

"Gavin Anthony Wright."

"Mr. Wright, how are you employed?"

"I'm a special agent with the Federal Bureau of Investigation."

"And how long have you been a special agent with the FBI?"

"Approximately eight years."

"As a special agent with the FBI, what are your responsibilities?"

"I work drugs, violent crimes, kidnappings, extortions, those types of offenses."

"And where are you assigned as a special agent?"

"I'm assigned to the Dallas Division, Dallas Resident Agency."

"How long have you been assigned in Dallas?"

"Approximately eight years."

"I want to take you back to April of 2002. Specifically, April 6 and 7 of 2002, did you have occasion to be assigned to assist in the investigation of an allegation of kidnapping of a sixteen-year-old girl by the name of Deandra Knight?"

"Yes, ma'am, I did."

"And that allegation involves the alleged kidnapping at 3401 Partridge Parkway in DeSoto, Texas?"

"Yes, ma'am."

"Now, let me move you to April 11, 2002, which I believe is a Thursday, and specifically refer you to the early morning hours of that day. Did you have occasion to be working with a detective in the DeSoto Police Department by the name of Frank Fargo?"

"Yes, ma'am, I did."

"And what were y'all doing that day or early that morning?"

"We were putting together the probable cause for the issuance of a warrant."

"And specifically, who were the arrest warrants for?"

"Rolando Connors, Malcolm Connors, and Calvin Stewart."

Marissa walked from around the podium. "About what time of the morning were those warrants obtained?"

"Approximately 2:45 a.m."

"And then what did you do, Agent Wright?"

"We called the Ponca City Police Department and advised them that we had felony arrest warrants for three individuals. I then advised my supervisor of the situation and requested that I fly to Ponca City, Oklahoma."

"And what happened? Were you able to go?"

"Yes, ma'am," Gavin answered.

"What did you do after you arrived in Ponca City?"

"I proceeded to the Ponca City Police Department in order to conduct an interview."

"And who did you interview at that time?"

"I interviewed Calvin Stewart for approximately two to three hours."

"Okay. Let's move forward to April 12, which is a Friday. Where did you go in regards to the investigation of this case?"

"We received a tip that Roland Connors was flying into Ponca City, to turn himself in, I suppose."

"And where did you go after receiving that phone call?"

"With a warrant, we arrested Roland Connors once he landed and took him to Ponca City Police Department."

"And did there come a time when you were able to talk to him?"

"Yes, ma'am."

"And was he by himself when you spoke with him?"

"No, ma'am."

"Who was with him?"

"He was with his attorney."

"Okay, wait. Is the Roland Connors that you spoke to on April 12, 2002 here in the courtroom?"

"He is, yes, ma'am."

"Would you point him out for the judge and jury?"

"Yes, ma'am. He's the black male sitting at the defense table with a brown jacket, a white striped shirt, navy tie, short haircut, somewhat of a medium-skinned black male."

Marissa looked to the bench. "The government asks that the record reflect that the witness has identified the defendant, Roland Connors."

"The record will so reflect," Judge Stagner responded.

"When you met with him, was the defendant read his Miranda warning, Agent Wright?"

"Yes, ma'am."

"And after they were read, what action was taken after that?"

"It was requested that everyone present sign and/or initial the card."

"And are those initials on Government's Exhibit 84?"

"Yes, ma'am, they are."

"Are your initials on there?"

"Yes, ma'am, they are," Gavin repeated.

"Is Government's Exhibit Number 84 one and the same card containing the warnings that were read to defendant Roland Connors?"

"It is."

Turning again to the bench, Marissa said, "The government would move to introduce Government's Exhibit 84."

"Government's Exhibit 84 is admitted."

"Agent Wright, would you read to the jury the warnings that were read to the defendant off that card on April 12?"

"Yes, ma'am," he responded, and read the requested evidence into the record.

"Okay, hang on a second," Marissa interrupted. "Did the defendant appear to understand those warnings?"

"He did."

"How could you tell that?"

"Because he signed his name on the card," Gavin shrugged. Several snickers were heard both throughout the courtroom and the jury box. It took a concentrated effort for Marissa not to smile herself.

"After that, did you and Detective Fargo speak with the defendant?" She walked back to the podium.

"Yes, ma'am."

"And what did you tell him?"

"We told him the facts as we knew them at that point concerning the kidnapping."

"Let me stop you there. On, April 12, 2002, did you know where the location of Deandra Knight was?"

"No, ma'am, we did not."

"Did you know whether she was alive or dead?"

"No, ma'am, we did not."

"What did you tell Roland Connors at that time?"

"I told Mr. Connors that at the bottom of it all, it was a dope deal that had gone bad, and that we needed to find Deandra Knight."

"And what happened at that time?"

"He looked at us as if he wanted to respond but did not, and we continued to talk about the facts as we know it."

"And what else did you say?"

"I just told him it was a bad deal that, you know, it shouldn't have happened that way, we needed to find her. We're looking for her, we would like to find her alive, you know, we need your help. Things like that"

"And how did he respond, or did he respond at all?"

"I believe that at that time, his eyes became watery."

"And then what happened."

"Then the interview was, in essence, terminated."

"And what happened at that point?"

"He stated, 'Come see me in Texas. I'll tell you all about it.'"

"Okay, what happened after that?"

"I had an additional conversation with him where, when he said 'it wasn't supposed to be like that.'"

"After that, Agent Wright, where did you go?"

"I went to the county jail."

"And what happened at that time?"

"We requested permission to see Calvin Stewart."

"And did you interview Calvin Stewart?"

"Yes, ma'am, I did."

"About how long did that interview take?"

"In the jail, it only took about thirty minutes."

"Okay. Did you leave at that time?"

"Yes, ma'am, I did."

"Where did you go?"

"We checked Mr. Stewart out, went to a sandwich shop and waited for a local patrol unit to meet us there."

"And after that, where did you go?"

"We went to the park that Mr. Stewart described for us."

"Now, prior to speaking with Mr. Stewart, did you have any idea about Faurot Lake?"

"No, ma'am, I did not."

"How long did you stay out there with Mr. Stewart?"

"We stayed out there some five hours. About four to five hours. We were out there a long time."

"What were y'all looking for?"

"We were trying to find Deandra Knight."

"Were you able to find her?"

Gavin looked at the jury. "No, ma'am, we were not."

"What happened next?"

"It was early in the morning, and we couldn't find her. We carried Mr. Stewart back to jail and we left, got a couple hours' sleep."

"Did you think Deandra Knight was alive or dead at that time?"

Gavin shifted in his seat. "I didn't know, ma'am. Training tells you one thing, but I was hoping she was still alive, but it had been so long, we were just hoping she was still alive."

"Okay," Marissa nodded. She sensed his uncomfort. "What did you do after you left the park?"

"I went to the Oklahoma City county jail."

"And who did you meet there?"

"I met with Nikko Hollis."

"How long did you meet with him?"

"Approximately two hours at the jail."

"After you met with him, did you go anywhere?"

"Yes, ma'am."

"Where did you go?"

"Well, I called to the hotel where the agents and the DeSoto police officers were staying and told them to get as many flashlights and as much light as we could, that we were going back to Faurot Lake to look for Deandra Knight."

"About what time did you get back to Ponca City?"

"Approximately 10:30 p.m."

"And what happened at that time?"

"Well, Mr. Hollis stated, 'You don't believe me. I'll take you to where I have some evidence.'"

"And what happened next?"

"We drove to a field where he told me her clothes had been burned up, that he had burned her clothes in a field."

"And what happened at that location? Did you stop at that time with Mr. Hollis?"

"Yes, ma'am."

"And what happened at that time?"

"He said, 'I burned the clothes up in the field, and the yellow anti-freeze jug that we used is out there, too.'"

"So, what happened?"

"Well, the agent that was with me couldn't find it, so Nikko said, 'come on, you and I will go get it,' and he and I walked out in the field."

"And what did you discover at that time?"

"Well, he said, 'here's the paint bucket where I burned her clothes up and the sheets. This is the yellow gas can that we brought from DeSoto that I used to set it on fire.' And he pointed up and said, 'look, the trees are scorched from the flame.'"

"Let me show you Government's Exhibit Number 65-D." Marissa handed it to Gavin. "Describe that for the court, if you would please."

Gavin looked at the picture. "This is a close-up picture of the same area. You're walking out into the woods, into the field area. There's a fence right there," pointing to the referenced area, "you can see the fence post, small row of trees, and then on the other side you can see among the yellow flowers is where the paint bucket and the anti-freeze container were recovered."

"Here's 65-I. Describe this, please."

"Yes, ma'am. This is a photograph of the scorched leaves as the circumference of the paint bucket was so hot it burned the leaves on the ground. Here, it's the same picture in relationship to the leaves on the trees that were scorched."

Turning to the judge, Marissa asked, "With permission of the court, could he point it out closer to the jury since it's so small?

"Yes," Judge Stagner nodded.

"Agent Wright, please do so briefly."

Gavin left the witness stand and repeated his statement, pointing out to the jury where the evidence was found on the picture. One by one, the jurors leaned closer to look at the picture, one juror, perhaps wearing bifocals, raised her glasses.

When Gavin returned to the stand, Marissa continued, "After leaving, where did you go at that time?"

"We went back to Faurot Lake."

"And what happened then?"

"Well, Mr. Hollis said, 'I'll show you where she's buried.'"

"And then?"

"Again, I called the motel and got more agents and police officers. We all met at the park, and he walked us out in the park to her grave."

"Let me stop you for a second." Marissa held up her hand and walked over to stand in front of the jury box. "Was that a similar or different location from where Calvin Stewart was?"

"It was the same location, the same park, same area."

"Okay. You said that Nikko Hollis took you up to the grave. What happened at that time?"

Gavin rubbed his chin. "Well, it was in the middle of the night, and we walked down the nature trail, went up the incline, over an old logging road into another thicket. He said, 'I can't find it tonight.' But, . . . "

"But, what, Agent Wright?"

"We didn't know we were standing on top of her grave."

•••

Lydia felt the air leave the room, and she put her hand on her throat. Her mind's eye created pictures of people walking on top of Deandra as she gasped for breath. Her throat burned and her eyes watered, imagining Deandra whimpering for help.

William looked over and his heart fell as he saw the visible hurt over his future mother-in-law's face. He put his arm around her, rubbing her shoulder.

She absently patted his arm, never taking her eyes away from the front of the room.

•••

"And so what happened at that point?"

"We carried him back and told the patrolmen that were stationed at the lake that we would be back in the morning."

"All right. Did you know at the time that you all were standing on her grave?"

"No, ma'am, we did not."

Marissa paused a moment, letting that soak in with the jury. "All right. After that, what happened?"

"The next day, which I believe was the afternoon of April 14, about 3:00 p.m., they brought Mr. Hollis back to the park, and I said 'Nikko, are you going to take us to the grave today?' And he said, 'Yeah, come on.'"

"So what did you observe at that time?"

"We walked right back out to the same area we had been the night before, and he said, 'she's right here.' We looked around, kind of in disbelief."

"Now, at that point, did you have occasion to go get another one of the subjects?"

"Yes, ma'am."

"And who was that?"

"Calvin Stewart."

"And what happened?"

"We carried Calvin Stewart back out to the grave area. He looked around, and he said, 'yeah, this is it.' And we asked him to describe to us how she was laying in the grave and how she was prior to the attack that placed her in the grave."

"And then what did you guys do?"

"We marked it, took pictures, put up crime scene tape, photographed it, then removed the o-lookers out of the area and got together to decide how we were going to exhume her body."

"Let me show you Government's Exhibit Numbers 37-A through -E, and ask if you recognize those photographs?"

Marissa walked up to the witness stand and handed Gavin several photographs. After looking them over, he described for the jury the area surrounding the grave, identifying several landmarks such as the concrete walkway and a nature trail. He pointed out to the jury the length of the park where the evidence tape ran, and described the picture of the grave area, pointing out to the jury the actual grave. There were pictures depicting how the defendants placed pine tags and loose leaves and broken branches over the grave to disguise it, attempting to make it look as if the soil had not

been disturbed. And pictures where the officers placed little crime scene flags, marking the area where they believed the body was.

"Let me show you Government's Exhibit 37-G. Describe that for us, please."

"After Calvin Stewart described the approximate size of the grave, we placed markers at what we thought was her head and at the bottom of her feet, the length of the grave."

"Was that consistent with what was ultimately discovered?"

"Yes, ma'am."

"Approximately how long did it take before the body of Deandra Knight was discovered?"

"As we were digging through the layers of dirt, ma'am?"

"Yes."

"About two to three hours."

"Okay, let's move on," Marissa continued. "On April 17, did you return to the Dallas/Fort Worth area?"

"Yes, ma'am, I did."

"Where did you go?"

"We went to the DeSoto City Jail and requested permission to see Roland Connors."

"And what happened at that time?"

"When Roland Connors walked up to the desk area, he said, 'what's taken you guys so long?' I told him not to say anything else until we can get him upstairs and advise him of his warnings."

"Agent Wright, this is Government's Exhibit 87." Marissa placed it in front of Gavin. "Is this a true and accurate copy of the adult warning form signed by you and the defendant and Detective Fargo on April 17, 2002?"

"Yes, ma'am, it is."

"The government would move to introduce Government's Exhibit 87."

"87 is admitted," the judge replied.

"Agent Wright, if you could, would you please read Government's Exhibit 87 to the jury?"

Gavin read the advice of rights into the record. At the end, he looked first at the jury and then back at Marissa.

"And there's a box there that says, 'signed,' correct?"

"Yes, ma'am."

"Who signed it there?"

"Roland Connors."

"And who signed as witnesses?"

"Special Agent Gavin A. Wright, FBI Dallas Division, and Detective Frank Fargo, DeSoto Police Department."

"And what was the time this document was executed?"

"3:11 p.m."

"All right. Let me show you what's been marked as Government's Exhibit Number 85. Do you recognize the signature on that document?"

"Yes, ma'am, I do."

"And what is that?"

"The signature of Roland Connors."

"Is Government's Exhibit Number 85 a true and accurate copy of the warning that was given earlier in the day to Roland Connors by Municipal Judge Allison Bradshaw of the DeSoto City Jail, located at the DeSoto City Jail?"

"Yes, ma'am."

"Your honor, the government would move to introduce Government's Exhibit Number 85."

"85 is admitted."

"Without going into the reading of the whole document, does that also contain what's commonly known as the Miranda warnings?"

"Yes, ma'am, it does."

"And that was the procedure that was read to the defendant before the municipal judge, is that right?"

"Yes, ma'am,"

"After he had been warned by Judge Bradshaw and by you and the Miranda warnings, what happened at that time?"

"Well, Mr. Connors started to tell us about the drug deal, the kidnapping, . . ."

"Your honor, we're going to object to that." Montgomery stood up. "We're going to object to what he said at that time for all the reasons previously stated."

Judge Stagner looked at Montgomery. "Overruled," he said.

"Let me stop and ask you some questions about that." Marissa was seething, but she forced herself not to look over at Montgomery. "Did you or Detective Fargo force Mr. Connors to talk to you?"

"No, ma'am."

"Did you promise him anything to get him to talk to you?"

"No, ma'am."

"Did you threaten him in any way?"

"No, ma'am."

"Did you display your handguns or do anything to force him to give you that statement?"

"No, ma'am, we did not."

"To your knowledge, did anyone else?"

"No, ma'am, no one did."

"All right." She gave her jacket a slight, satisfied tug. "After he had signed all those warnings, you said he talked to you. What did he tell you?"

"He started to tell us about the facts surrounding this case."

"Ms. Elliott," Judge Stagner held up a hand, "let me interrupt you for a moment, because this seems like a good place to take a break."

Marissa nodded, and walked back to sit beside Austin.

While the judge addressed the jury, Gavin sat back in his chair and took a drink of water from the decanter on the stand. Once Judge Stagner and the jury left the courtroom, he left the witness stand and walked up to the prosecution table.

"Well, if I were wearing a tie, I'd be ready to take it off now!" He rubbed his hand over his head.

"You're doing great." Marissa smiled over her glass of water.

"How much longer?"

Looking over her notes, she replied, "Umm, I'm guesstimating another thirty minutes on our end."

Gavin nodded, looking around.

●●●

After the break and everyone was back in the courtroom, Judge Stagner rapped his gavel a couple of times and called the courtroom to order. He looked at Marissa and said, "Ms. Elliott, you may continue."

"Thank you, your honor." Facing Gavin, Marissa smiled and said, "Agent Wright, I want to go into a couple of things in the statement Roland Connors gave you, some of the additional stuff that he said to you, a portion of it, anyway, all right?"

"Yes, ma'am," Gavin nodded.

"Did he mention to you why he recruited Hollis to come down to Texas?"

"Yes, ma'am, he did."

"And what was that?"

"Your honor," Montgomery interrupted, "we have the same objections that we made earlier."

"Overruled."

Glancing at Montgomery, Gavin answered, "He stated that Nikko Hollis had a reputation for pistol whipping people, kicking in doors and collecting drug debts."

"Did he say if anybody else recruited Hollis besides himself?"

"No, ma'am, he did not."

"Did he tell you what their intent was in using the gasoline?"

"Yes, ma'am."

"What was that?"

"Same objections, your honor," said Montgomery.

"Overruled, counselor."

"May we have a running objection to this line of questioning?"

"Yes, sir." Judge Stagner nodded at Marissa. "Go on."

"What did he tell you in regards to that?"

"He told me that the intent was to duct tape both Kyle and Rider, the brothers, pour gasoline on them and make them give them their money back."

Marissa walked to the prosecution table where Austin handed her more photographs. "Now, during the course of your investigation, Agent Wright, did you have occasion to go over to 1812 Holliday Lane in Oklahoma City, Oklahoma?"

"Yes, ma'am."

"And who lives there?"

"Jeremy Spencer and his wife."

"Okay." Looking at Judge Stagner, she asked, "May I approach the witness, your honor?"

"You may."

Walking to the witness stand, Marissa asked, "why did you go there?"

"Because from the statements that we had taken from Calvin Stewart, we knew that Deandra Knight had been to that house as they travelled from Texas to Oklahoma prior to going to the Ponca City Inn."

"If I could, I want to show you what's been marked as Government's Exhibit Number 33, and ask you if you recognize that map?"

"Yes, ma'am, I recognize it."

"And what is that?"

"It's a map of the city of Ponca City, Oklahoma."

"Okay. How many times were you up in Ponca City during the course of this investigation?"

"In excess of six times."

"And this map was actually obtained from the police department, is that right?"

"Yes, ma'am."

Marissa turned to the jury box. "Agent Wright, please describe to the ladies and gentlemen of this jury the general layout of this map."

Gavin walked the jury through the map and pinpointed the streets of the city, pointing out where the hotels were in proximity to the residence of Jeremy Spencer and the lake where Deandra was found.

"All right, Agent Wright, thank you. Now, you had mentioned earlier in your testimony about a bucket, is that right?"

"Yes, ma'am, I did."

"Okay. I want to show you Government's Exhibit Number 67." She took the box from Austin and placed it on the table next to the witness stand. "Agent Wright, do you recognize the contents of this box?"

Gavin peered inside. "Yes, ma'am, I do," he nodded.

"What is in that box?"

"This is the actual paint bucket that was recovered in the field that Nikko Hollis led us to."

"And is this the one and the same bucket that was retrieved by you and other law enforcement officers on April 13?"

"Yes."

"The government would move to introduce Government's Exhibit 67 into evidence."

"67 is admitted," Judge Stagner replied.

To Gavin, Marissa asked, "When you went to the home of Jeremy Spencer on Holliday Lane, did you talk to him?"

"Yes, ma'am."

"Did you have occasion at that time to retrieve any evidence?"

"Yes, ma'am."

"What did y'all do at that time besides talk to him?"

"We asked Mr. Spencer had Roland Connors left any clothing or any personal items at his residence."

"And did you obtain any items from the home of Jeremy Spencer?"

"Yes, ma'am, we did."

"Who gave them to you? Who gave you the items?"

"Jeremy Spencer and his wife."

"And what did he and his wife give you?"

"They gave us an overnight garment bag."

"And did you have occasion to take certain items out of that garment bag and place them in evidence, you and another detective?"

"Yes, ma'am."

"Who would that detective be?"

"Detective Christian Parker."

"Okay. Now I want to show you what's been marked as Government's Exhibit Number 11, and ask if you recognize that exhibit?"

"Yes ma'am, I do."

"All right. And where have you seen that exhibit before?"

"This exhibit was on top of the clothing in the bag that was recovered at 1812 Holliday Lane, the residence of Jeremy Spencer."

"Did you take that into custody?"

"Yes, ma'am."

"Is that the one and the same item that was retrieved that day?"

"Yes, ma'am, it is." Gavin took a drink of water.

"Your honor, the government would move to introduce Government's Exhibit 11."

"Government's 11 is admitted."

"Agent Wright, what is Government's Exhibit Number 11?"

"It's a Texas personal identification card. It gives a description of a black male, a name and a photograph."

"What's the name on there?"

"Calvin Stewart, signed by Calvin Stewart."

"Who's photograph is on that identification card?"

"Roland Connors."

"Your honor, may we publish this to the jury?"

"You may."

Marissa walked to the end of the row and handed the exhibit to the foreman. Turning to Gavin, she said, "Let's move forward, while the jury is looking at that exhibit. Let's talk about your return to the Dallas/Fort Worth area. Did you have occasion to go to Pomegranate Way?"

"Yes, ma'am."

"And why did you go there?"

"I had a conversation with Calvin Stewart."

"And the result of that conversation?"

"I went to the Pomegranate Way address in Duncanville, Texas, specifically to a field."

"Wait. Who lives there?"

"Vanessa and Marcus Nelson."

"What happened at that time when you got there?"

"We proceeded to search a large field."

"And did you have occasion to discover anything at that time?"

"Yes, ma'am."

"And what was that?"

"We discovered Deandra Knight's eyeglasses."

"Your honor, we're going to object to that." Montgomery stood up, holding out his hand towards the witness stand. "That's a conclusion at this point."

Judge Stagner pushed up his glasses. "Sustained."

"And please ask the jury to disregard," Montgomery finished.

The judge held up his hand and nodded. Looking at the jury, he said, "You are to disregard the last answer."

Montgomery sat down. Marissa said, "Let me back up. Were there eyeglasses discovered?"

"Yes, ma'am."

"Okay, let me show you three photographs, Government's Exhibit 16-A through C. Do you recognize the subject matter of those photographs?"

"Yes, ma'am, I do."

"Do these photographs fairly and accurately depict the field there and some eyeglasses that were found during the course of your investigation at Pomegranate Way in Duncanville, Texas?"

"Yes, ma'am."

"The government would move to introduce Government's Exhibit 16-A through -C."

"Objection your honor, relevance," said Montgomery.

Leaning back, the judge replied, "I'm going to admit them conditionally, subject to tying up later. I'll consider the objection and motion to strike." Gesturing to Marissa, he said, "Conditionally admitted."

"Let me show you Government's Exhibit Number 15. Can you identify those?"

"Yes, ma'am."

"And what is Government's Exhibit Number 15?"

"Those are the eyeglasses we found in the field."

"Your honor, we move to introduce Government's Exhibit Number 15 conditionally upon them being proven up."

"Objection, your honor, relevance." Marissa could have sworn she heard a tinge of whining in Montgomery's voice.

"Overruled as to relevance, admitted conditionally."

"Let me show you what's been marked as Government's Exhibits 14-G and -H, and ask you if you can recognize the subject matter of those photographs?"

"Yes, ma'am, I do."

"And what are those photographs of?"

"These are area photographs of the Pomegranate Way address in Duncanville, Texas.

"The government would move to admit Government's Exhibits 14-G and -H."

"14-G and -H are admitted."

"Okay. If you could, for the members of the jury, describe what's depicted in that photograph."

"This is the field area where the eyeglasses were retrieved," Gavin pointed at the picture, "and this is the Pomegranate Way address where Vanessa and Marcus Nelson live."

Marissa turned to the bench. "We pass the witness, your honor."

The judge looked at Montgomery. "Cross examination?"

"Yes, your honor." Montgomery walked to the podium and opened his notebook.

"Good morning, Mr. Wright," he addressed Gavin.

"Good morning, sir."

"I want you to think back now to when you first met Roland Connors in the police department, and that was in Oklahoma City, is that correct?"

"That is correct, sir."

"And you first met him in a room, one of the captain's offices or detective's offices or a police officer's office there in the police station, is that correct?"

"That is correct."

"And he had a lawyer with him?"

"That is correct."

"A Mr. Griffins, that was his name, is that right?"

"That is correct."

"And you had a conversation with Mr. Griffins before you spoke to Roland Connors, isn't that right?"

"That is correct."

"And Mr. Griffins told you that he was not going to let Roland talk to you, but that you could talk to Roland or something to that effect, isn't that right?"

"No, that's not correct, sir." Gavin shook his head.

"Okay. What was it Mr. Griffins told you?"

"Objection, your honor." Austin stood up. "Hearsay."

"Overruled."

"He said we could tell his client about what had occurred, and that he was going to be in the room," Gavin responded. "It was up to him as to how his client would respond."

"You weren't there earlier when Mr. Griffins had had any conversation with Mr. Connors, were you?"

"No, sir, I was not."

"You did sit there and talk to Roland Connors, is that correct?"

"Yes, sir."

"And he did not respond to you verbally, did he?"

"That is correct."

"But you did and were able to observe an emotional response on his part, isn't that correct?"

"During the initial part of the interview, sir?"

"During the interview."

Gavin nodded, "Yes, sir, that is correct."

"And as a matter of fact, during the interview as you talked to him about what you thought had happened, that you saw tears coming up in the corner of his eyes, isn't that right?"

"I saw a tear in his eye, that is correct, sir."

"Well, have you ever said anything different under oath, Mr. Wright, than a tear in his eye?"

"I think I may have said tears came to his eyes, plural, sir."

"As a matter of fact, on two occasions under oath talking about this very thing, you said that tears came to the corners of his eyes, isn't that right? Tears?"

"Yes, sir."

Montgomery flipped some pages in his notebook before continuing. "Near the end of that conversation or that monologue you had with Roland Connors, his lawyer stepped out of the room, is that correct?"

"Yes, sir."

"Detective Fargo of the DeSoto Police Department also stepped out of the room, is that correct?"

"Yes, sir."

"And you and Roland were alone in that office in the Oklahoma City Police Department for a brief time, isn't that right?"

"We were in the doorway, sir, yes, sir."

"And he said to you at that time, 'it wasn't supposed to be like that. I'll talk to you about it when I get to Texas.' Isn't that what he said?"

"That's correct."

"And then you alone took Roland Connors from the detective's office back to the holding area or jail area of the Oklahoma City Police Department, didn't you?"

"No, sir."

"Did you walk with him from that area to a holding area or jail area?"

"Yes, sir."

"And who was with you?"

"Detective Fargo was with us in a close proximity. I don't remember how close he was, but he was walking down the stairs with us, sir."

"Did he walk all the way to the end of the walk where you left Roland at the jail or holding area?"

"No, sir, he did not."

"So then you were alone with Roland Connors as you got to the end of the walk?" Montgomery walked towards the jury as he spoke.

"That is correct."

"And at that time he said, 'I'll tell you all about it when I get to Texas, come and see me,' isn't that right?"

"That's correct, sir."

"And you told us when you got to Texas and went to see him, he said, 'what took you so long? I want to tell you all about it.'"

"Yes, sir."

"And that's when he gave this statement that's in evidence, isn't that right?"

"No, sir."

"Okay, or shortly thereafter?" Montgomery waived his hand in the air, annoyed.

"Yes, sir."

"And as a matter of fact, you told us that you had to stop him and say, 'let me stop you and give you these warnings first,' or did Detective Fargo say that?"

"I said that, yes, sir, that's correct."

"Now, I want to take you to the time that you first talked to Calvin Stewart."

"Yes, sir."

"Do you remember that?"

"Yes, sir."

"And that was in," Montgomery made a show of shuffling his papers on the podium. "Agent Wright, where was that, Oklahoma City or Ponca City?"

"Oklahoma City, sir."

"And you had a conversation with Calvin Stewart for two or three hours, isn't that right?"

"That's correct, sir."

"And during that period of time, you were asking him for information about the Deandra Knight kidnapping, is that right?"

"Yes, sir, I was."

"Okay. And during that conversation that you had with Calvin Stewart for all that time, he didn't tell you where Deandra Knight was, did he, that first conversation?"

"Yes, sir, he did. He told me the last time he saw her, sir."

"Okay. He told you the last time he saw her?"

"Yes, sir."

"Where did he tell you that was?"

"That was at the Ponca City Inn."

"And he lied to you during that conversation, didn't he?"

"Yes, sir."

"Because he didn't tell you about being out at the site where she was buried, did he?"

"That is correct, sir."

"He didn't tell you about hitting her with that shovel, did he?"

"No, he did not."

"He lied to you during that two- or three-hour conversation he had with you. Isn't that right?"

"Yes, sir."

"Did you have anything to do with having Nikko Hollis arrested?"

"Yes sir."

"Tell us about your part in that."

"Well, at that particular time, we were looking for Calvin Stewart and Malcolm Connors. Malcolm was the only one in the motel room with a key to the room."

"Had you had a warrant for Stewart at that time?"

"No, sir, we had not."

Montgomery pointed at the table beside the witness stand. "Do you have Government's Exhibit 52-E there? It's going to be the large photograph of the two guns in the trunk of Stewart's car."

Gavin retrieved the photograph, and held it up.

"Is that a revolver?

"Yes, sir, it is."

"And does it have tape around the handle?"

"It does."

"Now, is that black electrician's tape, is that what that looks like to you?"

"Yes, it is."

"And during the course of your investigation, did you find out that that looks like a gun that was described as regularly being carried by Calvin Stewart, the one with the tape on the handle?"

"That is correct, sir."

"Thank you, sir." Directing his attention to the bench, Montgomery said, "pass the witness, your honor."

"Redirect?"

"Just a couple of questions." Marissa walked to the podium. "Agent Wright, Mr. Montgomery asked you about Calvin Stewart's statement."

"Yes, ma'am."

"Was it the first or second time that you interviewed Calvin Stewart that he told you about the murder of Deandra Knight?"

"It was the second time, ma'am."

"Okay. Describe his demeanor at that time."

"We had gone to the county jail to talk to him, and I walked in, and he looked at me and he said..."

"Objection, your honor." Montgomery shot out of his chair. "I object to it being relevant, your honor, what his demeanor was at that time."

"Overruled."

"I mean a subsequent statement that I didn't ask him about."

Judge Stagner looked at Montgomery. "Overruled, counselor," he repeated.

Marissa nodded at Gavin, who then said, "He looked at me and said, 'you knew I lied.' And I said, 'yes.' He started crying, and I told him it was all right, but he needed to tell me about it."

"No more questions, your honor."

Judge Stagner looked at Montgomery and gestured to the podium. He was already half-way there.

"Agent Wright, you also found out that on subsequent interviews by the FBI or FBI agents or FBI technicians or operators that Mr. Stewart also lied and was deceitful. Don't you know that?"

"No, sir."

"You do not?"

"No sir, I do not know that."

"May we approach the bench, your honor?"

Judge Stagner beckoned both attorneys to the bench.

"Your honor, I think we're entitled to get into the polygraph examinations at this time," Montgomery said, "because the polygraph examinations were conducted by government agents, FBI agents, wherein he was deceitful to them, in their own opinion. Ms. Elliot got up and asked about it, and I think she opened it right up."

"My response to that, your Honor, is that I deny I opened any door." Marissa was flustered. "He is the one that brought up the part about Stewart, and I just responded to it. I think if I'd opened the door and brought it in that way, then okay, yes, maybe we would be dealing with that, but I don't think I raised it. Certainly he hasn't, and it's not admissible for any other reason under 403. He was the guy that brought in the issue, and I just responded to the same degree and nothing further. I didn't go into any of those subsequent statements." She tried hard not to turn and glare at Montgomery.

"What impact is there if Mr. Wright just said no in answer to that question," the judge probed.

"But he did just say no," Marissa implored. "It was calling for a hearsay response on his part anyway. He would say do you know from any other time he's lying. He wasn't present during those interviews. That's a hearsay response."

Judge Stagner held up his hand. "Thank you, counselor, but my question was really directed to you," pointing at Montgomery. "He denied it, so, where are you?"

"Well, I think that if I can ask him the question about the polygraph test that Stewart failed, then he will know because he knows he failed it."

"He knows by hearsay," Marissa responded.

"No, your honor, it's a statement by an FBI agent, a written statement by a party opponent under 801 (d)(2). . ."

"No," Marissa repeated, shaking her head.

"It absolutely is!" Montgomery argued. His cheeks were bright red. "801(d)(2)(D) takes it out of hearsay. It's a written report by an FBI agent during the course of his agency or employment relating to this subject matter. It is, Marissa."

"It is hearsay to him right now, and you opened the door," countered Marissa. "I do not think it's admissible."

"Okay, boys and girls," the judge interjected, "here's what we're gonna do. We'll take an early lunch break, and I'll settle this over lunch. We'll come back at 1:00 and I'll have a decision for you." He waved them back to their respective tables.

Addressing the court as a whole, the judge said, "Ladies and gentlemen, we're going to take an early lunch. A point has been raised that I need to do some research on, so we'll come back at 1:30. So please remember all of your instructions about your conduct as jurors. You're excused at this time."

Austin looked at Marissa. "What's going on?"

"Hang on a second," Marissa watched as the last juror left the courtroom. Turning to the bench, she said, "your honor, may we approach?"

Sighing, the judge sat back down. "You may."

At the bench, Marissa said, "Your honor, I have submitted my brief on this argument of the polygraph. I think this is a classic case of bootstrapping where he put it in issue, and now he wants to use it as the vehicle to just try to get in the polygraph test. And I think my brief speaks to it, but not in a situation of a classic bootstrapping that Mr. Montgomery did to try to place this in issue, and I object to it."

"Thank you, counselor. You'll have a decision at 1:00."

"For the purpose of the record, your honor, Agent Wright went into another conversation that I never asked him about," Montgomery countered. "I asked Mr. Wright about the first two- or three-hour conversation he had with Calvin Stewart. You went into the subsequent conversation that he had with Calvin Stewart," pointing at Marissa, "and that's when you came out with this," he waved his hands, "this idea about the truthfulness."

"Okay, I don't want to hear anymore." Judge Stagner stood up. "I'll see you at 1:00." With that, the judge turned and walked through the door behind his chair.

Shit, thought Marissa as she walked back to her table. It took all she had not to stick her foot out as Montgomery strolled by.

CHAPTER TWELVE

Marissa rapped on the door before opening it. She walked into the judge's conference room, finding William and Lydia having lunch. Or, judging by the food still in front of Lydia, trying to have lunch. Both of them looked up when she opened the door.

"Hi," she smiled. Looking at William, she asked, "Could you give us a minute, please?"

"Of course." William touched Lydia's shoulder before walking out of the room, closing the door behind him.

She indicated to a chair across from her. "May I?"

"Please."

Marissa sank down in the chair, letting out a huge sigh. "How are you holding up?" She looked across the table at the lady in front of her, read the worry and concern in her eyes, the sorrow over her face.

Lydia offered a slight smile. "This is not as easy as I thought it would be. Sitting there, listening to all of this."

Marissa glanced at her food. "You haven't touched your lunch."

She gave an absent nod, looking down. "The mind is a terrible thing, you know. It creates startling pictures and images you cannot shake, no matter how hard you try."

Nodding herself, Marissa remained silent.

Lydia pushed herself away from the table, walked to the opposite end of the room. "You know, I keep thinking, more than anything, that if only I hadn't let her live with her sister. If she had stayed with me, would she still be alive?"

"If I may ask, Mrs. Knight, why was she living with Adena?"

"She wanted to study early childhood development," she chuckled. "Become a child psychologist. So, she wore me down over a year to let her to the School of Health Professions in Dallas." Lydia shrugged. "Adena sided with Deandra after about four months, mostly because she lives closer to the school than I do." Sighing, she continued, "And over time, it just started to make sense."

"You cannot blame yourself over this," Marissa said to her back.

"I know," Lydia nodded. "She paced the length of the conference room. "How do I erase the image of them walking on top of her," she exclaimed. "Was she breathing? Or, on her last breath?" She stopped pacing and covered her face with her hands, struggling to compose herself.

Marissa's heart went out to her.

"This is only going to get worse, isn't it?" She spoke from behind her hands.

"What do you mean?"

"This, the testimony. It's only going to get worse?" Her hands fell down to her sides, yet she still didn't turn around.

Marissa shifted in her seat. Resigned, she simply said, "Yes."

"Thank you, Ms. Elliott."

"For?"

"For being honest with me. I was expecting you to say no. Or, talk me into going home."

"Would you listen if I did?" Marissa grinned.

"Probably not." She turned around to face her, also grinning.

Marissa held up her hands. "So, why try?"

Lydia nodded and sat down again, this time next to Marissa. "So, what happens next?"

"Well, you're going to try to eat some lunch." She felt a little lighter when Lydia laughed. "I will do my job, and try to get you through this. Somehow."

"That's fair." She reached across the table, sliding the bag towards Marissa. "Chip?"

● ● ●

After the lunch break, Judge Stagner addressed the attorneys before the jury was brought in.

"The question that Mr. Montgomery asked to provoke the discussion at the bench was, 'you also found out that on subsequent interviews by the FBI, or FBI agents or FBI technicians or operators that Mr. Stewart also lied and was deceitful. Don't you know that?'

ANSWER: 'No, sir.'

QUESTION: 'You do not?'

ANSWER: 'No, sir, I do not know that.'

Judge Stagner looked back and forth between Marissa and Montgomery. "Now, it seems to the court that if Mr. Montgomery wants to impeach the witness on the question and the answer, he may do that subject to the Rules of Evidence. So think about that, the question and the answer. If Mr. Montgomery intends to show a polygraph examination through this witness, who didn't take the exam and may not know about the exam, I don't know, and that doesn't seem to me to be proper. The polygraph question, it seems to me, is going to have to come up either from Agent Wright or from some other witness. I won't get into where. So, the long and short of it is I will allow the question pursuant to the Rules of Evidence."

"We still have an *in limine* order in place on the polygraph, is that right," Marissa asked, willing defeat from her voice.

"Yes, ma'am, and I don't necessarily see a conflict between the *in limine* order and what I just said about the Rules of Evidence."

"No. I just wanted to make clear, Mr. Montgomery was using operator and technician, and I think that's skirting close to the *in limine*."

"But I don't think it was over the line."

"It certainly wasn't intended to, your honor," Montgomery drawled. Marissa was hard-pressed to keep a straight face and not growl.

"I'm sure it wasn't."

"May I ask him a question outside the presence of the jury, sir?"

Judge Stagner propped his chin on his hand, and said, "you want a dry run?"

"Because I can't ask him this in front of the jury."

The judge waved his hand. "All right."

Walking towards the witness stand, Montgomery asked, "Special Agent Wright?"

Gavin turned to him. "Yes, sir."

"Are you aware that on the first of August of last year that Calvin Stewart was given a polygraph examination by FBI polygraph examiners Ellen Peppers and Raymond York, and that in that examination that they found that he was deceitful in his answers to three relevant questions?"

"No, sir."

"That was kinda my point," the judge said.

"Okay," Montgomery said. "I couldn't ask that in front of the jury."

"I agree. All right." Turning to his bailiff, the judge said, "Bring the jury down."

Once the jury was seated, the judge turned to Montgomery. "Is there additional questioning for Agent Wright?"

"Yes, sir." To Gavin, he said, "Two quick areas, Special Agent Wright. One area, I want to call your attention back to an earlier question I asked about a conversation you had with Mr. Griffins, who was Roland Connors' lawyer at Oklahoma City, Oklahoma."

"Yes, sir."

"This is the first occasion you met Roland Connors in the police station at Oklahoma City?"

"No, sir."

"No?"

"No, sir. The first occasion I met with Mr. Connors was when I arrested him on his plane in Oklahoma City."

"Okay. At an earlier hearing under oath in this courtroom, didn't you say that, 'we asked Mr. Griffins could we talk to him. Mr. Griffins said, yes, you can talk to him. You know he's not going to tell you anything about the offense here because I'm representing him, but you can talk to him. Tell him whatever you want to tell him.' Is that what you said earlier?"

"That is correct, sir."

"And is that what the lawyer in Oklahoma City told you?"

"Yes, sir, that's correct."

"One other area, on redirect examination, Ms. Elliot asked you about your confrontation with Calvin Stewart, about the second meeting with him, about the fact that he was not honest with you in the first meeting."

"Calvin Stewart, sir," Gavin asked.

"Yes."

"Yes, sir."

"And let me see if I've got this picture right from what you're saying. That you walk into the room and he says, 'you know I lied'?"

"Yes, sir."

"And you say, 'yes'?"

"Yes, sir."

"And he starts to cry?"

"Yes, sir."

"This man that you know at this point in time is involved in the kidnapping and the murder of Deandra Knight, you put your arm around him and say, 'it will be all right. You need to tell me about it.'"

"Yes, sir."

"And that's before you ever found the body of Deandra Knight?"

"That is correct."

"And that's before you ever completed your investigation?"

"That's correct."

"And your investigation was in the early states at that time?"

"That's correct, sir."

"Pass the witness, your honor." Looking at Gavin, he nods and says, "Thank you."

"Is there redirect," Judge Stagner asked Marissa.

"No, your honor," she answered.

"You may step down, sir."

"Your honor, a recess of ten minutes, please," Austin stood up to address the judge as Gavin crossed the well and sat next to Marissa.

"What for, counselor? We just got back from the lunch break."

"Approach, your honor?"

Judge Stagner motioned for him to approach and Montgomery was right on Austin's heels. Moving his microphone, the judge looked at him. "Okay, Mr. Gregory, explain."

"Briefly, our next witness is one of the co-defendants in this case, Calvin Stewart. He's going to testify to everything that happened during and after Deandra Knight's kidnapping and murder. I thought it would be appropriate to advise Mrs. Knight of this testimony, as I'm sure she will find it quite disturbing."

The judge removed his glasses. Looking at Montgomery, he asked, "Any objections?"

"No, sir, your honor."

"Very well, then. I'll give you your ten minutes. But," the judge put his glasses back on, "let me have the jury taken out. They do not need to see you, basically, talking to the mother of the victim. Even," he held up his hand anticipating Austin's protest, "if you are taking her out of the courtroom to do so."

The attorneys walked back to their respective tables, and Judge Stagner released the jury for the requested break. Marissa and Gavin stepped out of the well. Marissa kept walking out of the courtroom while Gavin stopped and spoke to Lydia.

Guiding her by the small of her back, he led her to the judge's conference room where Marissa, Adena, and William were waiting. Whispering to Adena, she got up and followed Gavin outside into the hallway.

Once he closed the door, Lydia turned to Marissa and said, "Okay. What's going on?"

First looking at William, then Lydia, she said, "Mrs. Knight, we wanted to advise you that our next witness is going to be one of the co-defendants in this case. This witness was one of the kidnappers that also assisted in the murder." She swallowed some of the thickness down her throat. Never taking her eyes from Mrs. Knight's, she added, "His testimony will be graphic and detailed." She glanced again at William. "Mrs. Knight, the court fully understands if you choose to be out of the courtroom during this testimony."

Without hesitation, Lydia shook her head. "No, no, I want to be in there."

William walked over and touched her arm. "Are you sure?"

"Yes, I'm sure. I want to be in there. I want to hear it."

Looking into her eyes, Marissa saw resilience and determination.

William gave a nod, and said, "Well, that's what I'm here for. To be in there with you. So, let's go."

"Okay." Marissa nodded at them both. "Okay," she repeated, "let's go."

●●●

Back in the courtroom, the jury was seated and Austin stood at the podium.

"Your honor, the government will call Calvin Stewart, and he'll testify to all counts of the indictment."

The courtroom door opened, and in walked a young man wearing black slacks, a white button-down shirt, and a black tie. He looked neither to the left nor right, but stared straight ahead as he walked to the front. He stopped in front of Judge Stagner, then proceeded to the witness stand after being sworn in.

"Could you state your name for the judge and jury," Austin began.

"Calvin Michael Stewart."

"How old are you, sir?"

"Twenty-five."

"Where were you raised?"

"St. Louis, Missouri."

"How did you end up down here in Texas?"

"My mother's job moved down here."

"Before you were arrested, where were you living?"

"In DeSoto, Texas."

"I have before you Government's Exhibit Number 6-B, a plea agreement. Please pick that up and turn to the back page. Does that exhibit contain your signature?"

"Yes, sir."

"Is that a true and accurate copy of the plea agreement you entered into in this case?"

"Yes, sir."

Turning to the judge, Austin said, "The government would move to introduce Government's Exhibit Number 6-B."

"6-B is admitted," the judge responded.

Austin read the plea agreement into the record. After he finished, he looked at the witness. "Was that your plea agreement?"

"Yes, sir."

"Are there any other agreements?"

"No, sir."

"Are there any other promises that have been made to you by anybody?"

"No, sir."

"Okay. I want to take you back to the summer and remaining months in 2001, up to around January, February of 2002. Were you working anywhere then, sir?"

"Yes, sir."

"And where were you working?"

"Taco Bell."

"How long had you been working there?"

"For about year, just a little over a year."

"What did you do?"

"Mostly worked the first window of the drive-thru, took people's order, then took their money, gave change as needed."

"Okay. Let me take you to the earlier part of 2002. Did you have occasion to meet a man by the name of Roland Connors?"

"Yes, sir."

"Is he here in the courtroom?"

"Yes, sir."

"Would you point him out for the judge and jury, please?"

The witness pointed to the defendant sitting on the other side of Montgomery.

"Okay, how many people is he from my left?"

"He's the second one."

"The government would ask the record to reflect that the witness has identified the defendant, Roland Connors."

The judge nodded, "The record will so reflect."

Austin flipped several pages in his binder. "Where did you first meet Roland?"

With that, Austin and the witness wove the tale of how Calvin became acquainted with Roland, the friendship that developed into a lucrative marijuana business. Calvin described for the jury how they got it started and the funding it took to launch it off the ground. He explained who were the key personnel and their levels of involvement, and gave minute details of where the money went, who made what, and the bank accounts that held the money. The jury appeared deeply engrossed, and Marissa hoped it was in their favor.

"Okay, so no one showed up at the appointed place behind the Wal-Mart," Austin continued. "What happened next?"

The witness fidgeted in his chair. "I called Mac on the cellular phone, and he was surprised that, that Rider hadn't shown up yet. So, he said he would keep trying to get in touch with him. So we drove – me and Malcolm – drove to where Roland was supposed to be with his girl. He came out and he asked us did everything go all right, and we told him that they hadn't shown up yet."

"How did Roland react to that?"

"He just went off! He was mad, and he said, 'I knew it. I knew it. I knew they got me.' I was talking to him, trying to calm him down."

"So, what happened after that?"

"We got on the phone and I called Mac back up, and by this time he had found Rider. He put him on the phone, and he was hollering, saying that somebody had jacked him, had took some marijuana, some money from him, and stole his car. I could hear somebody crying in the background, you know, shouting and hollering. So, I was telling Roland what Rider said, and he wanted to speak to him. He just kept asking him what happened. Over and over again, what happened."

"So, then what," Austin coaxed.

"Okay. Roland got off the phone and he was just saying that he heard some guy hollering and crying in the background, saying they took my car, too. But when Roland got off the phone, we sat around and he just kept saying, 'I know he took it. I know he got me.'" He wanted me to call him back and set up a meeting. So, I called Rider back, but Mac answered the phone. I told him that we wanted to set up a meet with them the next day so we could try to find a solution to this. Mac said okay, so . . ."

"After that, did you and Roland have occasion to speak in private?"

"Yes, sir."

"What happened at that time?"

"At that time, Roland was mad, and he's saying that 'I don't have nothing else to do.' He said 'I don't have nothing else to lose, and I'm not going back to Ponca City until I got my money, my marijuana, or some blood on my hands.' And I just sat there, looking at him."

"Do you think he was joking when he said that?"

"No, sir."

"Okay, so then what happened next?"

"The next morning, me, Malcolm and Roland drove to where we were supposed to meet Rider and Mac. When we got there, they never showed up. So right there, Roland knew that they had beat him. We called Rider, and the phone had been cut off, so we didn't have no way to get in contact with them. And right then he knew for sure that they had beat him for the money."

"Had there been any decision or attempt to obtain the address where Rider and Mac lived?"

"Yes, sir."

"And what were they?"

"Well, Roland had this girl he would hook up with from time to time, she worked at the electric company. I guess he asked her to look into it, 'cause he kept saying 'that bitch Diane, I knew that bitch would come in good for something.'"

"And then?"

"After he got the address, he told me and Malcolm to go out and try to see if we could find some guns."

"Who told you that?"

"Roland."

"So what happened?"

"Me and Malcolm, we went out and tried to see if I could find anybody that had any guns that we could use. But we didn't find anything the first time when we went out."

"Okay, back to the address Roland acquired. Did y'all ever drive there?"

"Yes, sir. We found the building, and as we drove around, we saw the Camaro backed into the fence with a 'for sale' sign on it."

"Who's Camaro was it, Mr. Stewart?"

"Rider's, sir."

"Okay. What was said at that time?"

"Roland said, 'I knew it, and now I know for sure now.' After that we just kept driving, and eventually went back to Vanessa's apartment."

"And what happened at that time?"

"Me and Malcolm went back out to look for some guns. My boy DJ said he could score us some, but we had to wait awhile."

"So, did you have occasion after that to go to any stores?"

"Yes, sir."

"And what was that?"

"Me and Malcolm went to Academy Sports in Dallas."

"Why was that?"

"That was to buy some ammunition for the gun."

"Were you able to purchase any ammunition?"

"Yes, sir."

"And what happened after that?"

"I got a call from my boy DJ that he had a gun. Me and Malcolm went to his apartment. I told DJ I got into it with some dude and that I needed a gun just in case he tried something on me. So he said okay, gave me the gun, and I told him I'd have it back by Saturday."

"Let me stop you for a second. What kind of gun was it?"

"A .380."

"Okay, then what did you do once you got the gun?"

"I took the gun over to Vanessa's apartment. Then I got a text from DJ, saying he had acquired another gun for me. Me and Malcolm went back to his place and he gave me the black .380. I gave it to Malcolm and we drove back to Vanessa's house."

"What did you do with the guns?

"We took them into one of the bedroom of Vanessa's apartment and hid them in there."

Austin turned several pages in his binder, and Judge Stagner spoke into his microphone. "Mr. Gregory, we've been in here at this about an hour and a half now. Let's take a break."

Austin nodded and joined Marissa at their table.

●●●

"Your honor, before the jury is called in," Marissa said after the court's break, "to try to save some time with some other witnesses, we've entered into an agreement with the defense where Mr. Gregory is going to offer some documentary exhibits at this time.

"All right," responded Judge Stagner.

Austin read off the agreed exhibits, such as the airline tickets the defendant used to fly to Texas, the receipts for the purchases of ammunition from various stores, the ski masks used in the kidnapping, and the receipts from the motels used to house the defendants prior to the murder.

Afterwards, the jury was brought in, and Judge Stagner gestured to Austin. "Okay, counselor, are we ready to proceed with this witness?"

"Yes, your honor," Austin replied. "Mr. Stewart, we left off with your hiding the guns at Vanessa Nelson's apartment. After that, did you go back out to the apartment where you saw Mac and Rider's car later that night?

"Yes, sir."

"Who with?"

"Me and Malcolm."

"And why did you go out there?"

"We wanted to find exactly what apartment number they was in."

"Okay. Let's move forward. What happened the next day?"

"Well, that next night, we all dressed up in camouflage top and bottom, camouflage hat, and we had a ski mask in our pocket. Roland had the chrome .380, and I had the black .380, and we drove out to Rider and Mac's apartment."

"Why did y'all put on camouflage outfits?"

"It was supposed to disguise who we were."

"Where did y'all get the camouflage outfits?"

"I had 'em over at my mother's apartment."

Austin looked puzzled. "How did you come across them?"

"I was in the Army Reserves for four years. Well, I was still in the Reserves at the time when this took place."

"Okay, so after y'all came out, dressed up in camouflage, and you and Roland each had a pistol, where did y'all go?"

"We drove to Mac and Rider's apartment."

"So, what happened when you got there?"

"After we parked, we were sitting in the car waiting to see if somebody was going to come out. We were leaning down all the way in the seats. We saw Mac and Rider and another man come outside, and they walked over to some cars, including the Camaro they said was stolen, and they were like wiping them down with towels like they were just cleaning them up."

"So, what did y'all say at that time?"

"So at that time, Malcolm wanted to do something like jump out of the car, put a gun up to one of them, and say, where's the money, or some dumb shit like that." The witness promptly looked at Judge Stagner. "My bad, your honor, I apologize for that."

"Just be careful, son," the judge nodded.

Austin cleared his throat. "What did Roland say," he asked.

"He told Malcolm to 'just wait, wait, we can't rush into this.'"

"And what happened after that?"

"So after that, Malcolm got out of the car to look for the apartment. He came back and said that he had found the place."

"How did you know that he'd found it?"

"He said he knocked on the door and asked to speak to Felicia, and they said no Felicia lived there, and he said okay and came back to the car."

"And what happened at that time? No, wait, let me stop you there. Nikko Hollis wasn't with you that night, was he?"

"No, sir."

"Did the subject of Nikko Hollis ever come up that night?"

"Yes, sir."

"Explain that, please."

"Well, Malcolm was mad and he was telling Roland, 'Let's go do something now.' Roland was telling him, 'No, you can't rush into this. We need to know what we're doing.' He said 'I wish I had Nickels down here.' At that time, I was trying to calm Malcolm down because I didn't want to do nothing. So I told him to just wait and let Nickels come, somebody like him that got experience in doing something like this."

"Now, Nickels, are you referring to Nikko Hollis?"

"Yes, sir."

"Okay, what happened the next day?"

"The next morning, Roland woke me up and told me to go pick up Nickels from the airport, from Love Field airport, that he was coming in 'round 12:45. So, I went to the airport, and picked up Nickels. I took him to the Holiday Inn Express off 67. He gave me the money, and I went inside and rented a room. Then both of us went up to the room, and he dropped his bag off up there.

"Then we went back to Vanessa's apartment, and Roland, Nickels, and Malcolm were, like, discussing ways to, you know, if you want to torture somebody, how would you do it. And Nickels asked me how would I do it if I wanted to torture somebody or make somebody talk."

"And what did you say?"

"I told him tie 'em up and put 'em in the bathroom and pour gas on 'em and then they will talk."

"So what happened after that?"

"Well, we drove straight to the apartment 'cause Roland wanted to show Nickels the place. He told him 'this is the apartment right here.' And then Nickels said, 'Oh, this will be simple. This is a piece of cake.' Then we went to the Luby's right off 67 and we sat there and ate. Then we took Nickels back to his hotel at the Holiday Inn Express."

"Do you know who brought Nickels down?"

"To my knowledge, I thought it was Roland."

"Objection." Montgomery stood up.

"I'm sorry?" Judge Stagner looked at him.

"Objection if he doesn't know. He's speculating."

Austin looked back at Calvin. "Do you know?"

He responded, "No," the same time Judge Stagner said "Sustained."

Austin held up his hand. "Let me back up a second. Have you ever been with Roland and seen Nikko Hollis do anything violent?"

"No, sir."

"Well, let's move on. Did there come a time when you went back to the Holiday Inn?"

"Yes, sir."

"And what happened at that time?"

"We get to the Holiday Inn, and Nickels, he opens the bag he brought and pulled out a full set of camouflage, the top and bottom, and a hat and some Army-style jump boots. And we was sitting there, and Nickels mentioned that it would be better if we had some rope instead of tape. So, Roland gave me and Malcolm some money, and we went to Wal-Mart and purchased a pair of brown gloves and some white rope."

"Okay. What happened after that?"

"After that, me and Malcolm went back to the hotel, and all of us got dressed in camouflage, top and bottom, and we each had a camouflage hat, and we had masks with us. Roland had the chrome .380 and Nickels had the black .380."

"Let me stop you there. Was anything done in relation to those guns while you were at the hotel?"

"Yes, sir."

"What happened?"

"We had some WD 40, and Roland and Nickels sprayed down the guns and oiled the guns down."

"Why did they do that? Oil the guns down?"

"It lubricates the gun so it doesn't jam. When you shoot, you wanna make sure you get the shot off. So," he shrugged his shoulders, "you oil it down."

"Were the guns loaded when you left?"

"Yes, sir."

"What happened after that?"

"So we get to the apartment and we see these guys working on the cars right across from us, and after a little while, Roland says, 'Let's go get some beer,' so we left. We go to a Texaco and Malcolm gets a little anti-freeze container and wants to put some gas in it and get the beer. As they do that, Roland and Nickels go into the Texaco, but come out with no beer. Malcolm puts the container of gas in the car, and we all drive over to the Chevron across the street. When we get there, Roland, Nickels, and Malcolm get out of the car. When they come back, Nickels has a six pack of beer."

"All right. What happened after that?"

"We drive back over to the apartments. This time, we park kind of closer to Rider and Mac's apartment."

Using the laser pointer, Calvin showed the jury where they were parked at the apartment from the exhibit of the various aerial views.

"Okay, so what happened after you backed into the parking spot by the dumpster?"

"We all sat in the car and drank beer, waiting til it got dark."

"And what happened when it got dark?"

"As soon as it got dark, we pulled up to a closer parking spot and sat there for a little while. So myself, Roland, Nickels, and Malcolm got out of the car and we walked up to the apartment."

"Okay. What were you carrying?"

"I was carrying the container of gas."

"What was Roland carrying?"

"He had the chrome .380."

"What was Hollis carrying?"

"He had the black .380."

"And what did Malcolm have?"

"He had a two-by-four plank of wood."

"So what happened after you started walking up there?"

"So as we walked up to the apartment, Roland, he positioned himself on the left side of the area where the door is, and I positioned myself on the right side by the brick wall, and Nickels walked up to the door with Malcolm right behind him.

"So then Nickels started knocking on the door, and he knocked on the door hard and nobody answered, so then he just started kicking on it like trying to kick the door in. And he couldn't kick it in, so Nickels, . . ."

"Could you hear anything inside the apartment," Jonathan interrupted.

"No, sir."

"Alright, please continue."

"So then Nickels and Malcolm walked around to like, the side of the apartment, and me and Roland were still in the same position watching the door to see if anybody was going to come running out. So, I'd say about maybe twenty or thirty seconds later, I heard a loud noise that sounded like glass breaking, so as soon as that happened, Roland pulled his mask down and told me to go start the car and he walked around back. So I went to the car and started it, and I was just sitting in the car looking around to see what was going on. And the next thing I know, Nickels and Malcolm is dragging this girl out of the apartment, almost like half dragging, half carrying her."

"What was she doing?"

"Her head was bobbling around, like she was sleep or out of it or something."

"How was she dressed?"

"She had on some shorts and a tank top, and she had on some glasses, and her hair was like in big braids."

"I want to show you what's been introduced as Government's Exhibit Number 4-B." Holding up a photograph, Austin asked, "Have you seen the girl in this picture before?"

"Yes, sir."

"Was that the person Nickels and Malcolm were pulling out?"

"Yes, sir."

Austin turned to the jury. "Let the record reflect that the witness has identified Government's Exhibit Number 4-B as Deandra Knight." Spinning back towards the witness, he continued. "Okay. What happened when they got to the car with Deandra?"

"When they got to the car, Nickels opened the door and I lifted up the back seat and he put her in."

"All right. During the course of driving, was there any conversation with Deandra?"

"Yes, sir."

"And what happened?"

"Well, Nickels was kinda hitting her, not hard, just like, trying to wake her up. He started asking her her name, and she said Deandra, and asked how old she was, and she said sixteen."

"So what happened after that?"

"So we got to Vanessa's apartment, I just pulled the car in, just parked in straight ahead, and we got out of the car. Roland told me to go get my car, and back it in, so I did and Roland brought Deandra to my car. Roland and Deandra got in the back seat of my car, and Nickels got in the front passenger seat."

"Okay, and what happened next?"

"Nickels started asking me did I know where like a secluded place is, a place where it's dark where nobody goes. And I told him I would try, try to find a place. So, I'm driving around, but I couldn't find no place. So Nikko got mad, and he's hollering, so I just keep on driving. And as I was driving, Roland, he started raping Deandra in the back seat."

"What did you see?"

"I could see Roland making Deandra perform oral sex on him, and then I could see Roland on top of Deandra raping her."

"And tell the members of the jury what you saw."

This made Calvin squirm in his seat. "Roland asked me if I had any condoms, and I told him they were in a bag under the seat. And then I kind of looked back, and Roland was sitting behind the front passenger seat, and Deandra was laying down with her head on his lap, but her face was facing down on his lap, and Roland was making her give him oral sex. I could see Deandra's head moving up and down.

"And then after that, I saw like Deandra laying on her back, her head still facing towards the front passenger seat and Roland was on top of her, and I could see him going up and down. I remember him asking her if she had a boyfriend, and she told him no."

"After Roland assaulted Deandra, what happened in regards to Deandra's clothes? Were they on or off, or what happened?"

"They were on her."

"And what was she wearing?"

"She was wearing a tank top and some shorts."

"Did she have any shoes on?"

"No, sir."

"Okay. What did you and Nikko Hollis do at the Holiday Inn Express?"

"We go upstairs, and Nickels got his clothes and got his bag and got all of his stuff, and he checked to make sure we didn't leave anything. And he left the key to the room on the table. Outside, Roland told us to put all the clothes we wore in the bag, put everything in the bag. So, after I put my clothes in the bag, I just reached my hand in there to see if both the guns were in there, and I only found the chrome .380. So, after I put some more clothes back on, Roland was standing around. He was talking about how he raped Deandra saying that, he said, 'That little bitch got some good shit, man. You can tell she ain't been fucked too many times.'"

Austin held up his hand. "Okay, we get the picture. What happened after that?"

"Roland told me to take her up to Ponca City and that he would get there the next day. I told him okay. Me, Nickels, and Malcolm and Deandra got in my car. And we left."

"Who was sitting where?"

"Huh?"

"Who was sitting on the passenger side?"

"Malcolm."

"And . . ."

"And Nickels and Deandra were in the back, and Deandra was laying with her head on Nickels' lap, and, . . ."

"Wait. Why did she have her head on his lap, do you know?"

"That's just the way he made her lay down."

"So what happened at that point?"

"We started driving. Nickels kept telling me to slow down and do the speed limit, and not speed. At that time, Nickels began to rape Deandra. He made her give him oral sex, and then he got on top of her and he raped her. We get to a gas station, Malcolm got out and filled up the car. So, after we drive a little ways, Malcolm told Nickels that he wanted to go in the back seat."

"So what happened?"

"While I'm driving, I scooted my chair all the way up, and Malcolm and Nickels switched places. Malcolm went to the back seat, and Nickels went to the front. So after that happened, Malcolm started raping Deandra, and he made her give him oral sex and he got on top of her."

"What happened after that time?"

"So after that, after Malcolm finished, we were still driving, and Nickels like leaned over to me and said 'I know a place where we can take her and burn her and nobody will find her.' And I just looked at him and just shook my head like okay."

"Where did you go when you got to Ponca City?"

"We went to Jeremy Spencer's house.

"Why did you go to Jeremy Spencer's house?"

"Because Nickels had to get some money for a hotel room."

"How did you know to go to Jeremy Spencer's house?"

"That's where he told me to go." Calvin shrugged his shoulders.

"Who's 'he?'"

"Nickels."

"So, what happened when you got to Jeremy Spencer's house?"

"Well, when we get there, Nickels gets out and he goes inside, for like fifteen, twenty minutes. And he comes out and we drive to the motel. I went to use the restroom in the main office. When I came out, Malcolm had got in the driver's seat, and Nickels was still in the front passenger seat, and I got in the back seat with Deandra. And her head was facing the same way, towards the passenger's, and her head was laying on my lap, and I put my jacket over her head so nobody could see her.

"So while I was in the restroom, Nickels had gotten a room. Malcolm drives over to the room and backs into the parking spot. Nickels told me to just hold Deandra's hand and casually walk her over to the room like she was my girlfriend or something. So I grabbed her hand and walked into the room, and Nickels came in the room and closed the door.

"After that, Deandra just sat down in a chair right by the door, I sat on the bed, and Malcolm sat on the bed. And Nickels started asking her questions, started asking Deandra 'Where's the money at?' And she kept telling him that she didn't know what he was talking about. She started crying and saying that she would show him where her brothers were. And he told her to stop lying and she just cried harder.

"After we was sitting around for a while, Malcolm took Deandra in the bathroom. He came out, then went back in the bathroom like about fifteen, maybe twenty minutes."

"And then what happened after that?"

"So then after he came out of the bathroom, he told me, 'Go ahead, it's your turn.' So I got up and went in the bathroom, and I told Deandra to take her clothes off. And right as I was going to attempt to rape her, I couldn't get an erection, you know."

He genuinely looks ashamed, Marissa noted.

He continued. "I just told her, 'Anybody asks you anything, say we did something.' And she said okay. So I told her to put her clothes back on, and I came out of the room. Nickels went back in for about fifteen, twenty minutes and came back out. So then he said, 'Y'all hungry,' and we were like yeah. So Nickels asked to use my car to get something to eat. When he got back, he had some chicken with him and something to drink. So me and Malcolm ate, and then Malcolm said 'Here, I'm going to take this to Deandra.' Nickels said, 'Don't give her anything,' but he took it to her anyway."

"So then what happened?"

"So then after that we were just sitting around talking, and maybe a couple hours after that, Roland and Jeremy Spencer showed up."

"Okay, what happened then?"

"Roland, Spencer, and Nickels went into the bathroom where Deandra was sitting. They were in there for about fifteen, maybe twenty minutes. After they came out, I asked Jeremy did he hit it, meaning did he rape Deandra, and he was just sitting there smiling. And then Malcolm said, 'You know he like to do it standing up.' So Jeremy didn't say nothing, he was just sitting there smiling."

"All right. What happened at that point?"

"So at that point, Roland came and sat next to me, and he told me that if anything had to happen to Deandra, me and his brother, Malcolm, wouldn't have to be there. So, I said, 'What's up?' And he said, 'She know too much.'"

"Who said that?"

"Roland. So then he says, 'Things like this you do by yourself anyway.' So I said, 'All right.' So Roland and Spencer were getting ready to leave and Roland said, 'If you need me, I'll be at Spencer's house or I'll be calling y'all later, whichever,' so Roland and Spencer left."

"So after that, where was Deandra?"

"She was still in the bathroom at that time."

"Did there come a time when y'all tied her up?"

"Yes, sir."

"Was that later that day?"

"About fifteen, twenty minutes after Roland and Spencer left."

"All right. And where was she tied up?"

"There was, like, a little closet where a chair is, right next to the sink. And right next to the door going into the bathroom, she was tied up to that chair."

"Now, let's move into later in the day. Did there come a time when Malcolm and Nikko left?"

"Yes, sir."

"And it was just you and Deandra there, is that right?"

"Right, yes, sir."

"Tell the members of the jury what happened at that point."

"So, after Nikko and Malcolm left, I untied Deandra and I told her to lay down on the floor. I told her to take off her clothes, lay down on the floor. And before I did anything, she said, 'Don't do it hard.' I told her, 'okay.' So I began to rape her, and then she started crying. And when she started crying, I just stopped, and I told her to put her clothes back on."

Austin swallowed hard. "All right. After that, did you do anything else with her?"

"Yeah, I talked to her for a little bit."

"All right. Now, let's go forward. Did there come a time when Malcolm and Nikko come back?"

"Yes, sir."

"And what happened next, at that time?"

"At that time when they came back, Nickels had his car and Malcolm was driving my car. When they got back, Nickels asked me to use my car again. He said there something wrong with his. So, he left in my car. So we was sitting there, me and Malcolm had the TV on. . ."

"And where was Deandra at that point?"

"At this time, she was tied up sitting in a chair, and before Nickels left, he placed that camouflage mask over her face."

"What happened next?"

"At that time, we were just sitting there, we had the TV on. And then, like, she could hear the TV, and when she started laughing, Malcolm turned the TV down, because Deandra had the impression that she was in California, and we didn't want her to hear the TV and know that she was in Oklahoma, so we turned it down."

"Did you observe Deandra later that day?"

"Yes, sir."

"What was she doing?"

"I just looked around the corner to check on her, and she was sitting there with her hands in a prayer formation, praying. And I went and told Malcolm that she was praying, and he told me don't look at her, don't let it get to me, don't look at her. So I sat back down. And after a while we were sitting there, and we started getting hungry, and Malcolm called Nickels to see where he was and all."

"Now, was Malcolm ever successful in getting a hold of Nikko Hollis?"

"Yes, sir."

"Okay. What happened at that point?"

"Malcolm called over to Jeremy Spencer's house, and he talked to Roland, and said, "Tell Nickels to get over here, man, because we've been watching her all day, and we're hungry and want to go get something to eat." And Malcolm also told Roland to send some marijuana over with Nickels for me and him to smoke. So Roland said okay, that Nickels was on the way.

"So after that, Nickels finally shows up. He gives the marijuana to Malcolm, and Malcolm asked Deandra if she wanted something to eat, if she was hungry, and she said no. And then he asked her if she wanted some candy, and she said yes. So, me and Malcolm got in my car and we drove to McDonald's, got something to eat, and we stopped at a store to buy some cigars and got some candy, and we went back to the room."

"And what happened after that, after you got back to the room?"

"When we got back to the room, Deandra was still tied up and sitting in the same space. Malcolm tried to give her some food, she didn't want it, and he gave her a candy bar and she ate a little bit. So Nickels told him, 'Don't give it to her,' but he gave it to her anyway.

"So after that, Nickels said, 'I'll be right back.' He was gone for a little while, and me and Malcolm was sitting there and we smoked some weed. And then Nickels came back, and he said, 'Come on, let's do this.' He was talking to me. And I said, 'What you talking about?' And he just started laughing, and he said, 'You know what I'm talking about.' So I said, 'I thought I wasn't going to have to go for that.' And he just looked at me and he was like kind of smiling.

"So I called Roland and I said, 'I thought I wasn't going to have to be there if something happened to her.' And he said, 'No, man, just hold her down in the car.'"

"And what happened after you talked to Roland?"

"I just told him 'Okay,' and hung up the phone. Nickels told me to go get Deandra, untie her and just walk her out to the car like nothing was going on. I did and I told Deandra to get in the car. I told her to get in and just lay down, head facing the front passenger seat in the back seat. So I like laid down kind of halfway on the seat and halfway on the floorboard next to her. And Nickels gets in the car."

"Now, Malcolm didn't go with you?"

"No, sir."

"What was the reason for that?"

"At that time, there was no reason. Roland just wanted me to go."

"So what happened at that time, after you got down on the floorboard with Deandra?"

"So after that, Nickels got in the car and we go pick up Roland. And then we drive to this park, like forest area. When we get there, Nickels told me to get out of the car and take Deandra out of the car. I tried to open the door but it wouldn't open from the inside. Nickels started going off on me and cursing me out and telling me to get out of the car. So Roland opened the door, and we got out of the car, and he told me to start walking Deandra down. There's a little pathway, and to start walking her down there."

"Had you ever been to that park before?"

"No, sir."

"And what happened as you walked down there? Where was Deandra?"

"She was in front of me and I was standing behind her with my hands on her shoulder."

"And what happened at that time?"

"Nickels and Roland had flashlights so they were walking in front of us. And then they cut off in the woods, cut off the path into the woods. When they cut off in the woods, they told me and Deandra to stand right there and that they would be right back."

"All right. Did they come back?"

"Yes, sir."

"And what happened at that time?"

"When they came back, they just said, 'Damn, we can't find it.' And they said, 'Let's go.' So I'm behind Deandra telling her which way to go until we got back to the car."

"Now, was she wearing shoes at that time?"

"No, sir."

Austin had Calvin point to the area on the map where they took Deandra.

"What time of the night was that?"

"I'm not certain, like around ten, eleven at night."

"Was it completely dark outside?"

"Yes, sir."

"Well, what happened after you came back out?"

"After we came back out, me and Deandra got in the car, Roland and Nickels put the things they had in the trunk of Nickels' car, and we drove off and dropped Roland off, and Nickels drove back to the Ponca City Inn. When we get there, he just told me to stay in the car, and he got out and walked off."

"Okay. What happened after Nickels walked off?"

"Well, Malcolm comes and stands on the outside of the car, like leaning against it. He was telling me 'Calvin, just stay down in the car. Don't get out yet. Don't get out til I tell you.' He kept saying to stay down til he tells me to come out. After a while, Malcolm says, 'Come on, hurry up, go.' And I grabbed Deandra's hands and I said, 'Come on, let's go.'

"So we walked to the room real quick. When we walked into the room, I asked Malcolm what was going on. Well, first I put Deandra in the bathroom and closed the door, and Malcolm said there was a security guard down there walking around."

"So what happened after that?"

"So we were in the room, and the next thing we know somebody knocks on the door. I laid down on the bed like I was asleep. And Malcolm opened the door, and it was the security guard. He said, 'Is everything okay in here?' And Malcolm said 'Yeah.' He kind of just looked around in the room and said 'All right,' and he left.

"So after that happened, me and Malcolm started like panicking and Malcolm called Roland and told him that the security guard was acting suspicious and we needed to get out of there. So, Roland told Malcolm to get everything out of the room and just go over to Spencer's house."

"And what happened when you got over to Spencer's house?"

"When we got over there, Roland came outside and gave Malcolm some money and told him he was going to show him how to get to another motel."

"Okay, at that time, where did y'all go?"

"We went to a motel. Malcolm gave me the money, and I went up to the window and I rented a room. And when I came back, I drove over to the front of the room, and I parked the car, and me, Malcolm and Deandra got out. I put a chair in the bathroom and just told Deandra to sit down in the chair. Malcolm got some duct tape and tied Deandra up to a chair in the bathroom. Then me and Roland started putting the chairs and the table up to the door, up against the door of the hotel room."

"Why were you doing that?"

"So if we fell asleep, Deandra couldn't get out. We could hear her trying to get out."

"After that happened, did Nickels arrive?"

"Yes, sir."

"And what happened at that point?"

"Nickels came over, and Roland kept telling him, 'Just stay here, man. Just stay here so we can do Deandra in the morning.' Nickels kept making up excuses, 'No, I've got to go over to my girl's house. No, man, I'll be here early in the morning. So after that Nickels left. Roland told me and Malcolm 'Just go to sleep. Tomorrow all of this will be over.' So we went to sleep, and the next thing I know Roland was waking me up. And as soon as I got up, Nickels showed up. Nickels told me to go untie Deandra and walk her out to the car casually like she's my girlfriend. So, I went and got Deandra and walked her out to the car. I told her to lay down on the seat, then I laid halfway on the seat and on the floorboard and had my arm like on Deandra's back holding her on the seat. Then Nickels and Roland got in the car."

"What happened to Malcolm?"

"Roland told Malcolm to stay in the room and clean the room up."

"Did you go to the same or different park than the one you had been in the night before?"

"Same one."

"So what happened at that time?"

"So when we get there, Nickels told me and Deandra to get out of the car. So when we got out of the car, he told me to just start walking her down the path and that they would meet up with us. So I got behind Deandra and put my hand on her shoulders and started walking her down the path."

"And what happened at that time?"

"And at that time, Malcolm and Nickels, they walked past me and Deandra. They had a shovel and rakes, and Nickels had like, something balled up, like some kind of material balled up under his arm, and Roland had the yellow gas container in his hand."

"Let me stop you at that point. Was Deandra gagged or did she have anything over her face at that time?"

"She had the green mask over her face at that time."

"Was she wearing shoes at that time?"

"No, sir."

"And so what happened next?"

"So they walked off into the woods and I'm behind Deandra telling her 'Step over this branch right here,' and which way to step. So finally we go walking up and we arrive at a grave. It's like a rectangular hole in the ground."

"Had you ever seen that grave before?"

"No, sir."

"And then what happened when you got there?"

"I could see like two big mounds of dirt dug up on each side of the grave. And when we get there, Roland turned her like facing the opposite direction of the grave, and her back was facing the grave. Roland put a sheet over her head, then he grabbed the shovel and he hit her in the head one time."

"What happened at that point?"

"As he hit her on the head, she screamed and she started running. And Roland shouted at me, 'Grab that bitch, grab that bitch,' like that. So I ran and grabbed her, and as I grabbed her, I tripped over a branch and we fell back. She was hollering and screaming. Nickels was yelling at me, 'Shut that bitch up, man, shut her up.' So the only think I could think of to do was just put my hand over her mouth and she was still screaming under my hand. The only thing I could do is tell her, 'Please don't fight, don't fight.'"

"All right. At that point, what happened after that?"

"After that, she just kind of, she just started looking straight up. She had stop screaming and everything and she was just laying there looking straight up."

"All right. And what happened after you saw that?"

"As I got up, I noticed I had some blood on my t-shirt under my sweatshirt. So when I got up, Roland handed me the shovel and told me to hit her."

"Who was holding her at that time?"

"No one. She was laying down on the ground."

"And then what happened?"

"When I got up, I looked over at Nickels, and he was staring at me. So I just took the shovel, and I swung at Deandra's head. I hit her in the head twice. After I hit her, I handed the shovel back to Roland, and then Roland gave the shovel to Nickels. I took a couple of steps back, and turned my head, and Nickels started hitting her, like hitting her in the head. I was looking out of the corner of my eye, but the way I saw it, it was like he was hitting her on her head. And then Roland started hitting her, they took turns hitting her."

"Could you tell for sure? Do you think she was being hit in the head?"

"Yes, sir."

"So what happened then?"

"So when I looked back, Nickels was the last one hitting her. After he finished hitting her, I kind of heard like a gasp come out of Deandra like someone was fainting or something."

"Okay, let's stop there. After that happened, where was Roland Connors and Hollis?"

"Roland was standing at the end of the grave."

"And what happened then?"

"Nickels had his legs standing over her head, and his hands were like in front of her head. It looked to me like he was tying something round her face."

"Were you looking directly at him?"

"No, sir."

"Why not?"

"Because I didn't want to see whatever he was doing."

"What happened after that?"

"After that, Nickels looked at me and told me to put her in the grave. I told him, 'I can't do that.' And he said, 'Man, just pull her in the grave.' So I walked over to Deandra, and I didn't even look down at her face. I just grabbed her hands but I just couldn't, I couldn't force myself to pull her in the grave. I just couldn't do it. So, Nickels told me to quit acting like a little bitch, man, and he came over and pushed me out of the way and he just grabbed Deandra and just yanked her into the grave. Then he said, 'See, that wasn't hard.'

"So after that happened, Nickels grabbed Deandra's shorts and her panties and just snatched them off, then he grabbed her shirt and he pulled it off along with her bra. She's laying in the grave naked now, and I noticed she had a gag tied around her mouth. She was kind of laying not all the way in the fetal position, but her legs were kind of curled and her hands were like this." Calvin indicated to the jury how her hands were folded in front of her.

"What happened after that?"

"Nickels took the gas, the yellow thing, and started pouring it on Deandra. After that, Nickels told me to start shoveling dirt on her. So I grabbed a shovel, and I started shoveling down where her feet were. And Nickels saw that I really wasn't getting nothing done, so Roland told me to go check on the car. So, I turned around and ran to where I thought the car was, but I couldn't find it, so I walked back to where the grave was. It was fully covered and the dirt was packed down, was only sticking up about, like, half an inch."

"Now, let me stop you at that time. How many blows were struck all together on Deandra that you could see?"

"It looked like all together was fifteen, maybe twenty. I'm just guessing."

"Whatever it was, were you counting the blows?"

"No, sir."

"What kind of shovel was it that they had out there?"

Calvin shrugged. "It was like this digging shovel. It was square, the tip of it was curved, and it had a small little dent in the middle of it, like a dip in the middle of it."

"Did you ever see what happened to that shovel?"

"The last I saw of it, Nickels placed it in the trunk of his car."

Judge Stagner held up his hand. "Mr. Gregory, how much longer do you think you're going to be?"

"Maybe fifteen minutes, your honor."

"I was hoping we would finish direct today, but we've been here for two hours, and I think everybody is exhausted. Let's go home. We'll pick up here tomorrow at nine a.m." Judge Stagner cracked his gavel on his desk.

CHAPTER THIRTEEN

"Well, I, for one, am glad today is over." Gavin let his head flop back onto the headrest.

"Easy for you to say," Marissa responded. She also had her head laid back on her headrest, eyes closed. They were sitting in front of her house later that evening after a very long day in court and after a very short dinner.

In slow motion, she rolled her head towards Gavin and opened one eye. "Do you wanna come in for a glass of wine?"

He thought for a moment, and then shut off the engine. He got out of the car, and walked around to Marissa's side. Opening her door, he stuck out his hand, to which she put hers in his and got out of the car.

They both were slow in walking to the front door until Marissa said, "Hang on a second." Using his forearm for leverage, she stepped out of the leopard pumps. "That feels so much better," she grinned as she scooped up the shoes and continued towards the house.

Once inside, she tossed her briefcase, purse and jacket on the love seat, turning on lamps as she walked through the living room.

"Have a seat. I'll be right back." She walked down the hall towards her room.

Gavin leafed through a couple magazines on the table, then walked over to the large window looking out onto the street.

"Much, much better!" He saw her re-enter the room through the reflection of the glass.

Turning around, he flashed a huge grin. "Why, thank you!"

"I meant these." She lifted a leg, pointing to her foot, now covered in bright orange fuzzy slippers. He raised an eyebrow in question, and she giggled and replied, "They're fun!" Continuing into the kitchen, she called out, "White or red?"

"White."

"Moscato?"

"Perfect."

He heard glasses clinking, a couple of drawers open and close, and she appeared with a couple of wine glasses, the bottle of Moscato, a couple of apples and a knife.

"You open." She handed over the bottle and opener.

"So, how do you think it's going?" Gavin looked at her as he poured the wine, first for her then for himself.

Marissa laid back, propping her feet on the ottoman. "Tell you what, Agent Wright. My feet hurt and my brain hurts. Let's talk about something else."

Nodding, he said, "Okay, what do you want to talk about?"

"Why did you stop playing football?"

Surprised by the question, he absently took her legs and put them on his lap, massaging one foot at a time. "Well, about six or seven games into my third season, I blew out my knee. By the end of the season," he shrugged, "doctors told me I was done."

Marissa laid her head back on the sofa. The foot rub felt too good for her to be shocked or offended. Sighing, she let her eyes flutter closed. "Do you miss it?"

His hand slid from her foot up her leg, and he rubbed her lower calf. "Sometimes. Not the morning-after aches or long, grueling practices in a hundred, fifty-degree heat, but, . . ." He stopped and looked at her, who was faintly snoring. He moved one of her curls that had fallen across her eyes. He felt a quick tug of, something, as he continued rubbing her leg. He watched her sleep, observed how her lashes fanned her face. She's beautiful, he thought to himself, just plain beautiful. Gavin laid his head back on the sofa until the something passed over.

After a few minutes, he sighed and removed her legs from his lap, careful not to wake her. He scooped her up, and felt that something again when she wound her arms around his neck and nestled her head into the crook of his neck. He walked down the hall, and gently laid her on the bed, right away missing her soft breath that whispered on his neck. Spotting a throw on the window seat, he covered her as she burrowed into the pillows. He stood over her, watching her, and had a thought: why do women need so many pillows? He felt that something stir again when she sighed, snuggling deeper into those dozen pillows.

Get out now, he told himself as he retraced his steps back to the living room. He removed her house key from the set of keys on the counter. He wrote a note on the back of his card and left it on the remaining keys. He locked the door behind him, pocketing the house key. He smiled at the thought of her eyelashes, and he let the something take over his grin as he drove home.

•••

The next morning, Austin and Marissa were in the courtroom going over their notes, waiting for the judge to begin another small hearing. She jumped a little when someone tapped her on her shoulder. She turned around to find Gavin smiling at her. "Good morning," she said. Her stomach fluttered, a little embarrassed that she fell asleep on him the night before, and that he put her to bed.

"Good morning!" He replied, taking the chair next to her. He leaned over and laid her house key on her notebook.

Mumbling 'thank you,' she took the key and dropped it in her purse. Austin looked at her, raising his eyebrows. "It's not like that," she replied, cheeks flushed.

"All rise!" The court's bailiff announced.

Standing, she felt her cheeks grow hotter.

"It's not like that," she repeated.

Judge Stagner instructed everyone to sit down. As he took his seat, Austin leaned over and said, "Uh, huh."

"Before I bring the jury in, Mr. Montgomery, I believe you have something for me," Judge Stagner began.

Montgomery stood up. "Your honor, Mr. Gregory has informed me that at some point today, he intends to begin offering some of the more explicit photographs in this case, I suppose from some of the different crime scenes. I also believe Mr. Gregory and Ms. Elliott had agreed to take this up with the court, that before he begins to offer those photographs, before they're in any way displayed to the jury, that we be able to make our objections outside the presence of the jury to those photographs, and that they not be displayed to the jury in any shape, form or fashion until we're able to do that."

"I agree to that," Austin replied.

"Are you going to do that this morning?"

"No, later this afternoon, your honor."

"After the noon break, let's take it up then. And I'll have full context then, and I'd rather do that than take a break and look at them. Anything else, gentlemen?"

"Your honor, I can provide smaller photographs if you want to take them back to chambers," Austin offered, "but they're not numbered. And these would be photographs of the crime scene, not autopsy photographs. That's a completely separate issue. If it does come up, it would come up with Dr. Miller, the medical examiner."

"So, the only ones you're talking about are the ones at the grave site?"

"That is correct, your honor," Austin nodded.

"All right." The judge turned to his bailiff. "Henry, bring in the jury." Once they were seated, he looked at the witness. "Mr. Stewart, you remember that you're still under oath."

"Yes, sir."

Austin nodded at Judge Stagner. "May it please the court."

Looking now at Calvin, Austin said, "Mr. Stewart, I just have a few more questions for you. I want to take you back, if I could, to the Ponca

City Inn on Sunday, April 7, 2002. I've displayed two photographs before you to your left, showing two scenes. It shows a chair. Was that the chair Deandra was tied up in?"

Looking down at the photograph, Calvin replied, "Yes, sir."

"Now, with the court's permission, I would ask you to come down here and show how Deandra Knight was bound in that room."

Walking over to the indicated chair, Calvin sat down, pulling his arms on the arms of the chair. "She was sitting down with her arms tied up like this, and her ankles were tied to the legs of the chairs."

"Thank you, you can go back over to the witness stand. Where was she tied?"

"There was a little closet right next to the door entering the bathroom. She was in there."

"All right. Is it depicted on any of those photographs that are up there on the bulletin board?"

"Yes, sir."

"Okay. Show the members of the jury, please."

He pointed to the picture. "Right here."

"Was she facing in or out?"

"She was facing out."

"Okay, is there a time when you went back to the grave site?"

"Yes, sir."

Okay. What happened at that time?"

"Well, when I went with the agents, they took me to an area that was marked off, and I identified it as being the grave site. They asked me questions about how her body was positioned, and that was about it."

"Did the agents do anything in regards to the position you said you recall the body in?"

"Yes, sir. They put these sticks down as I told them the position."

"Okay. And what did these sticks signify?"

Pointing to the picture, Calvin replied, "This stick signified where her head would be positioned, and this is where her legs would be."

"And at that point, was one of her knees up in the air some when you saw her?"

"Yes, sir."

"And that would be to the right or to the left?"

"The left."

"How was she positioned the last time you saw her?"

"She was tilted a little to the right, and I could see her head. I could see her eyes."

Austin nodded, turning to the judge. "Pass the witness, your honor."

Looking at Montgomery, Judge Stagner asked, "Cross examination?"

"Yes, your honor." Montgomery strode to the podium.

"Mr. Stewart, you lied to the FBI many times during this investigation, is that right?"

"Yes, sir."

"And you lied about your involvement and your knowledge regarding the death of Deandra Knight, isn't that right?"

"Yes, sir."

"And the reason you at last told them some more about your knowledge regarding the death of Deandra Knight is because they made you take a polygraph about which you told them about those issues, isn't that right?"

"No, sir."

Montgomery stopped, a look of puzzlement on his face. "You didn't take a polygraph?"

"Yes, sir."

"And after you took that polygraph, the FBI polygraph operator told you you were being deceptive in your answers to some of those questions, isn't that right?"

"No, sir."

"Nobody ever told you you were being deceptive in your answers?"

"No, sir."

"Well, after the polygraph test, did the polygraph examiner then interview you further about those areas?"

"Yes, sir."

"And did you state to him that there was information that you did not disclose beforehand?"

"I can't recall for sure." Calvin twisted in his chair.

"You certainly recalled a lot of details, Mr. Stewart. You can't recall the polygraph examination you took on this very important subject?"

"I can recall the test."

"But you didn't tell them about this conversation that you had with Nickels, when Roland Connors wasn't even around, when you and Nickels talked about a plan to kill Deandra Knight. You didn't tell them about that until after you failed a polygraph test, isn't that right?"

"Right."

"The money that was taken by Kyle and Rider at the Wal-Mart that was stolen, that was your money?"

"No sir."

"How much of it was your money?"

"None of it."

"Had you given a written statement that you signed and said that it was true to the FBI on the eleventh of April, 2002, to Special Agent Wright — you do know who Special Agent Wright is, don't you?"

"Yes, sir."

"And Detective Fargo, didn't you tell them that two thousand dollars of that money was your money?"

"Yes."

"And didn't you refer throughout the statement, 'We were going to get our money back'?"

"Yes."

"That was the truth, wasn't it?"

"No, sir."

"So, you're saying you were lying then and you're not lying now? Is that what you're saying?"

"Yes, sir."

"You also told them that you and Roland pooled your money together to buy the marijuana, isn't that right?"

"No, sir."

"You didn't tell them that?"

"No, sir."

"You didn't say to them in writing that, 'We pooled our money together, and then we would reinvest the money to buy more dope'?"

"Well, I said that, but it was a lie."

"Oh, that was a lie, too." Montgomery nodded his head. "That wouldn't make you look too good in front of the jury, would it? If you told them that was the truth, that wouldn't make you look too good in front of the jury, would it?"

"I don't know," Calvin shrugged.

"Well, you certainly want the jury to believe you now, don't you?"

"Yes, sir."

"That's important to you."

"Yes, sir."

"Okay. We're going to talk later about why that's so important to you. Well, let's see." Montgomery flipped some pages. "You gave another statement to the FBI a few days later, on April 13, another written statement that you signed and said was true. And throughout that statement, you referred to the money that Kyle and Rider took as 'our money,' isn't that right?"

"Yes, sir."

"That implies that it was your money, too, isn't that right?"

"Yes, sir."

"Are you telling the jury now you were lying about that then, but you're telling the truth now?"

"Yes, sir."

"And then when you spent all of that time with Special Agent Wright, you told him that some of the money was yours, too, didn't you?"

"After a while, I told him that it wasn't mine."

"After a while?" Montgomery blinked several times.

"Right."

"Do you have any idea why he would put in his final report that you told him that part of the money was yours?"

Calvin shook his head.

"Do you think they just made that up, and these FBI agents put that in there as a lie?" Montgomery waved his hand in the air. "Wait, before you answer that, let me ask you this. You gave a written statement, a lengthy written statement, on April 13. Nowhere in that statement do you ever mention that you saw Roland Connors have sex with Deandra Knight, did you?"

"I don't think so, no."

"And then April 23, you had another lengthy interview with Agent Wright, you didn't tell him anything about that, did you?"

"I'm not sure. I don't recall."

"Well, if he didn't put it anywhere in his report, do you believe maybe you didn't tell him about it?"

"I guess I didn't tell him."

"And it wasn't until the end of May when you spent four or five days with these agents, maybe forty hours, would that be fair to say?"

"Yes, sir."

"That's the first time this comes up, is that right?"

"No, sir."

"That's the first time it's ever reflected in any report that the FBI made, isn't that right?"

"I guess so. I don't know."

"Well, then how come you went and spent forty hours with these agents in May?"

"To tell them the truth."

Montgomery held up his hands. "All right, help me with something here. You've told us a number of times you're lying, and now you're saying a number of times you're telling the truth. Help us a little bit. Is there something that you do that we can tell when you're telling the truth and when you're lying? Do you lick your lips? Do you swallow? Scratch the side of your nose? Is there something that we can see that will help us know when you're telling the truth and when you're lying?"

"No. The thing is, when I would tell them the whole story, and then after I thought I told them the whole story, I would remember something, but then I didn't want to tell them because I thought they wouldn't believe me if I just came out of the blue with something."

"Isn't it true that when you spent those forty hours with these agents, with Agent Wright in particular, you had a lawyer at that time?"

"Yes, sir."

"Mr. Aiden Benjamin, isn't that right?"

"Yes, sir."

"Sitting right here on the front row?" Montgomery pointed to a man with glasses and a crew cut sitting behind Gavin.

"Yes, sir."

"This is your lawyer, isn't it?"

"Yes, sir."

"And he told you it would be to your benefit if you would cooperate with the government and help them with their prosecution of Roland Connors, didn't he?"

"He said it was up to me."

"I know, but he said if you did help them, that they could help you, it would be to your benefit, didn't he?

"He said it couldn't hurt me."

"And it was on his advice that you sat down and spent forty hours with the FBI, isn't that right?"

"He left it up to me."

"You mean this experienced, able lawyer here, this criminal practitioner," Montgomery waved his arm behind him, pointing to the attorney, "he didn't discuss with you whether or not it might help you or hurt you to talk to them?"

"He advised me of everything, but he left it up to me."

"And he had been engaged in conversations with Ms. Elliott, hadn't he, before you spent forty hours with them? Your lawyer had been talking to the prosecution, isn't that right?"

"Yes, sir."

"When you talked to Gavin Wright and gave him that written statement, you told him that you had raped Deandra Knight in the motel room, taking turns with Nickels and Malcolm and you when you were all three there, isn't that right?"

"Yes, sir."

"And when you talked to the FBI for forty hours, you told them that you and Nickels and . . ."

Austin stood up. "Judge, he never said it was forty hours. I object to that. He's testifying."

"Overruled."

Montgomery did little to hide his satisfaction. "Approximately forty hours is what you agreed to, right?

"Yes, I guess so."

"You told them right after getting in the room, that you, Calvin, Nickels and Malcolm raped Deandra Knight, and you told the agents that you . . . that Malcolm Connors was the one with her for twenty minutes, that you followed him for about twenty-five minutes in raping her, and then Nickels did, isn't that right, what you told them?"

"Yes, sir."

"But you told this jury yesterday that you didn't do that. You said that when you went in there, you didn't do it."

"Yes, I told them that I couldn't get an erection and that I told her just don't say anything."

"Well, that's what you told the jury yesterday."

"Yes."

"But you didn't tell the FBI agents that. You told them you raped her, didn't you?"

"No, I told them that, also."

"And when you put it in your statement on April 11, you told them that you raped her, isn't that right?"

"I'm not sure. I might have. I'm not sure."

"As a matter of fact, you told the FBI during that lengthy interview for many days that you had sex with her twice, isn't that right?"

"I told them the second time I did have sex with her."

"Well, the first time you told them you had sex with her is when you, Nickels, and Malcolm took turns, and you were with her raping her for twenty-five minutes. You told them that, isn't that right?"

"I might have told them that at first, but when I finally told the truth, I told them that I couldn't get an erection."

"So you told them at first that you did rape her, and then later you changed your story, is that what you're saying?"

"Yeah. I told them the truth later."

Montgomery let out an exaggerated sigh. "Is there any way that they knew when you were telling the truth? Did you do something special to let them know when you were not telling the truth and when you were telling the truth?"

"When I was telling the story and I would remember something after I told the whole thing, I thought they'd think I was lying if I just brought something up."

"So, you went ahead and told them that you did rape her when, in fact, you didn't, and then you told them you didn't, right?"

"Would you repeat that question"

Montgomery waved his hand. "I'll ask you another one. You also told them that after you and Malcolm and Nickels all raped her, that you were then later on alone with her, right?"

"Right."

"And you also told them that you raped her again, isn't that right, that there was a second time?"

"Yes, sir."

Montgomery held up two fingers. "That's two times. But now, you're telling us you only did it once, is that right?"

"Judge, I object." Austin stood up again. "He's arguing with the witness."

"Overruled, counselor."

"Isn't that right," Montgomery repeated.

"No. I'm telling you that I only had intercourse with her once."

"But you told the agents that you did twice, right?"

"Yes."

"You also sometimes use different names, isn't that right?"

Caught off guard, Calvin leaned forward. "Huh?"

"Calvin."

"Yes?"

"Any other names you use or go by?"

"No."

"Well, isn't it true that you told Special Agent Wright and Detective Fargo, when you gave them your statement on April 11, that 'I usually go by Calvin, but if I don't want somebody to know my real name, I use the name 'Thomas' or 'Philip' or something like that'? Did you tell them that?"

"Yes, I told them that."

"I guess that's not true either."

"No, that was a lie, also."

"You knew Nickels before all of this happened, didn't you?"

"Yeah, I had met him a couple times."

"And you had seen Nickels carry this pistol with the tape wrapped around the handle, didn't you?"

"Yes."

"When you found out that your money had been taken by Rider and Kyle, you were on the phone talking to Rider and Kyle, weren't you?"

"Yes."

"You were calling them, isn't that right?"

"Yes."

"As a matter of fact, Mr. Stewart, you played the most active role in all of this, didn't you?"

"No."

"You didn't?"

"No."

"Well, let's see. It was your car that was used to go to Wal-Mart to give the money to Kyle and Rider that was taken, isn't that right?"

"Yes."

"When they didn't return, you made three calls trying to find out where your money was, isn't that right?"

"Not my money, but I made the calls."

"Well, the money you claimed was yours before, many times before."

"Yeah."

"And you're the one that arranged the meeting between Roland and Kyle and Rider that never took place because Kyle and Rider didn't show up, isn't that right?"

"Yes."

"You, Calvin Stewart."

"Yes."

"And you're the one that got the address from Roland's girlfriend, isn't that right, where Kyle and Rider lived?"

"No, that was Roland."

"Well, didn't you tell Detective Fargo and Special Agent Wright, when you gave a written statement on the eleventh, that, 'I called Diane on the telephone and asked her for Kyle and Rider's home address'? Did you tell the police that and sign your name to that as true?"

"Yes."

"Because that was true, wasn't it?"

"No, it wasn't true."

"Did you just make that story up on the spot?"

"Yeah."

"Are you pretty good at doing that? Making up stories on the spot?"

"No, sir."

"If you're in a bind, can you come up with a story that detailed pretty quick like that?"

"No."

"Well, you just told us that you just made this story up on the spot. Have you had a lot of practice doing that?"

"No."

"People involved in the drug business, they have to be deceptive don't they, or they get caught?"

"I don't know."

"They have to come up with stories real quick, don't they? Think on their feet?"

"I don't know," Calvin repeated.

"So, you just came up with that intricate lie all of a sudden, is that what you're telling us?"

"Yes."

"And you tell us that that wasn't the truth then, and what you're saying today is the truth?"

"Yes."

"Wasn't it through your contacts, your friends and your acquaintances that got two .380 automatic pistols?"

"Yes."

"You went to your friend DJ, isn't that right?"

"Yes."

"Certainly he was a good enough friend for you to go get some pistols from him, isn't that right?"

"Yes.

"It was you that made up the story real quick about why you needed the pistol, isn't that right?"

"Yes."

"You, Calvin Stewart?"

"Yes."

"It was you who went to your mother's house to get those camouflage uniforms, isn't that right?"

"Yes, sir."

"You just have three, or four, camouflage uniforms there, just laying around?"

"No. They were in the closet."

"Are these camouflage uniforms that the U.S. government issued to you?"

"Yes."

"It was you that went to Academy Sports and bought the ammunition, isn't that right?"

"Yes."

"It was you that went and bought the rope, and the ski masks, and the gloves, isn't that right?"

"Me and Malcolm."

"But, you were there, is that correct?"

"Yes, sir."

"It was you that picked up Nickels at the airport, right?"

"Yes."

"It was you that took Nickels to the Holiday Inn Express, isn't that right?"

"Yes."

"Roland wasn't there, was he?"

"No, sir."

"It was you that went to the room and rented the room, isn't that right?"

"Yes."

"And you're the one that had the duct tape and the rope and the gasoline when you went over to Villa Wind Apartments, isn't that right?"

"No."

"Did you tell Special Agent Wright of the FBI during those approximate forty hours that you talked to them that you had the rope, the duct tape, and the container of gasoline at Villa Wind?"

"Yes."

"So, you lied?"

"Yes."

"And it was you and your car that drove all over the metroplex with Deandra Knight in the car after she was kidnapped. It was you that drove around with her in your car, isn't that right?"

"Yes."

"It was you that led Deandra Knight down that path with your arms on her shoulder, isn't that right?"

"Yes."

"It was you that hit her in the head with the shovel twice, isn't that right?"

"Yes."

"It was you that started to cover her up in the grave, isn't that right?"

"Yes."

"It was you that when she tried to run that grabbed her and held her, isn't that right?"

"Yes."

"And it was you that took your clothes to Stacey Barnett and told her to destroy them, isn't that right?"

"I took them over there, but I told her to hold them for me."

"Did you tell the FBI during those forty hours that you took the clothes to Stacey Barnett and told her to destroy the clothes that you had given her?"

"Yes."

"Are you telling the jury that's not true now?"

"Yes."

"Was that another one of those things you just made up on the spur of the moment to tell Agent Wright because you thought that would be a good thing to tell him at the time?"

Calvin sat back in his chair. "That's just what I told him at that time."

"The reason you just told him a lot of these thing at the time was you were trying to make a deal with the government, weren't you?"

"No."

"Well, I'm having a little problem here. Help me with this."

"Your honor," Austin said, "I object to his argument . . ."

Montgomery held up his hand. "I'll withdraw it." Flipping some pages in his notebook, he turned back to the witness. "You told us earlier that your lawyer said to go talk to these people, and it can't hurt you if you tell them the truth, is that right?"

"Yes."

"The FBI agents, right?"

"Right."

"And now you tell us that some of the things you told them was a lie, isn't that right?"

"Yes."

"And the reason you told them some lies during that interview, well, if they were lies, I don't know because I can't tell . . ."

This time, both Marissa and Austin stood up. "Argumentative," they said simultaneously.

Their dual response both surprised and amused Judge Stagner. "Sustained and sustained," he nodded at each attorney.

"Well, some of the things that you told them that you now tell us are lies, did you tell them that just so you would look better in their eyes so that you would get a better deal from them?"

"No."

"Well, you understand that the plea agreement you have with them requires you to cooperate and be truthful, is that right?"

"Your honor," Austin said, "It doesn't say cooperate. It says testify truthfully. That's a misstatement."

"Well, he can ask him the question, and he can answer whether it says that or not." Judge Stagner gestured to the podium. "Go ahead, Mr. Montgomery."

"Well, you did agree to be interviewed by the government, that's these people over here, the FBI agents and the prosecutors, right?"

"Yes."

"And to provide truthful and complete information and testimony if you're asked to, isn't that right?"

"Yes."

"And that's why they had you go take this polygraph test that you failed, isn't that right?"

"Yes."

"Your honor." Austin was beyond irritated. "I'm going to object to that, that he failed the polygraph test. That's not true. It's on those specific questions that he failed, not the entire test. And I ask that the jury be instructed to disregard his comment."

Judge Stagner took off his glasses and leaned forward. "Mr. Gregory, I don't want you to testify, I want him to testify. So if it's not the truth, you'll have an opportunity to reexamine him. Counsel asked him a question, and he got an answer. If you don't like the answer, you can ask your own question when it's your turn." Austin sat down, adjusting his tie. Judge Stagner put back on his glasses. "Go ahead," gesturing to Montgomery.

"It was your idea to take the gasoline, to tie up Mac and Rider and pour gasoline on them, isn't that right?"

"Yes, sir."

"To get your money back."

"No, sir."

"Are you sure?"

Austin stood up, but the judge beat him to the punch. "Argumentative, counselor." Turning to the jury box, he instructed them, "You are to disregard that question."

Montgomery closed his notebook. "Pass the witness, your honor."

Judge Stagner nodded at Austin. "Mr. Gregory, you may proceed."

"Thank you, your honor." Austin took his place at the podium. "Mr. Stewart, Mr. Montgomery asked you about the April 11th statement that you gave to Detective Fargo?"

"Yes, sir."

"And he specifically asked you about getting the address 3401 Partridge Parkway. Were you intentionally deceiving the officers at that time?"

"Yes, sir."

"Why was that?"

"Because at that time I was confused and I was scared. I didn't know if they were still going to put me in the same cage with my co-defendants, put me in the same jail with them or not. I just didn't know."

"Have you ever heard what happens to people who snitch on somebody else?"

"Yes, sir."

"What happens to them?"

"They get killed."

"Judge, we're going to object to what he might have heard about what might happen." Montgomery held out his hands.

"Sustained."

"What do you think might happen?"

Calvin looked down. "Something might happen to me."

"Mr. Montgomery brought up the fact that you were interviewed after you were charged with this case, after the second statement that you gave, you were interviewed by the FBI agents for several days, is that right?"

"Yes, sir."

"At that time you had been charged with kidnapping resulting in death, is that right?"

"Yes, sir."

"Now, when you were interviewed by the agents, had there been any promises at that time?"

"No, sir."

"Did you know that anything you told us we could use against you if we decided to turn around and seek the death penalty?"

"Yes, sir."

"And when you took the polygraph test, was there an agreement with you not to seek the death penalty?"

"No, sir."

"Did we force you to take the polygraph test?"

"No, sir."

"Regarding the question concerning the gag, that was one of the questions about how Deandra was gagged. You answered false to that question at the polygraph test, isn't that correct?"

"Yes, sir."

"Why did you do that?"

"Because at first I couldn't remember about the gag. And when I did remember, I didn't want to tell it because I had already said that I don't remember and make the FBI think I was lying. I was scared that if I told them, they just wouldn't believe anything I said."

"What was the most important thing that I, or Ms. Elliott and the other agents told you during the interview?"

"That you just wanted the truth."

"Mr. Montgomery asked you about raping Deandra, and you testified at trial earlier, and on cross-examination, that when everybody else was gone you did rape Deandra, is that right?"

"Yes, sir."

"Were there any witnesses to that at all?"

"No, sir."

"Were you helping yourself when you told us that you raped Deandra and no one else was around?"

"No, sir."

"Did you know we could use that to prosecute you to seek the death penalty?"

"Yes, sir."

"Well, why did you tell us that if there were no witnesses to that?"

"Because I wanted to tell the whole truth about everything that happened."

"Does your plea agreement call for you to testify against Roland Connors and perhaps send him to the death chamber? Is that what it calls for?"

"No, sir."

"What does it call for?"

"To give truthful testimony."

"On April 13, after you had not told the agents earlier about the murder, why did you change your mind and tell them about the murder?"

"Because I knew that what happened to Deandra was wrong, and I felt like that was something that I didn't want to happen. But I was a part of it because I was scared for my life, but I knew what happened to her was wrong, so I just wanted to tell the truth."

"Pass the witness," Austin said, and left the podium.

Judge Stagner sat forward and adjusted his microphone. "Gentlemen, I'm getting to the stage now with this witness where we're tending to be repetitious. I'm serving notice on both of you that I'm going to discourage that. Mr. Montgomery, let's wrap this up."

Montgomery bowed his head towards the bench and said, "Your honor, I will make this quick, as I only have one or two more questions."

"You may proceed." Judge Stagner gestured with his hand and sat back in his chair.

Montgomery turned to the witness stand. "The truth is when you were told that you failed the polygraph, and only then did you tell the agents about your conversation with Nickels on the way to Oklahoma about how he would kill Deandra Knight, isn't that right?"

"Yeah, a little bit later on after that." Calvin shifted in his chair.

"And the reason you didn't tell them before is not because you forgot. The reason you didn't tell them before was because you knew that you and Nickels, when you were alone and not in the presence of Roland Connors, had formed the plan to kill Deandra Knight, and Roland wasn't even around, and that would look awfully bad for Calvin Stewart, isn't that right?"

"No, sir."

"And when you started talking to the government agents and spent all this time with them, you were still looking at the death penalty, isn't that right?"

"Yes, sir."

"And after you were through talking with them, you were no longer looking at the death penalty, isn't that right?"

"Yes, sir."

Montgomery smiled and turned to Judge Stagner. "Pass the witness, your honor."

Austin stood and said, "No further questions."

"You may step down, sir. The government may call its next witness."

CHAPTER FOURTEEN

"Your honor, the government calls Malcolm Connors."

William's involuntary "whoa" did not go unnoticed by Lydia. The far side door of the courtroom opened, and they along with everyone else watched as a medium-size, medium-built man entered the room. He had a fresh haircut, cut low with sharp lines on the side. Malcolm was wearing a navy blue suit, white shirt with a smart navy and maroon tie. He was not handcuffed, yet two deputy U.S. Marshal's flanked both sides, escorting him to the front of the bench. Malcolm raised his right hand and was sworn. As he took his seat on the witness stand, the two deputies retreated to stand in the back of the courtroom. Lydia and William looked at each other in amazement as they turned their attention back to the proceedings.

Austin let a few seconds pass before he began. "Would you state your name, please for the jury and the court."

"Malcolm Robert Connors."

"Okay. And Malcolm, do you have a brother by the name of Roland Connors?"

"Yes, sir."

"Is he here in the courtroom?"

"Yes, sir."

"Would you point him out to the judge and jury, please."

Without a word, Malcolm pointed to his brother sitting between Montgomery and Ms. Williams. Roland lifted his chin and nodded back at his brother.

"From my left, how many people over is he," Austin asked.

"Two."

Austin looked at Judge Stagner. "The government would ask the record to reflect the witness has identified the defendant, Roland Connors."

"The record will so reflect," replied the judge.

"Is Roland younger or older than you?"

"Older."

"How much older is he than you?"

"Six years."

"Malcolm, did you plead guilty to an offense of conspiracy to commit kidnapping?"

"Yes, sir."

"And that involves the kidnapping and death of Deandra Knight, is that right?"

"Yes, sir."

Austin picked up the witness's plea agreement and read it into the record. Malcolm did not look at anyone in the courtroom, but held his gaze to the back. Turning to the witness, Austin asked, "Is that the agreement that you entered into with the government?"

"Yes, sir."

"Are there any other agreements by anyone else that we haven't brought up?"

"No, sir."

"Have there been any promises made by anybody what sentence you will get?"

"No, sir."

"Do you know who you're going to be sentenced by in this case?"

"The judge."

"That will be Judge Stagner?"

"Yes, sir." Malcolm sat back in his chair. So far, he looked bored.

"Okay. Let's look at Thursday, March 27, 2002. Did you have occasion to receive a call from your brother, Roland?"

"Yes, sir."

"And what did he tell you in that conversation?"

"To call Calvin and ask Calvin to get in touch with Rider."

"Did he say why to call him?"

"No, sir. He just told me to have Calvin get in touch with Rider."

"Do you know what he meant?"

"Yes, sir."

Gesturing towards the jury box, Austin said, "Tell the members of the jury what he meant."

"To buy some marijuana."

"So, what did you do in turn?"

Malcolm shrugged his shoulders. "I texted Calvin."

"Okay. Did Calvin Stewart respond to that?"

"Yes, sir."

"What happened after that?"

"I picked up Calvin and he and I went to meet Rider."

"Where was that meeting to take place?"

"Behind the Wal-mart."

"What was your purpose in going to Wal-mart?"

"To give him the money to buy some marijuana."

"And what were you instructed to do at that time?

"Rider told us to come back in two hours, and he'd have the marijuana."

"After the two hours, did you and Calvin go back?"

"Yes, sir."

"Did Roland go with you?"

"Yes, sir."

"Well, did Rider ever come?"

"No, sir."

"How long did y'all wait?"

Malcolm shifted in his chair, shaking his head. "I can't recall the exact time, but it was a long time."

"Did anything happen after you had waited for a time?"

"Yes, sir. Calvin called Rider."

"Was he able to get hold of anybody that you could see?"

"Yes, sir."

"And what happened at that time?"

"Well, he talked to somebody on the other end, I don't know who, but when he hung up, he told me that one of the guys said he was going to go find the other one and to call back."

"And what happened after that?"

"Well, we waited for a while, and we called back, and the guy told us that the other guy had been robbed."

"Who's money was it that had been given to Rider?"

"I don't know whose money it was."

Austin shrugged his shoulders. "Well, it wasn't your money, was it?"

"No, sir."

"Was it Calvin's money?"

"Not that I know of."

"Was it Roland's?"

"I think so."

"What was Roland's reaction to what happened?"

"He was mad about it."

"Well, what did he say?"

"That he knew he shouldn't have given them the money."

"Was there ever an effort to contact Rider again?"

"Yes, sir."

"And were you able to get in touch with him?"

"Yes, sir."

"Who talked to him?"

"My brother, Roland."

"Where were you when Roland was talking to him?"

"Sitting in the car."

"How long did Roland talk to him on the telephone?"

Shrugging, he replied, "I can't recall how long."

"All right. Well, what happened? Did he tell you what had transpired on the phone?"

"Yes, sir. It was the same story that we had heard before, that he had got robbed."

"How did Roland react to the story at that time?"

"Well, he believed him at that time."

"What happened after that?"

"We went to my sister's, Vanessa's house."

"And what happened when you were there at that time?"

"Well, he talked to Rider and Mac again on the phone."

"Your brother did?"

"Yes, sir, my brother and Calvin."

"And what was said at that time?"

He smirked and said, "Well, I wasn't on the phone, but my brother told me that they said they were going to go get the guys who robbed them, and he heard guns in the background, that they had guns in the background."

"All right. Was there any plans made that night about what to do?"

"No, sir."

"Okay. Let's move forward to the next day, Thursday, the 28th. Had there been any arrangements made to again meet with Rider and Mac?"

"Yes, sir."

"And what arrangements, to your knowledge, had been made?"

Ms. Williams stood up. "Your honor, we're going to object unless the identity of the speakers is made."

Austin held up his hands and said, "I'll rephrase the question." Turning back at the witness, he asked "Who told you about their arrangements?"

"I believe it was Stewart," Malcolm responded.

"What were the arrangements that had been made?"

"Well, to meet Rider and Mac, I don't know where, just to meet them."

"Was there ever a discovery of the address?"

"Yes, sir."

"Please tell the members of the jury how that happened."

"My brother ended up getting the address from a girl that he knew."

"And who was that?"

"Your honor," Ms. Williams interrupted, "I'm going to object unless the basis of his knowledge is established."

"Sustained," Judge Stagner agreed.

"How did you find out that Roland had gotten the address," Austin asked.

Malcolm shrugged his shoulders and replied, "He told us, he told me and Stewart."

"What did he tell you?"

"Basically that he had gotten the address from a girl, Diane."

"Do you know where she worked? Did Roland tell you where she worked?"

"I believe he said at the electric company."

"Did Roland make a comment about Diane in regards to getting that address?"

"Yes, sir," he nodded.

"What did he say?"

Ms. Williams stood once again. "Your honor, I'm going to object as irrelevant."

"Overruled."

"He said that . . . ," Malcolm started before Ms. Williams interjected again.

"Your honor, may I approach the bench?"

The judge frowned over at Ms. Williams. "For what purpose?"

"To state the basis of my objection."

Judge Stagner waved his hand, and said, "State it now."

"Under Rule 403, your honor."

Judge Stagner sighed before saying, "Approach."

Ms. Williams began immediately. "Judge, I think that his response to that is that Roland said, 'I knew that bitch would come in handy for something,' and I think the prejudicial effect of that outweighs any probative."

"No, he's not going to say bitch. He didn't tell me that," Austin defended.

Judge Stagner held up a hand. "Even if he did, I don't think the prejudicial substantially outweighs the probative, so, . . ."

"Let me add something since we're out of the presence of the jury," Ms. Williams interjected. "The statements have to not only be made during the course of the conspiracy, but they have to be statements that are in furtherance of the conspiracy."

Austin shook his head. "It's an admission of a party opponent."

"Well, it has to be something that's relevant to the furtherance of this conspiracy," countered Ms. Williams, "not just puff talk, smart-aleck comments or something like that. There's a big difference."

"I think there is, too. Let's move on." The judge waved the attorneys back to their tables.

"Mr. Connors," Austin started when he returned to the podium, "we were talking about Diane. Did Roland tell you what he said about Diane Murphy giving him the address?"

"Yes, sir, he did. He said he knew she would be good for something."

"After receiving that address, did you go anywhere with anybody?"

"Yes, sir."

"All right. Where did you go?"

"To their apartment."

"And where is that apartment located?"

"In DeSoto."

"Who went?"

"Me, Stewart, and my brother, Roland."

"What did y'all do when you got there, to the apartments?"

"We parked in a parking space."

"Let me stop and ask you, was it during the daytime or at night?"

"It was during the nighttime."

"Tell the members of the jury what happened when you got there?"

"We just parked the car in a parking space."

"And what happened at that time?"

"We sat in the car for a while. I can't recall how long it was."

"All right. Did anything happen while you were sitting there?"

"Yes, sir."

"What happened?"

He scoffed. "We seen Rider and Mac come out of the apartment and stand in the parking lot while we was out there."

"At what time were efforts made to get firearms?"

"I can't recall if any efforts were made at that moment, but later on there were."

"When was that," Austin pressed, "Would that have been Thursday night or Friday?"

"Friday, I believe."

Shifting gears, Austin asked, "Did you ever go to Academy Sports?"

"Yes, sir."

"Why did you go there?"

"To get some bullets for a gun."

"Okay, let's go to Friday. That morning, did you have occasion to go anywhere with Calvin?"

"Yes, sir."

"And where was that?"

"To look for a gun."

"Why was there a need to look for a gun?"

"Because we found out that Rider and Mac didn't get robbed."

"How did you find that out?"

"Well, when they were talking to Stewart and my brother on the phone, they had told them that they had got robbed for their car and money and everything. When we went over there, we seen their car."

"Would that have been on Thursday evening you saw the car?"

"Yes, sir."

"Thursday out there at the apartments, when y'all saw the car and you knew Rider and Mac were lying, what was the reaction?"

"Well, everybody in the car acted like it was a shock that they was lying."

"What did Roland say, if anything?"

"That they was lying. They had the car right there, so they got to be lying."

"Was there any plans made there or later at Vanessa's about what to do about that lying?"

"No, sir. Not just what to do, no sir."

"Okay. Back to Friday. You said you and Calvin left to get the guns?"

"Yes, sir."

"Whose decision was it to get the guns?"

"I can't recall who brought it up."

"Well, where did you go to get the guns?"

"Calvin took me around to some people that he knew. I don't know their names."

"All right. Do you know where you went to get the guns?"

"Yes, sir."

"And where was that?"

"Well, it was a guy that lived near Calvin's apartment that we got one gun from."

"Do you remember his name?"

"No, sir."

"And were you able to get the gun, you and Calvin?"

"Yes, sir."

"What kind of gun was it?"

"A .380."

"Okay. After you got that gun, what did you do with it?"

"We took it back to the apartment?"

"Who did you give it to?"

"My brother."

"Did there ever come a time when you could get another gun?"

"Yes, sir."

"When did that happen?"

"Later on, Calvin got another text from his hook up, again and told him that he had another gun for him."

"Now, after you got that gun, where did you go?"

"Back to the apartment."

"Okay. What did y'all do the rest of the day?"

"The rest of the day," Malcolm paused for a moment, "we went back to their apartment later on that night."

"Who went?"

"Me, Stewart, and my brother, Roland."

"How were you dressed when you went out there?"

"In camouflage."

"Where did you get the camouflage?"

"From Stewart."

"Why did y'all go out in camouflage?"

"I have no idea," Malcolm half chuckled.

"After you got out there to the apartments, was it daylight or dark?"

"It was dark outside."

"What was the purpose in going out there?"

"To see if we could see Rider and Mac, again."

"And were you able to see them?"

"Yes, sir."

"And what happened? What was said in the car at that time in relation to seeing those guys out there?"

"Well, we was like, 'There they go right there.' And we was all ducked down in the seats where they couldn't see us."

"Were you ready to take action at that time?"

"No, sir."

"So, what happened after that?"

"Well, one guy left in the car and two guys went off into the apartment, and at that moment I got out of the car and walked up and knocked on the apartment."

"Who told you to go up there?"

"My brother, Roland."

"Well, why you? Why were you supposed to go up there?"

"Because they knew Calvin and they knew my brother, Roland."

"Did you know which apartment to go to?"

"No sir."

"Did somebody answer the door?"

"Yes, sir."

"Who was that person?"

"A black female."

"Did you later see that black female again?"

"Yes, sir."

"Who was that?"

"Deandra Knight."

"When Deandra Knight answered the door, what did you do? What did you say?"

"I asked for Felicia."

"And how did she respond?"

"She said Felicia didn't live there."

"What did you observe while talking to Deandra Knight?"

"I saw Rider and Mac sitting in the living room, watching TV."

"And then what did you do?"

"I went back to the car and said it was the right apartment."

"How did Roland and Calvin respond? Was there any desire to go on and take some action at that time?"

"No, sir."

"Do you know a man by the name of Nikko Hollis?"

"Yes, sir."

"When did you first meet Nikko Hollis?"

"I can't recall when, but I know it was after my brother, Roland, got home from the penitentiary."

Montgomery shot up off his chair. "Your honor, may we approach?"

"Yes."

The attorneys barely were all at the bench when Montgomery exclaimed, "Your honor, we're going to object at this time to any reference to our client having been in the penitentiary. That was a nonresponsive answer and we're going to ask, . . ."

Austin interrupted, "I think it was responsive. I didn't . . ."

Montgomery cut him off. "We're going to ask that the jury be instructed to disregard that last response, and we're going to ask for a mistrial at this time."

The judge looked at him in disbelief. "A mistrial? Now, that would be dandy. Denied, of course." Waving away any further argument, he added, "I will, however, give the instruction." The attorneys retreated back to their tables, as the judge spoke to the jury. "We have an objection to the last answer. Please strike it from the record."

"And we ask for further relief, your honor," Montgomery insisted.

"It's denied." Gesturing to Austin, he said, "Go ahead, Mr. Gregory."

"Was there any other conversation about Nikko Hollis?"

"Yes, sir."

"Tell the members of the jury what that was."

"My brother said that Nikko Hollis was coming up to handle this, to get the money back from the guys."

"Okay, let's back up for just a second. You mentioned you got some guns. Was there ever any attempt besides going to Academy Sports to get ammunition for those guns?"

"Yes, sir."

"Where'd y'all go?"

"Wal-Mart.

"Who went?"

"Me and Stewart."

"Were you able to purchase any?"

"Yes, sir."

"And what did you do after you purchased the bullets at Wal-Mart?"

"We went back to the apartment."

"And what did you do with the bullets?"

"I can't recall," he shrugged, bored again.

"Let's move to Saturday morning. What happened after Hollis got there?"

"We went out to eat."

"And what happened then?"

"We went to the Holiday Inn Express."

"And what happened at that time?"

"Well, Nickels and my brother, Roland, went up to the room, and me and Stewart went to the store."

"What did you buy at the store?"

"Some gloves and duct tape."

"What store did you go to?"

"Wal-Mart."

"The same Wal-Mart where you bought the ammunition?"

"No, sir, we went to a different one, one in Irving this time."

"Okay, now, after you got those items, what did you do next?"

"We went back to the Holiday Inn Express."

"And what happened when you got there?"

"Well, I can't recall how long we stayed, but after that we got ready, put the camouflage clothes on and we left."

"Where did you guys go first?"

"I can't recall what store, sir, but we went to a store."

"What was purchased at the store?"

"We bought some beer and gasoline."

"And then what? Where did you go?"

"We went to the apartment."

"Who was driving at that time?"

"I was driving."

"Why were you driving?"

"Like I said before, they knew my brother, Roland, and they knew Stewart."

"So what happened after you got there?"

"We sat in the car, drinking and talking. We was waiting until it got dark."

"Why?"

"We was going to knock on the apartment door."

"Tell the members of the jury how y'all went up there."

206

"Me and Nickels knocked on the door."

"What were you carrying?"

"A two-by-four plank of wood."

"What did Nickels have?"

"One of the guns."

"What did Stewart have?"

"I believe the tape and the gasoline."

"And what did your brother, Roland, have?"

"The other gun."

"Was there an attempt made by Nickels to open the door?"

"Yes, sir."

"Was he able to kick it open?"

"No, sir."

"So, after Nickels tried to kick the door open, what happened at that time?"

"We went around to the patio glass."

"Could you see inside there at the time?"

"Yes, sir."

"What did you see?"

"I saw a black female on the telephone."

"Who was it?"

"Deandra Knight."

"At the time you saw Deandra Knight on the telephone, did she have a gun in her hand?"

Shaking his head, Malcolm replied, "Not that I could tell, no sir."

"Did you ever see a gun in her hand?"

"No, sir."

"You said she was talking on the phone. Was she standing or sitting?"

"She was standing up."

"Who broke the patio glass door?"

"I did."

"How?"

"I chunked the two-by-four into the door."

"So, what happened after you broke the glass?"

"Nickels went in the house first, and it looked to me like he chased her down the hall because she ran to the back."

"Now, you heard the 911 tape, isn't that right?"

"Yes, sir."

"Could you make out any other voices on the tape besides Deandra's"

"Yes, sir."

"Whose was that?"

"Nickels' voice and my voice."

"What happened at that time?"

"Me and Nickels ran to the back of the house. There was only one door closed, and we couldn't open it, so Nickels kicked it in. We could hear her in the closet, so he kicked that door in, too. We went into the closet and dragged her out to the door."

"Did she go with you peacefully? What was she doing?"

"No, sir. She was squirming and kicking and screaming for help."

"And then what happened?"

"When we got to the door, Roland came in and punched Deandra in the face."

"Why did he do that?"

He shrugged and said, "I guess because she was screaming. To shut her up."

"And then what happened?"

"Me and Nickels dragged her to the car. My brother, Roland, was driving, Stewart was in the passenger seat, I was in the back seat, and Nickels was in the back seat."

"And where was Deandra?"

"In between Nickels' legs."

"And what was Nickels doing?"

"Asking her where was her brothers at."

The judge tapped his microphone. "Mr. Gregory, we need to take a break. Look for the earliest opportunity to take a break in your questioning."

"Yes, your honor." Looking back at the witness, Austin asked, "What was her demeanor? Was she happy, crying, or how would you describe it?"

"I can't recall if she was crying, but she was scared."

"What was Nickels doing in relation to the gun?"

"I didn't see the gun in the car."

"Did there come a time when you got to your sister Vanessa's place?"

"Yes, sir."

"And what happened after you got there?"

"Everybody got out of the car."

"May I approach the witness, your honor?" At Judge Stagner's nod, Austin walked up to the witness stand and handed him a picture. "Do you recognize this?"

"Yes, sir."

"And what is that?"

"That's what we had the gas in. The anti-freeze can."

"Did y'all let Deandra Knight go?"

"No, sir."

Austin nodded at the bench. "Now is a good time to take that break, sir."

Judge Stagner moved his microphone closer to his mouth and said, "Ladies and gentlemen, we'll take a fifteen-minute break now. Let's try to resume at 3:00, or as close to that as we can."

●●●

After the break, and after everyone settled back into their seats, Austin continued his examination of Malcolm. "Mr. Connors, what happened after y'all arrived at your sister's apartment?"

"I went into the house. Everybody else left."

"Did you know what they did with Deandra at that time?"

"No, sir."

"About how long were they gone?"

He shrugged, "I can't recall."

"Well, what did you do?"

"I was in the house, in the bathroom."

"Did you notice anything in your pockets at that time?"

"Yes, sir,"

"What was that?"

"Some glasses and glass."

"What did you do with those glasses?"

"Later on, once my brother and everybody got back, I told them about the glasses, and Vanessa ended up throwing them away."

Austin stood directly in front of the witness stand. "Now, the glasses that were in your pocket, were they your glasses?"

"No, sir."

"Had you ever seen those glasses before?"

"No, sir," Malcolm replied, shaking his head.

"Did you have them before Deandra was kidnapped?"

"No, sir."

"Did you see those glasses on Deandra?"

"Not that I can recall, no, sir."

"I want to show you Government's Exhibit Number 15, which is an envelope containing something." Austin placed the envelope on the ledge of the witness stand, and looked at Malcolm. "Now, I've shown these to you before, is that right?"

"Yes, sir."

He removed the contents of the envelope, placing them on top of the envelope. "Are those the glasses that you had in your pocket?"

"Yes, sir."

"Your honor," Austin looked at the bench, "the government would move to introduce Government's Exhibit Number 15."

Ms. Williams stood up. "Your honor, at this time we're going to object on relevancy."

Judge Stagner paused a moment, then said, "Sustained."

Damn, Austin thought as he walked back to the podium. Frustrated, he flipped a few pages in his notebook. He then looked back at Malcolm and asked, "Did there come a time when Roland, Calvin Stewart, Nikko Hollis and Deandra returned?"

"Yes, sir."

"And what happened at that time?"

"At that time, my brother, Roland, came into the apartment and told me to get my clothes and get ready to go."

"And what did you say in response to that?"

"I believe I asked why."

"And his response?"

"That it's time for me to get out of Texas."

"And then what happened at that time?"

"At that time, I went and packed my stuff and me and him walked out the door together."

"And where was Calvin Stewart and Nikko Hollis?"

"They was outside."

"And what happened at that time when you walked outside?"

"My brother, Roland, told me that he would be there by the time that we get there, and he gave me a hug."

"Did you say anything to him?"

"No, sir, not that I can recall."

"Now, when he said you were getting out of Texas, where did you think you were going?"

"I had mentioned a while ago that I wanted to find a job somewhere out in Jersey. To sortta start over somewhere fresh."

"Was there any discussion about letting Deandra Knight go at that time?"

"No, sir."

"What happened at that time after you got in the car?"

"At that time, we drove off to go to Oklahoma."

"Who was driving?"

"Stewart."

"And where were you sitting?"

"In the passenger seat."

"And where was Deandra Knight and Nikko Hollis?"

"In the back seat."

"And as you went up toward Oklahoma, what happened in the car that you saw?"

"Well, I looked in the back seat, and Nickels was having sex with her."

"What did you do or say at that time?"

"Asked him why was he doing that on the highway."

"And what did he say?"

"He told me to shut up and turn around."

"Now, when you said he had sex, did he rape her?"

"Yes, sir."

"After raping her, did he do anything else in relation to her as far as sexual acts?"

"Yes, sir."

"What did you see him do?"

"He put her head down below his legs."

"Did he make her perform oral sex on him?"

"Yes, sir."

"After that what happened?"

"Well, he stayed back there for a little while, and me and Stewart kept driving."

"After that point, did you switch places with Hollis?"

"Yes, sir."

"Tell the members of the jury what happened."

"At that time, Nickels got in the front seat, and I got in the back seat. When I got in the back seat, Nickels told me to grab some condoms."

"And what did you do?"

"I grabbed the condoms."

"And then what?"

"I put them on. Nickels said put three of them on."

"And what happened?"

Malcolm looked off, away from the jury. He lowered his head and replied, "I had sex with her."

"Did you force her to?"

Swallowing down the sudden thickness, he said, "Yes, sir."

"What happened after that?"

"I had her give me oral sex."

"And what happened?"

"She started to. . ."

Impatient, Austin repeated, "What happened?"

"She started to cry, and I got up and laid on the floor of the car, and she laid in the seat of the car."

"What happened after that?"

"We kept driving to Oklahoma."

"Okay. Now, what happened when you got to Ponca City, Oklahoma?"

"We went over to Jeremy Spencer's house."

"Why did you go to Jeremy Spencer's house?"

"I have no idea." He slowly shook his head.

"Okay, what happened when you got to Jeremy Spencer's house?"

"Nickels went in the house. Me and Stewart stayed in the car, and he was in the house for a while."

"What happened when he came out?"

"He told Stewart to drive to a motel."

"And then what?"

"Well, we went to a motel. He rented a room, and then we went inside there and chilled out for a minute."

"What happened after you got the room?"

"Well, after we got the room, me, Nickels, Stewart and Ms. Knight were inside the room, and at that time, Stewart went in the bathroom and had sex with her."

"Did you see him having sex with her?"

"No, sir."

"So, how do you know he had sex with her?"

Malcolm flung his hands and shrugged. "He came out and told us."

"Okay. Where was Deandra kept initially when she was brought in after Stewart sexually assaulted her?"

"In the bathroom."

"And how was she kept in the bathroom?"

"On a sheet."

"Was she bound or unbound?"

"She was bound."

"What was used to bind her?"

"We used more duct tape."

"Who bought the duct tape?"

"Nickels."

"Did Roland and Jeremy ever show up?"

"Yes, sir."

"What happened when Roland and Jeremy came?"

"They went in the bathroom."

"And where was Deandra?"

"In the bathroom."

"What happened when they came out?"

"Nickels asked what was they going to do with me."

"Referring to you?"

"Yes, sir."

"Well, what happened after that?"

"After that they left."

"Where was Deandra put after they left?"

"In the closet area."

"Okay. How was she tied up?"

"In a chair."

"Who tied her up?"

"Stewart."

"Did there come a time when Hollis left?"

"Yes, sir."

"And what happened at that time?"

"He left, I don't know where he went, but later on he came back."

"And then what happened?"

"When he came back, him and Nickels left with Deandra."

"Did you know where they were going?"

"No, sir."

Austin paced before the jury box. "Why didn't you go?"

"He told me to stay there and clean up the room."

"Was this daylight or dark when they left?"

"It was dark."

"Did they return?"

"Yes, sir."

"And what happened then?"

"Nickels came into the room and told me that my brother, Roland, and Stewart had got . . ."

"Your honor," Ms. Williams stood up, "We object to any hearsay."

Turning to Austin, Judge Stagner replied, "Response?"

"I don't believe it's hearsay."

Judge Stagner looked pointedly at Austin over the rim of his glasses. "Well, that's helpful, counselor."

Clearing his throat, Austin responded, "Sir, I think it's a co-conspirator's statement."

"Overruled, Ms. Williams," Judge Stagner nodded.

"Where was Deandra Knight placed at that time," Austin asked Malcolm.

"Back in the closet."

"Okay. Let's move down through the night to the early morning hours. At that time, did Roland have occasion to text Hollis?"

"Yes, sir."

"And did Hollis show up?"

"Yes, sir."

"And what happened at that time?"

"When Nickels came in the room, he told Stewart to go get Miss Knight. And while he was in there getting Miss Knight, me, my brother, and Nickels was out in the bedroom area."

"And what happened then?"

"Stewart came out of the bathroom with Miss Knight and they all got in the car and left."

"Why didn't you go with them this time?"

"I don't know."

"You don't?"

"No, sir."

"Do you know where they were going?"

"No, sir."

"How long were they gone?"

"I don't know the exact time."

"What happened when they came back?"

"When they came back, Stewart was the first one to come in the room."

"And what happened at that time?"

"Well, when he walked in, the first thing he said was that he had hit her."

"He said he hit her?"

"Yes, sir."

"How did he look?"

"He looked sad."

"And what did you do?"

He looked down at his hands, then looked back at Austin and replied, "I gave him a hug."

"And then what did he do?"

"He went and took a shower."

"Could you see anything on Stewart's clothes?"

"I seen mud on his shoes."

"So what happened at that time?"

"After that, we all got into Stewart's car and went over to Jeremy's house."

"And what happened when you got over to Jeremy's house?"

"Well, Jeremy told Stewart to go clean the car. I went with Stewart."

"And what did y'all do?"

"We cleaned the car."

"Did you ever see Deandra Knight again?"

"No, sir."

"Now, after you cleaned up the car, what happened at that point?"

"Me and Stewart went back over to Jeremy's house."

"And what happened when you got over to Jeremy's house?"

"Me and Stewart got out of the car, and Jeremy walked up to the car and told Stewart he did what he had to do."

"Okay, let's skip forward. Did there come a time when you met Roland in Oklahoma City?"

"Yes, sir. We all met over my uncle's house."

"What was the subject of the conversation?"

"About the cops going to Stewart's house and to my sister's house back in Texas."

"What else did you guys talk about?"

"We was talking about what we should say. And I can't recall who made the exact story up but," Malcolm shook his head, "I can't remember everybody else's version of the story but my own at the time."

"What was your version?"

"To say that my uncle picked me up in Norman."

"And that was the version you were going to tell the police?"

"Yes, sir."

"Did everyone have a version?"

"Yes, sir."

"And then what happened?"

"Later that afternoon, the cops were at my motel room, and they took me to jail."

"You were arrested?"

"Yes, sir."

"When you had the meeting to get your story straight, was there any kind of discussion about telling them the truth about the murder of Deandra Knight?"

"No, sir."

"The kidnapping?"

"No, sir."

"Now, you said when you and Roland and Calvin met to get your story straight that you remembered your story?"

"Yes, sir."

"Did you ever tell that story to the police?"

"Yes, sir."

"And when was that?"

"The day that I got arrested."

"Was that the truth you told them?"

"No, sir."

"You also, in the end, gave a written statement, is that correct?"

"Yes, sir."

"Who did you give your statement to?"

"Agent Gavin Wright and another officer."

"Did those officers force you to give a statement?"

"No, sir."

"Was all in that statement you gave true?"

"No, sir."

"You didn't admit breaking out the door with the two-by-four, did you, in that statement?"

"No, sir."

"And you didn't admit meeting Deandra Friday night when you went to the door to check the residence, is that right?"

"No, sir."

Austin closed his notebook. "Pass the witness."

The judge adjusted his glasses. "We'll take a break. Let's return here as close to 4:30 as we can. We'll try to shut down around 5:30."

CHAPTER FIFTEEN

Lydia and William made their way back into the courtroom after the break to find Marissa standing in the aisle waiting for them.

"How are you holding up?" She flashed a bright smile. Her eyes, though, Lydia thought, looked tired.

"Well, I'm just now getting over the shock of his brother testifying against him!" William rubbed his chin. "Your own brother . . . shouldn't this be a slam dunk for us?"

Shaking her head, Marissa held up her hands. "I wish it were that simple. The defense has to make their cross of our witness, so, . . . there's still some work to do."

William looked past Marissa to the woman standing at the podium. Gretchen Williams was a medium-built woman with mousy brown hair cut in a chin-length chic bob. Her ill-fitted suit blended with her hair color, and the cobalt blue blouse underneath matched her glasses.

"All rise!"

Marissa made her way across the well to the attorney table, and William and Lydia made their way to their pew seats as Judge Stagner walked through the door. Malcolm was already seated at the witness stand. The judge said, "The court is ready for cross examination, Ms. Williams."

"Thank you, your honor." She adjusted her glasses and smiled at Malcolm. "Good afternoon, Mr. Connors. My name is Gretchen Williams, one of the attorneys for your brother."

Malcolm stared back at her, mute.

"Mr. Connors," she continued, "you've indicated that when you were arrested, you told law enforcement officers a lie about what had happened, is that correct?"

"Yes, ma'am."

"And what you told them was that you, in essence, were not involved in any of this and you didn't know about any of this because you had gone to Norman the Friday before Deandra Knight was abducted, is that correct?"

"Yes, ma'am."

"And that was a story that you told to protect yourself, is that a fair statement?'

"Yes, ma'am."

"A couple of days later, you were taken from the Norman jail to the DeSoto, Texas jail, is that correct?"

"Yes, ma'am."

"And the next day, you had a brief conversation with law enforcement officers, is that correct?"

"Yes, ma'am."

"And at that time, you told them a little bit more about the trip, is that correct?"

"Yes, ma'am."

"You didn't tell them much, but what you did tell them was true, is that . . ."

"Some of it, yes, ma'am," he interrupted.

"And then the next day, by then your brother had been arrested, is that correct?"

"Yes, ma'am."

"And the next day at the DeSoto Police Department, law enforcement officers put you and your brother together, did they not?"

"Yes, ma'am."

"And they left y'all alone for a while, did they not?"

"Yes, ma'am."

"And it was during that time that your brother urged you to tell these law enforcement officers the truth about what had happened, is that correct?"

"Yes, ma'am."

"And he also told you to not only tell them the truth, but to take care of yourself, is that correct?"

"Yes, ma'am."

"And he told you that if telling them the truth hurt him, Roland, to tell the truth anyway, is that correct?"

"Yes, ma'am."

"And you believed he meant all that, don't you?"

"Yes, ma'am."

"And after the law enforcement officers put you and your brother together and left y'all alone, after that talk, you came out and told them the truth, did you not?"

"Yes, ma'am."

"That's when you gave your written statement, you signed a written statement, admitting your involvement, is that correct?"

"Yes, ma'am."

"And there may have been some things since that time you've changed or some things since that time you realized you've omitted, but for the most part that was a full and truthful statement of what occurred, is that correct?"

"No, ma'am."

"One of the things that's not in your written statement is you don't talk much about Jeremy Spencer, do you?"

"No, ma'am."

"And you know that Jeremy Spencer was pretty involved in all this, don't you?"

"Yes, ma'am."

"You also know that Jeremy Spencer has made a deal where he's not going to be tried for the death penalty, don't you?"

"Yes, ma'am."

"Let me ask you this. You knew Nikko Hollis to be a very violent individual, did you not?"

"Yes, ma'am."

"And you believed that this was a situation that you and Roland and Calvin Stewart could take care of yourselves, is that correct?"

"Yes, ma'am."

"And that's really what you wanted to do, is the three of y'all take care of this yourself?"

"Yes, ma'am."

"Now, if that meant getting the money back by force, you were willing to do that, but you wanted to take care of it yourself, is that correct?"

"Yes, ma'am."

"And it's your understanding that Jeremy wanted Nickels to come down here?"

"Judge, I object to that," Austin said, standing. "That calls for a hearsay response."

"I agree." Judge Stagner nodded his head. "Sustained."

"When y'all went to the Villa Winds Apartments on that Saturday after Nickels had gotten to town, you and Calvin, prior to that time, you and Calvin Stewart had, in all fairness, done quite a bit of preparation, had you not?"

"Yes, ma'am."

"Calvin Stewart found a friend that had guns, and you and he went and got them, is that correct?"

"Yes, ma'am."

"And then there was ammunition and duct tape purchased, that you and Calvin Stewart purchased, is that correct?"

"Yes, ma'am."

"And there were other items that have been offered into evidence up there, camouflage masks and that sort of thing, that you and Calvin Stewart purchased, is that correct?"

"Yes, ma'am."

"And it was your understanding that when y'all went to the Villa Winds Apartments on Saturday, the plan was to confront, by physical force, if necessary, and possibly tie up Mac and Rider, is that correct?"

"Ma'am, I can't say we were gonna tie them up, but it was to go there to make them give the money back."

"So number one, y'all knew that the story that they had been robbed of their car was not true, is that correct?"

"Yes, ma'am."

"And number two, y'all believed that Mac and Rider lived there, did you not?"

"Yes, ma'am."

"And when y'all approached the apartment, the fact of the business is nobody had a clue that Nickels was going to take that girl hostage, did they?"

"No, ma'am."

"Roland didn't have a clue . . ."

"Your honor," Austin interrupted again, "I object. That calls for a conclusion on his part on what Roland . . ."

"Sustained." Austin adjusted his tie as he sat back down.

"Okay," Ms. Williams tilted her head, "nobody knew that Nickels was going to take that girl and abduct that girl except for Nickels, is that correct?"

"Yes, ma'am."

"And when he did that, everybody ran to the car, is that correct?"

"Yes, ma'am."

"And another fact of the business is, once y'all left the apartment with Deandra Knight, Roland didn't know where he was going or where he was, is that correct?"

"Yes, ma'am."

"So, he and Calvin Stewart switched places, and Calvin started driving the car?"

"Yes, ma'am."

"Because Calvin Stewart was from that area and knew where he was and exactly where he was going?"

"Yes, ma'am."

"Would it be fair to say at that point everybody but Nickels was scared?"

"Yes, ma'am."

"And was Nickels, Nikko Hollis, essentially telling everybody what to do, what they needed to do and what was going to happen?"

"Yes, ma'am."

"Ms. Williams," Judge Stagner moved the microphone closer to his mouth, causing loud feedback from the speakers. "Some repetition is necessary for you to conduct a sufficient cross-examination, but to just review each step along the way that the government has already shown is more repetitious than I think there needs to be. Please try to focus on those parts of the direct examination about which you can offer additional enlightenment."

"Yes, sir," she bowed towards the bench. Turning back to the witness, she asked, "When you and Calvin Stewart and Nikko Hollis drove from Dallas to Ponca City, Oklahoma, was your brother, my client, Roland Connors, with you?"

"No, ma'am."

"Before y'all had gotten out of Dallas, Nikko Hollis had sexually assaulted Deandra Knight, is that correct?"

"Yes, ma'am."

"And, of course, Roland wasn't anywhere around when that occurred."

He shook his head no1.

"And you, you likewise, sexually assaulted Deandra Knight in the car prior to the time you got to Ponca City, is that correct?"

"Yes, ma'am."

"And again, Roland wasn't anywhere around when that occurred, was he?"

"No, ma'am."

"And in Ponca City at the motel, Roland and Jeremy Spencer showed up. And you know that at that time Jeremy Spencer sexually assaulted Deandra Knight, don't you?"

He frowned, twisting in his chair. "Well, I seen him go in the bathroom."

"Did you likewise see him pick up a condom before he went into the bathroom?"

"Yes, ma'am."

"Do you remember telling a representative from the FBI on October 28th of 2002 that you got up off the bed when Jeremy Spencer was there and watched Jeremy Spencer and Deandra Knight having sex in the bathroom?"

"Yes, ma'am."

"And do you remember telling the FBI at that time, on October 28 or so, that as you watched Jeremy Spencer having sex with Deandra Knight in the bathroom, do you remember saying to Spencer, 'Go 'head, Jeremy?'"

"Yes, ma'am."

"When Calvin Stewart and your brother and Nickels left with Deandra the last time when you didn't see her again, when Stewart came back, he told you he had hit Deandra, is that correct?"

"Yes, ma'am."

"And at some point soon after that, Jeremy told Stewart something to the effect of you were just taking care of business, you just did what you had to do, is that correct?"

"Yes, ma'am."

"Do you believe that Roland is sorry about this?"

He shifted his gaze downward, then back at Ms. Williams. "Yes, ma'am."

Closing her notebook, she said, "Pass the witness."

"Is there redirect," Judge Stagner asked Austin.

"Yes, sir."

"Only on the subject of cross," the judge emphasized, looking over the top of his glasses.

Nodding, Austin replied, "Yes, sir." Walking back to the podium, he looked at the witness and said, "We talked earlier about the time you gave a statement to the police when you got down to DeSoto from Ponca City. I believe the question was if you knew Roland had given a full confession and you said yes, is that correct?"

"Yes, sir," he nodded.

"Okay. Now, at that time, did you know and did Roland know that Calvin Stewart had already given a statement to the police explaining what happened in the case?"

"I'm going to object to him leading his own witness, your honor." Ms. Williams stood up.

"Sustained."

"What did you know about Stewart and what he had told the police?" Austin continued.

"Your honor," Ms. Williams interrupted, still standing, "objection as that's outside the scope of cross."

"It is?" Judge Stagner appeared confused.

"I don't believe it is," Austin replied.

"What did she go into that you're responding to?"

"The idea that Roland Connors was remorseful and gave a full confession," Austin clarified. "I'm trying to go in and develop just why he did give the confession."

"I'm going to allow it," Judge Stagner replied carefully, "but I'm going to watch you closely. Go ahead," he gestured to the witness.

Austin nodded at Malcolm and said, "At the time before you gave a confession, did you know about what Calvin Stewart had already said?"

Shaking his head, he replied, "I didn't know what he had said, but I knew he made a statement."

"Did you and Roland talk about what Calvin Stewart said?"

"No, sir."

"What was your understanding of what he had said?"

"Well, my understanding," he said, lifting his hands, "I didn't know what he said. I just knew he gave a confession about whatever had happened."

"Did you think it was consistent with the earlier story that y'all had made up to say, or was it different from that?"

"Your honor, once again, I'm going to object to him leading his own witness," Ms. Williams said, standing up.

The judge slightly shook his head. "No, I don't think so. I'm going to allow that."

They all looked at Malcolm, who visibly ducked his head. "Will you repeat the question?"

"Okay," Austin agreed. "With what you thought Roland or Calvin had said, was that consistent with the stories y'all had gotten together and made up in Ponca City, or was it something different from that?"

"No, I thought it was something different."

"Did you think it was any use, then, to keep saying the same story that y'all had made up?"

"Leading again, your honor." Ms. Williams kept her seat this time.

"Sustained."

"Yes, your honor," Austin held up his hand. "Ms. Williams asked you about what you told an FBI agent about seeing Jeremy have sex with Deandra. Was that the truth?"

"No, sir."

"Why did you tell the FBI agent that?"

"I really don't know, sir."

"Ms. Williams asked you that when you and Calvin Stewart were with Nikko Hollis after they came back from the last time you saw Deandra, and you went over to the house on Monday and you said that Nikko had said something to Stewart that you had to do what you had to do. Do you remember him saying that?"

"Yes, sir."

"Do you remember Ms. Williams also added that he said that you were just taking care of business. Now, do you ever remember Jeremy Spencer ever telling him that, you're just taking care of business?"

"No, sir."

"Did Nickels or anybody else, Hollis or anybody else ever prevent y'all from releasing Deandra Knight at that time there on the parking lot at Villa Winds Apartment on April 6th?"

"No, sir."

"Did anyone ever prevent you or Roland Connors or anybody from releasing Deandra Knight before y'all took her up to Ponca City, Oklahoma?"

"No, sir."

"Do you think Roland Connors was concerned for you when he told you to get in that car and drive up to Ponca City, Oklahoma with Deandra Knight, yet, he did not go?"

"No, sir."

"No further questions, your honor."

"Recross?"

"Just one question, your honor." Ms. Williams passed Austin on the way to the podium. "The fact of the business is whether you actually saw Jeremy Stewart have sex with Deandra Knight in the bathroom or not, you know he took a condom and was with her in the bathroom for about fifteen minutes, is that correct?"

"I don't know how long, but yes, he took some condoms in the bathroom with him."

"That's all I have your honor."

"Is there redirect? And remember the hour, Mr. Gregory."

"I, too, just have one question, sir." Standing at the podium, with his hands in his pockets, Austin looked at Malcolm and asked, "Who went in the bathroom with Jeremy?"

"My brother, Roland."

He nodded at the judge, and said, "Pass the witness, your honor."

Before anyone could say anything else, Judge Stagner turned to the witness stand. "Thank you, young man. You're excused." He nodded to the deputies in the back, and they met Malcolm at the jury box next to the door he entered in. Looking over at his brother, he threw up the peace sign. Roland, in turn, nodded his head, then looked back at the bench.

The judge gave the jurors their departing instructions and dismissed court for the day.

● ● ●

Later that evening, Lydia sat in her living room, sipping a cup of tea. The room was dimly lit, the candles on the table surrounding Deandra's picture were the only light source in the room. She watched her eyes come alive in the candlelight the flames flickered and danced, causing her smile to sparkle. Such a beautiful girl, Lydia thought, shaking her head, her own eyes burning with tears. Looking at the picture, she chuckled to herself, remembering Deandra's excitement when she brought the package of pictures home from school. She saw Norecce in her eyes, in her smile.

CHAPTER SIXTEEN

The next morning, Gavin, Marissa and Austin sat at their table, waiting for the day's session to begin. Her eyes darted between the clock on the wall in front of her, and the empty chair behind the bench right below. It was 9:03 am, and the judge was late. Marissa rested her chin on her hand and looked around. Her eyes fell on Montgomery, who extended his arm in the air, raising his paper coffee cup in salute. His gaughty too big, too much bling watch caught the light, the glass added more blitz and shine. She gave a polite nod and averted her eyes back to the clock. Gavin laid his hand on top of hers, and she realized she'd been tapping her pen on the table. She laid it down and threw him a helpless smile. Austin took the pen, putting it on the other side of his pad. The clock clicked to 9:05 am.

The side door swung open, and the court bailiff stepped into the courtroom.

"All rise!" he announced.

Judge Stagner marched to the vacant chair on the bench, his robe wafting in the breeze. Marissa smoothed out her animal-print skirt and bowed her head as the bailiff recited the beginning prayer.

"Good morning, everyone," Judge Stagner started as he took his seat. Marissa ran her fingers along her smooth updo as she also took her seat. "I'm sorry I'm late, there was some business I had to attend to that took longer than I thought. Is everyone ready?"

"We are, your honor," Montgomery drawled.

"Yes, your honor." Austin replied, standing.

"Very well, Mr. Gregory. You may proceed."

"Your honor, the United States call Theresa Solomon."

Ms. Solomon walked in, wearing a police uniform, hair pulled back from her face. She stopped in front of the bench and raised her hand. After she was sworn in, the witness sat down at the stand.

"Ms. Solomon," Austin began, "for the record, how are you employed?"

"I'm a detention officer with the DeSoto Police Department."

"And were you employed with the City of DeSoto Police Department in April of 2002?"

"Yes, sir, I was."

"At that time did you take any fingerprint impressions, ink fingerprint impressions of an individual named Roland Loenthal Connors?"

"Yes, I did."

"May I approach the witness, your honor?"

"You may."

"Ms. Solomon, would you look at what's been marked as Government's Exhibit 57-A in front of you, and I ask if you can identify that, please?"

"Yes. It's the fingerprints that I took."

"Okay, is that a Xerox copy of the fingerprint car that you took?"

"Yes, it is."

"What's the date on that, ma'am?"

"April 16th."

"And would you look at Government's Exhibit 57-B, please. Can you identify that?"

"Yes, sir."

Austin gestured to the witness. "Please tell the jury what that is, ma'am."

"That is a Xerox copy of the palm print card that we take."

"And is that also the palm print that you took from an individual named Roland Loenthal Connors on April 16th, 2002?"

"Yes, it is."

"Do you see the individual in the courtroom today who you took the ink fingerprint impressions from on April 16th, 2002 named Roland Loenthal Connors?"

"Yes, I do."

"Would you describe where he's sitting and what he's wearing for the jury, please."

"He's sitting to my right wearing a brown jacket and blue tie."

Glancing at the bench, Austin said, "Your honor, I would ask the record to reflect that she's identified the defendant."

"The record will so reflect."

"I pass the witness."

Montgomery stood up. "We have no questions of this witness, your honor."

Judge Stagner turned to the witness stand. "Ms. Solomon, you may step down. You're free to go." To Austin, he said, "You may call your next witness."

Marissa stood up, changing places with Austin. "The government calls Kyle MacKenzie to the stand."

The bailiff opened the courtroom door and the witness strolled down the aisle up to the bench. His dark blue jeans sagged a little in the back, and his blue and white ginger-gram shirt was tucked in. He lowered his hand after he was sworn in. Marissa swallowed her impatience as he sauntered up to the witness stand and sat down, almost sliding into the chair.

"Would you state your name for the judge and the jury?"

"Kyle MacKenzie."

"How old are you, Mr. MacKenzie?"

"I'm thirty-one years old."

"Are you the eldest brother of Deandra Knight?

"Yes, ma'am."

"Is that her picture over to your left, sir, on the bulletin board there?"

"Yes, ma'am."

"Do you know a man by the name of Victor Howard?"

"Yes, ma'am," he responded, talking almost as slow as he walked.

"How did you know him?"

"Through my brother, Ryan Knight."

"Does Ryan go by the nickname 'Rider'?"

"Yes, ma'am."

"I want to take you back to around February of 2002. At that time, did Victor contact you regarding obtaining some marijuana?"

"Yes, ma'am."

"What did he tell you?"

"Well, he told me he had some cousins coming from out of town, and he wanted to know if I could get him about four pounds of marijuana. I told him I'll check with somebody and I'll let him know."

"Well, why did he come to you, Mr. MacKenzie?"

Shrugging his shoulders, Kyle replied, "I've sold some to him before."

"Were you able to get the marijuana for him?"

"Yes, I was."

Marissa turned, gestured to the jury box. "Explain to the jury how this deal, in fact, works, or how it went down, if you will."

"He would ask me about it, then I tell him I'll check. I check with my guy, and then I call Victor back and tell him I can get it. So then I meet him and he gives me the money. I take the money, go get the dope, and then meet him behind the Wal-Mart and give him the marijuana. Then after he looked at it, and after he said it's good, then he would leave."

"Okay," she nodded, "tell us about the deal that went down at the end of March, 2002."

"I had sold some marijuana to Victor about a week prior. He called me and told me the product was really good, and they sold it as fast as they could, so they wanted some more. So he tells me they wanted about ten more pounds."

"And then?"

"I told him I'll check with my source to see if he could deliver that much. Source said it was no problem."

"And what happened next?"

"I met him and got the money. We counted it, and there was nine thousand dollars. After that, I tell him when I get it, I'll call him and he said okay."

"And after that?"

"Before I met him, he called me and told me they didn't want ten pounds, they only wanted six. After I got the six pounds, I met Vic, gave him the six pounds and three thousand dollars back."

"Where did y'all meet for that exchange?"

"The usual place, behind the Wal-Mart."

"What happened at that time when you got to the Wal-Mart?"

"I got there first. After a while, Victor Howard pulled up. He came, I gave him the money. He counted it, saw it was all there, then I gave him the marijuana. He counted that, then he said okay and left."

"Was anybody with him at that time?"

"Yeah."

"One of the people you met that day, is he here in the courtroom?"

"Yes, ma'am."

"Would you point him out for the judge and jury, please."

He pointed to the defendant.

"What is he wearing?"

"A suit with a blue tie."

Marissa looked over the Judge Stagner. "The government would ask the record reflect the witness has identified the defendant."

"The record will so reflect."

"All right. Let's move forward to March of 2002. Was your apartment raided by the police?"

"Yes, ma'am."

"And as a result of that, did you plead guilty to possession of marijuana with intent to distribute?"

"Yes, ma'am."

"And what was your sentence in that case?"

"I got five years' probation." He looked down into his open hands.

"Okay. After that time, did you stay at your apartment?"

"No, I had to move, so I was staying with my sister for a while."

"At the time you moved in with your sister, who lived there?"

"Deandra and Ryan and Adena."

"Did Adena or Deandra have anything to do with the drug deals you made?"

"No, ma'am," he replied.

"Or the marijuana?"

"No, ma'am," he repeated.

"Okay, let's talk about the weekend of March 29 and 30. Did you have occasion to speak to Ryan in regards to Roland and Calvin?"

"Yeah," he nodded. "My brother came to me and told me that Calvin Stewart was trying to get in touch with him. So after they finally got in touch, they discussed some deal, and I guess Stewart said his cousins were coming from out of town and they wanted some marijuana. They wanted about ten pounds."

"Now, what happened to your source for marijuana, Victor?"

"Well, about a week before my apartment got raided, Vic went to jail. He was my only source, so I didn't have no source for marijuana after that."

"But your brother set up a deal with them anyway?"

"Yes, he did."

"And what was the purpose? What were y'all going to do, the bottom line?"

Shrugging his shoulders, Kyle replied, "We was just going to con them."

"What did y'all do to get the money from them?"

"Well, we told them that we could get them some marijuana at a cheaper price. So when Stewart called him that evening and told him that his cousins was there, we met them behind the Wal-Mart. At that time, it was Stewart and Roland."

"What happened?"

"Well, at first, they didn't want to give my brother the money, and then after they gave him the money, they wanted to follow us. And then we said they can't because our source didn't want anybody to know where he stays or nothing like that. So then after they gave my brother the money and he had it in his hands, then we took off."

"What happened after that?"

"They called me and asked where is my brother, asked me if he had got there yet. I tell them something must be wrong. Then after they call back later again, I told them my brother said he got robbed."

"I'm going to object unless he identifies who the speaker was." Montgomery interrupted, standing up.

"Sustain the objection."

"Who were you talking to?"

"The first time was Stewart. Then after, Roland Connors called."

"And what did you tell Roland Connors?"

"I told him that we got robbed, that my brother got robbed, they took the car and the money and everything. And after, he said 'what are you going to do about my money,' what was he supposed to tell his people. I told him I'll try to get the money back. Then he kept asking me what was he going to tell his source. I said 'let me talk to your source,' but he wouldn't let me talk to anybody. That's the last time I heard from him."

"Alright. That Friday night. What happened?"

"Me and my brother and a friend of ours was outside standing around Ryan's car, and I saw a guy in a camouflage suit, and he was walking by. He kept looking at the car. It thought he was trying to steal something from the car, but when he saw me, he just walked up faster, turned his head and walked faster. I didn't recognize the person."

"Did you ever leave the apartment?"

"About two hours later, we did."

"Did you ever see Deandra again after you left that night?"

"No, ma'am."

"Who was at the apartment when you left?"

"Adena and Deandra."

"Okay. Saturday. What happened?"

"Saturday night, Adena called me and told me Deandra was kidnapped and to come home."

"When you got there, were you met with the police and the FBI agents?"

"Yes, ma'am."

"Did they ask you about if you knew anything that could have happened?"

"Because they knew of my dealings and my previous conviction, they wanted to know could it, the kidnapping, somehow be connected to the dealings."

"Did you ever volunteer about the rip off to them?"

"No, not at first." He shook his head.

"In fact, you lied to them or withheld information about what was really going on, isn't that right?" Marissa paced in front of the jury box.

"Yes, ma'am."

"What happened that night?"

"We were driving through Duncanville, and we saw the Camero, my brother said that was the Camero he saw at our apartment. We had heard some of the license plate numbers from the news, so we drove back around again and we looked at it. So after seeing the GF on the license plate, I called 911 and told them I just saw the Camero that they've been looking for, and that's the people who got my sister. So then they told me to leave the area, go to a convenience store and the police were on their way."

"Did you eventually tell the police the whole story, that it was a rip-off dope deal?"

"No, I didn't."

Feigning surprise, Marissa arched an eyebrow and asked, "Why not?"

"At first, Ryan thought the FBI was playing a game trying to sting us about the marijuana dealings."

"That was a stupid thing to think, wasn't it?"

"That's what I'm saying right now." He lowered his head, shaking it slightly.

"Did the police come to the convenience store?"

Looking back at Marissa, Kyle simply replied, "Yeah."

"Okay, later on, did you at last tell the police what really happened?"

"Yes, I did."

"Do you realize that if you told the police about the true things, maybe Deandra could be alive right now?"

"Yes, ma'am." Kyle shifted his gaze downward.

"Do you feel like you ripping them off justified them in killing your sister?"

"Objection, your honor!" Montgomery stood up so fast, his chair crashed to the floor.

"Sustained." The judge waved his hand in the air. "Ignore the answer."

"Your honor, we are going to ask for a mistrial." Montgomery's face was blood-red, almost purple with anger.

"Overruled." Judge Stagner looked at Montgomery over his glasses.

"The government passes the witness, your honor." Marissa walked back to her table and sat beside Gavin.

Before she sat down, though, Montgomery was already at the podium and barged straight into his cross examination. "When the police raided your apartment, there was a substantial amount of marijuana there at that time, was there not?"

"There was less than four ounces of marijuana."

"And you pled guilty to that in federal court, did you not?"

"Yes, I did."

"And you also told the police that the gun they found was yours, is that right?'

Marissa half-stood. "I object as irrelevant at this time, that's beyond the scope of this trial."

"Your honor, I think they opened this up," Montgomery retorted, gesturing behind him.

"Overruled," Judge Stagner replied.

Looking back at the witness, Montgomery continued. "They found the gun at that time, did they not?"

"Yes, they did."

"You told them that was your gun, didn't you?"

"Yeah."

"And at the time they searched the apartment, they found some scales, is that correct?"

"Yes."

"And they seized the scales as well, did they not?"

"Yes."

"And those were the kind of scales that you would use to weigh the drugs that you were going to sell, is that correct?"

"Yeah."

"And when they searched your apartment, they found approximately five thousand dollars in cash on the table, is that correct?"

"No, not on the table."

"Okay, then, where was it?" Montgomery squinted.

"It was in my apartment. I had it in my jackets, in my clothing."

"And they took that, too, didn't they?"

"Yes, they did."

"And you needed the five thousand dollars that you stole from my client to replace that five thousand the police took, did you not?"

"No."

"Would you tell the jury where you got that five thousand dollars?" Montgomery folded his hands on the podium.

"Objection," Marissa said, "irrelevant."

"Sustained."

"You don't have it back now, do you?"

"No, I don't."

"The government's trying to keep it, aren't they?"

Marissa fully stood up. "Objection, your honor, irrelevant."

"Your honor, she's the one . . ."

"If we're going to argue about it, can we approach the bench," Marissa fired back.

The judge waved his hand. "No. Sustained."

Ms. Williams stood up and cleared her throat. "Your honor, I think that we have something else to offer in support of that question."

Judge Stagner paused for a moment. "I'm going to allow it subject to it being stricken." Gesturing to Montgomery, he nodded. "Go ahead."

"You indicated you were in the process of getting that five thousand dollars back, is that correct?"

"Yes, sir."

"And that's because law enforcement is holding on to that money, is that correct?"

"Your honor, please! We object to relevance!" Marissa implored.

"I'll carry the objection. Go on."

"Is that correct," Montgomery repeated.

"That's correct. My lawyer contacted me about a week ago. We went to court for that, and he tells me I'll get it pretty soon," Kyle smirked.

"Did you tell the police where you got that five thousand?"

"That question is asked and answered. You sustained the objection," urged Marissa.

"Well, I'm not now," Judge Stagner countered. Looking at Montgomery, he said, "Go ahead."

"Did you tell the police where you got that five thousand dollars?"

"Yes, sir."

"And what you told them is that you embezzled that five grand, isn't that right?"

"No, sir."

"You didn't tell the police that?"

"No, I did not tell them that."

"Do you know why they would put that in their report, then?"

"I object to that. That calls for a hearsay response," Marissa said from her seat, not bothering to stand this time.

"That's sustained," said Judge Stagner. "But your relevance objections are overruled."

Turning his attention back to Kyle, Montgomery asked, "When your apartment was raided back in 2001, you hadn't worked for eight months, had you?

"That's correct."

"You had been unemployed for eight months, yet you had five thousand dollars in your jacket?'

"Yeah," Kyle replied smugly, nodding, "I had five thousand dollars."

"When you talked to the police, they asked you if you had any idea who would have a motive to kidnap your sister, is that correct?"

"Yes, sir."

"And you said you had no idea?"

"Yes, sir."

"You knew what Calvin Stewart looked like didn't you?"

"Yes, sir."

"You knew what kind of car he drove, correct?"

"Yes, sir."

"You were able to drive straight to his house, where he lived, and pointed out his car, is that correct?"

"Yes, sir."

"Did you tell the police at that time that you had a strong suspicion Calvin Stewart was involved?"

"No, I didn't."

"But you drove by his house?"

"Yes, I did."

"Without talking to the police?"

"Yeah."

"Okay, let me get this straight. You know what Calvin Stewart looked like. You know what his car looked like. You knew where he lived. You call the police and turned in the car. Yet, you are telling this jury that you did not have a strong suspicion that Calvin Stewart was involved, is that correct?"

"Correct."

"You knew what Roland Connors looked like, did you not?"

"Yes, sir."

"And at that time, you never described Roland Connors to the police, did you?"

"No, I didn't."

"You knew that Calvin Stewart had introduced Roland Connors as his cousin from Oklahoma, didn't you?"

"Yes, I did."

"But, you didn't tell the police that, did you?"

"No, I didn't."

"Okay. After you called 911 and the police arrived, they wanted to know how y'all found the Camaro so fast, is that correct?"

"Yes, sir."

"And what did you tell them?"

"I told them we had got in a fight with somebody, and we remembered where he stayed at."

"Do you remember telling them that your brother, Ryan, had a dispute with a guy named Calvin over a car?"

"I remember telling them we had a dispute over a car, but I can't remember calling any names."

"Yet, your brother denied that he had had a dispute with anybody over a car, and he denied that he knew anybody named Calvin, is that correct?"

"No, sir."

"So the police report that reflects that as incorrect?"

"Judge, I object to what the police report reflects," Marissa interjected. "It calls for a hearsay response."

"Sustained."

"The Monday after your sister went missing, you and your brother went down to give fingerprints at the police station, is that correct?"

"Yes, sir."

"Do you recall that once again, the police, in essence, begged you and your brother to tell them everything that you knew?"

"Yes, sir."

"Do you recall that Detective Fargo told you that he believed your sister's life was at stake and would you please tell the police everything that y'all knew?"

"I can't remember that."

"Do you recall that your brother, Ryan, started crying?"

"I can't remember that."

"You withheld all this information because you thought the FBI was trying to trick you, is that what you're telling this jury?"

"No, that's not the only reason."

"Well, another reason was you were afraid you were going to get into trouble, isn't that right?"

"Yeah, and there's more reasons than that."

"Whatever the reasons were, they weren't good enough for you to be honest with the police, were they?"

"No, sir."

"I'll pass the witness." Montgomery shook his head as he walked back to his chair.

"Redirect."

"Briefly, your honor." Marissa walked to the podium and looked pointedly at Kyle. "Do you feel like you did the right thing by withholding information from the police?"

"No ma'am."

"Were you trying to suggest that to the jury?"

"No, ma'am."

"Your sister, Adena. Did she have anything to do with any of the drugs that were discovered at your apartment or those scales?"

"No, ma'am."

"To your knowledge, did the police find anything in that apartment with her name on it or anything linking her to any drugs?"

Montgomery stood up. "I'm going to object as irrelevant, as outside to scope of cross."

"Sustained."

"Did Deandra Knight have anything to do with any of the drugs that were found over at the apartment?"

"Same objection your honor," Montgomery interrupted.

"Sustained."

"Well, was there anything signifying that those were Deandra's scales or those were Adena's scales?"

"No, ma'am."

"Same objection, your honor."

"Overruled there." Judge Stagner shook his head.

"When you moved in with your sister, did you conduct any narcotic transactions there?"

"Objection, your honor. Leading question."

"Sustained."

"Well, did you conduct any business over there at all?"

"No, ma'am."

"Earlier before court I showed you a picture taken of a park. Do you recall that?"

"Yes, ma'am."

"A grave site picture?"

"Yes, ma'am."

"Were you able to identify the person depicted in that picture, Government's Exhibit 37-BB?"

"Yes, ma'am."

"And who was that?"

"That was my sister, Deandra."

"No further questions, your honor."

"Is there re-cross?

"No, sir," Montgomery responded, shaking his head.

"You may step down, sir."

CHAPTER SEVENTEEN

In Lydia's opinion, the afternoon's court session was imbedded with technical testimony. She listened to the testimony of several FBI agents that assisted in the investigation of the kidnapping and recovery of evidence at the various places Deandra was held. There were fingerprint experts flown in from Washington, D.C., that explained things like print card copies and ridge points. She had no idea what any of it meant, and she was even more amazed and curious why the defense attorney did not ask these witnesses any questions! None!

The day ended a little earlier than normal as the judge explained he had other business to attend to. Through the chaos of everyone gathering their belongings and leaving the courtroom, Lydia and William managed to meet Adena at the elevator without incident. And since the judicial chastisement the media received a few days ago, they were able to reach their car and leave the courthouse in peace. They all were more than a little tired, and she didn't have to do much convincing to have Adena and William go on to dinner without her. Truth be told, she needed a little quiet now, perhaps a nap and a little dinner.

Later that evening, she gave the door a light tap at first, and then knocked a little harder to be heard over the voices inside. She received a "come in!" and opened the door.

"Mrs. Knight, hello!" Marissa stood up from her table. Also present were Gavin sitting at the table, and her pretty assistant, who, from the look of things, was gathering the remnants of a Chinese dinner.

"I'm sorry to interrupt you," Lydia started. For a moment, she thought coming there was a bad idea.

"No, no, no! Please, come in." Marissa escorted her to the chair in front of her desk.

"I'll just take these to the break room on my way out." Grace gathered the remaining carts and napkins off the table.

"I'll walk you to your car." Gavin swung his suit coat across his shoulder and took some of the cartons from Grace. Lydia noticed he had ditched the tie he wore earlier that day.

"Why, thank you, Agent Wright," Grace smiled. Turning to Marissa, she asked, "What time do you need me in the morning, boss?"

"Umm, let's make it eight, all right?" Marissa walked to the door with Gavin and Grace, who nodded at the requested arrival time.

Lydia overheard Gavin say, "Call you later, Maury" before departing. She smiled at the soft "okay," followed by the click of the closing door.

"I seem to make this a habit, coming to your office unannounced," she said as Marissa took the chair next to her. Lydia took comfort again when Marissa chose to sit next to her verses across from her at her desk.

"Don't give it another thought." Marissa crossed her ankles and sat back in the chair. "What can I do for you, Mrs. Knight?"

"Well, I really just wanted to talk about how it's going. How do you think it's going?"

"I think it's going well," she consented. "I know today was filled with high-tech testimony, so it might have been difficult to sit through without glazing over." Marissa crossed her eyes, and Lydia chuckled, thankful for the lightness of the moment.

"There was a lot about fingerprint cards. I may not understand it," she chuckled again, "but I can say it was interesting." Shifting in her seat, she cocked her head. "How much longer do you think the trial will last?"

Marissa frowned a little. "Well, I believe we can finish presenting our case in a couple of days. That's on the just-in-case side."

Lydia agreed.

"As a matter of fact, I'm glad you stopped by. I can use this opportunity to prepare you for our next witness." Marissa leaned over and touched the arm of Lydia's chair.

"Okay," she hesitated.

"Tomorrow, we're putting on the medical examiner. Doctor Miller will be testifying in detail about the examination of Deandra's body. It will be intimate, it will be extremely detailed, and," she leaned over again, this time gently grasping Lydia's arm, "I really, really think you should sit this one out."

"Thank you for caring so much." Lydia patted her hand. "And thank you for the heads' up. But I want to be there. I have to be there." She squeezed Marissa's arm just a little, causing her to look up into her eyes. Releasing her hold, she repeated, "I have to be there."

"I kinda figured you would still want to come." Marissa let out a sigh and sat back, "but, like last time, I could not not tell you what to expect."

"Thanks for that." She also sat back. "When will Adena testify?"

"After Dr. Miller. She's our last witness."

Lydia paused a moment. "Does it mean anything that the defense attorney isn't asking any questions?"

"Well, it could mean that they have no argument to that particular testimony. I mean, why argue with fingerprint experts," Marissa asked matter-of-factly. "They are his client's fingerprints, they were found in the hotel and in the car, what is there to dispute?"

"That makes sense." She mulled over what Marissa said. Gazing out the window, she watched the traffic come and go, people going about their business, living their lives.

"Are you okay?" Marissa raised an eyebrow.

"Long day," she replied. Lydia then turned and looked hard at Marissa. "May I ask you a personal question?"

"Uh, sure."

"What's going on between you and Agent Wright?" Her voice was almost a whisper.

"Nothing," Marissa responded, a little too quick. "We work together, that's all."

Lydia caught the instant flush of her cheeks, the red tinged tips of her ears. "Really? Well, when both of you showed up at my house, I thought you were together. I must admit, you make a very handsome couple."

Marissa tried to blink away her shock.

"He's very handsome, isn't he," Lydia continued.

Marissa couldn't find her voice. Her mind gravitated to the morning after Gavin put her to bed, the slight disappointment she felt the next morning. Swallowing heavily, she nodded. "I can't dispute that, Mrs. Knight, he is." She watched Lydia's slow smile spread across her face. Holding up a hand, she said, "But we just work together. That's it."

"Okay, okay. Curiosity got the best of me. Did I offend you?"

Feeling the heat rise in her cheeks, she shook her head. "No," she stammered, "no, you didn't."

Lydia nodded. "Okay. I'm going home, so you can lock up and go home." She patted her arm one last time and stood up.

Marissa stood up with her. "Wait, I'll walk out with you." She gathered her purse and briefcase, stopped briefly to turn out a lamp in the corner.

Lydia looked at her and asked, "Are you ready for tomorrow?"

Marissa smiled. "I'll let you know tomorrow."

Lydia chuckled and Marissa closed the door behind them.

●●●

The next morning, Lydia and William walked into the courtroom and sat in their usual seats. Taking off her trench coat, she adjusted her dress and looked at her watch. They still had a few minutes before court was set to begin.

She watched Marissa talk to the other attorney at her table. The courtroom doors opened, and Gavin strode in. She liked his chocolate brown suit. Very handsome, she smiled to herself. He walked up to stand between Marissa and Austin, and Lydia caught herself smiling wider when he briefly touched the small of her back. They must have felt her watching because they both turned and looked at her. Gavin threw up a wave, and Marissa offered a nod, which she responded in kind, noting her blush.

The side door opened, and the court's bailiff appeared. "All rise," he announced, beginning the day.

Lydia and the rest of the room sat down after the jury was seated, and waited as Marissa announced her next witness. "The United States calls Dr. Clifton Miller."

Doctor Miller walked in, hospital scrubs replaced with a charcoal gray suit and yellow tie. He stood in front of Judge Stagner and was sworn in. He then proceeded to the witness stand and sat down, folding his hands on the desk in front of him.

"Good morning, Doctor," Marissa nodded in his direction. "Please, state your name for the record."

"Dr. Clifton David Miller."

"And the nature of your profession or occupation, sir?"

"I'm the chief medical examiner and forensic pathologist for the State of Oklahoma."

"And how long have you been employed in that capacity, sir?"

"In the State of Oklahoma, since January of 1997."

"And where is your office located, sir?"

"At the Oklahoma State Crime Laboratory in Oklahoma City." Doctor Miller looked at the jury and briefly explained his educational background and medical experience for the court.

Marissa nodded. "Sir, did you have an occasion to perform an autopsy on April 16, on the body of an individual identified to you as Deandra Knight?"

"Yes, I did."

"Doctor, there are two photographs there, they should be on the ledge down at your feet there. Let me ask you to look at those, but please don't display them to the jury at this time, please."

"Okay," said Dr. Miller, looking down at his feet.

"Let me ask you if you recognize those as photographs of Deandra Knight?"

He nodded. "Yes. They are photographs of Deandra Knight."

"That's the person you performed the autopsy on, is that correct?"

"That's correct."

"All right. Why don't you, if you can, walk us through an autopsy when one is performed in your laboratory."

"Well, any body that comes into the Oklahoma State Crime Laboratory goes through a protocol, depending on the type of case it is. The first thing we do is we take the height and weight of the individuals, then we take the as-is photographs of the individual as they come in the office. Now, depending on the type of case it is, we may elect to do postmortem X-rays. For example, if it's a case involving a gunshot wound, we would do a gunshot residue kit. If it's a suspected sexual assault, we would do a rape kit. So, we have different protocols for different types of cases that come in the office. After the body has been documented in photographs as-is, then what we do is undress the body, clean the body up and take the clean photographs of the individual.

"After the photography and other necessary tests that need to be done have been completed, we proceed with the actual autopsy. The autopsy is divided into two parts. We have an external examination, and we have the internal examination. During the external examination, we note the height and weight of the individual, the color of the hair, the color of the eyes, any unusual features or injuries situated on the external aspects of the body, tattoos, body piercings, scars. After that's been completed and documented, we proceed with the actual autopsy when we make incisions into the body, and there we examine the structures of the neck, chest, abdomen, pelvis and the brain.

"During that time, we look for any evidence of natural disease, injury and general malformations. We also take specimens of body fluids to determine the presence of alcohol or drugs in the body fluids. What we do as a rule is take blood from the heart, we take bio from the gallbladder, we take urine from the urinary bladder, if it's available, any stomach contents or gastric contents, small bowel contents, if it's there, and the vitreous, which is the fluid behind the eyeball. After that's been completed and documented, we take the necessary photographs of the internal examination, if there's something that needs to be photographed.

"I then submit the evidence that I receive off the body to the appropriate section of the crime laboratory. After that has been completed, I issue a death certificate stating the cause and manner of death, then I generate an autopsy report for criminal and civil proceedings."

"Okay." Marissa nodded. "Is that autopsy report the report that you referred to which would then be reviewed by the other members of the professional staff of the laboratory?"

"Yes. After I finish with the case, after I review it, the other physicians in the laboratory will review the autopsy report. In certain cases, where they are difficult, we always call the other doctors into the autopsy room so they can examine the body and the organs while the body is still there. This way all the doctors in the office have a clear understanding of the type of cases we're dealing with."

"All right. Do you have before you a copy of the autopsy report for Deandra Knight?"

"Yes, ma'am."

"Let me ask you to refer to that, if you would, please, and I'll ask you if you would turn to the second page of that particular document. Please start with the external examination and briefly acquaint the members of the jury what it was that you recall about the external examination that you performed."

Dr. Miller took a pair of reading glasses from his breast pocket. Putting them on, he began to read from the report. "Deandra was received nude in a green body bag. She was covered with dirt and plant roots. The body was on two white dirty sheets, and under the sheets was a piece of greenish plastic. There was an odor of accelerates about the body."

Marissa held up a hand. "Hang on a second, Doctor. What do you mean by accelerant in common language or common terms?"

"Well, there was an odor of gasoline about the body."

"It was obvious, wasn't it?"

"Yes."

"All right. Go ahead, I'm sorry."

"The body was in a state of decomposition. The rigor mortis was absent or the stiffening of the body was absent, and lividity or the settling of the blood out of the blood vessels was barely perceivable. Upon cleaning the body, Deandra was a well-developed, well-nourished black female. A mouth gag was in place.

"There was diffuse decomposition involved in her body. There were also seven very think hair braids which contained twigs and dirt, and they also had a very strong odor of accelerates or gasoline. The braids measured between ten and thirteen inches in length. One yellow metal earring was in place. Her eyes were brown. The corneas were cloudy. The conjunctiva and sclera showed red discoloration but petechial hemorrhages could not be identified."

Looking up, Dr. Miller removed his glasses. "What that means is the sclera, which is the white of your eye, and the conjunctiva is when you lift the eyelids up. So what we look for when someone has a gag in their mouth or any type of object around the neck is petechial hemorrhages.

"Petechial hemorrhages are the very small pinpoint hemorrhages that are commonly seen in the face, and more specifically in the eyes and in the larynx or your voice box. When you see these small hemorrhages about the size of a pinhead, they indicate an asphyxia-type death, meaning death associated with the lack of oxygen."

"All right." Marissa walked to the jury box. "And you said upon examination of her eyes that you did not detect any petechial hemorrhages in her eyes, am I correct, sir," she asked, leaning on the rail.

"Yes, ma'am, because of decomposition. There may have been petechial hemorrhages there, but I couldn't see them due to the degree of decomposition."

"Okay. Now, let me ask you, Doctor, were you able to determine whether or not there was a presence or absence of needle marks, puncture marks on her arms, or anything that would indicate the injection of any substance into her body?"

"There were no needle tracks or puncture marks located on her body or extremities."

"And did you do a pelvic examination, as well?"

"Yes, I did," he replied.

"Tell us about that, if you would, please."

"The external aspects of the vagina showed no evidence of injury. Oozing blood, blood was just coming out of the vaginal orifice. At the vaginal orifice, or the beginning of the vagina in the underlying soft tissues, there was hemorrhage, and an incision of the tissue showed it to be a contusion. A contusion in layman's terms is a bruise or black and blue."

"And do you have an opinion, based on your experience, what could have or might have caused that sort of injury to Deandra Knight," Marissa asked.

"Well, that type of injury is seen during sexual activity, whether forcible or not."

"Doctor Miller, did you then go into your protocol or your results in your autopsy report into evidence of injury?"

"Yes. The injuries, I divided them into sections. There are head injuries, then I will describe the gag, then I will describe the chest injuries and the injuries of the extremities."

"Let's start with the head injuries."

"Okay. The way I'll do it is I'll explain the medical term first, then I'll put it in layman's terms so you can understand what I'm talking about.

"Situated over the right posterior parietal scalp was a vertical-oriented laceration measuring one and three-eighths of an inch. The margins of the wound were abraded. There was prominent tissue bridging and undermining the soft tissues. So we're saying, the scalp is divided into regions. You have the frontal region where your forehead is; you have the temporal region where your ears are; you have the parietal region, which is, in essence, found at the top of the skull; and then you have the occipital region, which is the back of the skull.

"On the right parietal, on her right side, on this area right here," he pointed to the right side of his own head, "we have a laceration. The difference between a cut and a laceration is big. A cut is when, if you have a knife or a razor blade and you cut yourself, you bleed and have nice, clean wound margins. A laceration indicates some sort of blunt force injury. What happens is when the object hits the scalp or any other part of the body and the tissue bleeds, the tissue is not cut nice and clean. It's torn, and when you open the wound, you can see bridges of tissue connecting the wound together. It's not a nice clean, straight module like you would see, for example, on someone who has been cut with a knife. And there was also abrasion. The margins of the wound were abraded. In layman's terms, I mean a scrape. So, as the object is hitting her scalp, it's causing a scrape to the scalp tissue, and it's causing a laceration or tearing of the underlying tissue.

"Now, situated over the left occipital scalp region, on the left side, or this side right here," again, using his own head for the jury's observation, "in this region here, there was another vertically oriented, laceration measuring one and three-quarters by one and one-half inch, a vertical direction going up and down. The margins of this were also abraded or scraped, and there was prominent tissue bridging."

"Doctor, let me stop you for just a second," Marissa interrupted. "The first injury you noted was a head injury to the right back side of the head, is that correct?"

"That's correct."

"You described that as a laceration?"

"Yes, ma'am."

"Let me ask you, sir, if that sort of injury would be consistent, for example, with having been struck on the head in that area with a blunt object, or consistent even with being struck in the head with a shovel?"

"Yes," Dr. Miller nodded. "It is consistent with being struck on the head with a blunt object such as a shovel."

"Are you able to state on the basis of your examination for certain what would have caused that?"

"What I can tell you on examination, that a piece of wood, a two-by-four, can cause that or a baseball bat, and also a shovel can cause that type of injury."

"But that would be consistent, is that correct," Marissa pressed.

"Yes, ma'am."

"What about the second injury, the one I believe you said was vertically oriented on the left side of the scalp?"

"Yes. That is consistent with being struck in the head with a blunt object as well."

"Are we talking about two separate and distinct injuries at that time?"

"Yes."

"One on the left and one on the right?"

"Yes."

"Okay. Was there evidence of a third injury?"

"Yes. On the external aspects of the skull there were no other injuries except for those two lacerations. When I made the incision in the back of the head, we flipped the scalp up. Now, we're looking at the scalp from the inside out. What I saw was over the right side temporal region, or where your ear is, your parietal region and occipital region on the back on the right. And it's the scalp tissue as you're looking at it from the inside out. There was a large area of contusion or hemorrhage measuring up to ten inches. The right temporalis muscle was contused. The temporalis muscle, if you put your hands above your ears, you can feel that muscle. So that muscle is bruised, or black and blue.

"The two scalp lacerations that I mentioned on both the right and left side of the head in the back, they were just superficial. They measured only up to about a quarter of an inch in depth. There were no associated skull fractures associated with these wounds.

"Now, because Deandra was decomposing, the brain was liquefied, well, semi-liquefied. And what happens is the brain is surrounded by a thick membrane called the dura. It's very pliable. And when we used the saw to remove the skull bone, as soon as I took off the top of the head, the calvarium, you have to look at it, and you can see the dura, and the brain for a few minutes retains its shape. I could see how the brain was semi-liquefied, yet retained its shape. However, when I remove the dura, it oozes out liquid. So as soon as I remove the top of the skull, what I want to look for is epidural hemorrhage, or hemorrhage between the durum itself, or subdural hemorrhage between the brain and the durum. There was no evidence of that type of hemorrhage, nor was there any other evidence, of hemorrhage inside the brain as I examined it. Even though the brain is liquid to semi-liquefied, you can still see areas of hemorrhaging in the brain. It's not as pronounced as if it were a fresh brain, but on careful examination you can see it. And her body wasn't in a really advanced state of decomposition. If she was very, very decomposed, you wouldn't see anything at all."

"Doctor, let me stop you again for just a moment. With regard to your statement just a moment ago about the state of decomposition, let me ask you if that has an effect on your ability to accurately detect the full extent of injuries such as the laceration and contusion you referred to?"

"Well, even though the body is decomposed, you can see the lacerations. However, when the body is green, black, and red, and goes through all the different color changes after death, it obscures or covers up the injuries. So, if there was an injury on one part of the body, due to the extent of the decomposition, it may just cover it up and you cannot tell it was there due to the decomposition."

"Okay. You mentioned at first the injuries on the left side and the right side. Then you mentioned that when you incised the scalp, you found it was hemorrhaging beneath the surface, is that correct?"

"Yes, that is correct."

"What is that evidence of to you, Doctor?"

"Well, it indicates that there's a site of impact."

"Can you tell how many impacts would have caused the type of injury you saw that would be what we referred to as injury number three?"

"We have a large area of confluent hemorrhaging or bruising. What's happening is the contusions or bruisings are overlapping each other, and it's really hard to say exactly how many impact sites there are because the body is decomposing. There are at least several impact sites there, but because of the condition of the body, it's really hard to discern the exact number."

"Okay." Marissa paced before the jury. "Before we leave that particular part of the autopsy, let me ask you this: I believe you did say that there were no fractures of her skull, is that correct?"

"That is correct."

"And let me ask you if the injuries that you've described to this jury here, with regard to the head injuries were, in your opinion, of a fatal nature?"

"Well, these type of head injuries, the scalp lacerations are superficial. We do have some bruising on the inside of the scalp; however, there are no skull fractures and there were no hemorrhages to the brain, so these injuries are not necessarily fatal injuries."

"Now, the next area you have there is a description of the gag. Let's pass over that for just a second, if we could, and go to the injuries on the chest if you could, please. What evidence is there of injuries to her chest?"

"Okay. Underneath the skin you have the fatty tissues and under the fatty tissues, you have the muscle. On the front of the chest over the midline, they showed multi-focal areas of contusion measuring about one-half to three-quarters of an inch. So, we have many areas of bruising ranging from one-half inch to three-quarters of an inch. When I use the term 'multi-focal,' it's greater than five. So I know we had greater than five contusions on the chest in the underlying soft tissues. You cannot see them externally because of the decomposition, however, when you make an incision into the tissue, you could see the hemorrhage in the fat and in the muscles."

"Are you saying, Doctor, then that just with regard to that particular injury or series of injuries, we're talking about the possibility, at least, of the existence of five blows to that particular area?"

"Yes, ma'am."

"Let me ask you if those blows in particular would be consistent with having been struck, also, with a blunt instrument such as a shovel?"

"Yes. Any time you have a contusion or bruise, it indicates blunt force injury, an impact to the body."

"All right. Go on to the next injury or series of injuries, if you would, please."

"Okay. And situated in the subcutaneous tissues or the fatty tissues above the right clavicle, or collarbone, there was also a two-inch area of hemorrhage in the muscle or bruising in the muscle."

"And would that be the type of the injury, again, consistent with having been struck with a shovel?"

"Yes."

"Let's talk about the injuries regarding the left arm, please." Marissa walked back to the podium.

Doctor Miller put back on his glasses. "On the lateral surface or the side of the left arm, okay, we had a one-quarter by one-half inch greenish contusion. The reason why the contusion is green is because of the decomposition. The decomposition is starting to cover over. Normally contusions are red or blue, but if the body is decomposing, it begins to turn green. It's starting to cover, and the contusion looks green. There was a greenish red contusion on the anterior surface of the left wrist. So the left wrist, anterior surface in anatomical terms, is right here."

"So, that would be the third injury, I gather, on the left arm, is that correct?"

"Yes, ma'am."

"Would all three of those injuries be consistent with having been struck with a shovel?"

"Yes," Dr. Miller nodded. He pushed his glasses onto the bridge of his nose.

"Based on your experience, is there a description that you use in the field of forensic pathology to describe the type of injury that you observed there on her left forearm?"

"These types of wounds we normally describe as defense wounds."

Nodding, Marissa asked, "And how would that occur, based on your experience, Dr. Miller?"

"Defensive wounds are injuries that we see on individuals who are trying to protect themselves. The human reaction is if someone is coming at you with an object or a fist, your first inclination is to protect yourself, and most people put their hands up in some fashion to protect that part of the body."

"So are there more than three?"

"Excuse me?"

"We talked about three. Are there more contusions on the left arm?"

"Yes. On the back of the left hand, there was an area of skin slippage. There was a pink-red-green contusion or bruise measuring four inches."

"Okay. Again, would you describe that as a defensive wound?"

"Yes, ma'am."

"Consistent with having been struck with a shovel?"

"Yes."

"Any more injuries there to the left arm in that area?"

"No."

"The bottom of that paragraph, the last paragraph in the middle of page four, Doctor, references some reference to 'showed hemorrhage.' Can you tell us about that, please?"

"Okay. What we do is, because the body is in a state of decomposition, I'm trying to look for hemorrhage or bruising in the underlying fat or muscle tissue. So what we do is we make incisions of the body along the arms in the back and back of the legs to look for hemorrhage, to look for impact sites. So when I did that, I saw the hemorrhage in the underlying soft issues in the regions that I just described to you. I found no other area of impact on her body."

"Doctor, just a recap, I believe you said there were at least two lacerations of the skull, but as many as five contusions on the right side of the head, am I correct in that regard?"

"Yes."

"Okay. And then with regard to chest injuries, I believe you said there were at least two, is that correct?"

"At least five, because they're multi-focal."

"Five?"

"Yes, on the front of the chest."

"And one, two, three, four identifiable defensive wounds, is that correct?"

"Yes, ma'am."

"So, Doctor, are we talking, just in general terms, that you observed, well over ten and as many as fifteen individual wounds on her body?"

Dr. Miller removed his glasses, nodding. "That's correct."

●●●

The room started spinning. Lydia couldn't catch her breath. Her throat burned with familiar acid, and she was afraid that she would get sick right then and there. Her forehead beaded with sweat, and she quickly stood up, excusing herself from the pew.

She almost didn't make it to the ladies' room in time, and crashed into a stall before the bile and acid found their way out of her insides. She retched for several moments until nothing was left. Spent, she laid her head on her forearm on the commode, willing herself to stop shaking as she caught big gulps of air.

"Mama?" The door burst open and Adena knelt down next to her, stroking the back of her mother's head. "Mama, are you all right? What happened in there? What's going on?"

Lydia didn't trust her voice, and she continued her slow breathing.

Adena wrapped her arms around her, rocking them both. She gave it a few seconds, and asked again, "What happened?"

"I had no idea," Lydia whispered.

"About what?"

"I had no idea," she repeated, "no idea that she fought back." Lydia felt another wave of nausea.

Adena said nothing, waiting for her continue.

"The doctor is on the stand. The medical examiner." Lydia spoke between deep breaths. "He described these wounds on her body. Wounds that prove she fought back against them. Defensive wounds. She fought back." She raked her arm across her face, wiping her eyes. "She fought back."

Adena stood up and then reached down and helped Lydia to her feet. She walked to the sink and rinsed her mouth. The cold water felt good as she splashed her neck. She looked at her reflection in the mirror, but what she saw was the image of her daughter fighting off the attackers, blocking the blows of the shovel until it became too much. She lowered her eyes.

"I don't know if this will make any sense to you," she explained, her head still down, "but I had always thought Deandra," Lydia fought the bile that threatened to rise again, "I had always thought that she died peacefully. That she turned her back, they hit her on the head, and she died. I had no idea, no,. . ." she trailed off.

"You had no idea it was so violent," Adena finished. She walked over to stand behind her mother. "I know." Smoothing the back of her hair, her hand rested on her mother's shoulder. "We can either think of the violence of it all, or we can choose to believe she fought to the very end. That she was strong, and she didn't chose to wimp out or let them kill her without trying to fight." Adena wiped her own cheek and smiled. "She died strong." Chuckling, she added, "You know she liked to wear people down."

Remembering her conversation with Marissa, Lydia shook her head. "Yes, she did."

"Mama, you don't have to go back in there, you know."

"I know," Lydia let her eyes fall back onto the sink.

"No one will think any different of you if you just stay outside for a little while longer."

"I know," she repeated.

●●●

In the meantime, Marissa continued her examination. "Now, let's go and talk about the gag. Tell us about that."

"What I found was a gag consisting of a multi-folded piece of white cloth appearing blood soiled and marked with secretions which was fashioned in a single one-half inch knot over the back of the neck. The gag completely occluded the posterior pharynx. The posterior pharynx is when you open your mouth and look inside where your tonsils are. That's the posterior pharynx way in the back of the mouth. The gag

extended just about two and one-quarter inches in the oral cavity or into the mouth or into the pharynx. When I removed the gag, its diameter was more or less four by four inches. Dirt was present on the external aspects of the gag. There were no injuries noted to the inner surfaces of the lips or inside the mouth. Multiple petechial hemorrhages, those small pinpoint hemorrhages that I described earlier, were present on the lining of her voice box."

"Let's put a pause there for a moment, Doctor. You said that you would expect to find these petechial hemorrhages under circumstances where someone was suffering from asphyxia?"

Nodding, he responded, "That's correct."

"Can you tell us a little bit more about that? About how long you would expect someone to be deprived of oxygen or air in normal breathing processes for those particular hemorrhages to appear?"

"It has been proven in scientific literature that it takes approximately forty-five to sixty seconds for petechial hemorrhages to develop."

"Now, with regard to the gag and the type of gag that you observed on the body of Deandra Knight, would you expect that type of gag and the placement of that gag to cause those sorts of petechial hemorrhages within a minute?"

"Within forty-five seconds or a minute, yes, ma'am."

"On the basis of the use of that gag alone, Doctor? Please explain that for us."

"When a gag is just placed in the mouth, the person, of course, doesn't die right away. What happens is as the mouth is gagged, the normal reaction of the body is that you tend to swallow. So what you're doing is you're trying to swallow the gag, and what happens is your body produces a lot of saliva, and the gag gets very, very wet. And as the gag becomes wet, it gets heavy, and as it gets heavy, the wetness is blocking the air to pass through the mouth into the air passages. Although you can still breath through your nose up to a certain point, as the gag is going farther into the back of your mouth and it's wet with the secretions, after a while, it's going to occlude breathing through the nose because your nasal passages are connected to your oral cavity. So, you have obstruction of air flow, with time, through the nose and through the mouth."

"We're not talking about just forty-five or sixty seconds, then, are we, Doctor?"

"No, it takes time. It can take anywhere up to twenty to thirty minutes."

"But the petechial hemorrhaging would be present after forty-five to sixty seconds, is that correct?"

"That's correct," Dr. Miller nodded.

"Now, once again about the head injuries and those other injuries of blunt force trauma, do you have an opinion as to whether or not those alone would cause the death of Deandra Knight?"

"My opinion is that the blunt force head injuries and the blunt force injuries to other parts of her body, in conjunction with the asphyxia mechanism, contributed to her death but did not cause her death."

"Did the test on Deandra Knight reveal the existence or presence of any drugs in her system?"

"No drugs were present."

"Any alcohol?"

"There was a trace amount of alcohol detected, but a result of postmortem production."

"That's decomposition. That's not ingested alcohol, is it?"

"Yes, from decomposition. And no, it's not."

"Okay. Let me ask you what you would have expected, based on your experience, having been struck in the upper body and the head as few as five and as many as fifteen times with a shovel? What would you expect based on your experience and your training, sir?"

"Based on these type of injuries, they may have rendered her unconscious or dazed."

"Would she still be breathing, Doctor?"

"Yes."

"Would there be something different about the rate of breathing after being struck in that manner?"

"Well, her respiration or breathing would decrease."

"You mentioned earlier that she had very thick, heavy hair braids. In your opinion, those types of braids that you observed on her would be capable of cushioning, an injury, even one as a result of a shovel?"

"Yes, they would. They were very, very thick braids, so, yes, they would soften or cushion the blow."

"Now, you said you thought she would be unconscious, is that correct?"

"That's correct."

"Can you say with any degree of certainty that she would be unconscious?"

"With reasonable medical certainty, yes."

"Okay. I want you to assume further, Doctor, that soon after losing consciousness, a cloth gag, the kind of cloth gag that you observed on Deandra Knight, was soon afterward applied to her mouth, okay? Would you assume that, Doctor?"

"Yes," he nodded.

"Doctor, with regard to the gasoline, do you have an opinion as to what effect the gasoline would have been on the body?"

"When gasoline comes in contact with the skin, a number of things happen. First of all, you would experience pain and a burning sensation, but most of all what happens is the gasoline causes the skin to slip off and just literally burns the skin. If you pour gas on your hand, a few minutes later you'll see the skin will just peel off."

"You mentioned earlier that in your opinion, the type of blows sustained by Deandra Knight would render her unconscious. Doctor Miller, let me ask you this: are you able to determine, or can you give us an opinion as to whether or not she would be capable or had been capable of regaining consciousness after having been buried?"

"There is the likelihood that she may have regained some consciousness, yes."

"And how long after being buried, Doctor, would you have expected her to live under those circumstances?"

"Well, not very long. I know at least forty-five to sixty seconds, but the with the amount of dirt and weight on you, you wouldn't be able to breathe. You would have complete compression of your chest and abdomen, and you wouldn't be able to breathe properly."

"Because of the weight of the dirt on top of her, Doctor?"

"Yes."

"One last question, Doctor Miller. Your laboratory examination, were there swabs or smears taken from her body to determine whether or not there was the presence or absence of seminal fluid or spermatozoa?"

"Yes."

"And what were the results of those tests, Doctor?"

"No seminal fluid was detected."

"Thank you very much." Marissa closed her file.

"You're welcome."

"I believe that's all the questions I have of this witness." She looked to the bench.

"Cross examination?" Judge Stagner gestured to Montgomery.

"No questions, your honor." He kept his seat.

Judge Stagner did a double-take at Montgomery over his glasses. Pushing them up onto the bridge of his nose, he turned to Dr. Miller. "You may step down, sir."

"Thank you. Your honor, am I excused to go back to Oklahoma City?"

"Yes, sir."

•••

Lydia and Adena were walking arm-in-arm down the hall when they were approached by the court's bailiff.

"Ms. Knight, they're ready for you inside," he said, looking at Adena.

Adena stopped walking. Lydia squeezed her arm, and Adena looked at her, trance-like.

"You can do this," Lydia gave her arm another gentle squeeze.

Adena just kept looked at her mother, shaking her head.

"Ms. Knight?" The court's bailiff waited for a response.

"Right, right." Adena snapped out of her trance. "Okay, I'm ready."

"I'm right there with you." Lydia smiled.

Nodding again, Adena followed the bailiff in silence with Lydia close behind.

They walked into the courtroom just as Marissa announced, "Your honor, the United States of America calls Adena Knight."

Lydia slid into the pew and sat down again next to William. His arm circled her shoulder, and he leaned down and whispered, "Are you okay?"

She shook her head, and responded, "Yes, I'm good now," before giving her attention to the front of the room.

Marissa smiled and nodded at Adena as she sat down. "Would you state your name for the judge and jury, please?"

"Adena Knight."

"I want to take you back to April of 2002. Where were you living?"

"3401 Partridge Parkway."

"And is that a location of apartments known as the Villa Winds Apartments?"

"Yes, it is."

"What was your particular apartment number?"

"212."

"Who did you live with there?"

"My little sister."

"And what was the name of your little sister?"

"Deandra Knight."

"When did she come to live with you there at the Villa Winds?"

"She moved in June of 2001."

"Did she enroll in school at that time?"

"Yes, she did."

"Okay. Let's move on to Saturday, April 6, 2002. Were you home during the day Saturday?"

Nodding, she replied, "I was until 4:30."

"Why did you leave at that time, Ms. Knight," Marissa inquired.

"I had to go to work."

"Where was Deandra during the day Saturday?"

"She was with me."

"And what did you two do that day?"

"We went to a sports store, to the dry cleaners, picked up a couple things from the market, then went home."

"And after that, what were the plans for the day?"

"Again, I had to be at work at five, so I left the apartment at 4:30."

"What were Deandra's plans?"

"She was going to a party for the school's basketball team."

"After you got to work, did you talk to Deandra after that by telephone?"

"Yes, I did."

"And when did she call you, or when did you talk to her by phone?"

"It was around 9:30, 10:00. I called her to see how she was, what she was doing, and we were talking about the party."

"All right. Tell the members of the jury what happened during that conversation."

"Well," she started, "Deandra was talking about . . ."

"Hearsay, your honor." Montgomery stood up, interrupting the testimony.

"I beg your pardon?" Judge Stagner took his chin off his hand, looking at Montgomery.

"This is hearsay."

"Overruled." Turning to the witness stand, the judge said, "Please continue, Ms. Knight."

"Deandra told me that she thought she heard something at the door. Seconds later, she became very frantic and she told me to come home because someone was breaking into the house."

"You say she was frantic. Describe it for the members of the jury."

"She said things like 'I'm looking at them right now,' and 'Adena, help me,' 'please come home." Adena grabbed a tissue from the desk and wiped her cheek.

"And what did you say?"

"I told her to grab the house phone and go hide in the closet and call 911."

"What phone did she call you from initially?"

"We were talking on her cell phone."

Marissa nodded. "And then what happened?"

"I listened to her talk to 911."

"What else could you hear?"

"I heard her scream, I could hear her scream for help. She kept calling for me to help her." Adena again wiped her cheek, her voice just above a whisper.

"What did you do then?"

"I left work and went home."

"How long did it take for you to get to the apartment?"

"Twelve minutes."

Marissa turned to face the jury. "Tell the court and members of the jury what you saw when you got there."

"There were police officers outside the apartment," Adena started, taking a deep breath. "At that point, I got out of my car, and I ran towards them, and I asked them where was my sister, and they told me to stand back. I asked one of the officers if he wanted my key, my key to the front door, and he said yes, so I gave it to him."

"Did you ever see your sister, Deandra, when you came back?"

"I beg your pardon?"

"Did you ever see your sister, Deandra, when you came back," Marissa repeated.

"No, I did not." She shook her head.

"May I approach the witness," Marissa asked the Judge.

"You may."

Walking up to the witness stand, Marissa asked, "Ma'am, did your sister wear glasses?"

"Yes, she did."

"I want to show you what's been marked as Government's Exhibit Number 15, and ask if you can identify it?" Marissa placed the exhibit on the stand.

"Yes. Those are her glasses." Adena wiped her nose and took another deep breath.

"Did she have those on on April 6, the last time you saw her?"

"Yes, before I left work, she was wearing them," Adena sniffled.

Nodding, Marissa handed her a little clear bag. "Now, let me show you what's been marked as Government's Exhibit Number 60, which I believe is already admitted into evidence. I ask if you can look at that. Do you recognize this exhibit?"

"Yes, I do." Adena brushed her cheek with the tissue.

"Have you seen that before?"

She simply nodded her head in response.

"Where have you seen it?"

"It was Deandra's."

Glancing again at the jury, Marissa asked, "Describe to the members of the jury what this is, please."

"It is a link chain necklace with a diamond pendant."

"Did Deandra wear it all the time?"

"Yes, she did."

Marissa cocked her head to the side. "Why?"

"It was the first purchase she made for herself with her own babysitting money."

"I want to ask you, ma'am, did Deandra on April 6 have her hair styled in any particular manner?"

"Yes, she did."

"Describe for the members of the jury how her hair was styled."

"Her hair was braided up, and it was rolled up in a bun on the top of her head."

"And who did her hair, who made that style for her?"

"I did." Adena coughed. "I did, for the party."

"Finally, ma'am. I want to show you what's been introduced as Government's Exhibit Number 4. Do you recognize the person depicted in that photograph?"

"Yes, I do."

"And who is that?"

She hesitated, then said, "That's Deandra," barely above a whisper.

"Your honor, pass the witness." Marissa left the podium and walked to her table.

"Cross examination," the judge looked at Montgomery.

Ms. Williams stood up. "No questions, your honor."

Marissa stood up. "Your honor, the United States of America rests."

Judge Stagner nodded. "The government having rested, the court calls upon the defendant to call its first witness."

"We need to make a motion on the record before we do that," Montgomery replied.

"All right, counselor."

"Side bar, your honor."

"Very well," Judge Stagner sighed, motioning them to the bench. "Approach."

"Your honor, comes now the defendant, Roland Loenthal Connors, by and through his attorneys of record, we would move for a motion for judgment of acquittal under Rule 29 as to each and every count that the government's proceeded on. That would be Counts One, Two, Three, and Six. And in each and every one of those counts the evidence is legally insufficient to get past a Rule 29, in that we would move for judgment of acquittal at this time."

"Denied." The judge arched his eyebrow "Is that it?"

"Yes, your honor."

Montgomery and Marissa walked back to their respective table. Montgomery remained standing. "Your honor, the defendant rests."

"Ladies and gentlemen, the government and the defendant have rested." Judge Stagner turned, addressing the jury. "That concludes the evidence in this case, and you will have the case to begin deliberations, but not today. The case having been completed as far as for the evidence, it's very tempting to start deliberating. Please do not start deliberating among yourselves. Please avoid media coverage, as I am sure there will be additional broadcasts and newspaper articles written today and probably tomorrow, too. Let's keep this trial pristine and free of all outside influences. You've been very patient and I appreciate that. The lawyers and I have to work on the charge, and we will have it ready for you Monday morning. So, if there be nothing further, enjoy your weekend, and we will see you on Monday morning. Please assemble in the jury room by 8:45 a.m. on the dot. Thank you. You're excused at this time." Judge Stagner pounded his gavel on the desk.

CHAPTER EIGHTEEN

"Please be seated."

Marissa unbuttoned the coat of her black pinstriped pantsuit as she sat between Austin and Gavin. It was the last official day of court, and this morning, they were scheduled for closing arguments. She glanced over at Austin, who adjusted his turquoise paisley tie, his signature nervous move. She placed an 'X' in the top right-hand space of the grid she drew on Austin's note pad. He smiled and marked an 'O' underneath.

Judge Stagner adjusted his microphone and put on his glasses. He cleared his throat and looked out into the courtroom. "Ladies and gentlemen, good morning. We will begin with the closing arguments of the United States, followed by Mr. Montgomery for the defendant." He looked at Austin and nodded. "Mr. Gregory, you have the floor."

Austin stood up and buttoned his black suit coat. He drew a line through the three diagonal 'O's' on the tic-tac-toe board, and set down his pen before walking to the podium. He turned to the judge and said, "May it please the court." Giving his full attention to the jury, he smiled.

"Ladies and gentlemen, good morning. I'm going to try to keep my remarks brief because I submit to you at this point in this trial there should be no doubt the defendant, Roland Loenthal Connors, is guilty of all the counts charged in the indictment in this case. I submit to you that Count One is what this case really is about, whether Roland Connors kidnapped Deandra Knight, transported her to Oklahoma, and whether her death resulted from that kidnapping.

"The four elements of kidnapping are: Number one, that the defendant knowingly, acting contrary to law, kidnapped, seized and confined Deandra Knight. Number two, that the defendant held Deandra Knight for ransom, reward or any other benefit that the defendant intended to derive from the kidnapping. Number three, that the defendant intentionally transported Deandra Knight in interstate commerce. And number four, that the death of Deandra Knight resulted from that kidnapping.

"Now, the government does not have to prove that the victim, Deandra Knight, was taken for ransom in the traditional sense of how we think of the word 'ransom.' In fact, we don't have to show that Deandra Knight

259

was taken for any monetary purpose whatsoever. We simply have to show that she was kidnapped, and that this kidnapping was done for some benefit for the perpetrators of the kidnapping.

"Retribution, revenge, sexual gratification," he counted off on his fingers, "any of those motives are all sufficient to satisfy that second element of kidnapping. And I submit to you, ladies and gentlemen, in this case, you have at least four or five motives for this kidnapping. The most obvious ones, retribution, revenge. Thinking back to the testimony in this case, ladies and gentlemen, Roland Connors kidnapped Deandra Knight, had her transported to Oklahoma for the purpose of getting back at Deandra Knight's brothers because he was cheated in a dope deal. That's why she was abducted from her apartment. That's why she was transported to Oklahoma. She was also kidnapped for the purpose of ransom or reward in the sense that she was taken to try to force her brothers to give the money back or the marijuana back that Roland Connors was cheated out of. Also taken for reward in the sense that she might know where that money was, she might have also known where the marijuana was. You heard the testimony that they asked her where's the money, where's the dope, where were her brothers. She was taken for that purpose.

"Also, ladies and gentlemen, I submit to you that once she was taken, she was continuously held by the defendants in this case, and that is a kidnapping. Not just the abduction, but the holding of Deandra Knight. And they held her for a number of reasons, one of which was their own sick, sexual gratification.

"And we also know why she died. She died, ladies and gentlemen, because they did too much to her, and that was the reason why she was held.

"Ladies and gentlemen, the government also does not have to prove that Connors himself transported Deandra Knight in interstate commerce. We don't have to prove that. We don't even have to prove that Roland Connors knew that she was transported. But you know from the evidence that he knew it. He instructed the other three defendants to take her to Ponca City, Oklahoma. In fact, ladies and gentlemen, the law also holds the defendant responsible as an aider and abettor for the conduct of the co-defendants acting under his direction or in concert with him, and that's exactly what happened in this case. They were all acting under his direction.

"The evidence shows that Roland Connors traveled from Oklahoma to DeSoto, Texas, in interstate travel for the purpose of participating in a dope deal where he was going to buy seven thousand dollars-worth of marijuana from Deandra Knight's brothers, Ryan Knight and Kyle MacKenzie. You also know that he was cheated out of the seven thousand dollars and the marijuana. You know from the evidence that Roland Connors used the telephone to get the address of the brothers, Deandra Knight's brothers. You know that Roland Connors asked Calvin Stewart to find some guns. You know that, at the direction of Roland Connors, Nikko Hollis, or Nickels, flew down to Texas to help take care of business, and that Roland Connors, Calvin Stewart, Malcolm Connors, and Nickels went to the Villa Wind Apartments dressed in camouflage and watched the apartment until dark. They went up to the apartment, tried to kick in the front door, but couldn't do it. So, they went around back to the sliding glass door and Malcolm Connors used the two-by-four that was put into evidence, smashed in the glass of the sliding glass door. It was Roland Connors that went into the apartment, punched Deandra Knight in the face, rendering her unconscious, and instructed Stewart and Malcolm to drag her out of the apartment.

"He forced her to perform oral sex on him, and then he raped her. On the trip to Ponca City, she was repeatedly sexually assaulted by Malcolm Connors and Nikko Hollis. And, ladies and gentlemen, it was Roland Connors who made the decision that Deandra Knight was going to die. It was Roland Connors and Nikko Hollis that went to Faurot Lake. They dug the grave. That evening Roland Connors, Nikko Hollis and Calvin Stewart tried to take Deandra Knight to Faurot Lake to kill her then, but they couldn't find the grave they had already dug.

"So, on the morning of April 8, Hollis, Roland Connors, and Calvin Stewart took Deandra Knight back to Faurot Lake. At that time, Roland Connors, Nickels and Calvin Stewart repeatedly hit her in the head with a shovel, they tried to kill her that way. When she fell to the ground, they took her clothes off. They stripped her of her clothes. They stripped her of her dignity.

"Roland Connors, Stewart, and Hollis threw her in the grave. Nickels tied a gag around her mouth, they poured gasoline on her and then they buried her. They had assumed that she was dead. But, she wasn't, ladies and gentlemen." Austin stopped walking and stretched his arms across the rail of the jury box. "She was buried alive."

He continued pacing. "Now, the defense may argue to you, ladies and gentlemen, that these witnesses or co-defendants each have something to gain by their testimony. The defense may argue that you need to blame somebody else for this horrible crime, that you need to blame somebody other than Roland Connors. Ladies and gentlemen, out of all the sorry and despicable people that could have saved this girl's life, out of all the sorry and despicable people who helped kill her, there's only one person who got the wheel rolling. There's only one person who said, 'I ain't leaving Texas until I get my money, my dope, or some blood on my hands.' There he is." Austin pointed across the room at Roland. "He's the reason why we're here, ladies and gentlemen. He's the reason why Deandra Knight is not here. He killed her, and he buried her alive.

"Ladies and gentlemen, I submit to you the evidence is overwhelming that this man is guilty of every count charged in the indictment." He paused, and looked at each juror. "It was this man who decided that Deandra Knight would die." He nodded his head in conclusion. "Thank you."

"Mr. Montgomery?" Judge Stagner cleared his throat.

Montgomery stood up half-way. "We don't have anything to present at this time."

"Okay," he hesitated. Judge Stagner looked at him over the top of his glasses. "I haven't had that happen before." Turning back to the jury, he said, "That concludes the argument in this case. The case is now yours."

Marissa exchanged a smile with Austin as Judge Stagner continued to give his instructions to the jury. She sat back in her chair and watched the jury listen to the instructions. Each appeared attentive and they were all looking at him. She'd always considered it a bad sign when one or two took this as an opportunity to observe the rest of the courtroom.

"All rise!" She stood along with the rest of the court as the judge and jury walked out.

"I'm headed back to my office." Austin cupped her elbow. "Call me if you hear anything?"

"Only if you do the same." She leaned down and gathered her belongings.

Gavin cupped the opposite elbow. "I'm gonna head to the bureau, check on some calls, my mail."

"Play online solitaire." Marissa chuckled.

"Shhh. . . someone may hear you." He looked around behind him.

She laughed out loud as he held open the well gate for her. Lydia and Adena stood waiting on the other side.

"What's next," Adena asked.

"Now, we wait." Marissa sighed. Looking from one to the other, she added, "Why don't you go home? There's no way to predict how long this will take. I promise. I will call you the minute we have some news."

William stepped up. "Will we have time to get back?"

"I'll make sure we don't start without you," she reassured all of them as they walked to the elevator. Gavin pushed both buttons as Marissa said, "Try to relax, run some errands." She glanced at her watch. "It's too early for lunch, so go have a late breakfast."

The elevator doors opened. It was going up, so Marissa stepped inside. She looked at Lydia and smiled. "Go, relax. I'll call you." She saw her nod before the doors slid closed.

●●●

Later that afternoon, back at her house alone, Lydia decided to repot some of the plants that have outgrown their homes. Placing the selected plants on her work table out in the room built onto the back of her house. She secured the apron around her middle. She pushed 'play' on the CD player and Charlie Wilson's velvet voice floated throughout the room. Reaching for the first post, she hummed along as her fingers dug in the rough dirt, searching for a good place to lift without tearing any roots. She gingerly placed the plant in the new pot atop soft soil and poured more soil to the desired level.

She replaced the humming with singing as she watered and pruned and fluffed soil until she was satisfied with the re-potted plant. She turned up the volume on the music and her singing and fell into a comfortable rhythm with her hands. Lydia put big pots of peach and white hydrangeas in beige stone urns to be moved to the front door this evening, she thought to herself with hope. Her arms full of deep violet tulips, she turned to head into the house to replace the wilting flowers in her bedroom with the fresh ones, and ran smack into Adena.

"Mama!"

Lydia screamed, jumped back almost knocking over several pots. Her eyes were saucers as she looked at Adena, purple tulips raining around them.

"I'm sorry! I'm sorry! I kept ringing the bell!" Adena waved her hands in front of her. Her mother covered her ears, yelling "turn that down!" She ran to the music and turned off the player, and the room was washed with deafening silence.

Lydia, still clutching her chest, leaned against the table. "What are you doing here?"

"The jury's back."

"So soon?" Lydia stayed just where she was, waiting to catch her breath that was suddenly stuck in her throat. Her eyes darted to the wall clock. "But it's only been a couple hours. What does this mean?"

Adena reached over, grabbing her mother's arm. "It means that this is almost over."

"How long do we have to get there?"

"We need to get there as soon as we can."

"Okay." Lydia started for the kitchen. "Okay. Where's my purse?"

"Uh, mama." Adena pulled the apron string as she walked by. "You can change first."

Lydia looked down and chuckled as she untied the apron and went into her room to get ready.

●●●

Across town, Marissa had just got back to her office from a quick lunch and was answering emails. She had shed her ruby red patent-leather pumps and her feet were propped on an open drawer at the bottom of her desk.

Her cell phone rang at her side. Without looking, she reached for it and answered, "Elliott."

"Hear anything yet?"

She smiled. "No, sir. Why, did you?" Her smile deepened when he chuckled. She'd always thought Gavin had a nice voice, especially on the telephone. "What's going on?"

"Just checking, seeing if there was any news. What're you doing?"

"Answering emails now. I need to look over notes for the next trial."

"Oh, yeah, Nickels. When does that one start?"

She sat back in the chair, tilting it back. "Right now, in four weeks."

Gavin paused for a moment. "Just switch out the names with your stuff from this one."

Marissa rolled her eyes and laughed. "Should I really explain this to you?" She chuckled again.

"Probably not. I'll just forget."

She looked up at the knock at her door. Montgomery stood on the other side of the doorframe.

"Umm, let me call you back." Marissa hung up before he could say anything else. "Mr. Montgomery. Come in."

He crossed the threshold and extended his hand to her. She shook it, as she remained seated. "Please," she gestured at one of the chairs.

"Sorry to barge in here unannounced, Ms. Eliott, he began. The way he pronounced "Ms." sounded like he was hissing to her.

"Not a problem. What can I do for you?"

"My client would like to plead this case out."

"Excuse me?" She stared at him blinking several times.

"My client wants to plead this case out." He repeated.

"Okay, so I did hear you right." Marissa was dumbfounded. "May I ask why?"

"Look, Marissa." She shot up an eyebrow when he said her name. "We just don't see how co-defendants were offered a deal and my client wasn't. They even testified to their participation in this hideous turn of events." She could swear she heard him hiss again. "We would just like to be afforded the same opportunity."

"This 'hideous turn of events,' as you called them," Marissa sat back in her chair, "were orchestrated by your client, not the others. It was his idea to take her when her brothers were not found in the apartment. It was his idea to kill her instead of letting her go because she knew too much. And yet, he did not stop anything that happened to her by the others that operated under his direction."

Montgomery pinched the bridge of his nose.

"But why the death penalty? Why not just ask for 999 years, let him serve out the remainder of his life in jail?"

"Because she was sixteen years old, Cecil." Marissa sat up and laid her hands on her desk. "She was sixteen years old, and he took her because she was home."

He was caught by surprise at the intensity in her eyes, the passion in her voice.

"Why is this so personal to you?"

Her tone was low but deliberate. "Because he saw her as inconvenient. When he made the decision to take her, he did so because he never thought she mattered. It is my duty to make sure he understands that she does."

There was another knock at the door. This time, it was Austin who gripped the doorframe. He looked from Marissa to Montgomery, not masking his curiosity. "Jury's back." Without saying anything else, he left.

She and Montgomery stood up at the same time.

"This is it, then." Montgomery offered his hand again. "Good luck, counselor."

Marissa looked at him as she shook his hand.

"Thank you."

• • •

"It's been reported to me that the jury has reached a verdict." Judge Stagner looked at the jury box. "Ladies and gentlemen, have you reached a verdict?"

A tiny, plump lady with gray hair and bifocals stood up. "Yes, we have, your honor."

"Who is the presiding juror?"

"I am," she responded.

"All right, Mrs. Brewer, if you'll hand the verdict form to Mr. Mehno."

The judge took the folded paper from his courtroom deputy and adjusted his glasses. "Will the defendant please rise?"

Roland stood between Mr. Montgomery and Ms. Williams.

"In the matter of the United States of America verses Roland Loenthal Connors, the jury finds the defendant, Roland Loenthal Connors, as to Count 1, guilty. As to Count 2, guilty. As to Count 3,. . ."

Lydia closed her eyes as the judge read one guilty after another. Adena clutched her arm in uncontained her excitement next to her, and William's arm circled her shoulder, squeezing her in his glee. Eyes still closed, she allowed the relief to wash over her. She felt the slow grin spread across her face. It was over. It was finished. Her smile deepened as she looked at Adena and William hugging each other.

"We did it, Mama!" Adena turned to her and engulfed her in her arms. "We did it! We won!" She rocked Lydia back and forth in her joy.

"Yes, we did!" For the first time in a long time, she laughed out of pure joy.

•••

Marissa sat back, elated. Guilty on all counts! Austin squeezed her arm, offered his congratulations. She beamed at him. "Congratulations, yourself!"

"Congratulations, Ms. Elliot, Mr. Gregory." Montgomery walked over. "Job well done."

She stood up and accepted his hand.

"Thank you, Mr. Montgomery." He shook her hand and gave a slight bow before retreating to gather his belongings.

"Congratulations, Maury." Gavin put his hand on Marissa's back.

"Today is a good day." She beamed back at him.

Lydia stood up the same time Marissa appeared in the pew in front of her. Eyes locked, she hesitated for just a moment before she opened her arms, and she embraced the woman that gave her daughter a voice.

"I told you, Mrs. Knight, she mattered," Marissa whispered. "Deandra matters."

Lydia nodded. Pulling herself away, she looked at Marissa through her tears. "Thank you."

Marissa's eyes glistened. She took Lydia's hand and said, "This belongs to you now."

She opened her hand and the diamond pendant of Deandra's necklace glittered back through her tears. She hugged Marissa again, and kissed her cheek. "Thank you," she repeated.

Marissa nodded, not trusting herself to speak. She accepted the embrace and thanks from Adena, and shook William's hand. She looked after them as they practically skipped out the door.

"That was a good thing you did, Charlie Brown." Gavin stood beside her.

"I do that, from time to time," she smiled after them. She looked up at him and said, "You owe me a drink."

"You know what, Maury?" Gavin draped his arm around her shoulders, steering her out of the well towards the exit. "I'll forget that it's your turn to buy. I'll even drive."

"I'm not even going to argue with you. Let's go."

•••

He pushed the lever, letting the window down, and looked out towards the courthouse. He saw her walk down the stairs, arm-in-arm with his sister. The smile on his mother's face was pure joy, and Kyle could almost hear her laugh. He could never take away the part he played in Deandra's death, but he was glad she received justice with the guilty verdicts.

"Hey, pal, you ready to go, or what?" The cab driver looked at him in the rearview mirror.

Kyle let the window back up, nodding to the driver. He took one last look at his mother, watching her and Adena cross the street, her head thrown back in another laugh.

"Where to?" The driver looked at him through the mirror again.

"The airport." Kyle faced forward, making eye contact with the driver.

He looked at the passing landscape. Kyle wished he could be there when his mother found the envelope of money in her purple tulips in the kitchen. She still leaves the key under the second flower pot on the left, he chuckled to himself. No, he couldn't take back his part. He was satisfied with what he left his mother. I'm ready, he decided with each passing building. I'm ready to start over. Get out of here, take his problems with him. Away from his family. Away from here.